on
last
second

BOOKS BY SAM VICKERY

The Promise
One More Tomorrow
Keep It Secret
The Things You Cannot See
Where There's Smoke

NOVELLAS
What You Never Knew

one last second

SAM VICKERY

bookouture

Published by Bookouture in 2020

An imprint of Storyfire Ltd.
Carmelite House
50 Victoria Embankment
London EC4Y 0DZ

www.bookouture.com

ISBN: 978-1-83888-814-5
eBook ISBN: 978-1-83888-813-8

For my husband, Jed, who is always *on my side.*

PROLOGUE

I don't remember the first time I realised they thought *I* was the problem. It happened so gradually, drip by drip, that by the time I saw what was happening, I was already drowning. There was no opportunity to defend myself, protest my innocence. I was lost in a pool of accusation so deep I couldn't reach the surface, however hard I tried.

There are certain things you believe as a parent. That your child will always look for you when they're in trouble. That no one else's child will ever seem as wonderful as your own, and that there's nobody in the world who knows your child as well as you do.

Mother knows best. That's the saying, isn't it? It's just accepted. Who else could know what they're like behind closed doors? Who knows more about their fears, their hopes, their struggles?

I never thought they wouldn't believe me – it hadn't even crossed my mind. That was the hardest part. The knowledge that they would take my words and taint them with a sheen of disbelief until I was all alone and fighting so many battles I didn't know which way to turn next. That I wouldn't be able to protect her, *save* her. I hadn't considered that they wouldn't listen.

But as it turns out, sometimes 'Mother knows best' is nothing more than a few meaningless words.

CHAPTER ONE

Madeline

Now

If I could have stopped him from taking her, I would have. Not because he was a bad father, but because these weekends without her were torture for me. I was utterly alone and I had nobody to blame but myself.

I fingered the bodice of what would become a sequinned octopus costume, moving it slowly beneath the needle, trying hard to keep my mind focused on the task at hand and failing miserably. The sewing machine jammed for the third time in a row and I hissed with frustration, throwing the cheap blue satin to one side and glancing up at the clock on the kitchen wall. Without the hum and whirr of the machine, the slow, methodical tick was the only sound to be heard in the empty house. Barely fifteen minutes had passed since I'd last looked at the wide purple clock face, willing it to speed up.

I hated these weekends alone. The ghostly creaks and moans of the old Victorian terrace that was far too big for just me. I'd known when Adam left that everything was going to change. But somehow I'd glossed over the realities of what my life would be like when we were no longer a family of three. I'd pictured me and Tilly together. Not him taking her for long weekends, me spending hours sitting on her vacant single bed, anxious and frightened in a way I hadn't been since I was a teenager.

I stood up, resisting the urge to go upstairs again. I'd developed a habit that was fast becoming an obsession of checking beneath the beds, inside the wardrobes multiple times throughout the day and night. What I was expecting to find there, I wasn't entirely sure, but still, my imagination played havoc with me any time I found a window I'd left unlocked, a door slightly more open than it had been when I last passed it.

I knew it was a symptom of being alone. I'd never had these fears before the divorce, and when Tilly was here, I was far too busy taking care of her to give in to the stories that ran wild in my mind. Adam would be appalled if he could see how far I'd let my anxieties escalate. It was thinking of him, the irritated roll of his eyes, that made me pause, forcing myself not to go through the ritual now.

Instead, I wandered through to the living room, pressing my face close to the window as if I could hurry them along. He would be on time. Adam was obsessed with punctuality, a fact that had been a constant source of conflict when we'd been married. It had seemed petty then. What difference did it make if we were ten minutes late to a party? Or if we missed the train to London and had to catch the next one? I had never been able to understand why it upset him so much – it wasn't as if we wouldn't get there in the end.

But now that fundamental part of his character, which I'd considered a flaw, was the only thing that kept me going on these endless weekends without our daughter. He would arrive at 6 p.m., as agreed. So why did I spend all afternoon waiting, hoping that this time he'd get here sooner?

I paced back to the kitchen, glancing at the clock again. Five minutes. I could manage five more minutes. The unfinished under-the-sea-themed costumes lay piled across the kitchen table, the shiny satin taunting me. The fabric was a nightmare to work with, but I *would* make it work. I always did in the end.

The parents who commissioned me to make the colourful costumes for their children's birthday parties and school plays didn't care that the material was cheap and had a short lifespan. They only cared that I could create something that looked incredible, that their child would be besotted with, that didn't cost the earth. I stacked the costumes, popping them into the big cardboard box I used to keep things out of Tilly's reach when I wasn't working, then picked up my empty coffee cup.

I washed it up at the sink rather than putting it in the dishwasher, desperate to keep my hands busy in those final few minutes. The warm water rushed over my fingers, soothing despite the August heat, and I let my eyes drift to the clock again.

The sound of tyres on the gravel of the driveway made my heart leap, and I placed the cup on the draining board, roughly drying my hands on a tea towel and rushing for the front door. I reached it before the engine cut out. Even a year on, Adam still refused to park out on the road. Just another of the little ways he dug his heels in and refused to let go of the life he'd left behind. It made no difference to me, but I worried that he wasn't moving forward. I knew he still held on to the hope that things would go back to how they were before.

Flinging open the door, I broke into a wide grin as Tilly clambered out of the back of Adam's BMW and ran to me with her arms outstretched. Her dark-blonde waist-length hair was matted and tangled again. She was blessed – or cursed – with the same wild curly tresses as me, an unruly lion's mane that looked perpetually messy no matter what you did to it. As a result, Adam deemed it a lost cause and frequently forgot that it *did* actually need a brush through it on a regular basis. The longer he left it, the harder it was to fix, and the grumpier Tilly would be about having it done.

I shook off my frustration, lifting Tilly into my arms, her six-year-old body still light and easy to scoop up. I dreaded the day I could no longer do this. Breathing in the musty scent of her, ascertaining that she hadn't been near a bar of soap since I'd bathed her last either, I pressed a kiss to her neck.

'Hey, sweetie. I missed you.'

'Me too,' she murmured. She threw a pointed glance over her shoulder towards Adam as he strolled towards us, then wriggled out of my hold and slipped under my arm. I heard her footsteps on the stairs as she disappeared from view.

'Tilly,' I called. 'Say goodbye to your daddy!'

'Don't bother. I'm in her bad books,' Adam said gruffly, folding his arms across his chest.

He was dressed in his usual chinos and Oxford-style shirt, his brown leather shoes buffed to a bright shine. His collar was open, a nod to the fact that it was Sunday, but for Adam, this was as far as dressed-down went. I was pretty sure he didn't even own a pair of jeans any more. He ran his fingers through his slicked-back chestnut hair and pursed his lips.

'Not again?' I said. 'What for this time?'

'I'll give you three guesses but you'll only need one.'

'Adam. We've talked about this.'

'You've talked. I didn't agree.'

'So, what? You've dug your heels in and she's gone hungry, is that it?'

Adam's eyes flashed angrily. 'No, that is not *it*.' He paused for a moment, taking a breath as if readying himself. We'd had this argument a thousand times since he'd moved out, but something felt different this time, as if he'd been preparing for this conversation, and now that it had started he wasn't going to stop without saying his piece. 'Quite frankly, I've had enough of it, Maddie,' he said, folding his arms. 'You're spoiling her.'

'Spoiling her?'

'She's learned that if she refuses to eat the food you give her, you'll just give in. You always do. Well, I'm sorry if it makes me the bad guy, but I'm not going to just bow to the demands of a six-year-old any more. She needs a balanced diet. Nutritious food. Not plain toast and bloody pancakes three times a day!'

'Of course she does,' I replied quickly, hoping to stop the argument before it really began. 'I'm not disagreeing with you, Adam. But it's better that she has something to eat than nothing at all. It's not as if she's got reserves – there's nothing of her.'

He gave a derisive snort and I gripped the door frame, trying to keep my cool. Adam and I had spoken time after time about how best to approach disagreements with Tilly. I didn't agree with his strict, unbendable approach. It made no allowances for her feelings, her needs, and as a parent I always wanted to understand the motives behind her behaviour. Adam, on the other hand, felt that she should do as she was told without question, something instilled in him by his grandparents, who had brought him up. He accused me of being too soft on her. I thought he needed to listen more and give her a break. It had been a bone of contention throughout our marriage and had only worsened since Adam had moved out.

The image of Tilly staring at a plate of food she wasn't able to eat, while her stomach spasmed from hunger pains, made my eyes sting with emotion. She had never been a great eater, but in the past year, it had escalated. I was the first to admit it, but I was certain it had nothing to do with being fussy.

She'd had so many tests as a baby to try to get to the bottom of her vomiting after feeds. I would spend hours breastfeeding her, only to have her throw up what seemed like everything. I'd cut dairy out of my diet so it wouldn't come through my milk. When that hadn't worked, I'd cut out spicy foods. Garlic. Nightshades. Nothing had made the slightest difference. Eventually, the gastro specialist we'd been referred to had written the vomiting off as reflux, but I hadn't agreed with her. If that had been the right diagnosis, her symptoms would have improved when she started eating solids. She would have got better, not worse.

It was true that she was sick less often after starting on solid foods, but only if we let her guide us at mealtimes. There were a handful of foods she was able to manage with no noticeable after-effects. Plain rice. Toast. Wholegrain pancakes and a couple of fruits and vegetables. But if we veered off the safe list, she'd suffer with bloating, constipation and, in some cases, projectile vomiting. Adam had insisted it was classic fussy toddler syndrome, while I'd continued to press for more investigation, but once we had the diagnosis of reflux down on paper, the doctors all seemed to lose interest in our complaints. And Adam, no longer worried that she was harbouring some awful condition, had stopped giving her the benefit of the doubt and gone head to head with her over every plate of food.

I knew that he considered it a bonus of our divorce that he could take control of Tilly's mealtimes without my interference during his days with her, and from what I'd heard from the pair of them, it wasn't going well. I'd noticed more and more that she would have hardly any appetite for days after she'd been to his flat, her stomach round and gassy, and over the past year, she'd been sick with increasing regularity. It had gone from once every couple of months to practically every few weeks now, and I was sure there were times she was sick in his care that he conveniently forgot to mention to me. He was pushing her too hard, but he just wouldn't listen to me.

'Maddie,' he said, taking a step towards the house as if he were going to try and come inside. I moved subtly to the right so there was no space to pass by me. He shook his head, frowning. 'Look, I know you worry. That's why you give in. You can't stand to see her go without a meal. But you're too soft on her. If she was really that hungry, she'd eat.'

'It's not that simple, Adam. You know that better than anyone.'

Adam sighed, his shoulders slumping. 'Do you really think I *want* to spend my weekends at loggerheads with her? I want to enjoy our time together. It's precious to me, the little access I get.'

I looked away, guilt flooding through me. The hardest part of ending our marriage was knowing that Adam would no longer see his daughter every day. It was cruel, really, and I got no pleasure from his pain. But how else could it have worked if I didn't want him under my roof? What choice did I have?

'I want to be able to have fun with her, Maddie. Do the normal dad stuff, you know? Not argue over a plate of food. All I'm asking is that we work together on this. We need to be consistent. United. Can't we do that?'

I sighed, rubbing my temples. 'I'm not going to gang up on her, Adam. We need to be on her side. Figure out *why* she struggles with eating.'

'I think making a big deal out of it is only making it worse.'

'No, it's not.' I rubbed my temples again, my head throbbing. 'I can't talk to you about this now. I need to feed our child before she wastes away, and you're missing the point completely.' *As usual.*

'No, Madeline. I'm not. And until we start working together on this, *she's* the one who's going to suffer. Think about it.' He turned away, walking slowly back to his car.

'What did you offer her to eat?' I called after him.

'Why does it matter? Like I said, she needs to learn to get what she's given.'

'You're too hard on her, Adam. You're not being fair.' I didn't wait for him to drive away before storming inside, slamming the door shut. I leaned my head back against it, trying to steady myself, breathing in slowly as I waited for my anger to disperse. I didn't want Tilly to see me like this, the frustration rippling through me in palpable waves. It wouldn't be fair to her – I would hate to think she might feel caught in the middle of our disagreement. I closed my eyes, determined to put Adam out of my mind, for now, at least. Finally I straightened up, running my fingers through my hair.

'Tilly!' I called. 'Are you in your room?'

'Yes, Mummy,' her sing-song voice answered from above.

'Come down here, please, darling.'

There was a thud, as if she'd dropped a toy on her bedroom floor, then slow footsteps. I waited at the bottom of the stairs, watching as she descended slowly.

'Has Daddy gone now?'

'Yes. Didn't you want to say goodbye?'

She shrugged, not meeting my eyes. I leaned against the banister.

'I heard you fell out.'

She folded her arms across her narrow chest. 'He won't listen to me. He never does.'

I breathed in deeply, feeling completely caught in the middle. As angry as I might be with Adam, I didn't want Tilly to pick up on that. I couldn't remember it ever being difficult like this with my own parents. They'd always been so in tune with each other, on the same page with every aspect of parenting. I was lucky. They'd never been strict or unfair with me; they were so easy-going, always happy to let me make my own choices, figure things out for myself. I had admired that and respected them all the more because they hadn't tried to tell me what to do but instead taught me how to make my own choices. I wished Adam and I could present a united front as my parents had, but he seemed to want to control Tilly in a way that appeared to border on unhealthy.

'Are you hungry?' I asked, dropping down to my haunches to look her in the eye. 'I can make you pancakes?'

Her serious little face broke into a smile. 'Yes please, Mummy.'

I watched her skip into the kitchen, relieved to have her home again. It was like a light had been flicked on in the house. No monsters were lurking in the dark corners of my imagination now. The creaks were nothing more than hot water expanding the pipes.

I mixed fresh batter, pouring it into the sizzling pan, watching it brown and bubble. It seemed ridiculous to me now that just an hour ago I'd been jumping at every noise: checking under the bed with a rounders bat grasped in my shaking hand, imagining predators that had snuck in the back door whilst I was working at my sewing machine. An empty house could be so intimidating at times, but Tilly's presence made my anxieties fade away.

I poured her a drink, using a dropper to add some liquid vitamins to it, keeping my back to the table so she didn't see what I was up to. She wouldn't like it if she thought I was trying to trick her. *See, Adam*, I thought, mixing the liquid briskly with a wooden chopstick. *I do care about her getting a balanced diet.*

Sliding the pancakes onto a plate, I carried them and the drink over to Tilly, placing them on the table and moving swiftly away. I made a show of clearing up, not wanting her to feel watched as she ate. She hated to feel under pressure. All the same, I cast covert glances her way every now and then, pleased to see her chewing thoughtfully as she watched the birds landing on the little wire feeder we'd hung by the back door. She swallowed a bite of pancake then took a deep drink from her glass.

'I bet that feels better?' I smiled as she popped the last bite into her mouth. She nodded, though she didn't tear her gaze away from the blue tits pecking at the nuts and seeds.

'Shall we get you in the bath, then? It's nearly bedtime and you've had a long day.'

She pushed the plate away and stood up. There was a glazed look to her eyes and I wondered how early Adam had got her out of bed. He was one of those perpetual early birds, and as such could never seem to grasp the fact that not everyone enjoyed rising at the crack of dawn.

'Mummy,' she began. She swayed a little, and her hand darted out towards the table for support. 'I… I feel funny.'

I opened my mouth to speak but didn't get the chance to. Tilly's eyes rolled back and I stood rooted to the spot as she fell forward, hitting the kitchen floor with a resounding smack. 'Tilly!' I screamed, my legs springing into action. I ran forward, scooping her into my arms, struggling with the dead weight of her as I tried to see her face. There was blood trickling from a cut above her eyebrow, but she was breathing.

'Tilly, darling, wake up, wake up!' I cried, rolling her onto her back on the cold kitchen floor. I brushed her hair from her face, panic coursing through my veins. Her eyelids flickered, then opened slowly, and she stared up at me, uncomprehending.

'What are you doing, Mummy?' she murmured.

I sucked in a shuddering breath and scooped her into my arms as if she were no bigger than a newborn baby. Grabbing my car keys from the hook, I made for the door. 'I'm taking you to hospital, that's what I'm doing.'

CHAPTER TWO

Laura

The café was filled with weekend tourists, who glared at me as I defended my table in the window. I watched exhausted parents argue with their small children over the extortionate prices of the cakes they were demanding. Elderly couples visiting on coach trips to see the swarming pavilion and check out the cute little lanes, caught their breath over a pot of tea before the return journey.

Not for the first time, I wished I lived somewhere quiet, rural even, a place where I could drink my coffee in peace, rather than smack bang in the most popular area of Brighton. Not that I didn't love the beach, the food, the beautiful countryside just a stone's throw away, but I could do without the tourists.

I glanced at my watch, then peered out of the window, wondering where Adam was. We'd arranged to meet at half past six, but it was getting on for seven now and there had been no message to warn me he was running late. He and I had a standing arrangement to meet twice a month for dinner after he dropped Tilly back with Maddie, so that we could catch up on each other's news. We'd got into the habit back when the two of them were still married, though it had been the three of us then, but Adam and I had continued to meet even after their divorce. It had been a relief to find that he was just as keen as I was to continue our friendship, and I was glad to have been able to be there for him through the divorce, though I sometimes got the feeling that Maddie would have preferred me to pick a side.

I usually chose a pub out in the countryside, preferring to escape the hubbub of town, but this was Adam's week to pick the place, and he'd sent a text first thing to say he was sick of sitting in traffic, telling me to meet him here. It was close, and convenient, but that was about all it had going for it. I sighed, sipping my coffee.

'Excuse me? Can I steal this seat?'

I looked up, shaking my head at the woman, who already had one hand on the frame of the chair. 'No, sorry, I'm saving it for a friend.'

She released it reluctantly, muttering something under her breath as she backed away. I looked down at my watch again, frowning. It wasn't like Adam to run behind schedule, and on the rare occasion he did, he would *always* call to apologise. I hoped he hadn't got caught up in some row with Maddie again. It was becoming more and more usual for them to fall out after his weekends with Tilly.

Madeline had been my best friend since we were seven, and when she'd started dating Adam at fifteen, he'd slotted into both of our lives. We became like the Three Musketeers, doing everything together. The two of them had been in the front row of the audience at my graduation ceremony, cheering louder than anyone else. Madeline and I had held sweaty hands as we huddled nervously together in the back of the small aeroplane Adam had chartered after getting his pilot's licence, quietly hoping he was as good as he claimed and we weren't about to plummet into the English Channel. The three of us had sat in silent awe at the first moments of their daughter's life, each of us knowing just how privileged we were to be a part of that moment. I had a thousand stories about our time together, their lives so interwoven with mine it was impossible to separate either one of them from my memories, but since they'd divorced a year ago, everything had changed.

Now, no matter which of them I spent time with, I felt guilty. For two people who had been in love to the point of obsession, the split had been anything but amicable. It had come suddenly, and I still didn't understand the reason for it, but it was clear that Adam still held on to a hope that Madeline would take him back. Privately, I didn't think he stood a chance. She was impulsive at times, but when she made a decision, she stuck with it.

A trickle of sweat ran between my breasts and I put my coffee down, wishing I'd bought an iced tea instead. The air conditioning was no match for the sweltering August evening. I glanced out of the window again and sighed in relief as I saw Adam striding confidently towards the café. He stood out from the crowd, not just because he was half a foot taller than anyone else, or because he was dressed in chinos and a shirt despite the fact that it was Sunday – it was his commanding presence that made him so noticeable.

I saw the way people moved aside as he passed, the double takes from women, who thrust back their shoulders, lowered their lashes. Not that Adam looked at them. He never seemed aware of the attention he drew. Even so, I pressed the back of my hand to my lips, hoping I didn't have froth from the coffee on them.

Adam walked into the café, spotted me and gestured to the counter, joining the queue to get a drink. I dragged my gaze away, determined not to stare like every other woman in the place. I waited impatiently, feeling increasingly claustrophobic as more people pushed inside, jostling for tables and calling to one another. Adam's voice carried as he ordered a black coffee, and I looked up, watching tensely as he made his way over to the table.

'I know, I know,' he said, placing his mug down and slumping into the empty chair. 'I'm late.'

'And let me guess, it's not your fault,' I teased, folding my arms, though I felt my lips curl into a smile. It was impossible not to smile at Adam.

'You know I'd much rather be here, catching up with you, than arguing with her.'

I shrugged. 'And I'd much rather the three of us could hang out like we used to, rather than me being piggy in the middle,' I said, handing him a laminated menu.

'You and me both,' he said with a frown. 'I miss it. The way it was before.'

I nodded. I did too. The ease of it all, the lack of conflict. I didn't bother to ask what the fight was about, despite my desire to be supportive. I knew well enough to stay out of their disagreements unless I wanted to find myself thrown into the ring.

A young waiter with spiky brown hair and a nose piercing came over to take our food order, saving us from having to queue up at the counter again. I put my menu aside, waiting for him to leave us alone before resuming our conversation. 'So, how was Barbados?' I asked, hoping to move onto lighter subjects.

'Windy,' he replied, taking a sip of his coffee. 'Loads of turbulence on the way over, but the return journey wasn't too bad.'

'No sightseeing?'

He grinned. 'No time. You know how it is – I barely see the world outside the hotel most of the time. It's a pretty short stopover.' He shrugged. 'I'm off to New York tonight.' His smile was tight and I got the distinct impression he was still simmering over his row with Madeline. He sighed, his gaze drifting towards the window, and I wondered if there might be more to his low mood than he was letting on. I let him brood in silence for a moment, unsure how to break through the tension. The waiter reappeared carrying two plates piled high with pasta, plonking them down in front of us and leaving without a word.

I picked up my fork, spearing a cherry tomato on the tip, then popped it in my mouth and bit down, the tart juice bursting over my tongue. 'But you do love it, right?' I probed, drawing his attention back to me. 'Being the captain of a commercial airline? It's what you've worked for.'

'I know. And I *do* love it. But honestly, Laur, I'd give it all up if I could have my family back.' He scooped up a forkful of the steaming pasta, chewing thoughtfully. 'I want to be there when my daughter wakes up in the morning. I'm sick of being made out to be the bad guy, the weekend dad who can never get it right.'

'Tilly doesn't think that, Adam. She loves you.'

'I know that. But… take today, for example. I fell out with her because she wouldn't eat her food, and now I've had to walk away with her still angry and upset with me. I won't get to see her again until next weekend. What is that going to do to our relationship in the long run, if I'm never there to make it up to her? I need to be in her life every day. I hate being out on the sidelines. Going home to an empty flat when all I want is to walk through my own front door, into the house *I* bought, and have dinner with my family.'

'Give it time. It will get easier. You'll find a way to make it work,' I said, reaching over the little round table and squeezing his hand.

He sighed. 'I don't have any choice, do I? So I guess I'll have to.' He put his fork down, shaking his head. 'I'm being terrible company, aren't I? Late, and then moaning from the moment I sit down. I give you permission to fire me as a friend.'

'As if I would.'

He managed a smile. 'Anyway, enough about me. Tell me about your week. Is it all adventure in the world of Dr Laura Burts?'

'Oh, hair-raising stuff,' I teased sardonically. 'Hay fever galore and a particularly nasty rash in the armpit of an eighty-year-old woman. And Friday afternoon we had to call the police because I wouldn't prescribe diazepam to a fifteen-year-old boy with no history of mental illness, and he got nasty.'

'You think he was being pushed into it by someone?'

'Probably. And I'm sure he was scared to go back empty-handed, but that fear made him aggressive. He refused to leave the surgery. Grabbed me by the collar and yelled in my face actually.'

'Jesus, Laur! And here's me talking about my little spats with my ex, when you've been strangled in your office.'

'Hardly strangled. He was a scrawny thing really, and the police were very efficient.' In truth, I'd been pretty shaken by the whole situation, but I didn't want to burden Adam with that. I wanted him to think of his chats with me as refreshing. Something to look forward to, when the rest of his life seemed increasingly hard.

His phone rang and he slipped it from his pocket, frowning. 'Maddie,' he announced, his eyes meeting mine as he lifted it to his ear. My stomach tensed as I watched, hoping she hadn't called to continue their row. It wouldn't be the first time I'd sat with one of them while they yelled down the phone at the other.

He was silent, his lips pursed as he listened to her speak. 'What?' he snapped, his tone sharp. He dropped the napkin he was holding, cutting the call and standing suddenly, yanking his wallet from his pocket and tossing a handful of notes on the table.

'Adam?' I asked, staring up at him. 'What is it? What did she say?'

'Tilly's in hospital. Maddie said that she collapsed. How can that be possible? I only saw her a couple of hours ago.'

My heart skipped, my mouth going dry as I pictured Tilly. If anything happened to her… I couldn't bear to even finish that thought. She was like a daughter to me. I'd rocked her to sleep as a baby. I'd brushed her hair and read her stories, played hide-and-seek and wiped the tears from her eyes after she'd fallen from her scooter, grazing her tiny round knees. I loved her like she was my own. I blinked back a wave of emotion and gripped the edge of the table, pulling myself up to stand. 'I'm coming with you,' I said, grabbing my bag and slinging it over my shoulder. I followed him through the crowded café, focusing on putting one foot in front of the other, not daring to imagine what might come next.

CHAPTER THREE

Madeline

'Tilly. Come and sit here,' I hissed under my breath as I watched her squat down beside the little plastic play kitchen in the waiting room. The cut on her forehead had stopped bleeding without any need for stitches, but I hadn't bothered to wipe the little flakes of dried blood from her skin.

Tilly ignored me, pulling a lurid pink plastic frying pan from the larder, then reaching into a basket of grubby-looking plastic fruit and vegetables. I cringed as she brought a squashed tomato to her face, sniffing as she'd seen me do a thousand times before at the farmers' market. I dreaded to think how many germ-ridden sticky fingers had handled the toys since they'd last seen a bit of disinfectant.

I should have called an ambulance. We would have been seen far quicker if I had. But no, I'd panicked and driven instead, and now we'd been kept waiting for so long that Tilly had seemingly made a full recovery and it was going to be all the more challenging to get one of the busy doctors to understand that despite current appearances, she wasn't well.

Something was wrong with her. I could feel it. I'd spent years being told I was making a big deal out of nothing, but now I was certain they had missed something and I had been right all along. It was as if I'd finally given myself permission to listen to my intuition, to the uneasy feeling in my gut that screamed that something far more serious than anyone had realised was going on with my child.

The thought should have shocked me, but instead, it felt like relief. Like finally confessing a dirty secret after years of repressing it. Healthy children didn't throw up their meals on a regular basis. They didn't need to rest after walking half a mile. And they certainly didn't collapse in a dead faint on a perfectly ordinary Sunday evening.

I chewed my fingernails, my eyes flicking between Tilly and the clock on the wall. *An hour.* We'd been here a whole hour, and other than the nurse taking her observations when we'd first arrived, we'd been utterly ignored. It wasn't good enough.

'Mummy, look.' Tilly grinned, placing a bright green plate on my lap. 'I made salmon en croûte.'

'Salmon on what?' I muttered, distracted.

'It's the thing Daddy wanted me to eat. And peas,' she added, pulling a face.

'Tilly, I really think you need to come and sit down. Are you feeling dizzy? Does your head hurt?' I asked, placing my palm flat on her forehead, careful not to rub away the trail of blood. It helped to showcase the extent of her collapse.

'I feel fine,' she said, wandering towards the Wendy house now. 'Are we going home soon?'

'Not yet.' I stood up, walking across the toy-strewn floor, stepping over a heap of Duplo to get to the desk, where the receptionist was scribbling something down on a notepad. I tapped my foot impatiently, and when she didn't look up, I cleared my throat. 'Excuse me. Can you tell me how much longer the doctor will be? My daughter really needs to be seen,' I said, folding my arms across my chest in a way that didn't come naturally to me. I felt like a little girl playing dress-up in her mother's clothes.

She paused her writing and peered owlishly up at me over the rim of her glasses, big brown plastic frames that obscured half her face. She seemed surprised to see me standing there. 'It can take a while,' she said with a shrug, tucking a loose strand of fine auburn hair behind her ear. 'There are several very poorly children being admitted right now. The general rule of thumb is the sicker the child, the more quickly they're seen. And,' she added, nodding in Tilly's direction, 'she doesn't seem to be in need of urgent medical attention right now. Consider yourself fortunate.'

I stared at her, shocked at her lack of professionalism. 'I'm sorry, but you didn't see what happened to her. It's not fair for you to just—'

'Maddie!'

I spun to see Laura making her way across the waiting room towards me, Adam following a few steps behind her. His eyes locked on Tilly and he walked briskly to where she was playing, crouching low to say something I couldn't hear.

'What's happening?' Laura asked, striding towards me and wrapping me in a brief hug.

'Nothing at this rate,' I sighed, taking in her flushed face as I guided her away from the unhelpful receptionist. She and Adam must have run from the car park. 'You came together?' I asked.

She nodded. 'We were just finishing dinner when you called. We were worried sick.'

I chewed my lip, trying not to feel jealous that Laura had continued her friendship with Adam, even after our split. I had no right to ask her to end all ties with him, and it wouldn't have been fair to either of them. Even so, it hurt to think of the two of them hanging out, like old times, only without me. It was embarrassing to admit that I'd assumed their friendship would fizzle out when Adam moved into his own place. I'd always thought I was the glue that held us all together. It was hard to imagine what they talked about without me there.

Laura's shoulder-length brown bob shone beneath the fluorescent lighting and I reached out to touch it with my fingertips. 'New cut?' I asked.

'Oh, yeah. I had this afternoon free, so…'

'It suits you. And the top,' I said, managing a smile. I exhaled, glancing over to Adam, who was pretending to drink from a miniature teacup. 'Thanks for coming, Laur. I've been out of my mind with worry.'

'I bet. I have too. You know how much I love that girl. But it looks like she's perked up a bit now?'

'You should have seen it. She just…' I clapped my hands together, remembering that awful sound of her hitting the floor.

'Oh, Maddie.' She reached forward, squeezing my hand. 'I'm sure it's nothing to worry about. Kids *do* faint, for all sorts of reasons, you know. And most of the time it's nothing serious.'

I nodded, sinking into a chair. She lowered herself into the seat beside me, waiting in silence. Adam looked up, his forehead furrowing. He murmured something to Tilly and then unfurled his long limbs, moving across the room. He took a seat opposite us, perching on the very edge, as if he were expecting to leave at any minute. 'She's fine,' he said. 'She said she doesn't even remember fainting. What happened?'

'I told you. She got up from the table, said she felt funny and then went down like a sack of potatoes. It was terrifying, Adam.'

'Well, she seems all right now. Are you sure they'll be able to tell you anything?'

'I don't know. I kind of hoped they'd do some tests, you know? Try and figure out what's going on with her.'

He pursed his lips. 'I have a 4 a.m. flight to New York, Maddie. When you called, you made it sound like it was life or death. I don't want to be sitting in a hospital waiting room all night, and Tilly needs to be in bed.'

I stared at him wordlessly, unable to comprehend how his daughter collapsing couldn't be considered life or death. I could feel Laura's eyes darting between us and willed her not to take his side. I couldn't bear to have both of them act like I was some hysterical mother. Laura took my hand, speaking softly. 'Let's just wait to see the doctor, shall we? Or I could take a look at her at home, if you prefer? It's kind of my job, you know?' she said with a little smile.

'But you can't do tests. Scans. And we both agreed it was better for you not to be Tilly's GP any more, Laur. It was you who said we needed to keep the boundaries in our friendship,' I reminded her. 'No, we'll wait,' I said, my voice firm.

Adam glanced at his watch and I felt a strong urge to scream. It wasn't like me to overreact. I wasn't the type to flap and fuss over a scraped knee or a crayon drawing up the hallway wall. But right now, I felt an impending sense of panic I couldn't begin to describe, and it frustrated me beyond belief that Adam didn't feel it too. It was as if he didn't care.

The door swung open behind us, bringing a burst of cool air into the room, and a woman in a tight pencil skirt and smart black blouse walked in. 'Hello.' She smiled, pausing by the desk. 'Do we have Tilly Parkes?'

'Yes,' I said, scrambling to my feet. 'Yes, here she is.'

'Hi, my name's Dr Moyes. I'm one of the junior doctors here. Let's go and have a chat, shall we, and you can tell me what's been going on.' She held the door open, waiting.

'Come on, Tilly,' I called. 'You can bring the doll with you.'

Tilly stood, staring uncertainly at the doctor, a bald baby doll clutched tightly in her arms, its cloth body greyed from years of handling.

'Come on, T,' Adam said, reaching down to grasp her hand. 'The sooner you let the doctor have a look at you, the sooner you can get home to bed. It's nearly nine. You're going to be tired tomorrow.'

I ignored the snide remark, following Dr Moyes as she led us through two sets of double doors and into a curtained-off cubicle.

'It's like a stage,' Tilly whispered.

'A little bit. Have you ever been to a pantomime, Tilly?' the doctor asked. Up close, she looked very young. Laura moved to the corner of the cubicle, taking a seat out of the way.

Tilly nodded as Adam lifted her onto the bed. 'At Christmas. It was *Snow White*.'

'And was it good?'

'It was funny. Dopey tripped over and fell off the stage. It wasn't supposed to happen, but he tripped on the curtain and landed on the man doing the music. It was the best bit.'

'It sounds like a lot of fun. So, Tilly, what's brought you in to see me today?' Dr Moyes asked.

'Not *what*. *Who*,' Tilly corrected. 'And the answer is my mummy.'

'Sorry,' Adam said, rolling his eyes. 'She can be a little bit pedantic at times. It's a phase, I hope.'

'She collapsed,' I said, stepping forward. I pointed to the remnants of blood on her head. 'She said she felt funny, and then she fainted. But that's not all. She's been complaining of pains in her hips and legs lately. And she's been struggling with eating. Being sick after meals.' I felt like I was talking far too fast, hyper-aware of Adam and Laura watching me.

Adam shook his head. 'The eating isn't a medical problem. It's an ongoing issue we've always struggled with. She's fussy,' he said, flashing a wry smile at the doctor. 'And even *I* know that isn't a reason to rush to hospital.'

'Adam.' I glared at him. 'We've waited a long time to see the doctor. Could you please just let *her* be the judge of what is and isn't wrong.'

Dr Moyes raised an eyebrow. 'Let's have a look at you, Tilly. Can you lie down and let me see your tummy?'

Tilly nodded, sinking back on the bed.

'And has she always been on the small side?'

'Yes,' Adam nodded. 'Small but perfectly formed.'

'She's only on the second percentile,' I said. 'She gets tired very easily.' I'd kept a close eye on her weight ever since she was a tiny baby, willing her to move up the chart, and though every doctor had tried to convince me her size wasn't an issue in itself, I always felt like they were too quick to write it off. After all, with a dad of Adam's height and bulk, and a mum who was decidedly average, it didn't make sense for her to be so petite.

'Maddie, calm down,' Adam interrupted. 'You're building this up.'

'No, I'm not,' I hissed through gritted teeth, wishing I hadn't bothered to call him. 'Can you do tests? Blood tests? Scans? I'm sure there's something going on with her.'

Dr Moyes was silent as she examined Tilly, prodding her abdomen, looking into her eyes and ears and throat, working methodically through a mental checklist. I wished I could read her thoughts. She finished listening to Tilly's chest, then looked up, hooking her stethoscope around her neck. 'Your daughter seems absolutely fine, and in my professional opinion, I really don't think it would be wise to put her through a series of unnecessary tests. She is stable and alert, and although she's on the small side, she seems well in herself.'

'But she collapsed!'

'And I'm sure that was very frightening for you, Mrs Parkes. When a child faints like that, it can be a scary thing to witness. But it's actually not all that uncommon, especially in the August heat. I expect she's had a busy day of playing, a bit too much sun and maybe not enough to drink. I think we adults forget how these little things can add up to overwhelm a young body. But as far as I can see, she is absolutely fine now. I wouldn't put her through scans and blood tests unless I felt it was really necessary, and I'm pleased to say, I don't.'

'But—'

'Maddie,' Laura said, standing up. 'This is good news. Trust the doctor's judgement. Believe me, I've seen some very poorly children this week alone. If she was really ill she wouldn't have recovered so quickly.'

'I'm not ill.' Tilly pouted. 'Not today.'

'See?' Adam said. 'So we're all in agreement. Tilly is perfect.' He grinned, reaching down to tickle her belly. She burst into peals of high-pitched laughter, and I could see that I would get nowhere tonight. 'Thank you, Doctor, you have been most helpful.' He flashed her one of his dazzling smiles. He'd always had the ability to use his charm to get his own way. I knew he couldn't stand the fact that it didn't work with me any more.

Dr Moyes flushed bright red, nodding to hide her face and mumbling a quick goodbye as she made a swift exit.

Adam turned to me with a satisfied smile. 'I'm glad that's sorted. Now, some of us have to fly a 747 across an ocean in' – he glanced at his watch – 'seven hours. So I'm going to shoot off.' He kissed Tilly goodbye and turned to Laura. 'You need a lift?'

'No, you go,' she said, glancing in my direction. 'Get some sleep. I can call a taxi.'

'I'll drop you home,' I said, my voice coming out in a flat monotone. I felt numb. Railroaded. If only I hadn't called Adam, the doctor might actually have listened to me. Instead, he'd gone out of his way to undermine me, and I'd come across like some neurotic woman looking for problems where there were none. I lifted Tilly into my arms, following Adam and Laura towards the exit, relieved that at least she was feeling better.

CHAPTER FOUR

Laura

In the end, I went back to Madeline's house rather than have her drop me home. There was a tense energy about her in the car as we drove back from the hospital, Tilly dozing in the back, and it felt wrong to leave her, despite the fact that Tilly had turned out to be fine. I knew she wasn't ready to be alone.

Maddie carried Tilly up to bed without saying a word and I went to the kitchen. Her mood didn't bother me. I was used to it by now. She was always working herself into a panic about Tilly and then getting angry when nobody else got as worried as she did. She'd gone two weeks without speaking to me when I'd refused to refer her back to the hospital for a third time after Tilly had been diagnosed with reflux as a toddler. She was adamant that they'd got it wrong, and when I told her that I couldn't in good conscience make another referral, especially when I'd suspected reflux to be the cause all along, she had accused me of not caring for Tilly or supporting her in getting the help she needed. Madeline could be stubborn, and more than a little fiery when she felt she was being wronged, and she had a tendency to cut herself off from anyone who she felt wasn't entirely on her side. This was no different.

I grabbed some nachos and dip from the larder, and opened a bottle of wine, pouring two generous glasses, while Maddie clattered around upstairs putting Tilly to bed. My stomach was rumbling loudly, and I doubted Maddie had found the time to eat dinner, what with everything that had happened this evening.

I carried the food and wine out to the garden, switching on the lights on the decking. The sky was clear, the stars bright, and the warmth of the long day had yet to dissipate. I lowered myself onto a sunlounger, the smell of jasmine and honeysuckle wafting around me as I sipped my wine slowly.

'She's asleep,' Maddie said, stepping out behind me. I nodded, handing her a glass, and she took it, holding it to her lips without taking a sip. Her eyes fixed on some point in the distance, a crease etched between her eyebrows.

'I'm sure she'll feel better in the morning. She was pretty chatty earlier,' I said.

Madeline shook her head, taking a seat on the sunlounger beside me. 'Can you believe Adam? Did you see the way he flirted with that doctor to get his own way? It was ridiculous. She should be struck off.'

I picked up a nacho from the bowl, scooping some salsa onto the tip to buy myself some time.

'I wish you'd been there when she collapsed. I know she bounced back quickly, but kids do, don't they? But if you'd seen her, you'd be on my side.'

'I *am* on your side,' I said, meeting her eyes. 'I believe you. It must have been horrible. But as a doctor, I can see Dr Moyes' point. It's hard to treat what you can't see, and Tilly looked fine. I'm not saying it wasn't scary for you when she fainted, but like Dr Moyes said, we're in a heatwave. This kind of thing is pretty common.'

Maddie stared at me, then shook her head, finally taking a sip of her wine. She was annoyed, with me, Adam, the whole situation. I could sense how close she was to losing her composure. We rarely argued; I was too uncomfortable around conflict for that. But when it came to Tilly, things could get pretty tense when I didn't agree with Madeline's concerns.

Not for the first time, I wished she would just relax a bit. It was so intense, the way she flapped around Tilly, begging her to eat, pandering to her every demand. It was exhausting. Sometimes I wished I'd chosen another profession so that I could actually relax around my best friend, rather than having to hear the details of Tilly's latest ailment every time I visited.

I'd been her GP up until last year, when I finally reached breaking point and told Maddie it wasn't serving our friendship for me to be Tilly's doctor any longer, but even now, she couldn't resist checking in with me about every little thing. Growing pains, new food aversions. It made her frantic with worry.

Not that I hadn't seen it first-hand. I couldn't deny Tilly was a nightmare when it came to mealtimes, but Maddie couldn't seem to understand that her own behaviour escalated the situation. It was mind games. Kids learn them young. They see their mummy or daddy begging them to eat, and they learn that it's a fun game to resist. They get more attention, and kids love that.

Tilly was a sweetheart, but if she were mine, she'd get what she was given or go hungry. I had spent a long time trying to explain this to Madeline, but she never listened. Now, I didn't even bother trying. I knew she wouldn't take my advice, so I kept my mouth shut.

She reached forward, grabbing a handful of nachos, snapping them into tiny pieces nervously before scattering them to the ground. 'I can't stand it, Laur. The way Adam is with her. I feel like he's trying to prove something. Going against everything we agreed about Tilly when we were married. He didn't get so involved with the parenting decisions back then. I wish he could just look after her properly, the way I do, without feeling like he's got to make up new rules. I mean, how is that fair on her? There's no consistency. It's confusing for her.'

'I don't think he wants to confuse her. And it makes sense that he's more involved in the decision-making now. He's alone with her for two full days a week – he doesn't have you there to lean on.'

'He could call me. I've told him that. Any time, day or night. I'd rather he woke me up than tried to figure things out for himself.'

I played with the stem of my wine glass, eyeing her cautiously. 'He knows that, Maddie. But that's no way to be a parent. He needs to work out his own way of doing things. And I promise you, he would never do anything to Tilly out of spite towards you. You *know* he wouldn't. Adam's a good dad. And Tilly is a smart girl. She'll adapt. Lots of kids have two sets of rules to follow. They work it out.'

'So I should just let her go to his place knowing that she might not eat all weekend?'

I sighed, leaning my head back against the sunlounger, staring up at the stars. There was no way for me to win, no right answer. Both Adam and Maddie were trying to do right by Tilly, only their ideas of what that looked like were so different they couldn't even grasp the other's point of view. I felt like the only child of a couple going through a nasty divorce. I doubted either of them had stopped to consider what the effect of their split had meant for me. The realisation that the people I considered family, the routines I'd been relying on, had suddenly been stolen from me.

No more Sunday lunches together, the three of us laughing over a burned pudding while Tilly chatted animatedly. No more summer holidays in Cornwall, Adam surfing while Maddie and I sunbathed and took turns to rinse a sticky, sand-covered Tilly under the chilly outdoor shower. No more camping trips or spontaneous parties. No more cosy nights in watching a movie and laughing until our sides hurt. Maddie and Adam had been my world. And now it was over, and neither one of them seemed to notice that I was just as lost as they were.

CHAPTER FIVE

Madeline

Then

The sun beat down on the back of my neck and I slipped another button open on my shirt with one hand, leaning back against the prickly grass. The air smelled of dirt and cut grass, vanilla Impulse spray and hot bodies. I squinted, shading my eyes with my hand to get a better view of the Year 11 boys in the centre of the playing field, half-heartedly kicking the ball around, none of them giving it their all in the stifling heatwave. I loved England when it was like this. The way my skin felt hot to the touch, the easy laughter and the sense that anything could happen.

Several of the boys had stripped off their rumpled school shirts, risking the wrath of Mrs Pennington if she caught them. I doubted they cared. At this point in the year, they were nearly free from East Gate Senior School. In some ways I envied them, but I was in no hurry to follow in their footsteps. For now, life was easy and I was happy to milk that a little while longer.

I hitched my hips off the grass, rolling the waistband of my pleated grey skirt over twice more, letting the sun warm my already tanned thighs. Beside me, Laura did the same, flashing me a grin. I let my gaze flick to her cleavage and held back a smile. For a while, we'd been the same cup size, swapping bras and bikinis back and forth, but this winter, hers had reached their peak, so to speak, and mine had kept growing. I was now a full cup bigger and I knew that pissed her off royally.

The ten-minute warning bell sounded, indicating that the blissfully lazy lunch break was coming to an end, and we sighed in unison.

Laura stretched out, feigning nonchalance. 'I wish we could just stay here for the rest of the day,' she said, wriggling her bare toes through the grass, her pillar-box-red nail polish glinting through the green blades. Around us, the other Year 10 girls were getting up, grunting and complaining, rolling skirts back to their knees and refastening buttons.

'At least we don't have to worry about that.' I grinned, nodding in their direction as they headed towards the English block. 'Mr Davidson is such a perv, you could walk in wearing nothing but your underwear and he wouldn't complain.'

'Tell me about it. I think he actually drooled down my shirt last week,' Laura said, screwing her face up. She made no attempt to follow the rest of the girls, but I didn't miss the way her eyes darted back and forth between me and the grey concrete building. She'd be waiting for me to move first, unwilling to look like she cared, though we both knew she would never dare to skip a lesson, let alone the whole afternoon.

I, on the other hand, had no such qualms. Where Laura's parents were mega strict and would ground her for a month for not doing her homework, mine were genuinely relaxed. They'd met and fallen in love in the sixties when they were my age, just fifteen, and though they'd both drifted in and out of flings with other people over the years, they'd never once given me any reason to think they weren't destined to spend their lives together. They weren't like other parents. They actually listened when I spoke. They cared about my opinions. And if I told them I'd taken the afternoon off school so I could lie in the grass and contemplate the meaning of life, they'd more likely hug me and ask what I'd discovered than send me to my room with my tail between my legs. I grinned. Laura could play it cool all she wanted, but she and I both knew that she was going to cave first.

I followed the direction of her gaze over to the gang of Year 11s, who'd finally stopped their game of football. Adam Parkes was glugging back Sprite, his thick brown hair slick with sweat, his tanned back glistening. I didn't need to be beside him to be able to imagine how he smelled.

In the past year, since my boobs had come in actually, I'd noticed that boys had a different kind of smell to them, something I'd never been aware of before. It was impossible to describe. Not bad, just noticeable, a smell I wanted more of. A nutty, masculine scent, strong and almost mouth-watering. It made my stomach tighten and my lips go dry. It made me want to get closer. To see if they tasted as good as they smelled.

'So?' I said casually, rolling over onto my belly to look Laura in the eye. 'You going to ask him, or what?'

'Huh? Ask who what?' she said, though her cheeks coloured instantly.

'Adam. You've had a crush on him for what? Five months now?' I said, pretending the details were fuzzy to me. As it happened, I could remember the exact moment she'd admitted her crush, down to the red liquorice we'd been eating and the Peter Andre song playing on her CD player. Because the truth was, I'd liked Adam myself for the past fifteen months, ever since I'd seen him stick up for one of the Year 7 kids who was being bullied at the bus stop. I'd been trying to get the group of older boys to leave her alone, trying to be brave, though I was terrified they would start on me instead, when Adam had turned up and told them to back off. I didn't think he remembered the look of relief on my face, or the mumbled thanks I'd managed as he held out his hand for the little girl to get on the bus, but *I* had. I'd seen him everywhere after that, watched him as he walked across the canteen and stopped to chat to the dinner ladies, willing him to look my way. I'd liked him for so long, though I'd never told a soul.

'So what?' Laura asked. 'I can't just ask him out, can I? He doesn't even know who I am. I doubt he's even noticed me.'

'And he won't. Unless you make him. Go on, Laura, ask him.'

'No!'

'It might be your last chance.' I shrugged.

'Why? What do you mean?'

'Well, think about it. There are seven weeks left until the summer holidays and he's a Year 11. You know they break up early once they've finished their GCSEs?'

'There's still the Year 10 and 11 prom,' she said, biting her lip. 'He'll go to that.'

'Maybe. But there's a whole lot of time between now and then. Long days at the beach. Pretty girls in bikinis. You see where I'm heading with this? You really need to make your move now. I mean, when you think about it, it's pretty much now or never...'

Laura pursed her lips. She swung her legs round so she was sitting up, glanced at her watch, then jumped up. For a nerve-racking instant, I thought she might actually do it. 'Come on,' she said, not meeting my eyes. 'We're going to be late to class.'

'Chicken.'

'I'm not.'

'You bloody are. You're a wuss.'

'Easy for you to say,' she scowled, slinging her bag over her shoulder. 'It's not like you'd do it.'

'I would.'

'Yeah, right, Maddie. You'd go up to Adam Parkes, the hottest guy in Year 11, a guy who's probably never even looked at you, and ask him out?' She smirked. 'You're so full of it.'

Slowly I got to my feet, brushing the grass off my skirt. Adam was heading across the field now, casually buttoning his shirt as he followed a little way behind his friends. It really was now or never. As much as I teased Laura, I was relieved that she hadn't called my bluff. It would have crushed me to watch her walking over to him, knowing that once she made a move, I never could. But I was sure that her crush on him was just that, a crush that she'd move on from in a matter of weeks. It wasn't like she knew him. The pep talk I'd given about this being her last chance was something I'd been thinking about for weeks now. If I let this moment slip through my fingers, I wouldn't get another opportunity. Adam's summer would be filled with beach parties and camping trips with his friends, and we didn't know any of them. If I didn't do it now, I would spend the next two months regretting not taking my chance when it was right in front of me, pining for something I could have had. I flashed Laura a confident smile, pinching myself hard on the wrist to keep from losing my nerve.

'Is that a dare?' I asked, hoping she would say yes. If she wanted to stop me, *this* was her opportunity. She could tell me to leave it. She could walk across the grass and go and ask him out herself.

I saw the uncertainty flash across her face. She jutted out her chin and smirked. 'You wouldn't do it.'

I pushed back my shoulders and winked. 'Oh yeah?' I smiled, relieved that she'd given me the permission I needed. 'Just watch me.' Then I turned, running across the hot, dry grass towards Adam Parkes, before I could lose my nerve.

CHAPTER SIX

Now

I gasped, blinking into the darkness, my heart racing as I tried to recall if I'd been having a nightmare. I didn't think so, and yet I felt a strange sense of tension creeping over my body, as if something wasn't quite right. Pulling myself up against the headboard, I flicked the switch on the bedside lamp and stifled a scream as I came face to face with Tilly. 'Oh!'

'Sorry, Mummy,' she said, her face pale in the amber glow of the Moroccan-inspired lamp.

'Tilly, sweetheart, how long have you been standing there?' I asked, reaching a hand out towards her. She gave a small shrug, looking down at the carpet, and I caught the unmistakable tang of urine. 'Sweetie, did you... Are you wet?' I asked softly. For a moment she didn't move, her eyes trained on the floor, but I didn't miss the embarrassed flush that spread across her cheeks, the way her fingers knotted together tightly, her knuckles blanching.

I slipped my feet out from beneath the warm duvet, moving into a crouch in front of her. 'It's okay, baby. It's only wee. It's not the end of the world.'

She raised her eyes uncertainly. 'You're not angry?'

'Of course not. You couldn't help it, could you?'

She shrugged again, her gaze sliding back to her feet. 'Daddy was angry,' she said softly.

'What? Has this happened before?' I asked, caught off guard. Tilly had been remarkably easy to potty-train. She'd outgrown the stash of cloth nappies my mum had passed down to me just before her second birthday, and rather than waste money on a new set, I'd just stopped bothering to use them. Instead, I'd popped her in a T-shirt and let her run free. It had been so much easier to mop up the occasional puddle on the floor than it had been trying to wrangle a wriggly toddler onto a changing mat. And it hadn't been more than a couple of months before she'd figured out the whole toilet thing. She'd done it herself really, despite Adam's accusations that I was turning her feral. It was the same thing my mum had done with me. But to start wetting the bed again now, after so long… It didn't seem right.

I pressed a kiss to her forehead, then rolled her nightdress up, slipping it deftly over her head.

'How many times has this happened?' I asked, trying to keep my voice from betraying my anxiety.

She gripped my shoulder for balance as I helped her out of her soaked underwear.

'Three, I think. Twice at Daddy's flat and now one time here.'

I bit back my irritation at the realisation that Adam hadn't bothered to discuss this with me. It was typical of him to think he could handle it alone. Hadn't I read somewhere that bed-wetting could be caused by fears? The thought of Tilly lying in the dark at Adam's stark flat, scared and homesick, filled me with guilt and nausea. She was the one who was suffering most in the wake of our divorce. And it was my fault for not having seen it sooner.

'What did Daddy say? When it happened at his?' I asked, taking her hand and leading her towards the bathroom. I ran a soft worn flannel under the tap, letting the warm water drench it.

Tilly rubbed the top of her foot against her ankle in a nervous gesture. 'He said I was lazy. And that I should know better. But I didn't mean for it to happen, Mummy. I really didn't. I woke up and it felt all warm on my legs and then I knew what I'd done and I was too late to stop it.' Her words caught in her throat and I saw the sheen of tears in her eyes.

'It's okay, sweetie. It happens. I'm sure even Daddy's had his fair share of accidents. I'll talk to him, okay?'

She shook her head, her eyes widening. 'No, Mummy, please, don't tell him. He'll be so angry with me.'

'Of course he won't,' I said, dropping down to look her in the eye. 'It's not your fault, Tilly. Has something frightened you, or, I don't know, been on your mind?'

She shrugged and gave a tiny shake of her head. 'No. But please promise not to tell Daddy.'

I breathed in slowly, wishing I knew what to do for the best. Finally I gave a nod. 'Okay,' I agreed. 'If you really don't want me to, I won't.'

'Promise?'

'I promise. It will be our secret. But I want you to tell me if it happens again, okay? Here or at Daddy's. Will you do that?'

'Yes, Mummy.'

'Thank you.' I kissed the top of her head. 'Now, let's get you cleaned up and back into bed. It's late.'

Tilly gave a nod and I watched as her shoulders finally relaxed, the tension rushing out of her body, making her sleepy with its departure. She yawned loudly and I squeezed the water from the flannel, watching it flow down the plughole, hoping I hadn't made a mistake.

There are certain jobs that seem to drum up more admiration than others. The kind that earn you a nod of respect from strangers. Doctor. Scientist. Even actor, if you happen to be successful at it. None of my jobs had ever earned me that nod. I'd had mums sidle up to me to try and negotiate a discount on my fancy-dress costumes, not grasping the fact that by the time I deducted materials and my labour, my hourly rate was already barely more than pennies. I'd had plenty of raised eyebrows and careless innuendoes during the six months I'd spent as a cuddle buddy, not even counting all the perverted men and women who'd called me hoping to tack on extras to their session.

The idea had appealed to me the moment I read about it. In a world where humans were becoming increasingly disconnected from one another, people were starting to understand just how important physical touch was to their well-being. 'It's about closeness,' the woman on the phone had explained. 'People can go days, *weeks* even, without so much as the touch of a hand. Cuddling not only calms our minds and reduces depression, but it makes us healthier all round.' The idea of bringing some platonic happiness to a lonely soul whilst paying my bills sounded like a dream job, but it certainly hadn't earned me any respect when I mentioned it in public. People couldn't seem to understand that it was about connection. Comfort. Closeness. Nothing to do with sex. But too often we don't respect what we can't understand.

I couldn't deny that I'd had a colourful work life so far. But out of all the jobs I'd tried over the years, the one that earned me the most disdain by far was the one that actually brought in the most cash and ensured my bills got paid every month. I'd signed up to the agency three weeks after Adam moved out, as an excuse to get out of the house more than anything. The job was simple. Turn up on a Wednesday morning – I never understood why it wasn't a Monday – collect the cardboard boxes filled with leaflets, and then deliver them door to door through various streets in Brighton. You never knew what you were going to get. Some weeks it was menus for the latest Indian takeaway. Sometimes beautician's pamphlets. Sometimes free newspapers.

I was perfectly aware that most of them would end up in the recycling bin without so much as a glance. But it was reliable, honest work, and I loved the fresh air and the brisk walk. I could never see why the simple act of delivering leaflets through letter boxes could incite so much scorn. There were far worse things I could do for a living.

I heaved the box onto the table now, peeling back the cheap brown tape to reveal the contents. *Life insurance at the click of a button.* I slid one off the top of the pile with a sudden feeling of inadequacy. This was the stuff grown-ups should be thinking about. Insurance. Wills. Savings accounts. None of which I'd ever bothered with. Adam had always dealt with that stuff, and I hadn't even thought to check if he'd left our joint savings account running or revised the wills he'd done for us back when we first moved in together. Somehow I couldn't imagine him leaving me as the sole beneficiary to his assets now.

I sighed, knowing the leaflet would sit on the table, taunting me, for a week or two before it ended up as scrap paper, the measurements for a pirate costume scribbled in the margins. Wheeling the kitsch old-lady trolley I used for my deliveries from the cupboard under the stairs, I flipped open the lid and began to fill it with the loot for the day. It wasn't yet 8 a.m., and I could already tell it was going to be stiflingly hot. Tilly would complain about having to walk so far – she always did – but I would just have to figure out a way to make it fun. I tried to do the leaflet drops when she was with Adam or my parents, to save her having to come, but I'd taken on extra recently, hoping to finally start putting some money aside for emergencies, and what with all the sewing projects I had lined up, sometimes I had no choice but to take her with me.

I pushed down the lid of the trolley and went into the living room. Tilly was curled up on the armchair, her plate of plain buttered toast sitting untouched on the floor. She was staring out of the window with a pitiful expression on her pale little face. I hoped she wasn't still worrying about wetting the bed. I wished I knew more about child psychology. Was it best to bring the subject up again? Make sure she knew I wasn't angry? Or should I keep quiet and wait for her to mention it? I sat down on the edge of the armchair. 'You haven't touched your toast, sweetie.'

'Not hungry.'

'Really?' I asked, thinking back to dinner last night. She'd barely had more than a few mouthfuls. 'Is your tummy queasy?'

'It hurts.'

'Again?' She nodded, pulling her knees up to her chest. 'Do you want to try something else? Cereal? I could cook you an egg?'

'No.'

'Fruit? You have to eat something,' I pushed, wondering how on earth she was going to walk the delivery route on an empty stomach. She'd be out of energy before we reached the end of the road.

'I said my tummy is sore!' she snapped suddenly. 'I can't eat *anything*.'

'Tilly,' I began, 'you would tell me if there was something worrying you, wouldn't you?' I had the horrible feeling there was something she wasn't saying. Something more behind her mood than just the usual nausea. She stared up at me with innocent eyes. When she spoke, her words sounded far too grown-up for the mouth of a six-year-old.

'I'm not worried. I told you, my tummy hurts. It hurts all over and I'm fed up of everyone trying to make me eat. I can't, Mummy. I just can't.'

'Okay,' I said. 'Then I'm taking you to the doctor.' It wasn't fair to Tilly that this was becoming normal to her, this inability to play and enjoy her life as other six-year-olds could. I hated seeing how subdued she'd become over the past months. It was as if she was slowly slipping away from me, and I had to do something to bring her back. This had gone on for too long, and if it meant being stubborn, sitting for hours every day in the doctor's surgery until somebody was prepared to take us seriously, then that was exactly what I was going to do.

'Why?' Tilly asked. 'They never help.'

'This time they will. I'll make them listen,' I promised.

CHAPTER SEVEN

Then

'What is *that*? Some kind of rat or something?'

I looked up, giving Adam a hard stare. We were squeezed into the rickety old shed at the bottom of my garden, and Adam looked well out of his comfort zone. It was nice to see actually. A flicker of vulnerability. We'd been dating for almost a month, and though I'd expected it – whatever *it* was – to fizzle out after a week or two, things were going better than ever. Those beach parties I'd warned Laura about, the ones with all the girls fawning over him, were no longer some abstract, out-of-reach thing to be envious of. Laura and I were now part of the gang. *Included.* And the only girl Adam seemed to have eyes for was me.

Thankfully, Laura seemed not to mind that I'd made my move before her. And the more I got to know Adam, *really* know him, the more I could see how badly suited the two of them would have been. Adam and I sparked off each other like fireworks. He was funny and flirty, but he also had a quiet side to him that I hadn't expected. And he was far more into his studies than any boy I'd ever known. I liked that about him. He wasn't shallow, not like so many of the guys in his circle.

It hadn't taken long for me to realise he was ambitious. He had goals that seemed so far out of reach to me that I sometimes wondered if he was setting himself up for a life of disappointment.

But something about the way he spoke, the flash of determination in his eyes when he told me he *would* be a pilot, and he would make enough money to live a very different kind of life to the one he had now, made me believe him. He was adamant that he'd never again have to set foot on the Ramsay estate, where he lived with his grandparents. His single-minded drive to succeed made me stop in my tracks. For him to make it would take a level of perseverance not many people were blessed with, but something about Adam led me to believe he might actually do it.

'A rat?' I repeated, lifting the creature out of the hay-lined cardboard box I'd placed on the workbench. 'I thought you were supposed to be smart?'

'I'm not a fan of animals.'

I laughed. 'Maybe you just haven't met the right ones yet. This is Bill. He's a hedgehog. Obviously.'

'And why, may I ask, do you have a hedgehog in your shed?'

'Found him,' I answered, running a palm along his quills. 'Did you know, if you see a hedgehog out during the day, it's almost always because something's wrong with it. You shouldn't leave them, you know. My dad taught me that.'

'So what's wrong with Bill?'

'Can't you see?' I held out the little bundle towards him. 'Go on, take him, he's pretty tame.'

Adam raised an eyebrow in that sexy way that always made my stomach clench and my mouth go dry. I leaned closer, kissing him, and he pressed against me, his eyes half closed. When I stepped back, he had Bill held awkwardly in his cupped palms. 'Now do you see?'

'He's only got three legs. What happened?'

'Your guess is as good as mine. Probably a seagull or a fox. He had a lucky escape.'

'So what, you just decided to keep him as a pet?'

'No, of course not. He'll go back out into the big wide world when he's all better. I called a rescue place, but they didn't have space to take him. I wasn't just going to let him die, was I?'

'But how did you know what to do?'

I shrugged. 'I took him to the vet. I'm good with animals. I can hand-feed a baby bird, I know the difference between a grass snake and an adder, but my talents don't stretch to administering stitches and IV antibiotics.'

'I'm surprised. I thought you could do anything,' he teased.

'Almost.' I winked.

Adam peered at Bill with a look of mingled disgust and fascination. 'Vet's bill can't have been cheap,' he said. 'Did your mum and dad have to fork out for it?'

'I had money from babysitting. I'd been saving it,' I said, busying myself with Bill's nest, refilling his food and water bowls. The truth was, I'd been saving for over a year, hoping to go to India when I turned sixteen. My cousin Dani had gone for six months when she left school and had returned with dreadlocks, an Australian boyfriend and such amazing stories that I wanted to go too, to see what all the fuss was about. But when I'd found Bill, there had been no choice. India could wait. He couldn't.'

'And you just spent it all on him? A half-dead hedgehog?'

'Why not?' I shrugged. 'Like I said, I wasn't about to let him bleed to death.'

'You're so weird. I feel like the more I get to know you, the more I realise how little I know. You're not like any girl I've ever met.'

'Good. I'll take that as a compliment, shall I?'

He hid a smile, his cheeks flushing. He was so confident in so many ways, but when it came to talking about his feelings, he seemed to struggle. It was alien to me. My parents were both sixties relics. They still wore flares and flower-printed shirts, when they weren't parading round in the nude. They'd taught me to be open, honest, never hide my true feelings, and that was a double-edged sword. I'd been told by plenty of people that I was hard to take. Abrasive at times and shocking at others. But if I liked you, you would know about it, and if I loved you, there was no hiding it. It didn't matter if you didn't feel the same way. Love was supposed to be unconditional. A gift. And the more I got to know Adam, the stronger I could feel my feelings growing for him.

Adam held Bill close to his face. 'He's funny-looking. Why did you call him Bill? Wouldn't Lucky or Trio suit him better?'

'Would you like to be named after your most obvious flaw?' I grinned. 'It's like calling Mr Bell "Sour Breath".'

'Or Lucy Minnows "Giant Tits".'

'That's not exactly a flaw,' I said, pushing him playfully in the stomach. 'Give him here – he should be sleeping anyway.' I slipped my hand beneath the little ball of spines, the back of my hand grazing Adam's palm. I still felt this incredible sense of electricity between us at the slightest touch. I hoped that would never fade.

'Yours are better anyway.' He grinned as I placed Bill back into his cosy nest and moved the box back under the tool shelf.

'Thanks. Come on, let's go to my room.'

'Aren't your parents in?'

'Yeah, so?'

'They won't mind?'

'Course not. Why would they?'

He shrugged. 'My grandparents would have a fit if I brought you home and took you upstairs.'

'Yeah, but they're pretty strict, aren't they? And I guess it's easy to see why.'

'What do you mean?'

'Well,' I said, opening the shed door and taking his hand. 'Being a parent, it's a big responsibility. But I bet it feels even bigger when you've got the pressure of raising someone else's child. They have to do even better than your parents, don't they?'

Adam snorted. 'That's not hard, is it? A drug-addicted mum and a dad in prison for burglary. They'd have to work pretty hard to fuck it up as much as that.'

'I know,' I said softly, stopping on the lawn to look up at him, our hands still clasped together. I could feel the tension in his muscles, the way he squeezed a little tighter. I wasn't sure he was even aware he was doing it. Adam hardly ever talked about his parents, though there had been nights sitting huddled beneath a blanket on the shingle, listening to the ebb and flow of the ocean while our friends drank and laughed nearby, when he'd opened up to me. He'd held me close and told me about his past, about his toxic relationship with his parents, the things he'd seen and experienced in their care, and I'd tried to keep quiet, let him talk, because I could sense just how desperate he was to share the truth with somebody.

He'd made the decision not to have any contact with them when he turned thirteen, and he had told me that even though he knew it was the right choice, it still hurt, even now. He never let it show, but in the tiny snippets he shared with me, I saw the pain he carried, the longing for the parents he wished he could have had. He felt let down, abandoned, and I was sure that his drive to succeed, his unstoppable work ethic, stemmed from wanting to break away from his past and create a fresh new future for himself. He was brave to make that choice and I admired him for it, but I sometimes wished I could take away his pain. He had scars that could never fully heal, and I wanted to make them disappear.

I ran my thumb over the back of his hand, pressing lightly against the tense muscles. 'I'm just saying. It makes sense that they're strict. They don't want to let you down. Not after everything you've already been through.'

He looked at me, his forehead furrowing. 'You're deep, Maddie. You know that?'

I laughed. 'You're only just seeing that?'

'No,' he murmured, leaning forward, his lips brushing against mine. His breath tasted sweet and his skin smelled like pheromones. 'Actually, I don't think I am.'

CHAPTER EIGHT

Now

'Mummy, carry me,' Tilly whined, pulling on my arm, her small fingers looping through the beaded strap of my watch, threatening to snap the thing in two. The sun was blazing already, and I could feel little trickles of sweat running down the back of my dress, the butter-yellow cotton turning itchy as it plastered itself to my skin. The car park in front of the doctor's surgery was only half full, but as I'd pulled up, a lorry delivering supplies to the pharmacy had cut in front of me, blocking the entrance. Not keen to wait for it to unload, I'd driven across the road, parking in the multistorey for the shopping centre. Now I was beginning to regret my decision.

'Tilly, it's not far – can't you try? Just for a little way?' She stood still, her eyes on the ground, her lower lip trembling, and I felt a wave of pity for her. 'Oh, fine. But no wriggling, okay?' I said, holding out my arms. I hitched her up onto my hip, my hands knotting beneath her bony bottom.

'Are we going to see Auntie Laura?' she asked, her mood instantly lifted now that she'd got her own way. Sometimes I could see how Adam might think she had me wound round her little finger. Not that I'd ever have admitted it to him.

'No, sweetie, I expect she's busy with her patients. She's not your doctor any more, is she?' I reminded her. Laura had made the decision for us, well over a year ago now, telling me she felt she needed to distance her professional life from her friendship with me. I'd been hurt at the time, shocked that she wouldn't want to do everything in her power to help Tilly, but once the initial wave of emotion had died down, I'd realised it was probably for the best.

Laura and I had never really been the type of friends who argued. Our differences were the foundations to a long-lasting friendship. Where I was fiery, she was calm. Where she thought long and hard before airing her grievances, phrasing her words with practised care, I was an open book and spoke my mind accordingly. Any disagreements that could have become arguments blew over because she was so calm and I was brutally honest. It worked. It always had, since we were little girls trying to figure out which game to play or where we should make our new den.

It was only when it came to Tilly's health that we ever got near to a real argument. When she was just a tiny baby, struggling to put on weight and screaming over her feeds, Laura had taken Adam's side, talking more about my hormones and mood swings than she ever did about Tilly's struggles. Adam was convinced that a strong mind could overcome any obstacle, a belief he'd managed to cement with his own success.

He'd set his goals, then proceeded to drag himself out of the life he was born to, and into something he considered far better. He didn't tolerate weak thinking, and as far as he was concerned, my focusing on Tilly's issues was exactly that.

I knew how conflicted Laura had been, pulled between my worries and Adam's inability to accept anything that wasn't perfect. But Adam's charm had won in the end. Laura had never taken my concerns seriously, and that, I realised now, could have made all the difference. If we'd made the break sooner, maybe we'd know what was causing Tilly's issues by now.

'We'll go to the drop-in surgery. I don't know who we'll see but I'm sure they'll be nice,' I said, crossing the road towards the surgery. My arms tingled, and I shifted Tilly to the other hip, trying to leave a gap between her body and mine for air to circulate. It wasn't ideal timing – we'd have to go out in the midday sun to deliver those life-insurance leaflets or I'd be in a whole lot of trouble. I couldn't afford to lose another job.

Adam was, admittedly, like clockwork when it came to paying child support. I knew him well enough to be confident that no matter how bitter he was towards me, he wouldn't let Tilly go without. We'd got to keep the house and the car when he moved out, and even though I knew he could afford to buy a decent place of his own, he had chosen to move into a rented flat, as if he were trying to prove to me that he knew I'd change my mind. That this whole divorce nonsense was just a temporary glitch, and there was no need for him to start afresh in the meantime.

If I asked, he would increase his monthly payments. He would *love* that. Knowing he was still supporting me. It would be one step closer to getting a foot back in the door. But I wanted to be independent, and that meant finding the time to get my handful of part-time jobs done. I wondered if Tilly could still fit in the old pushchair. She might have to if she wouldn't walk.

I approached the automatic doors to the surgery, sighing with temporary relief as a blast of cool air washed over me, before realising that the air con was concentrated solely on that spot. The waiting room was stifling, and smelled like TCP and cheese on toast. It wasn't yet 9 a.m., but I could see we were far from the first to arrive.

It didn't matter. I'd wait all day if only someone would give me some answers about my daughter. I plopped Tilly down on a seat in the children's area, her eyes glazing over instantly as she stared up at the brightly coloured cartoons playing on the television, then went to get a number. The receptionist handed me a laminated card, the number 23 printed across it. Trying to calculate how long it might be before we were seen, I headed back to Tilly, sitting down beside her, my mind busy working out how best to explain to the doctor the reason for our visit.

I needed to get across that this wasn't just some virus or tummy bug. To use my words carefully in order to make them see what *I* saw. To take us seriously. For once, I wished I had Laura's talent of offering up a perfectly rehearsed speech at the exact right moment. I always dived right in, like a bull at a gate, blurting out everything in one go. But not today. I had to get it right.

I was dragged out of my thoughts by the familiar sound of Laura's voice. Glancing up nervously, I watched as she gave an instruction to the receptionist before walking round the desk, heading into the office behind it.

Tilly, still glued to the screen, soaking up every minute of the coveted TV time, a treat she rarely got at home, hadn't noticed Laura's presence. I found myself sinking low in my seat, hoping she wouldn't look our way. I couldn't explain why, but I felt like she would be irritated after what had happened in A&E. And she'd definitely tell Adam. I didn't want to have to deal with her trying to pretend everything was fine when it wasn't.

After a moment, she reappeared and walked briskly through the waiting area back to the corridor that led to her consulting room, without so much as glancing our way. I released the breath I'd been holding. Was this what it was like to lie? To be the kind of person who snuck around behind their loved ones' backs? It was awful. I felt irritated that I'd been forced to feel like I had to hide my actions, but at the same time, I couldn't help but reason that I was justified. Being honest had got me nowhere so far.

Tilly rested against me and I wrapped my arm round her, waiting in tense silence as I practised my speech for the duty team.

'I'm worried,' I started as the nurse pulled the curtain around the cubicle. 'Something isn't right. She's barely eating, and this has been going on for months. She's frequently sick. She's complaining of pains, in her stomach, her joints, and,' I added, leaning close to the nurse, lowering my voice, 'she's started wetting the bed again.'

'Mummy!' Tilly said, her face flushing bright red.

'Sorry, sweetie, but I have to tell the nurse the truth. Don't worry, she's not going to tell anyone,' I promised, giving her shoulder a gentle squeeze. 'She's tired all the time and still has an afternoon nap most days. That's not normal for a six-year-old, is it?' I pushed.

The nurse smiled, placing her hand on the top of my arm. 'It could be. There are a few viruses that have been going round lately. Not to mention tummy bugs.'

'But this isn't just recent. It's been going on a long time. Please,' I said, meeting her eyes, realising they were filled with warmth. Kind eyes. 'I need someone to be on my side here. I feel like nobody is listening to me.'

She nodded, her expression filled with empathy. 'I'm on your side. Truly I am. And I'm of the opinion that nobody knows better than the parents when it comes to their children. If you're worried, we take that very seriously.' She gestured to a padded grey chair between the curtain and the trolley. 'Take a seat. I'm going to ask Dr Dove to come and have a look at Tilly. She can decide what to do from there. Is that okay?'

'Yes,' I breathed, sinking into the chair. Tilly climbed onto my lap, snuggling into me.

'I want to go home now, Mummy,' she whispered, her face pressed into my neck.

'Don't be afraid, darling. They're just going to have a look at you. Maybe ask you some questions about what's been happening – the tummy aches, the pain. You just tell them what we talked about, okay?'

'I don't want to,' she said, her voice barely audible.

I hoped she wasn't about to be uncooperative. Not after an hour and a half in the waiting room, not to mention putting off my leaflet rounds so I'd have to do this afternoon's sewing projects this evening. I could feel my patience ebbing, the heat making me irritable. I took a deep breath, determined to keep control of the situation. It wouldn't do to get cross.

'Come on now, sweetie. The doctors can't help you if you don't tell them what's wrong. There's no need to feel embarrassed, okay? And when we're finished here, I'll take you to the toy shop. You can choose something for being so well behaved. Deal?'

She nodded, just as the curtain opened. 'Good morning.' A woman dressed in grey slacks and a white coat stepped into the cubicle and pulled the curtain closed behind her. 'I'm Dr Dove.' She held out a hand to me and I shook it, wishing I'd remembered to wipe the sweat from my palm first. Hers was mysteriously dry. She slipped it inside her coat pocket and I wondered if she was surreptitiously wiping the moisture away. She smiled, her head tilting in a gesture of sympathy. 'My colleague tells me you've been having a hard time.'

'Yes, that's right,' I answered carefully, determined not to bombard her with a flurry of information all at once.

'Do you mind if I have a look at you, Tilly?'

Tilly glanced up at me, and I gave a small nod. She climbed off my lap, standing uncertainly before the doctor.

'Can you hop up on the bed?' Dr Dove asked gently.

She shook her head, and I stood, lifting her up onto the narrow trolley. 'She struggles with climbing. It hurts her legs, especially around her knees,' I explained.

I stood beside the doctor as she examined Tilly, relaying the conversation I'd just had with the nurse. I kept my voice slow, refusing to sound like some hysterical hypochondriac.

The doctor nodded, frowning. 'Hmm. It's interesting. Everything you've described could be just the complexities of growing. And it's possible she has some food allergies we haven't identified, though from her records, I see she's already been tested as a toddler.'

'That's right,' I replied, my body tensing as I prepared for her to give us the usual brush-off. I wasn't leaving without a fight – not this time.

'Her tummy *is* a little swollen. But other than that, there's nothing hugely concerning. However,' she added, before I could cut in, 'I take your point that we're not seeing the full picture, and it can't hurt to reassure you, if nothing else, so I'd like Tilly to have a blood test. We can see from that if there's anything untoward going unnoticed.'

'And what about scans?' I asked.

'I'll order an ultrasound. And a review with the gastro specialist. You'll have to go into the hospital for those. They should send you a letter with an appointment within the week – they're very good at rushing these sort of things through. If you haven't heard anything by, say, next Wednesday, give me a call and I'll chase it up for you. Does that sound okay to you, Mrs Parkes?'

'Yes.' I nodded. 'Thank you. I can't tell you how much of a relief it is to be listened to at last.'

She smiled. 'I'll have my colleague come and do the bloods now, if that's okay?'

I thanked her as she left, then wrapped Tilly in a hug, feeling a burst of excited energy at the prospect of finally moving forward.

'Can we go now, Mummy?'

'In just one minute. You need to have a little blood test and then we're off to the toy shop. What do you think you'll choose?' I asked as the nurse sidled in, a blue tray in her hand filled with a selection of tiny bottles and packets. I sat down on the trolley beside Tilly, trying to keep her focused on me as the nurse lifted her right arm, peering at the veins that ran in deep blue rivulets inside her elbow. Tilly watched her curiously.

'Tilly,' I said, waiting until she looked back towards me. 'So? What will the new toy be? A teddy? Some Lego?'

'Um, maybe a new baby?' she said, her face lighting up at the prospect. 'Or a till so we can play shops.' My gaze flicked to the nurse as she pulled on a pair of blue gloves, unwrapping the sterile needle from its packet. 'Daddy had one at his flat, but the ringer ran out of batteries and he said there's no point replacing them…'

I clamped my tongue between my teeth as the silver tip of the needle glinted, the nurse positioning it confidently. I hoped she was good at this. She looked up at me, and I gave a slight nod, willing her to get it over and done with. I forced myself to keep my hands in my lap, rather than grab Tilly to shower her in reassurance.

'… and that's silly, isn't it, Mummy?' Tilly continued, oblivious to what was about to happen. 'What's the point of a till with a broken—' She sucked in a sudden breath, her eyes widening as the needle pushed through her skin. All at once I felt every single muscle in her body tense up. She stared at a point ahead of her, frozen in shock, as the nurse drew back the blood, collecting her samples.

'You're being so brave,' I whispered, pressing my cheek to the side of her head, my lips against her ear. 'Nearly done.'

The nurse eased the needle out of her arm and gave a satisfied nod. 'All finished. That wasn't so bad, was it?' She smiled, pressing a wad of cotton wool to the pinprick wound, securing it with a strip of white tape.

Tilly turned her face slowly to look at me, her cheeks pale, her lower lip trembling. I saw the scream build inside her before she even released it.

'I'll get out of your way,' the nurse said, grabbing her tray just as Tilly let out a blood-curdling bellow. I nodded, leaning forward to envelop my daughter in my arms, unable to hold back a smile as I watched her blood samples being whisked away to where they needed to go.

CHAPTER NINE

Laura

'What have you done to your hair, dear?'

'Hi, Mum.' I did the usual awkward dance around her, leaning in as she offered a flustered air kiss, neither of us knowing whether to hug. I patted her arm before stepping into the house I'd grown up in and self-consciously smoothed down my carefully curled hair. I should have known not to try something new before dinner with my parents. They never let any little change pass without comment.

'It looks lovely,' Mum said, screwing up her face as if she didn't believe her own words. 'Very young.'

'Thanks, Mum. It's nothing really. Just messing around.' I handed her a bottle of wine, knowing I wouldn't see it again. She would store it away for when she had *proper* guests – Dad's colleagues from the hospital, or her book club meeting. I'd be palmed off with a tepid glass of supermarket own-brand Chardonnay, and as usual, I wouldn't point out the switch.

I followed her into the dining room, where Dad was already seated, glaring at the smartphone clutched in his hands. 'Trouble at the hospital?' I asked, taking a seat opposite him and waiting for him to notice me. He pressed a few buttons, then sighed, placing the phone on the table, where he could glance at it every now and then. He looked up, seemingly surprised to find me sitting opposite him.

'Laura was asking if you're having trouble at work, Peter. Because you looked so cross,' Mum added pointedly.

'Did I? Well I bloody well should be. Have you been keeping up with the cricket? Bloody bunch of oafs if you ask me.'

'I don't follow it.' I shrugged.

'Don't follow the Ashes? Why on earth not?'

'Here, dear, something to help you unwind,' Mum said, pressing the expected Chardonnay into my hand.

'Thank you.' I took a sip, swallowing quickly.

'So, are you getting anywhere at that place?' Dad asked, leaning back in his chair as Mum poured him half a lager.

'How do you mean? At the surgery?'

'Of course at the surgery. Are you bored of it yet? Must get terribly dull, day in, day out… I couldn't stand the monotony,' he added darkly.

He didn't need to add any further detail. I knew exactly how he felt about my career. It had once been my intention to follow in his footsteps and train as a surgeon. He'd gone into cardiothoracic surgery. I'd wanted to specialise in trauma. Save lives, step in during the aftermath of the worst moments of my patient's lives. It had been my dream for so long, I couldn't begin to imagine taking another path. But sometimes, I'd discovered, life has no interest in plans or dreams. Sometimes you're dragged from the route you'd intended to take, and no matter how hard you try to get back, you can't find your way. Dad had never forgiven me for that.

'It's fine. I'm not bored,' I said, offering a small smile as Mum served new potatoes onto my plate.

She put the bowl down, patting my shoulder. 'I think you've done wonderfully. I'm always hearing people praise that surgery, and I'm sure you're a big reason for its success.'

'It's rewarding work,' I muttered, helping myself to a portion of overcooked broccoli. I never knew how to take her praise.

Part of me wanted to believe she meant it, but I couldn't help but think she only said these things to bolster my confidence, the way mothers do when a child brings them a messy collage covered in glue and sequins.

When it came to my work, she seemed determined to over-compensate, brushing over any mention of the career I could have had, and offering up over-the-top compliments that somehow seemed a little excessive. I looked up to find her watching me, and smiled, my eyes crinkling. Whatever her motivation, I was grateful that she was making the effort.

Dad made a noise that sounded like a snort, and Mum sat down beside him, tutting. 'Eat your dinner, Peter. While it's still hot.'

We were silent for a moment, the only sound the tinkling of the serving spoon as Mum filled her own plate. I chewed slowly, waiting for what I knew was coming next.

'Charlie's doing well,' Dad announced through a mouthful of lamb chop. I glanced up, seeing the little flecks of green from the mint sauce lodged between his teeth. Self-conscious on his behalf, I ran my tongue over my own teeth, then took another sip of the syrupy wine.

'I heard,' I said, placing my glass gently on the table. Charlie was my brother. Five years my junior and, as far as my parents were concerned, a resounding success and overall winner at life – not that it should have been a competition. If I were honest with myself, I knew he'd won too. He had the career I'd never achieved, working as a paediatric surgeon in one of the best hospitals in New Zealand. He'd managed to escape the cloying attentions of our parents, moving to the opposite side of the planet whilst still maintaining his status as the clear favourite. And eighteen months ago, he'd blown me out of the water when he'd married Emma. She was a highly regarded obstetrician and had had both Mum and Dad eating out of the palm of her hand from the moment they met her.

It was hardly fair. To top it all off, Charlie was really a lovely guy. We'd never been massively close, but he was a good man and I couldn't hate him for doing well, leaving me in a cloud of dust as he got on with life with a gusto I seemed to be missing.

'He called today,' Dad continued, stabbing a potato on the tip of his fork.

'Peter,' Mum said, her tone tight as she flashed him a warning glare. I looked from her to my dad, a sudden coldness spreading through my limbs as I got a horrible premonition of what he was about to say.

'Emma's expecting. Our first grandchild! Would you believe that?' He beamed, his eyes trained on my face as he spoke. I knew he was watching for signs of guilt over my inadequacy as a daughter. As the elder child, it should have been *me* who'd settled down first. *Me* announcing the impending arrival of their first grandchild, seeing the joy on their faces. I chewed my lamb slowly, the flavour lost on me, the food I'd already swallowed sitting heavy in my stomach, threatening to make a second appearance.

'Peter,' Mum said, clearly angry now. 'We discussed this. I said *I* was going to tell Laura Charlie's news later.'

'Were you? I don't remember anything about that.' He shrugged. 'I don't see what the big deal is, June. This is happy news.'

I finally managed to force the mouthful of stringy meat down, chasing it with a deep glug of wine. 'It is,' I managed. 'I'll send them a card. It's good news.'

I tried to imagine my brother as a dad, to picture what his baby would look like. I could feel my father's challenging stare boring into the top of my head as I looked down at my plate, trying to hold my emotions in check. I was sure he had done it on purpose, broken the news himself because he wanted to see my reaction. He had always been like this, using guilt and shame, promoting competition between me and Charlie to get us to push that extra step further, try that little bit harder at everything we did. The more I veered from the life I knew he wanted for me, the more he put my brother on a pedestal under the mistaken assumption that it would make me want to change in order to please him. He didn't understand there was so much more to the choices I'd made than he could possibly realise. His tough-love approach only served to make me feel worthless.

If Mum had got her way and been the one to break the news, she would have done it gently, with empathy. She would have understood just how heartbreaking it was for me to hear those words. I was happy for Charlie and Emma. I *was*. But I couldn't squash down the longing I felt in the depths of my heart, the jealousy that simmered beneath the surface ready to explode from me with the slightest prodding. I couldn't let my dad see me crumble. I took another steadying sip of wine and looked up, meeting his eyes with a smile I hoped seemed genuine.

'There, see?' Dad said gruffly, picking up his beer and holding it aloft. 'How about a little toast. To Charlie and Emma, and their first baby.'

'Cheers,' Mum said, holding up her sherry awkwardly, her cheeks still flushed, as if she were embarrassed for me.

'Cheers,' I repeated, raising my wine. My hand was shaking and I took another sip, then placed it back on the table, meeting Mum's empathetic gaze.

'Sorry,' she mouthed as Dad focused on his plate. I shook my head, looking away, trying not to remember that this should never have been the first grandchild. That honour should have been mine.

CHAPTER TEN

Madeline

The doorbell rang for the third time in a row, and I rushed down the stairs, dropping a cloth on the banister and sweeping my tangled mess of curls up on top of my head with a scrunchy. Passing the mirror on the hallway wall, I saw a white mark emblazoned across the front pocket of my teal dungarees. Bending to sniff, I realised it was toothpaste. Tilly had developed a habit of using me as a face cloth, and I rarely noticed until some inconvenient time. I swung open the front door, coming face to face with Adam.

'Took you long enough,' he said, folding his arms. 'I was about to call you. Thought you'd gone out and lost track of the time.'

'I *had* lost track actually,' I replied, glancing over his shoulder. The sun was low in the sky, and I realised the afternoon had passed without my noticing.

'Well?'

'Well what?'

'Where is she? I'm desperate for a cup of tea and some dinner, and I expect she wants her bed.' He craned his neck to look around me. 'Don't say you've forgotten to pack her a bag again? I'm dead on my feet here.'

'Yeah, about that.' I paused, glancing behind me. I wished I'd remembered to send a text, rather than having to deal with this on the doorstep. 'Tilly can't come to you tonight. She's not well.

She's been sick twice since lunch, and she's already in bed. I'm sorry, Adam, but I couldn't make her wait.'

Adam's face froze. 'Madeline, I just got back from a twelve-hour flight, with a three-hour delay in Cape Town. I'm tired, I need a shower and I want to see my daughter. Is that really too much to ask?'

'No, of course it's not, but she's poorly. What was I supposed to do?'

'This is getting silly! You and I need to sit down and discuss a plan going forward. Tilly is not ill, she's *fussy*, and you've escalated it by pandering to her every demand. You want to know what I think?'

I really didn't, but I pursed my lips, hoping he'd tell me and leave if I let him have his little rant.

'Go on.'

'It's anxiety. You said yourself her relationship with food has gone downhill over the past year. Ever since you decided you didn't want to be married to me any more. You don't realise the impact a broken home has on a child, Maddie. It causes stress. A build-up of nerves. She doesn't know where she stands or what's happening to her, and that's probably having an impact on her health. It's no wonder she feels sick all the time when she knows you and I are at war.'

'We're not at war,' I said quietly. I breathed in deeply, meeting his eyes. 'I've considered that it could be anxiety. Of course I have – it's too obvious to ignore. And I haven't ruled it out. But I think it's something more, I really do. I would love to sit down with you, talk about what to do, what to try, but you never hear me out. You're so determined to gloss over it that you won't open your mind to the possibility that I might be right.'

He flared his nostrils, rubbing his palm across his eyes wearily. 'And you won't open your mind to the possibility that you're part of the problem. Your fears are making her worse. I mean, for goodness' sake, that scene at A&E – it was embarrassing. I think we need to discuss the fact that this might not be about Tilly.'

'What are you—'

'It's about your sister, Maddie.'

I felt my jaw drop open, shocked that he would dare to throw that in my face. I wanted to scream at him. Lash out. Instead, I swallowed thickly, taking a series of deep breaths as I stared down at my bare feet. Finally I looked up at him, praying that my face didn't betray how deep his words had cut. 'Adam, we're wasting our time. You know how this goes. We'll talk in circles and never come to an agreement. I think it's best we leave it.'

'Fine – give me my daughter and I'll be on my way.'

'I told you. She's sleeping.'

'So let me come up and get her. I'll carry her to the car and she can go straight back to sleep in her own bed at my place. I want her to start the weekend at mine.'

'I'm not going to let you disturb her for the sake of winning some battle. Come and get her tomorrow morning if you like. If she's better, that is. I'll call you, okay?'

'What? No! No, you won't *call* me. She's *my* daughter and if she's really ill, *I* can look after her.'

I shook my head again. I didn't want her out of my sight when she felt unwell. And I knew Adam didn't have the patience to deal with it. What if she wet the bed again or couldn't manage the food he tried to force on her? It was bad enough having her gone when she was at her best, knowing I wasn't there to stand up for her against her father's strict rules. But now? No, there was no way I could send her away. 'Adam, you're a grown man. Like you said, you've had a long day, you're tired and you need to get some sleep. I'm not going to send Tilly to you when she needs me.'

'That's not your choice. We have an agreement, Madeline. I have rights. I don't have to ask your permission – she's mine too!'

he said, his face reddening. The little veins on his temples were swollen and pulsing and I could see just how upset he was getting.

'I don't want to argue with you. And I have to get back to her. I'm sorry, Adam, but her needs have to come above your wants.'

I swung the door closed before he could say anything else, breathing heavily, my hand trembling as I slid the bolt across. I hated to row with him. I couldn't stand that things had become so fragile between us. I'd mistakenly assumed we could be civil after we ended our marriage. For the sixteen years we'd been together, we'd never been purposefully spiteful to one another, even in our worst arguments. He was a good man, stuck in his ways, yes, but fundamentally good. I never thought he would assume the worst in me. Treat me like a liar. I didn't want to stop him seeing his daughter and I would never try, but this was different.

I heard heavy footsteps on the gravel drive, followed by the slam of a car door. A few moments of silence passed, then finally the engine roared to life and Adam drove away. I sighed, relieved for now, though I couldn't help but think about what would happen in the morning.

'Mummy,' Tilly's voice called down from her room, 'can I have a drink please?'

I smiled, leaning my head back against the front door, closing my eyes. 'Coming, sweetie,' I called. 'I'm just getting it now.'

CHAPTER ELEVEN

My eyes itched with the desperate need to close, my head pounding after a long sleepless night, but none of that seemed to matter. I leaned forward on the mattress, my hands sliding through Tilly's damp hair, sweeping it back into a ponytail on top of her head as she gripped the bowl between her thighs, vomit dripping from her chapped lips.

'All done?' I asked softly. She gave the tiniest of nods, her pupils unfocused as she stared morosely down at the bowl. I moved it onto the floor and wiped her mouth with a towel. There were wet, acrid-smelling patches dotted over her fairy-printed duvet cover from when I'd grabbed the bowl a few seconds too late, and the room smelled sour despite the window being flung wide open. I tried to move so I was sitting in a dry spot, ignoring the splashes of yellow staining my white cotton pyjama bottoms.

The heatwave had continued all night, warming the sickroom to intensify the stench of stomach acid. I'd changed the bedding twice, but now I'd run out of both sheets and energy. Laying a towel over her pillow, I tried to guide her head back down to the soft contours. 'Do you feel like you could sleep?' I whispered as she lay back.

She shook her head. 'It hurts.'

'What does, baby? Your tummy?'

She let out a long breath. 'Everything.'

I sighed and stroked her matted hair off her forehead. Her skin was dry and papery and I tried to recall when she'd last managed to keep anything down. She'd been throwing up almost constantly since midnight, but she'd had a few sips of water around dinner time, just after I sent Adam on his way. It wasn't enough. Not even close. I watched her now, her eyes open, staring blankly up at the ceiling, her chest rising and falling as she took in shallow breaths.

She could die. The thought hit me hard and I felt panic ignite in my body, my own mouth going dry as I realised just how serious this could be. My stomach cramped painfully and I pulled my knees up to my chest, hugging them tightly. Dehydration in kids, especially ones Tilly's size, could be fatal. I should have taken her to hospital hours ago.

It had been fear that had stopped me. The offhand reaction I'd had at our last visit to A&E, when Adam had undermined me to the point where the young doctor, clearly infatuated by his charm, hadn't listened to a word I'd said. I should have fought harder then. Stood my ground. But no, I'd let them walk all over me, and now, just as I'd predicted, Tilly was suffering the consequences. My gut was screaming at me that we needed help, urgent medical intervention to rehydrate her, tests to determine what was wrong, as I'd begged for time and time again. But I was so afraid to make the call, to be brushed aside once again, accused of being an overprotective mother, to have Adam chastise me for wasting everyone's time and Laura try to make me believe this was normal. I knew Tilly needed help, but what if nobody would believe me? How could I protect her when nobody was willing to hear what I was trying to tell them? I had never felt so alone. So terrified.

I stood up slowly, stretching out my back, feeling the pop and crack of my spine from being hunched over all night. My neck throbbed and I kneaded my fingertips roughly into the muscle, then moved towards the window, pulling open the curtains. The sky was turning an inky blue, sunrise not far away. I picked up my phone from the dressing table and saw it had just gone five in the morning. Indecision gripped me. I felt paralysed by fear, but I had to make up my mind quickly. I was running out of time. I turned back to Tilly. 'Can you manage a drink, baby? Can you try a sip of water?'

She didn't answer, didn't even move; just continued to stare up at the ceiling. I bit my lip, gripping my phone hard, terror pulsing through every inch of my body, the urge to scream building somewhere deep within me.

I wished Adam were here. Or Laura. If they could see this, if they'd witnessed the night we'd just endured, the relentless vomiting, the way Tilly's eyes had turned flat and lifeless above her hollowed-out cheeks, they would never think to disagree with me. But they never had to deal with this part. It was *me* that was left with the difficult decisions, and I didn't care how angry it might make my ex-husband. I wasn't going to let my daughter suffer.

There had been so many nights when I'd held her hair back, whispering soothing words until her stomach finally relaxed, but this was different. This time, it wasn't easing as the hours passed. If anything, it was getting worse. I didn't understand how there could be anything left inside her to expel; her stomach seemed to constantly refill with the bright yellow bile that she couldn't stop bringing up. Each time, the force of it shocked me, the liquid cascading from her mouth like a fountain, leaving her shaking and breathless in the aftermath.

I bent down, kissing her cheek softly. Her breath smelled like bile and something far worse, and I pulled back, hoping she would say something, reassure me that she was holding on, but she didn't say a word. She just kept staring, her mouth hanging open, her tiny hands flat at her sides on the mattress. Swallowing down my fear, I lifted the phone, keying in the number. It rang just once.

'Nine nine nine, which service do you require?'

I took a breath and spoke. 'Ambulance, please. I need an ambulance.'

'We need an IV now,' the paramedic said, leaning over Tilly's single bed, pressing hard at her spindly arms. He seemed too large for her pretty green bedroom, and I watched in mingled horror and surprise as Tilly let him manhandle her. The ambulance had arrived in four and a half minutes, and during that time, Tilly hadn't moved an inch. She hadn't said a word as the two unfamiliar men entered her room, and now, as the first of them made his assessment of her, she didn't even turn her head to look at him. I knew that was a very bad sign. The second paramedic handed a tray to the first, and I saw the glint of a needle as I rushed around her bed to the opposite side.

'Tilly,' I began, hoping to distract her as I had before. The paramedic pushed the needle into her skin without preamble, and Tilly made a tiny grunt in the back of her throat.

He fiddled with the angle and I flinched as he stabbed at my baby girl. My hands clenched into tight fists as I watched him, forcing myself not to leap forward and yank his hands away from her. Finally he shook his head, tossing the hair-thin needle back into the plastic tray. 'No good,' he muttered. He looked up at me. 'When did she last drink?'

'Last night, but she's been sick at least fifteen times since then.'

'Fifteen?' he repeated. I nodded.

'And what's she bringing up?'

I held up the bowl I'd placed on her dresser to show him the yellowy-green liquid. He gave a grim nod. 'I'm sorry, Mrs...'

'Madeline – it's Madeline,' I told him.

'Right. Madeline.' He spoke fast, though not unkindly. 'Your daughter is very dehydrated. I know it's not fun, but I'm going to have to poke her again. It's vital we get a cannula into her so she can have some fluids. And the more dehydrated she becomes, the more difficult it is to get IV access.'

'Do it.' I nodded, my voice stronger than I'd expected. 'Just do what you have to do. Please.'

He lifted Tilly's little hand, pressing hard on the paper-dry skin. 'I'm going to need a tourniquet and a butterfly needle,' he instructed over his shoulder. Moments later, he made a second attempt. I gripped Tilly's free hand, watching as the blood began to trickle out from the vein on the back of her hand. His fingers trembled as he fiddled with the tiny tube, attaching the cannula and taping it down. He picked up a syringe filled with a clear liquid.

'What is that?'

'Just water. Sodium chloride.' He screwed the tip of the syringe to the end of the cannula and flushed half the liquid down it, then sat back, exhaling. Tilly moaned softly. 'Don't worry about that,' he reassured me. 'The flush is cold; it can sting a little, but the important thing is that it's working. We'll hook her up to a bag of fluids and then we'll get going.'

'To hospital?' I asked.

'Yes. This will take a minute. Grab your phone, toothbrush, whatever you need.'

I picked up my phone from where I'd dropped it on the mattress and ran through to my bedroom, tossing it into my handbag. I yanked my charger from the socket and shoved that in too.

The house was stifling, but I felt shivery and sick, so I yanked a thick pashmina from the top shelf of my wardrobe and rushed back to Tilly's room. The paramedic was screwing the end of a drip line onto her cannula. 'Ready?' he asked his colleague. He gave a nod and together they lifted Tilly onto the stretcher, strapping her down.

'Is that necessary? Can I not just carry her?' I asked, stepping forward, my arms already outstretched.

'We've got her,' he said, moving towards the door.

I nodded, biting the inside of my cheek to keep from arguing, and ran ahead of them to the stairs, taking them two at a time. I opened the front door, seeing the orange and pink streaks marking the start of a new day staining the horizon. The paramedics passed by me, settling Tilly in the ambulance as I stared at the sunrise.

'Madeline. We're ready.'

I nodded silently and got in the back, heading straight to Tilly, my fingers gripping her cold hand.

She blinked up at me, confusion clouding her features. 'What are we doing, Mummy?' she croaked.

I smiled, relief flooding through me at the sound of her voice. 'We're going for a ride in the ambulance, sweetheart. You're not very well, and we need to go and see the doctors.'

'I'm tired.'

'Then rest, darling. You can sleep.'

'Excuse me?' the second paramedic said from behind me. 'You need to sit here.' He pointed to a seat on the opposite side of the ambulance.

'Can't I stay here?'

He shook his head. 'It's our policy. Keeps us from getting sued when passengers fall over.' He flashed me a sympathetic smile. 'Don't worry, we're right here, and it looks to me like she's drifting off already.'

I nodded, unknotting my fingers from my daughter's, feeling the weight of their absence instantly. I sat down, my eyes never leaving her prone body as I fastened my lap belt. The paramedic picked up a portable monitor, unwinding the wire and clipping the end of it onto Tilly's big toe. Two numbers flashed up on the screen and he wrote them down.

'What do they mean?' I asked softly, trying to understand.

'This one is her heart rate. It's quite high, but that's probably down to dehydration. And this is her saturations. The oxygen levels in her blood. That's looking quite normal.'

I nodded again as the back doors slammed closed and the engine roared to life. My body veered to the left as the ambulance took a corner, and I saw the flash of the blue light reflected in the dark windows of my neighbours' homes. In an hour or two, Adam would be calling, demanding to come and collect his daughter, and I had no idea what I was going to tell him.

I glanced towards my bag, wedged between my feet, wondering if I should let him know what was going on. If it were the other way round, I'd want to know. I'd be livid if he didn't call me the instant he got the chance. But then I recalled just how hard he had made things last time, and I knew I wouldn't pick up the phone. Not yet. Not until I'd had the opportunity to speak to a doctor – a specialist, hopefully – without him talking over me.

CHAPTER TWELVE

The ambulance slowed and I blinked, seeing the lights of the hospital up ahead. I braced myself, knowing that the next few hours were going to be important. How seriously they took us once we got inside would come down to what I said and did now. I couldn't waste this chance to be heard. The doors opened with a bang and I unclipped my seat belt, grabbing my bag.

'Climb down first, and then we can get Tilly out,' the paramedic instructed.

'Oh, okay, yes,' I said, my throat croaky. I took his hand, accepting his help as I scrambled down to the pavement, my hands gripped tightly around the strap of my handbag. 'Are we going to A&E?' I asked as they lowered the stretcher to the ground. Tilly had managed to fall asleep, and I stepped up beside her and slipped my hand into hers again, determined not to let go.

'No, we're heading straight up to the children's ward. They're expecting her.'

I pressed my lips together, relieved. That sounded positive. There would be no waiting around in playrooms for someone to take notice of us. Not today. We were being pushed to the front of the queue. I couldn't help but think that if they'd just listened to me last time, we could have got a head start on investigating what was wrong, and perhaps prevented Tilly from getting so very poorly. They should have known just how important it was to act quickly. It wasn't good enough. But never mind, that didn't matter now. The important thing was that we were here and they were going to help Tilly. I didn't let myself think about any other possibility – I couldn't bear to. Later, once we'd got through this awful day, I would be able to process the events of the night. I'd give myself permission to recall the terrifying roll of my daughter's eyes, the way her skin felt paper thin beneath my fingers. I would cry then, give in to the bubbling vat of emotion rolling around my gut. But not yet. Right now I had to be strong, focused. How I felt was inconsequential; all that mattered was supporting Tilly, in any way I could. There was no other option.

I kept a firm grip on her hand as the paramedics wheeled her stretcher through the automatic doors, into the sprawling chaos of A&E. An old man was lying alone on a stretcher, his head bleeding through a thick white bandage. A few feet in front of him, a woman with what looked to be a heavily pregnant belly rolled onto her side with a loud moan. Doctors rushed from one cubicle to the next, emitting a frenzied energy that made my own heart race. We didn't pause to watch; we just kept walking in a straight line as if all hell wasn't breaking loose around us. I found myself shielding Tilly's eyes with my free hand, hoping she wouldn't wake up and see the patients with gaping wounds, the elderly people crying for help. She would have nightmares for years after a few minutes in here.

We came to another set of double doors and I sighed in relief as we emerged into a long, deserted corridor, eerily quiet after the hustle and bustle of the emergency ward. The paramedic who had given Tilly her cannula pressed a button, and I realised in a daze that we were heading inside a lift.

It all felt so surreal, so very odd to be standing inside a lift looking down at the gaunt, sleeping face of my daughter in the early hours of the morning. I felt as if I'd fallen into a bad dream I couldn't wake from, and I suddenly wished more than anything that I could go home. That I could tell them it had all been a dreadful mistake, Tilly was fine, she really was, and I was sorry for wasting their time, but I needed to take her home now because we both needed to go to bed.

The lift doors opened and we stepped out into the bright lights of a corridor. The first thing that hit me was the colour. The cheery posters on the walls, the swirling patterns in the floor; even the windows were adorned with transparent plastic designs in a kaleidoscope of colour. But there was no time to stop and look at any of it. I felt dizzy, my temples aching, my legs struggling to keep up with the fierce pace of the paramedics.

We turned a corner, and the second paramedic spoke into an intercom on the wall beside another set of doors. Seconds later, a buzzer sounded and we were admitted to the ward. A nurse rushed towards us, nodding to the paramedics, instructing them to follow her. The hall here was dim, the lights turned low, and I stared as we passed each bay, my gaze homing in on the beds where children lay sleeping, wires and monitors streaming from beneath their blankets. Beside them, on single camp beds, parents were sprawled, some sleeping, some staring mindlessly at their phone screens, haunted eyes in exhausted faces.

We were led into a bay beside a large window, facing out onto a tower block, and several more nurses joined us, helping to lift Tilly onto the thick mattress of the hospital bed. She woke briefly, her eyes still unfocused, her hands gripping tightly at my forearms, the half-moons of her nails digging into my skin.

'It's okay, sweetheart – go back to sleep,' I reassured her, and she turned her face into the pillow, giving in to her exhaustion. The paramedics spoke quickly to the nurses, using words I didn't know or understand, and I watched, trying to absorb it all.

The sound of a curtain being pulled back caught my attention, and I glanced towards the opposite bay as a woman in rumpled pyjamas stepped out carrying a wash bag. On the bed behind her, a small, dark-haired boy, no more than five or six years old, lay sleeping. She glanced at me, our eyes meeting briefly, and I knew at once that she understood. She knew what I was going through right now, better than any other person in the room. The agony of not knowing what would come next, of having to stand helpless as your child, the person you loved most in the world, faded before your very eyes and there was not a thing you could do to help. All either of us could do was just *be* here, keep going, continue putting the needs of our children above everything else in order to get them the help they needed. We had to be strong. Unbreakable. It was all we had left.

She dipped her head, tearing her eyes from mine and walking towards the hall, and I felt my throat tighten against a lump I would not give in to, my hands shaking as I turned back to my daughter, pulling the curtain shut behind me.

CHAPTER THIRTEEN

I didn't know how many hours had passed since we'd arrived at the hospital, but there had been a near-constant stream of people moving in and out of our cubicle, asking me the same questions, making me repeat the whole story and the events that had led to us being here over and over, like I was under police interview or something. I was tense and beyond exhausted, but I knew that even if I were left alone now, I would never be able to sleep. Too much had happened for me to be able to switch off.

Sometime after the day shift had arrived on the ward, we'd been moved out of the little bay and into a side room of our own. It was hospital policy that any child admitted with such severe vomiting was separated in case whatever they had turned out to be contagious. I knew it wasn't. Tilly had been getting sick more and more frequently over the last few months, the symptoms she'd always struggled with growing more pronounced, more obvious – to me at least. I knew this was all part of whatever had been going on with her. She didn't have a bug. I would have staked my life on that. But when they'd insisted on moving us to the side room, I hadn't bothered to argue. I'd been too tired, and I was certain that I was going to have many more battles ahead of me as the day progressed. I had to save my energy.

The room, in stark contrast to the bays, was quiet and lonely. Tilly had mercifully remained fast asleep throughout the transfer, and the nurse had instructed me to press the call button if we needed to use the toilets, as they had allocated Tilly her own so as to contain the spread of infection.

She was hooked up to a drip, which whirred incessantly, and beeped every now and then, and a monitor gave off a regular high-pitched alarm to let us know that her heart rate was still up. It seemed pointless to me, when we were already well aware of that. The number on the monitor had remained between 175 and 180, drawing tuts and frowns from every nurse who entered, clad in masks and aprons now, acting as though we were harbouring smallpox. I felt like I'd walked onto a stage in a foreign theatre, where everybody seemed to know their roles and their lines but I couldn't translate the words on the script.

I sat down on the blue padded chair near the window, grateful at least that this room had a better view. There was a public play area across the road, a few trees dotted around it, and I watched with a kind of desperate hunger as a mother and her small child walked up to the gate. The child – I couldn't tell if it was a boy or a girl – let go of her hand and ran for the swings, arms flailing to the sides, free as a bird. It was cruel to build a park in plain view of the children's ward. I glared down at them and released I was overcome with jealousy. Angry that *they* got to be out there, while I was in here terrified for my daughter's life. It wasn't fair that they were free to carry on as normal while we were forced to watch from our cage.

Tilly stirred and I rose from my seat automatically, reaching for the disposable sick bowl the nurse had left for us. I brushed the hair back from her forehead as her eyes flickered open, my hand sliding round the back of her neck, swinging her up to sit just as she gagged and threw up noisily.

The door opened as she retched, moaning incoherently before sinking her head back onto the pillow. I wiped her mouth with a paper towel before looking up to see who'd come in.

A man of around fifty, wearing a dark purple shirt and yellow polka-dot tie, stepped forward, flanked by a young woman holding a clipboard and a bearded man of no more than thirty-five. I placed the sick bowl on the table and waited for him to speak.

'Hello, I'm Dr Wallis,' he said, moving to the opposite side of the bed, not bothering to introduce his colleagues. 'I'm one of the gastro consultants here. I've just been going through Tilly's notes and it appears that her symptoms have been going on for long enough that we can rule out a sickness bug, is that correct?'

'Yes,' I said. 'It's not a bug. I'm absolutely certain it isn't.'

He gave a nod. 'So from what I gather, she has had difficulty eating, abdominal pain, vomiting and weight loss increasing in severity over the last twelve months, resulting in regular visits to her GP. Is that correct?'

'Yes. She also complains of pains in her hips and legs. And she gets tired. Much more than other children of her age.'

'Which is to be expected if she's not getting sufficient nutrition and hydration,' he said. 'I'd like to examine her, if I may?'

I nodded. 'Of course.'

Tilly's eyes half opened as he leaned forward.

'Don't worry, sweetie, the doctor just wants to have a little look at you.'

She made a sound and closed her eyes again. Dr Wallis felt along her throat, pressing gently on her glands. He lifted her vomit-stained pyjama top, his fingers moving lightly along her stomach, and she gave a squeak of discomfort.

He stepped back with a sigh and looked at me. 'Right now, the cause of Tilly's symptoms isn't obvious. She's a little distended, but not as much as I would expect if her bowel was twisted, for example, and as you say, this has been an issue for quite some time, so I believe we can rule that out. I would like to send her for an ultrasound and some X-rays to make sure we've got the full picture. Does she ever suffer from coughs that won't go away? Chest infections?'

I shook my head. 'No. But she fainted earlier this week, and her lips were a bit blue. What are you thinking?'

'We don't have enough information for me to be able to tell right now. We'll do some bloods—'

'She only just had some taken at the GP. I haven't had the results yet.'

He nodded. 'We'll find out the results for those, but I would like to do some more detailed blood work. There are conditions we can test for that could fit the bill here.'

I nodded, feeling sick at the thought of having to put her through yet another needle. 'What conditions?' I managed to croak.

'Too many to discuss now, and there's little point to it until we have all the facts in place. Our minds tend to jump to the worst conclusions, and that won't help you or Tilly.'

I wanted to disagree, to tell him that any answer, even if it wasn't the right one, was a step in the right direction. It would give me a starting point, something to focus on. But I could see that he was set on his decision, and I was grateful that finally a doctor – and a senior doctor at that – seemed to be taking us seriously.

He glanced at his watch. 'I'll order those scans for this afternoon,' he said. 'Do you have any questions?'

I had a thousand. *What happens if you don't find anything? What if you do? What happens if you can't cure her? What if I lose her?* Instead I shook my head and he turned for the door. 'Thank you,' I called as the two silent sidekicks followed him. The door closed, and once again we were all alone.

I slipped my phone out of my pocket, looking at it for the first time since we'd arrived. It was half past ten and I had six missed calls from Adam and three voicemails. I chewed my lip, looking back out of the window to the play area below, seeing that the mother and child had gone. With a sigh, I pressed a speed-dial number, holding the phone up to my ear. The line crackled and a voice answered.

'Laura,' I said. 'I need you to do something for me.'

CHAPTER FOURTEEN

Laura

'I had no idea things were this bad,' I said, leaning over Tilly's prone body, watching the slow rise and fall of her narrow chest. 'Why didn't you call me last night? You know I would have come with you.'

'It all happened so fast,' Maddie replied, sinking into a chair beside Tilly's bed.

I handed her the coffee I'd bought from the café on the ground floor. 'Americano,' I said, pressing the cup into her hand. 'Thought you might need the boost.'

She nodded but didn't take a sip. 'Did you call him?'

'Of course,' I said, looking down at Tilly so I didn't have to meet her eyes. 'He's on his way.'

'You didn't pick him up?' she asked, almost accusingly.

'No, it would have meant driving out of my way. I just wanted to get here as fast as possible. You know Tilly means the world to me.'

Madeline dipped her head, her shoulders slumping.

'Was it awful?' I asked softly.

She sipped her coffee, wincing as she rubbed wearily at her bloodshot eyes. 'It was the worst experience of my life,' she said softly. 'I thought I was going to lose her, Laur. I... I still might.'

'You won't! Don't even think it, Maddie. You're exactly where you need to be and she's surrounded by doctors. She's going to be fine.'

'You don't know that.'

'I know *her*. And she's strong, Maddie. Whatever this is, she will pull through it. She *will*.'

'Was he angry?'

'Adam?' I shook my head. 'He was scared, just like you would have been if the tables were turned.' I fixed her with what I hoped was an empathetic look, conscious of coming across as being on his side. 'You could have called him when you got here though, couldn't you?'

'It was too much of a rush. Everyone was dashing in and out, asking me questions, I didn't have a chance to think,' she said, her tone defensive.

I nodded. 'Of course; I understand that,' I said, tensing at the prospect of an argument. 'Adam will be fine. And obviously you have to put Tilly's needs first.'

Tilly stirred, as if I had called her, slowly opening her eyes.

'Hey, you.' I smiled, stepping forward to take her hand.

'Auntie Laura?'

'Thought you'd come and have a little adventure, did you?' I said, putting on a jolly tone that sounded ridiculous even to my own ears. Maddie looked away, rolling her eyes. 'How are you feeling?' I asked softly.

Tilly shrugged. 'I don't know.' She tried to sit up and Madeline jumped out of her seat, moving the line of her drip out of the way.

'Careful,' she said, showing Tilly the clear line running from the drip stand to the back of her hand.

'I don't want this,' Tilly said instantly, her eyes growing wide as she stared down at the tube protruding from the bandage around her wrist. 'What is it?'

'It's water, sweetie, just water that your body needs,' I told her, seeing the fear written on her pale little face. 'You can't drink at the moment because your tummy is sore, so this keeps you hydrated. It's only temporary.'

'That's right.' Madeline nodded.

'I bought some books for you at the shop downstairs. Do you want me to read you a story?'

Tilly gave a tired nod.

'Maddie,' I said, smiling, 'why don't you go and get something to eat? Stretch your legs and get a bit of air? I can take care of T.'

'No. I'm not leaving her. The doctor might come back and I don't want to miss him.'

'But I thought you said he's already been to see you? He won't come back again this morning.'

'I said no. Thank you, but no.'

I swallowed, looking back to Tilly. There was no point in pushing the issue; I'd only annoy her with my attempts at offering support. I could only imagine how exhausted she must be, how frayed her nerves after everything that had happened. It was clear to me that she could really do with a long nap, or a break from this poky little room at the very least. Her eyes were bloodshot and puffy and she looked ready to collapse, but if she wanted to play the martyr, that was up to her. It was ridiculous and she would burn herself out, but I knew just how stubborn she could be when she set her mind to something, and I wasn't about to waste my breath trying to convince her she was wrong. Instead, I raised the back of the hospital bed so Tilly was propped up, then lowered the side of it, clambering up on the mattress beside her.

'What are you doing?' Madeline asked, her forehead furrowing in an irritated frown.

'I'm reading Tilly a story,' I replied with a bright smile, then wrapped my arm around her back, letting her lean into me as I flipped open the first page. Madeline gave an audible sigh but said no more, turning back to the window to drink her coffee.

*

I was just finishing up the third fairy tale when the door opened and Adam rushed in, his gaze going instantly to Tilly. I gave him a reassuring nod and saw his shoulders slump in relief. His eyes flicked towards Madeline, still seated near the window, and I saw the unmistakable glint of fury in them. To his credit, he said nothing.

Instead he walked towards the bed, leaning across me to get to Tilly. His forearm brushed against mine and I could smell the clean, fresh scent of his hair, his expensive aftershave filling my nostrils. I felt the beginnings of a blush creep up my neck and shot out a hand, grabbing his forearm. 'Don't pick her up,' I warned. 'She's on a drip.' I pointed to the cannula and he shook his head.

'What for?'

Tilly held up her hand. 'They put a tube in me, Daddy, because I was too thirsty.'

Adam nodded grimly. 'I see. And how do you feel now?'

'My throat is sore. And my tummy too.'

He sighed, leaning across me again to kiss her cheek. 'We'll get you home soon, baby.' He straightened up, looking at me. I could tell it was going to be another one of those times when I was expected to become the mediator. It was wearing thin now, but both of them knew I couldn't stand the awkward silence that permeated the room. I always broke first.

'Maddie said that the doctor has ordered some scans for today, hasn't he, Maddie?'

She gave a nod, her eyes still trained on the window. Adam frowned, walking around the bed. 'Madeline, what happened?' he demanded in a low voice. I glanced down at Tilly, wary of her overhearing their conversation.

'I told you she wasn't well. It's what I've been trying to tell you for ages, but you don't listen. And now look where we've ended up.'

'But they'll send her home now, won't they?'

'No, Adam, they won't. I won't let them. We're staying until they get to the bottom of this, whether you agree or not. I'm sick of being walked over and pushed around, sick of you thinking you're always right. I'm her mother! I know her better than anyone, and I'm telling you, she's ill.'

'Maddie!' I said sharply. She looked towards me and I dipped my head in Tilly's direction. Tilly was staring wide-eyed at her mother.

'Am I dying?' she asked quietly. I gasped, my arm tightening around her narrow shoulders as Adam and Madeline sprang forward simultaneously.

'No, no, sweetie!' Madeline exclaimed, pulling Tilly's face to her chest, flashing Adam a furious glance as if it were he who'd said the wrong thing. She forgot sometimes just how much Tilly picked up on. How her battles with Adam affected their daughter. I wished they would just go outside and have it out without her having to witness their bitterness. And *I* could do without seeing it too.

I still couldn't understand why, after so many years together, Madeline had sent Adam packing. He'd proved he would do anything for her. He'd stuck by her when she was at her lowest ebb, and she'd just thrown him away like he didn't mean a thing to her. I wondered if she regretted letting him go, if she'd realised yet just how rare it was to find a man as supportive and caring as Adam was. It had to have been the biggest mistake of her life.

'Knock knock!'

We all looked up in unison as a chirpy voice trilled from the doorway. A blonde nurse walked into the room, grinning widely in a way that seemed totally out of place for the situation.

'Oh lovely, lots of visitors for you, Tilly.'

Tilly pulled back from Madeline's chest, eyeing the nurse suspiciously.

'Just wanted to do a quick set of obs, if that's okay?'

'Obs?' Adam frowned.

'Observations,' the nurse said, smiling confidently at him. 'Temperature, heart rate, blood pressure.'

'Does that mean a needle?' Tilly whispered.

'No, no needle.' The nurse smiled, overhearing. 'Nothing painful. I just pop this cuff on your arm and it gives you a little cuddle. Is that okay?'

Tilly nodded, and Madeline stepped back the slightest bit to let the nurse come closer. I saw her flash an irritated glance in my direction and realised she probably wanted me to get off the bed so she could trade places with me. I avoided her hard stare, concentrating on holding Tilly's hand instead.

The nurse took Tilly's temperature, read the heart-rate monitor and finally wrapped the blood pressure cuff around her thin little arm. 'You'll have to do her leg,' I told her. 'Unless you've got the baby cuffs to hand. The paediatric ones are always too big for her dinky arms.'

The nurse looked up at me, a smile on her lips. 'Are you a nurse?'

'GP.' I smiled as she fastened the cuff around Tilly's calf instead.

'Much better,' she agreed. 'You are a tiny little thing, aren't you, sweetie?'

'My daddy says good things come in small packages,' Tilly replied, flashing the nurse a self-assured smile.

'Your daddy is right.'

Madeline frowned. 'Is her blood pressure high? And her temperature?'

The nurse waited for the machine to finish doing its job. I couldn't see the screen from where I sat, but I could see the heart-rate monitor, and the numbers looked pretty good to me.

The nurse straightened. 'All looking absolutely fine. Temperature and blood pressure are normal, and that heart rate has come down nicely. Amazing what a couple of bags of fluid can do.'

'What about her scans?' Madeline said, gripping the bars of the bed. Her face was pinched and unsmiling. She looked so serious, so unlike the carefree girl I'd shared my pick 'n' mix with as a child.

'Scans?'

'Yes, X-ray, ultrasound. Dr Wallis said he was ordering them for today.'

'Ah, okay. Well, there's nothing in her notes, but these things can take a while.'

'But he said they'd be done today.'

'Maddie,' Adam said. 'Stop fussing, for goodness' sake. Leave the doctor to sort it, okay? You don't need to micro-manage everything.'

'I'm not micro-managing. I'm trying to make sure we don't get forgotten, shut away in this dank little room where nobody can see us. I mean, I've already said she isn't contagious! How are you supposed to keep an eye on her, stuck out here?' Maddie demanded. 'I think we should be moved back to the bay where she can get the attention she needs.'

For the first time, the nurse's smile faltered. 'I promise nobody is going to forget Tilly,' she said gently. 'We'll increase her to hourly checks, but the bay is full right now. We've had several very poorly children admitted this morning, and unfortunately, none of them are in a position to be swapped with Tilly.' She tilted her head to one side, pressing her lips together as she looked from Adam to Maddie. 'And I'm sure the scans will be ordered today. What usually happens is that the X-ray department call up and let us know when they have a space. Don't panic. If Dr Wallis said she needs them, she'll be seen soon enough.'

'Maddie,' I said softly, 'I know you're worried, but isn't this what you wanted? Things are getting done. She's safe here. But you have to be patient.'

Madeline glanced away, her expression unreadable, and the nurse picked up her tray. 'Tilly is stable now. She's doing far better than she was on admission, and that's a really positive thing.'

'So can we take her home soon?' Adam asked.

Madeline spun to face him, her face flushed, but the nurse spoke first. 'That's not my decision to make, but I don't think it will be today I'm afraid.' She wheeled the blood-pressure machine towards the door, pausing to look at him. 'I'll let you know the moment I hear anything.'

As she closed the door quietly behind her, Adam shook his head, his hands trembling. I looked meaningfully down towards Tilly, who was now flicking through the books I'd brought for her, warning him not to say anything that might upset her.

'Maddie,' I said quietly, 'are you sure you don't want to have a break? Adam and I can take over here. You could even pop home for a bit. Get some sleep. You look dead on your feet.'

'No,' she said, shaking her head, still staring at the door after the nurse. 'I'm not leaving her side. Not for one moment.'

CHAPTER FIFTEEN

Five hours later, I followed Adam along the brightly decorated corridor and through the double doors into the stairwell. He walked straight towards the wall, slamming his palm hard enough against it to make the window shudder in its frame.

'Adam,' I said softly, waiting for him to turn his face my way. His shoulders shook with the effort of holding his emotions in check, his breath unsteady. I had only seen him cry once before, and watching him so close to losing control now brought back a wave of feeling so strong I didn't think I could stand it. I squeezed my eyes shut, holding back the flood of memories that threatened to engulf me. 'Adam,' I said again, stepping forward. He turned to me slowly, his eyes wild and lost.

'I can't do this, Laur. I'm not cut out for this.'

'Nobody is. Do you think any of those parents would be here if they had a choice? Of course they wouldn't. They'd be at home, watching a healthy child running around, rather than putting them through hell for their own good.'

He shook his head, turning from me. I grabbed the collar of his shirt, forcing him to look at me. 'You *can* do this, Adam. You have to. Because as difficult as it is for you, imagine how much worse all of this will be for her. She's *six*. She doesn't understand what's going on, what's happening to her – all she wants is her normal life back.'

'So do I.'

'And you'll get it. You will, Adam. But for now, you have to be strong for your daughter, be there for her.'

'Like Maddie…'

'Yeah,' I agreed, glancing away. I knew Adam was thinking the same as me. That Madeline had found a strength neither of us had seen in her for years. The chirpy nurse with the unwavering self-confidence had come back an hour after her first visit, to take Tilly's bloods and inform us that her scans wouldn't be happening until tomorrow morning. Madeline had been almost frightening in her determination to advocate for Tilly. She'd forced the nurse to bleep the consultant so he could personally explain the reason for the delay, and then, as Tilly fought and screamed against the needle, Maddie had held her tightly, her face impassive and emotionless as Adam and I struggled to watch.

As a GP, blood tests were far from alien to me. I'd done more than I could count during my training and learned to put aside guilt and squeamishness. But this was Tilly, the person I loved more than anyone else on this planet, and I couldn't stop the niggling thought in the back of my mind that this, all of this, was unnecessary. That if we waited a little longer, she'd recover without all this prodding and poking. Madeline was always too quick to jump to the worst conclusions.

Adam turned towards the stairs, slumping down on the top one, his head resting against the wall. I sighed, then went to sit beside him, taking his hand. 'I'm scared,' he said, his gaze focused on his knees. 'I'm so fucking terrified, Laur. All this time I've been brushing Maddie off, thinking she's being overdramatic, but they wouldn't keep Tilly here if there wasn't something wrong, would they?'

I shrugged. 'They might. They're only doing tests, Adam. It could still be nothing.'

He squeezed my hand, then let go, rubbing his palms over his face. He looked exhausted.

'You don't have to fly tonight, do you?'

'I was supposed to. But how can I work when T's stuck in here?' He shook his head. 'I've asked for emergency cover. Not that my boss was happy about it, but what else could I do?' he muttered. 'I wanted to stay close.'

'I know. Me too. It isn't fair that they only let one adult stay overnight.'

'And of course it *would* be Maddie. She didn't even ask, she just assumed.'

'She's her mother,' I said loyally, though I knew how hard it had been for Adam to walk away after kissing Tilly goodnight. It had been the same for me. The fear over what would happen during the next twelve hours. It felt wrong to leave when every fibre of my being was crying out to stay by her side. 'We'll come back first thing tomorrow.'

'I thought I could master this, you know?' Adam said suddenly.

I shook my head, confused.

'Parenting. I thought it would be like anything else. If I studied hard enough, read enough books, dedicated myself to being successful, how could I go wrong?' He smiled wryly. 'But it's not like that. Every book you pick up contradicts the last one. Every few months a new scientific study is released telling you you've fucked it up when you thought you were getting it right. There's no right answer. It's not like flying.' He twisted his mouth, staring ahead at the stairwell wall. 'People always tell me they can't believe how I have the confidence to fly three hundred passengers across an ocean. Like *that's* scary. Flying is simple. There are variables, but you're trained to cope with them. It's safer than any other form of transport. Did you know that?'

'I think you've told me before,' I said softly. 'But it's hard to believe when you're up there. It's that feeling of being out of control that people hate. You can't do anything to save yourself if something goes wrong. You're at the mercy of the pilot.'

He nodded. 'Out of control… That's just how I feel now.' He shook his head, silent for a moment. 'When you're flying a plane, the rules never change. But parenting, it's so different. You think you've got the hang of it, but it's an illusion. Nobody really knows the right way. Not even Maddie, though I'm sure she would disagree.'

'Nobody knows everything. You just figure it out as each situation comes. Follow your instincts, Adam.'

'Yeah, and what if my instincts aren't the same as hers?'

I shrugged. 'Then you find a compromise, I suppose.'

'You're lucky you don't have kids, Laur. It tears your heart in two.'

My breath caught in my chest, the air growing thin around me as I stared wordlessly into his eyes.

'Oh shit. Laura, I… I didn't mean… I wasn't thinking…'

'It's fine,' I said, standing up, moving towards the banister.

He stood too, his face creased with concern. 'I'm upset, I'm not thinking straight, but that was stupid of me. I'm sorry…'

'I said it's fine.' I pursed my lips, breathing in hard through my nose, refusing to let his words hurt me. Those old wounds were boxed up nice and tight, and now was not the time to be letting them out in the open. 'Have you got food in? At home? Do you want me to cook you something?'

He looked at me, clearly weighing up whether to drop it or keep pushing. I didn't have the strength for this. He gave a small shake of his head, his eyes fixed on mine. 'No, I'll grab something. I have leftovers in the fridge.'

'Okay. Well, I'd better go then. See you in the morning.'

'Yeah.' He nodded.

I turned from him, walking down the stairs, my shoulders rigid as he watched me leave.

CHAPTER SIXTEEN

I slid the key into the lock of my flat, hearing Minnie's welcome greeting as she dashed to meet me at the door. She purred around my ankles and I scooped her up, carrying her like a baby into the small living room that boasted a view of a seven-storey tower block. When I'd rented it a decade ago, there had been a big green space opposite my window, with trees and birds to look out at. But a patch of land like that didn't go unnoticed around here for long.

I could have moved when I realised my pretty view was about to be replaced by a heap of concrete and metal. I *had* visited a few other flats when I got the planning notice, but there didn't seem much point to packing up my whole life to set up somewhere new.

I'd been working long hours at the time, desperate to prove myself in the surgery, and it didn't feel like the right time to go house-hunting. I'd reasoned I would buy a place of my own once I'd saved a deposit after a few years of working, but I never had. Now, the ugly grey building had been blocking my view of the sky for nearly six years, and I'd grudgingly accepted that it was never going to change.

I sat down, Minnie walking back and forth across my lap, cajoling me into stroking her between the ears. I felt deflated, my emotions raw, so close to the surface. My thoughts flitted between Tilly, what could be wrong with her, and Adam's face as he'd spoken those awful words. *You're lucky you don't have kids, Laur.*

I pulled Minnie close, glad when she nudged her little pink nose against my neck. 'At least you love me, pretty girl,' I murmured.

I'd never intended to become a cat lady, never even liked them before Minnie came along. But she'd snuck in through an open window one day, bony and matted and starving hungry, and after a fruitless search for her owners, she'd somehow adopted me.

I hadn't realised how much I needed her, needed some scrap of affection, until she'd arrived. Now, she was probably the only living being who would actually care if I disappeared off the face of the earth, and even then, I knew she'd move on and adopt a new family. She'd done it once already.

I edged her off my lap and stood, heading to the kitchen to pour some fresh biscuits into her bowl and change her water. I paused as I passed the fridge. Tacked to the door was a photograph of me holding Tilly when she was just a few days old. I looked flushed, my eyes sparkling as I stared down at the tiny, wide-eyed baby. I could still remember that visceral feeling of love, the realisation that this little girl was going to change everything for me. She called me Auntie Laura, but I had never been just an auntie. I'd been involved from the start, sharing her care, taking my turn and gladly.

That was another thing that had changed since the divorce. Maddie and Adam used to drop Tilly off to me for sleepovers whenever they wanted to go for a date. My jealousy at being left out had been far outweighed by my joy at having Tilly all to myself. We would play with bricks and dolls, read stories, laugh about nonsense until we gasped for air.

My favourite moments had been when she was all ready for bed, her hair brushed and plaited, her little pink pyjamas making her look so much smaller and younger than she did during the day, reminding me of when she was a toddler. She always made me roll the sleeves up at the wrists so that they didn't get in the way.

She would lie back against the pillow, her soft little hand in mine, holding on tight so that I wouldn't leave as she told me about whatever was on her mind that day. The boy who'd tried to steal her favourite doll at the park. The friend she'd made on the beach who'd showed her how to make sandcastles that didn't crumble apart as soon as you lifted the bucket. Her dreams, her interests, whatever she felt like sharing with me. And I would listen to her talk, offering little words of advice here and there, hiding my smile as her eyes grew heavy and her voice faded away. I would sit there long after her hand loosened in mine, just watching her, feeling so grateful that she was with me. That she trusted me enough to share her secrets with me.

I had treasured those nights, but since Madeline and Adam had split, the sleepovers had fizzled out. Now I could barely remember the last time Tilly was here on her own. Maddie had this obsession with control, which was why I knew I wouldn't get my turn staying with Tilly on the children's ward. Nor would Adam. She wasn't willing to let us in, and that hurt more than I had ever let on.

I picked up the photograph now, running my finger over the glossy surface. She'd been a beautiful baby. It had been hard to tell who she took after back then. It had been fascinating to watch her develop and change over the years. Her personality was far more like Madeline's than Adam's; she was a free spirit, wore her emotions on her sleeve and put more stock in adventure than academics. She also shared Madeline's wild, dirty-blonde curls, which remained forever untameable.

But the rest of her features were straight from her dad. Her deep ocean-blue eyes. Her full lips. Even her mannerisms were pure Adam, and that made her very easy to love.

I left Minnie with her dinner and poured a glass of wine, heading back to the living room. For once, I didn't turn on the TV to break the silence. I forced myself to sit in it rather than fight it, realising just how uncomfortable it made me. It was impossible not to feel alone, with the hum of the fridge and the creak of the hot-water tank the only sounds to break the deafening silence.

I could have met someone, could have married and had a family rather than clinging to the fringes of something that had never really been mine. But I hadn't, and part of the reason for that was Adam. Every man I met, I compared to him, and they never came out on top. How could they? So I sabotaged every relationship before it got off the ground. I walked away, fully aware that the man I wanted was so far out of my reach that he would never be mine. I needed to let him go. But I couldn't. So I stayed single. Alone. Longing for something I knew I could never have.

CHAPTER SEVENTEEN

Madeline

'I want to go home right now!' Tilly screamed, trying to clamber over the side bars of the bed. The junior doctor blocked her way and Tilly kicked out, her face red and wet with tears. A trail of snot ran down her face and I ached to wipe it away, but keeping her from diving head first onto the solid hospital floor was my first priority. The door to her room opened and I glanced up, my heart sinking. Adam. Why couldn't he have arrived twenty minutes later? I didn't have it in me to deal with him now, not on top of all this.

'What on earth is going on?' he demanded as he came face to face with the scene.

'Daddy!' Tilly screamed. She held out her arms and he rushed towards her, scooping her up as if she were a baby and holding her against his chest. His eyes were hard as he stared at me. The doctor looked from him to me and then down at the bed, fiddling with the contents of her plastic medical tray.

I sighed. I was too tired for this. My whole body shook, waves of dizziness washing over me every few minutes. I'd managed about an hour of sleep last night, what with all the monitors going off, the nurses coming in, Tilly crying and needing comfort. An hour in forty-eight. It wasn't enough.

'Tilly's cannula has stopped working,' I said matter-of-factly, holding his gaze. 'She needs a replacement so that she can have fluids, as she's still not eating or drinking. And earlier this morning, the lab called the ward to say that the blood samples they got yesterday were clotted and can't be used. So,' I continued, seeing the obvious fury in his expression, 'they need repeating. It's not ideal, I know.'

'Why have the samples clotted? Who let that happen?' he demanded, turning to the young junior doctor expectantly. She knocked over a sample bottle, staring wide-eyed back at him, clasping her hands in front of her, her mouth open.

'Don't you think I've asked the same thing already?' I said sharply. 'I'm not happy about this either, Adam. Apparently the nurse left them in the syringe for too long before transferring them into the blood sample bottles. I've already made a complaint, but that doesn't change the situation now. We need those results, Adam.'

He shook his head as Tilly squealed against his shirt, pulling at his sleeve in her desperation for him to carry her away. I should have known that I would end up being the bad guy in all this. That it would be me who had to make the tough choices, the decisions that left Tilly furious and hurt, so then Adam could swoop in and save the day.

'I don't see why they can't just use what they have. There must be some left that isn't clotted. It's ridiculous! Absolutely unacceptable. And what do you mean, she's still not eating? Why not?' he asked, his arm supporting Tilly easily as he stroked her dark-blonde curls.

'She's nil-by-mouth to rest her stomach. She doesn't want to eat anyway, and I agreed that it was a good idea. She's stopped throwing up now, so it's obviously helping.'

Adam frowned. 'Nil-by-mouth? What on earth does that mean?'

'It means she's not being given anything to eat or drink at the moment. The doctor thinks it's important to give her stomach a rest, and she's being hydrated via her drip so it's perfectly safe. It can't hurt to try it, and it's not like food is agreeing with her at the moment.'

'You can't starve the poor girl, Maddie!'

I breathed in through my nostrils, fighting the urge to lose my temper. 'It's not a permanent solution, for goodness' sake! Like I said, Dr Wallis thinks this is for the best, and I would think he would know. You said yourself we shouldn't interfere with the doctor's decisions. Now, are you going to help us get this over with or not?'

Adam turned to the junior doctor, still not releasing his grip on Tilly. 'Is this really necessary? If she's stopped being sick, do we even need to bother? It seems like overkill.'

'Adam!' I warned. I looked down at my daughter, still crying loudly against her father's chest. Those cries were heartbreaking, and the more upset she became, the more tense I grew. My muscles felt rigid, ready to snap with frustration. I hated this, every little part of it. I didn't want to put my child through another needle, to have to hold her down and break her trust, do the very thing she was begging me not to do. I didn't want to have to be the one who made all the hard decisions, and I sure as hell didn't want Tilly hearing me and Adam arguing over the top of her head as she cried her heart out.

I felt like screaming, bursting into tears and giving in to what he wanted, but I didn't have that luxury. This wasn't about me, it was for *her*, and it was the only way we were going to be able to move forward. I took a deep breath, fixing him with a look of sheer determination.

The doctor gripped her tray, meeting his demanding eyes. He could be so intimidating at times. I didn't think he even realised how nervous the poor girl was. Adam was a man who'd learned how to get his own way in life. To him, 'no' was just a barrier to be jumped, not an insurmountable wall. I knew it must be driving him crazy to find himself a helpless passenger with no idea where he was heading.

'As unpleasant as it might be, Mr Parkes, we wouldn't do it if we didn't believe it to be necessary,' she said bravely. 'Dr Wallis has asked me to place a new cannula and repeat the bloods. I can get him to come and discuss it with you before I go ahead if you prefer?'

Adam opened his mouth and I could see he was going to demand just that. I stepped forward, refusing to let him jeopardise things for Tilly again. 'That won't be necessary. He's already discussed it with me and I have agreed. I'm sure Dr Wallis has got far more important things to do than repeat information I've already passed on.' I glared at my ex-husband. 'Now, just stop making things worse and help me hold her. Please, Adam. The longer we discuss it, the harder it is for Tilly.'

He glanced down at her, his face creased with anxiety. I knew how much this was hurting him, because it was torture for me too. I didn't want to put her through this, but I had no choice. And she deserved strength from me. No matter how hard it got, no matter what they put her through, I would be there by her side, my own emotions locked up in a box while I focused on supporting her.

'Adam,' I pushed. 'Let's just get on with it, okay?'

He gave a defeated sigh, and I tried to keep my expression impassive to hide my relief. 'Fine. But I want to talk to Dr Wallis when he does the next round. I'm not letting you call all the shots here, Madeline.'

I refused to take the bait, ignoring his comment and indicating for him to sit on the bed. Tilly clung to him like a baby monkey, and I saw the flash of understanding in Adam's eyes. 'You want me to be the one to hold her?'

'You're stronger than me. Don't let her move.'

'Maddie, I…'

The junior doctor picked up her tray. 'Okay,' she said, reaching for Tilly's arm. Tilly let out a blood-curdling scream before she'd even touched her, pulling back hard.

'Hey, it's okay, it will only take a minute,' I said softly, walking round the bed to get closer to her. I stroked the back of her head as she pushed her face against Adam's chest, screaming her lungs out. Adam gripped her tight and looked up at me.

'Maddie, I can't do this.'

'Yes. You can. You can do it for her. Ready?'

'No,' he whispered. I nodded to the doctor, and she leaned forward, manoeuvring Tilly's arm. I didn't need to see the needle pierce her skin to know that it had. Tilly gave a high-pitched, panicked cry, and I saw the blood drain out of Adam's face, his eyes closing against the horrific sound.

I'd had to do this alone several times now, since that first occasion at the doctor's surgery. Adam had barely looked our way yesterday as I'd held Tilly still, offering no support until it was done and he could rush over to be the hero. I was glad he could finally experience what I'd been going through from this vantage point, understand that it had been bloody hard. Maybe he'd support me more now that he knew how tough things could get.

The doctor wiggled the needle-thin cannula with slow, careful nudges, and I held my breath, hoping she'd got it in the right position. Her hand squeezed Tilly's arm gently, encouraging the blood to flow through the tiny plastic tube, and I breathed out, relief flooding through me as the dark red liquid began to drip from the end. The doctor grabbed a syringe from her tray, using the glinting silver needle to draw back the blood until the syringe was almost full. She attached the end of the cannula with deft movements, working quickly to tape it down securely, then transferred the blood into the sample bottles right in front of us.

'At least we know they've been done properly this time,' I said. I placed a hand on Tilly's back. 'It's over, sweetie. It's all done.'

She looked up, her face blotchy and tear-stained, then pushed away from Adam, reaching out to me. I lifted her towards my chest, grateful that she still wanted me. Her hiccuping sobs caught in the back of her throat, making her body tremble, and I felt the all-too-familiar sting in my eyes. I pressed them shut, gripping her tighter, wishing I could take away her pain. I would swap places with her in an instant if I could.

'I'll get these off to the lab,' the doctor said, picking up her tray and walking briskly to the door. I wasn't surprised she wanted to rush off after the scene we'd put her through. She deserved a medal.

Adam sat defeated on the bed, his shoulders slumped. He raised his head slowly to meet my eyes. 'I don't want to have to do that again. Ever.'

'I can't promise that you won't,' I murmured.

Adam glared at me and stood up. 'T, I'm sorry, I really am,' he said as she raised her eyes to look at him. 'But look, if you get better, you can go home. Then we don't have to do any more tests, do we?'

'Don't make false promises,' I said sharply. 'We don't know what happens next. It's not fair on her.'

Adam ignored me, plucking Tilly from my arms. He placed her bare feet on the floor and she gave a startled cry, gripping onto his neck.

'She's too wobbly on her feet to walk yet! She's been in bed for days and she hasn't eaten. You need to hold on to her,' I said, irritable and cross.

He shook his head. 'No, this is the first step. Listen, T, if you can get back on your feet again and use your legs, you'll feel much better. You don't want to be sitting around in bed all day, do you?'

'But my legs *hurt*, Daddy,' she whispered. 'I don't think I can do it.'

'You *can*. You can do anything you set your mind to, baby. Come on, show me what you're capable of.'

Tilly glanced uncertainly at me, then back to Adam. 'Okaaay.' She took a tentative step and I saw the effort it cost her. She took another and wobbled, her arm darting out to hold on to the side of the bed.

'Be careful, sweetheart – go really slowly, okay?'

'Oh stop fussing, Maddie. Give her legs a chance to wake up. She's doing fine.'

'Can't you see what I see? She's struggling, Adam. She's in pain!'

'She's fine. Aren't you, Tilly?' He put his hands on his hips and smiled triumphantly as she took another cautious step. 'Keep this up and you'll be home before you know it.' He grinned and I shook my head.

'I'm going to grab a coffee from downstairs,' he announced, the confidence returned to his posture. He looked like the Adam I knew now, the man who would let nothing stand in his way to reach his goals. 'You want one?'

'No,' I lied. 'I don't want anything.'

He shrugged, moving towards the door, then stopped suddenly, as if he'd just remembered something. 'You… you are eating?' he asked softly, his dark eyes filled with concern as they met mine. 'You know how important it is, right? For you to eat properly? You can't fall into old habits…'

'I'm fine,' I snapped. I had no desire to become the focus of his meddling, not again.

'I'll get you something from the café.'

'There's no need,' I insisted, but he'd already disappeared through the door.

Tilly tried to take another step, lurching forward, and I grabbed her before she fell, lifting her into my arms. 'Ignore Daddy,' I told her. 'He just gets sad when he can't fix everything.'

'He's cross with me.'

'He isn't. He's just worried. He'll be fine, I promise.'

She shook her head. 'Mummy,' she said, looking up at me with fresh tears in her eyes, 'I don't know what I'm supposed to do.'

'You don't have to do anything, baby. Just let me take care of you.' I laid her on the bed and climbed up beside her, pulling her close against my side as I stroked her hair. 'You don't need to worry about a thing, sweetie,' I said quietly. 'Mummy is right here.'

CHAPTER EIGHTEEN

The atmosphere in the hospital room was thick with tension, Adam casting increasingly more pointed looks in my direction as he sat beside Tilly, reading her a story. The ham sandwich and full-fat cappuccino he'd brought back for me lay untouched on the side table, and I could almost hear his thoughts as he looked from me to the meal. I knew he thought I was being purposely difficult. Refusing to eat to spite him, or worse still, to garner his sympathy to get him on side. That was just the way his mind worked. Every little action had to have a reason, a bigger purpose, otherwise why would you bother?

But I wasn't quite as petty as that. No. The real reason I wasn't eating, that I had barely bothered with food all week, was that I was sick with fear. My stomach churned with anticipation as the hours ticked by with nothing to do but wait for whatever came next, the answers that would surely begin to trickle in soon. What would they find? Was I currently sitting on the edge of a drop, unaware of how far I was about to fall, how catastrophic the landing might turn out to be?

My body didn't want food. It wanted sleep. I could have shut my eyes and not opened them again for a week quite easily, if it weren't for the adrenaline keeping me going. But I couldn't rest. Couldn't even leave to get some air, see the blue sky without the grey tint of the hospital-room window. I didn't trust Adam to get this right, and I was excruciatingly aware that this opportunity was not one to be wasted. How hard had I fought to be heard? To be in the position that I had a specialist to discuss Tilly's health with? I might not get this chance again.

Adam cleared his throat and I looked up, meeting his eyes defiantly. Perhaps, I admitted to myself as I stared back silently, there was some small part of me that enjoyed the control of refusing the food. But if it was there, it was tiny. Just a minuscule factor in the great scheme of events. I liked the pain in my stomach that came with not eating. It gave me something to focus on outside of Tilly. And if it made Adam uncomfortable, nervous even, then wasn't that the icing on the cake?

I heard movement outside the door and looked away from Adam's pleading eyes. A moment later, a healthcare assistant popped her head in. 'We've had a call from X-ray – they want her there in fifteen minutes.'

'Oh, right.' I stood up, propelled into action. 'For both the X-ray and the ultrasound?' I checked.

'Yes, she'll have them back to back. First, though, the sister has asked me to do some swabs.'

'What for?' Adam asked, sitting up a little straighter. I wondered if he realised he was pulling Tilly closer against him or whether it was simply an unconscious need to protect her.

'It's just standard procedure, nothing invasive,' she explained, holding up some long sticks with cotton at the tip. 'One in the nostril, one in the mouth, one from the groin. It doesn't hurt.' She smiled reassuringly.

'But why does she need them?'

'To check for MRSA. It's really nothing to worry about – we do this for all the children who come through the ward.'

'MRSA? You're kidding? And how on earth would my daughter have picked up something like that? Are you telling me that this hospital is so unhygienic you need to check you haven't infected her with some horrendous disease?'

'Sir, it's really not like that, it's just standard procedure,' she replied, her expression emotionless, as if she'd seen a thousand similar outbursts before.

'Adam, don't cause a scene,' I said, nodding towards Tilly. 'You'll upset her.' After all the tests we'd put her through, a little cotton swab hardly seemed worth making a fuss over.

Adam looked down at Tilly, who was watching him with round eyes. He put a hand over her cheek, cupping it reassuringly, then moved his palm to subtly cover her ear. 'We're putting her at risk being here, Maddie. We need to get out of here before she really does become ill.'

The healthcare assistant placed one hand on the door. 'I'll tell you what, I'll do these a bit later. I don't want to upset Tilly before her scans.' She opened the door and turned to look at me. 'I'll get a wheelchair sorted so we can transfer her downstairs.' She disappeared without another word, and I turned to the bed, ignoring Adam as Tilly shoved his hand off her face crossly.

'Did you hear that, sweetheart? We're going on a little adventure.'

She folded her arms, her chin bowed to her chest. 'Your adventures never turn out to be much fun,' she said softly.

I felt Adam's eyes on me, but didn't glance up. 'No,' I admitted. 'I suppose they don't.'

Adam had finally left after the scan, muttering under his breath that if I wouldn't take a break, he may as well have one. It was a relief to have him out of the way and to resume my place beside Tilly on her comfortable single bed. She'd dozed off halfway through her ultrasound, the room peaceful and quiet, fairy lights twinkling from the ceiling and rainforest music playing softly as the radiologist worked quietly.

When I'd brought her back to the ward in the wheelchair, she'd fallen into a deep sleep and the healthcare assistant had taken the opportunity to get her MRSA swabs. I had already decided not to tell Adam that. He seemed determined to pick a fight, whatever the topic.

Now, with evening setting in, Tilly was sitting up, a selection of books and toys spread across her bed after a visit from a couple of sunny-faced play specialists who were determined to brighten her mood. It had worked.

Rather than shrink from them as she did with the nurses, Tilly had become animated, telling them all about her bedroom at home, the baby dolls who slept in her bed, and her old hamster, Butters, who'd escaped from an obstacle course she'd built for him in the garden last summer, never to be seen again. She looked like a different child to the one who'd been wheeled in on a stretcher in the early hours of yesterday morning. I was relieved to see her smiling again, but I couldn't help but hope they wouldn't try and discharge us before we had our answers. I wasn't ready to go yet.

The night shift had arrived half an hour before, and now a new nurse bustled into our room, her pillowy breasts pressing against her uniform, making her buttons stick out sideways. A notepad and two pens poked out of her pocket, and her fine mousy-brown hair was pulled back in a too-tight bun, making me think unkindly of the Trunchbull from Tilly's *Matilda* DVD.

I had become skilled at reading the various staff who came in to see us, knowing within moments whether they would be cheerful and chatty, brisk and efficient, forgetful or just plain incompetent. This one, I could instantly tell, had that matronly, no-nonsense vibe about her, and though her dress was light blue to signify she was a nurse, I was certain it wouldn't be long before she put herself forward for the role of sister. She gave me a brief nod, not a smile, and stepped up to the bed.

'Well, this is good to see,' she announced loudly, her voice reverberating through my aching head. 'On the mend, Tilly. Well done!'

Tilly's shoulders tensed, her smile disappearing as she stared down at her toy collection. The nurse turned to me. 'I'm Carrie. I'll be looking after Tilly tonight.'

I bit back my instinctive response that no, she would not actually, because *I*, her mother, would be looking after her tonight, as I did every night. I swallowed my irritation and forced my face into a smile. 'Any news on the scans she had this afternoon? Or the blood results?'

'The doctor will come round in the morning to discuss the scans, and I believe that some of the blood results should be back by then too. Several of the samples had to be sent to an outside lab for specialist tests, so they could take up to a week.'

'And we'll be here that long?'

'Who can say? But looking at Tilly now, I wouldn't think so. If she keeps this up, they'll likely send her home and contact you once her results are in,' she said, stepping forward to rub a beefy index finger beneath Tilly's chin. Tilly shrank back, glancing up at me with fear in her eyes. I stepped closer to the other side of the bed, pulling her across the mattress towards me, wrapping my arms around her.

'She hasn't eaten since we got here. I wouldn't jump to the conclusion that she's suddenly better because she's managed to sit up for a few minutes.'

'I'm not the type to jump to conclusions,' Carrie replied sharply. 'The doctor has said she may eat if she's up to it. I suggest we give it a try and see what happens.'

'I don't know if that's a good idea…'

'Well, we can't keep her nil-by-mouth forever, can we? I'll bring a cup of water and some toast and we can go from there.' She reached forward to pat Tilly on the head, but I blocked her hand.

'I'd rather you didn't do that. She's a little bit frightened of all the nurses right now. No offence, but she's had quite a stressful time of it.'

'Of course she has,' Carrie said, with a smile that didn't reach her eyes. 'Well, I'll get you that toast.'

She left without another word, and I sighed, half wondering if I should demand to see the doctor again. But it was gone eight, and I knew that Dr Wallis had gone home for the day just after five. Unless I wanted to go through the whole story with one of the night-shift doctors who didn't know our case, I would just have to wait until morning and hope that eating didn't throw Tilly back into a state of uncontrollable vomiting.

Carrie returned a few minutes later, again not bothering to knock as she entered carrying a blue tray containing a plate of toast, a selection of jams and spreads, a carton of orange juice and a cup of water.

'She can't have juice,' I said automatically, taking it from the tray and handing it back to her.

'Oh? There's nothing in her notes about that. Is it an allergy?'

'An intolerance.'

'Huh,' she said, raising an incredulous eyebrow. 'Tilly, love, I've brought you a little snack. There's loads of different jams for you to choose from. Why don't you come and sit up at the table?'

Tilly didn't even acknowledge her, and I was forced to hide a smug smile as I watched Carrie flounder. Did she think she could just walk in here and get my child to do the one thing I'd struggled to manage for six years?

'Or,' she continued, her voice growing incrementally louder, 'you can have it in bed.'

Tilly picked up a book, cracking the spine. I knew she was being rude, and that Carrie no doubt expected me to push her into giving an answer, but she couldn't help it. She was afraid, surrounded by people she neither knew nor trusted, and I wouldn't force her to speak if she didn't want to. It was her one source of control. The nurse would have to earn her trust, not expect it unconditionally right off the bat.

Carrie looked across at me expectantly, and I turned away, folding Tilly's clothes into a pile. She gave a pointed tut, placed the tray on the end of the mattress and put her hands on her hips. 'Well, I'll just leave it here then. I'm sure you don't want me watching over you as you eat. Let me know if you need anything else.'

Tilly glanced up as the nurse left the room and eyed the tray suspiciously. 'Do I have to eat that, Mummy? The smell is making me feel sick.'

'You don't have to,' I told her. 'Not if you can't manage it.'

'Can you get rid of it?'

I eyed the bin in the corner of the room, then shook my head. 'No, sorry, sweetie, I can't. If I throw it in the bin, they'll assume you've eaten it, and then they might send you home early.'

'But I *want* to go home.'

'Me too. And we will. But not until we have answers about how to help you feel better. That's what you want, isn't it, darling?'

She shrugged, her gaze fixed on the toast.

'Do you feel hungry?' I asked. 'I can get you something else maybe?'

'I feel sick. My tummy feels full and queasy. And my legs hurt again. Daddy said it would get better if I practised walking, but it didn't, did it?'

'Not yet. I think you need to rest them. Do what your body tells you to do, okay? If you feel like moving, then move. But if you can't, that's okay too.'

'Can I lie down?'

'Yes, sweetie, of course. But let me brush your teeth before you fall asleep, okay? I don't want them getting all yucky.' I rummaged in the bag that Adam had brought for her from his flat, digging out her yellow toothbrush and noting that it should have been replaced weeks ago. Tilly had a habit of chewing the bristles until they fell out completely, and this one looked like they were holding on by a thread.

My own mouth tasted furry, and I knew I was beginning to look and smell like a teenager on the last day of Glastonbury, but Adam hadn't thought to bring a change of clothes or any toiletries for me, and I hadn't wanted to leave Tilly even to go downstairs to the shop. I was still making do with my white cotton pyjama bottoms and grey vest top, hidden by the old comfy pashmina, which was far too hot for the ward. I would have to ask Laura to pick up some things from home tomorrow. She could use her spare key to pop to the house after she finished work.

I dabbed a little toothpaste onto the brush and handed it to Tilly. She shook her head. 'You do it, Mummy.'

It had been a long time since I'd brushed her teeth for her. She'd been keen to be independent from a young age, dressing herself, learning how to put her shoes and coat on, and even do the buttons up, when she was barely more than a toddler. These days, the only thing she needed my help with was brushing her hair. It was far too wild for her to manage by herself. I cupped her chin gently, angling the brush between her chapped parted lips. With slow, measured strokes, I brushed her tiny white teeth, smiling as I passed over the gap where she'd recently lost her first baby tooth.

Her wide blue eyes, Adam's eyes, stared up at me, and I felt the familiar warmth that always came from being needed. Being valuable to someone. These simple little acts gave meaning to my life in a way nothing else could. I held up a sick bowl for her to spit, then wiped her mouth with a paper towel. 'All done. You can sleep now, sweetie.'

I leaned close, kissing her rosebud mouth, then pulled back. Her cheeks were taut, her forehead creased, and it took me only a second to recognise the look of panic that crossed her features. I grabbed the bowl again, thrusting it back under her chin just as a fountain of bile erupted from her mouth. She heaved with violent spasms, a cry of pain escaping her lips between retches.

Finally, she gasped, leaning back, tears streaming from her eyes. I put the bowl on the table and wiped her face, drying her tears with a rough piece of tissue. 'It hurts again, Mummy,' she sobbed. 'My legs hurt so much and my tummy's sore. Make it go away, please!'

Pressing down hard on the call button, I pulled her close to me, whispering softly, 'It's okay, it's okay,' until her sobs slowly dissipated. I massaged her legs, focusing on the joints where the pain seemed to be accumulating, watching her grimace and moan as she lay back against the mountain of pillows. The door opened and Carrie walked in, heading straight for the wall. She pressed a switch, turning off the buzzer, and spun to face us. I dragged a blanket over Tilly and reached for the sick bowl. 'Here,' I said, thrusting it towards the nurse. 'She's throwing up again.'

'After eating?'

'No, we didn't get that far.'

Carrie eyed the bowl of yellow liquid distastefully. 'Pop it down and I'll take it to the sluice in a second. I'll need to put on some gloves for that. First, let's have a look at you, Tilly.' She unhooked the thermometer from the holster on the wall, holding it to Tilly's ear. It beeped almost instantly, and Carrie nodded to herself as she put it back. She read the heart-rate monitor and frowned. 'Well, she seems to be all right now.'

'She isn't. She may not have a temperature, but she's certainly not all right. Her legs are hurting again. I want her to have some pain relief.'

'I can bring some oral paracetamol.'

I let out an incredulous laugh. 'Oral? She's not keeping anything down – she can't have that. She needs an IV,' I said, repeating the words I'd overheard from the day nurses. 'She's got the cannula – we may as well make use of it.'

Carrie shook her head. 'I wouldn't normally give intravenous pain relief for growing pains.'

'It *isn't* growing pains. That's why we're here; they're investigating the cause, but you can't expect her to wait for a diagnosis before you give her something to ease her discomfort, can you? You said yourself the blood results could take a week to come back, if not longer. She needs something now, and Calpol, or whatever you're offering, won't work. She'll just bring it back up.'

Carrie shrugged dismissively. 'I'll have to speak to the doctors and see what they think.'

'Fine.' I folded my arms and watched her leave, frustrated and annoyed with her lack of compassion. I'd been feeling listened to, the doctors and nurses treating both me and Tilly with such empathy and understanding ever since we'd arrived. But Carrie seemed to think she knew better than I did, and I didn't like that. I turned back to Tilly with a smile.

'Don't worry, baby. We'll get you some medicine and you'll feel better soon. You just let me look after you.'

CHAPTER NINETEEN

'What do you mean you're sending us home?' I demanded, trying to keep my voice calm as the panic surged through my body. Dr Wallis was dressed in a fuchsia shirt today, his turquoise tie ridiculous. It wasn't professional. I wondered if he kept a change of clothes in his office in case he needed to break bad news to a family. Nobody wanted to hear a life-limiting diagnosis delivered by a man who looked like he belonged on a West End stage.

'We've spent the morning going over Tilly's scans and blood-test results. There's nothing at all that we can see that has caused us any alarm. We do still have one blood test outstanding, for a condition called cystic fibrosis – you've probably heard of it – but having looked at the whole picture now, I'm pretty confident that it won't be positive. Tilly doesn't seem to have the key characteristics of that particular condition, which is a good thing. A very good thing.'

'But you haven't found what *is* wrong with her,' I replied. 'Why would you send us home now when she was sick just last night?'

Adam cleared his throat. 'She seems better this morning though. She did eat the pancakes I brought in for her,' he pointed out, folding his arms in a gesture of triumph. 'She ate a whole one and drank some water, and she's kept it all down.'

'For now. Obviously she eats, Adam, otherwise she'd be dead by now, wouldn't she?' I spat, grateful that the play specialists had taken Tilly off to the playroom so I didn't have to sugar-coat my words. Dr Wallis had watched her walk out on her own two feet, without the slightest hint of a wobble, which wasn't helping my cause, but it wasn't like I could force her to use the wheelchair. She was having a good morning, that was all. It didn't mean the issue was fixed.

'The problem is ongoing,' I said firmly. 'She does eat and drink, of course she does. But she struggles. Frequently. I thought you were going to help us, Doctor?'

'I understand your reluctance to leave, really I do. But myself and the rest of the team feel that Tilly's particular issues surrounding food may be more psychosomatic than physical.'

'What? You're saying my daughter is mad, is that it?' I demanded.

'Maddie, be quiet and listen to the man,' Adam said, stepping closer to me. He placed a hand on my shoulder and I shrugged it off roughly, furious with him for his complete ignorance of what was happening. He should have been working *with* me, pushing just as hard as I was to get answers for our daughter, not grasping at the first opportunity to leave. How could he stand there and listen to the nonsense the doctor was spouting and not say a word in Tilly's defence? I needed him to support me, to care as much as I did, but he seemed utterly oblivious to my panic.

'Absolutely not, not at all,' Dr Wallis continued, unperturbed. 'But Adam told us that Tilly has always had a fussy relationship with food. These things can start off small and, if not managed correctly, can easily grow into fears around food.'

'What do you mean, not managed correctly? You're saying this is my fault? I'm a shitty parent, is that it?'

'No, no,' he said, shaking his head quickly. 'But if you've been unconsciously validating her fussy habits, you could have unintentionally contributed to them escalating. Listen, this is not about blame, not at all, Madeline. I've seen how you are with Tilly – you're a wonderful mother. But these things are not always easy to cope with.'

'She's not just fussy! She's sick – frequently. You've seen it yourself. And so have the nurses. Ask them! Ask Carrie what she was like last night. She had to be given intravenous paracetamol to stop the pains in her legs. You're telling me that's all in her head?'

He nodded patiently. 'I understand that she's experiencing physical symptoms. Nobody is denying that. But anxiety can have a huge effect on our bodies. Tilly already had a poor relationship with food, but Adam has explained to me that things seemed to escalate for her in the period following your… your separation?'

I spun, glaring at Adam, wishing we were alone so I could scream at him. His insistence on fixating on the break-up of our marriage was jeopardising Tilly's health. I could not believe he would sink so low. 'It isn't about that, and you know it, Adam!'

He shrugged casually, as if he were disagreeing over which restaurant to go to for dinner, not the health of our only child. 'I don't agree. It's too much of a coincidence that she started to get worse when you made me leave.'

'Made you—' I stopped myself, aware of Dr Wallis watching us closely. I sucked in a deep breath and gripped the bars on the side of Tilly's empty bed, counting to ten in my head before I finally spoke. 'With all due respect, Dr Wallis, I can see how easy it would be for you to jump to this conclusion. But I *know* my daughter, and this isn't just a simple case of anxiety. It's more than that. And if you send us home now, you are letting her down. If the tests that have been done show nothing, surely you need to do more? Keep searching? Not just give up, for goodness' sake!'

Dr Wallis's eyes were warm as they met mine, and I felt myself beginning to crumble, determined not to cry.

'I'm not giving up on you or her,' he said kindly as I blinked away the moisture that was threatening to overspill, angry at myself for losing my composure. 'I promise you will have our support. I've arranged for the dietician to come and speak to you – she has a few ideas that might help, especially around breaking these ingrained responses to food. I want you to offer Tilly a water bottle with a lid she can suck from, or a cup with a straw. Many children find this easier to cope with, and it will prevent her from becoming dehydrated again. That is important.' He opened Tilly's file and pulled out a small blue leaflet. 'This is a drop-in group for children with food anxiety. I highly recommend you pop along there on a weekly basis. They will give you excellent support and they're associated with us. We send a lot of patients their way and have seen some good results.'

I stared at the leaflet in his outstretched hand, not bothering to reach for it. Adam took it instead, folding it in half and slipping it into his trouser pocket. 'Thank you, Doctor. You've been a great help.' He nodded. 'We'll definitely pay them a visit.'

'The pains,' I said suddenly. 'You've not found a reason for the pains.'

I didn't miss the look that passed between Adam and the doctor. 'I believe, as I mentioned to you before, that they are partly down to dehydration. Cramps are a common symptom of not drinking enough, which certainly seems to fit the bill here. And also she's at an age where she's growing a lot. Growing pains are quite normal in her age group. I do think that you should try not to worry about them, or to let Tilly know you're worried.'

'Dr Wallis thinks she could be picking up on your anxiety,' Adam said. 'She's a smart girl, Maddie. If she thinks you're worried, she will be too, and the pain might seem worse than it actually is. I think it's very telling that she barely mentions it when she's staying with me.'

'I think that *is* telling, yes,' I said, spinning to face him. 'Because she's too afraid to mention it. Just like she was scared to tell you that she'd been wetting the bed. She knows you'll brush it off, or worse, chastise her. Just because she hides it doesn't mean it isn't still going on. Like I've told you a thousand times before, pretending there isn't a problem won't make it magically disappear!'

Dr Wallis looked pointedly at his watch. 'I have to go to clinic now,' he said, already stepping back from us towards the open door.

'But...' I shook my head.

He smiled. 'As I said, you won't be alone. You'll get support in dealing with this, I can assure you. But for now, Tilly doesn't need to be here. I wouldn't discharge you if there was the slightest doubt in my mind.'

'Thank you, Doctor,' Adam said with a smile, walking across the room and shaking his hand firmly. 'We'll be fine.'

Dr Wallis nodded and left without glancing back. Adam turned to me with what appeared to be the hint of a smile on his face. 'You went behind my back,' I accused. 'You searched him out and spoke to him before he came here, didn't you?'

'I called his secretary, yes. I wanted to make sure he had the full picture.'

'Do you realise what you've done? You're putting her at risk, Adam. You know this isn't just anxiety.'

He shook his head, already shoving Tilly's things into her backpack. 'I don't agree. I'm sorry, Maddie, but I have to be honest. I think you make her worked up. You pander to her so much. Maybe she's doing it for attention, maybe it's unconscious, but she is not ill. She's confused.'

I stared at him, wondering how we'd got here. How we could think so differently. There was a time when I would have trusted Adam more than I trusted myself. When I knew he would do anything for me and never dream of letting me down. I couldn't understand how we'd reached this point, where he was so determined to hurt me that he would place our daughter in the middle. Surely he knew me well enough to know I would never do anything to harm her. How could he believe that I was the reason she was anxious? That I was the root of her health problems?

'I don't know how to talk to you any more,' I whispered, clasping my hands under my chin. 'You're like a stranger to me.'

He shook his head, his eyes narrowing. 'I'm the same man I always was. I just don't agree with you now. It doesn't have to be some great war between us. We both want what's best for Tilly, don't we?'

'I'm not sure you do.' I turned from him, heading to the door, a sudden need to find my daughter making me tense. I wanted her with me.

I hadn't considered how we would get home, but Adam had insisted on driving us once we got the discharge paperwork. The journey back to the house was tense, Tilly talking animatedly to each of us, but Adam and I studiously ignoring each other. I could smell his aftershave in the tight confines of the car and knew he would be aware of the musty, unwashed scent of my own skin. I should have been embarrassed, but I was too angry to care.

I tried to picture the last time we'd been in a car together and realised I couldn't bring to mind a clear memory. There had been so many journeys together, they'd all blurred in my mind. Back when we were younger, in the early years of our relationship, I had loved going out on drives, just the two of us. I'd made the effort to pass my test, determined to have the option of driving if I needed it, but nine times out of ten it had been Adam in the driver's seat. He would take me out into the countryside, through curving tree-lined lanes, and I'd kick off my shoes, propping my feet up on the dashboard, my hand resting on his thigh as we listened to music, or talked about anything and everything.

Laura had always commented on it, long after we were married, how it seemed like we always had to be touching somehow, connected physically, even when it would have been easier not to. It had never been a conscious decision; it was just instinct. I had simply needed to feel close to him.

I couldn't pinpoint the moment when it stopped, that need to feel his pulse beneath my fingers, to be close enough to absorb the warmth of his body evaporating like a half-forgotten dream, but when I did eventually notice that it was gone, it had been a shock to realise that I was okay with it. I didn't want to go back. I was grateful for what we'd had, but it was gone, and no amount of pretending or recreating the past was going to fix what we had lost.

Adam pulled up on the driveway behind my red Fiesta and switched off the ignition.

'I'll come in for a bit, shall I? Get you settled.'

'No,' I said quickly, before Tilly could jump on the idea. She would love nothing more than the three of us home together, like the old days, Adam drinking coffee as he read the paper, bringing up current news stories for debate, while I cut material for the latest costume I was making or painted watercolours with Tilly at the kitchen table. But that was the past and it wouldn't do to go backwards. Besides, if Adam came in now, we would definitely argue. I was still furious with him.

'We're fine. You can go,' I said, opening the passenger door and stepping out.

'Here, Tilly, take your teddy.' I unlocked the front door and Tilly ran inside, shouting something about checking nobody had moved her babies.

I turned to find Adam standing behind me. 'Adam, I said you should go.'

'I want to talk to you. You think I'm doing this because of some grudge. Because I'm angry with you over the divorce.' He stepped forward. 'I'm not. I wouldn't do that. You know I wouldn't.'

'Then why are you making this so hard? It's difficult enough to get the doctors to listen to me, but when you don't take my side, it's impossible. You should be supporting me, but instead I'm having to fight you too. It's not fair.'

'I love her too, you know. I want the best for her. I just don't always agree that you're right about what's happening. Maybe you're too close to the situation to see it for what it really is. I don't know. But you can't keep trying to do it alone, cutting me out like I don't matter. She's mine too, Maddie, and I will never stop reminding you of that.'

'As if I could forget.'

He shook his head. 'You aren't her only parent. You can't play this role of saviour, martyr, whatever you think it is you're being. You need to let me in. If not to your life, then to hers.' He watched my face, waiting for a response. When I didn't offer one, he shook his head, his lips pressing together, then turned and walked away. I closed the door, leaning my head back against the wood as I finally let out the breath I'd been holding.

CHAPTER TWENTY

Laura

Then

'Laura, come on!' Maddie grinned, wiggling her hips in my face as I cringed against the high-backed chair in Pete Roley's living room. His parents had gone on a three-week camping holiday in the South of France, leaving Pete to hold the fort at home. I couldn't imagine my parents ever trusting me enough to let me have free rein of their house for a day, let alone the best part of a full month. At nineteen, they still treated me like a flighty eleven-year-old, Mum insisting on doing all my washing and throwing a fit if I even used the oven when she wasn't there to supervise me, while Dad gave me a firm curfew of midnight and lost his mind if I came back even two minutes late.

Even if they *had* allowed me a weekend home alone, I would never have dreamed of throwing a party, let alone the four Pete had held so far. His kitchen was a sea of empty cans and overflowing ashtrays, and I dreaded to imagine the state of the bed sheets upstairs. There'd been a near-constant stream of couples closing themselves off in his parents' room.

I blushed now, looking up at Madeline. She and Adam had disappeared upstairs an hour before, and she'd emerged forty-five minutes later with flushed cheeks and swollen bee-stung lips. I couldn't help but imagine Adam naked, knowing what they'd been doing just moments before.

She was dressed in a layered minidress, the rah-rah skirts a sea of pink, purple and green silk, offering glimpses of her bum cheeks every time she bent over. She sashayed suggestively in front of me, trying to lure me up to dance with her, but I shook my head, my eyes sliding to Adam, who was watching us with unfiltered interest.

I wished I had her guts. Her ability to just do whatever came into her head without shame or reservation. She'd always been more confident than me, but since she and Adam had got together, it was as if she'd become a woman, while I still felt like a silly little girl most of the time. That vulnerability she'd had when we were younger had been replaced by an unshakeable self-assurance, not cockiness or vanity, but something deeper, as if she knew exactly who she was and was comfortable in her own skin. If she wanted to strip off naked and dance on the coffee table, I had no doubt she would do just that. No wonder Adam was obsessed with her.

She flashed me a wink, then turned and walked over to the stereo, rifling through the collection of CDs on the shelf beside it. She passed over the pop music, the typical choices I knew *I* would go for if I had to pick something. I would choose based on what people would think of me, whether it was cool enough. Madeline didn't think that way. She didn't give a fuck what people thought of her, and somehow that made everyone love her all the more.

She slid the CD into the stereo, and I cringed as Tom Jones's 'You Can Leave Your Hat On' started up.

Adam and Pete gave a cheer as Madeline threw her arms into the air, dancing like there was nobody else in the room. She turned to me, smiling wickedly, shimmying her way back across the sticky carpet. I could feel the eyes of everyone in the room on her, and on me as a by-product, and I hated her for it. I didn't want to be the star of the show; I wanted to shrivel up and die.

I fixed a smile on my face, hoping I wasn't too red and blotchy. Madeline tossed back her wild curly hair, leaning over me, her hips moving to the music. She was giving me a lap dance in front of a room full of people! I wanted the ground to open and swallow me whole, but I just kept smiling, pretending I didn't care. That I was the kind of person who could let myself go.

Just like her.

My gaze flicked towards Adam again, and he stared back at me, eyes sparkling. He winked at me and I felt myself flush even redder, looking down at my lap. Madeline spun away from my chair, and I felt a mixture of relief and abandonment as all eyes followed her, leaving me behind. She whirled in a circle, laughing as she sauntered over to Adam and collapsed in his lap. She kissed him, completely unselfconsciously, then rested her head against his shoulder, watching as other couples got up to dance now that she'd broken the ice.

She was always the first. *Always.* In all the time we'd been friends, I had never been able to beat her to the finish line. She'd been the first to kiss a boy, the first to have a boyfriend, the first to try alcohol and subsequently pass out from overindulging. She'd also been the first to lose her virginity. She'd beaten me to all of it. Somehow it took the shine off of everything I did, and I felt like I was always catching up, reaching the goal as she moved the posts another fifty feet back. I took a swig of my drink, a warm bottle of beer I'd found in the cupboard under the stairs, and watched her lean close to Adam, whispering something that made him grin. His arm snaked around her waist, pulling her close.

I looked down at my lap, picking at a loose thread of cotton on my own dress, which might as well have been a sack compared to her frills and ruffles. Madeline was free and uninhibited in a way I could never master, though I'd spent my whole life trying to fake it. But there was a reason it worked for her and never did for me: she wasn't just playing a role, creating some character to present to the world. She was real. Never less than one hundred per cent authentic, and *that* was what made her special.

She never failed to show exactly what she was feeling in the moment, and people couldn't help but gravitate towards her. Unlike the rest of us, she wasn't hiding behind a mask, fighting to be seen as cool, confident, unflustered when really she was cringing inside. She wouldn't do that. She was exactly what she seemed, and that took a level of self-assurance not many people had. I was in awe of her, but I was also jealous, because I wanted it too.

I swallowed another sip of my beer, unable to resist looking her way again. Adam was running a hand up her thigh, his fingertips grazing the hem of her dress, trying to keep her attention. She was chatting to a group of his friends now, who'd settled beside his chair the instant she'd joined him.

I sighed. I could never be as brave as her, and even if I magically found the confidence, I knew it wouldn't produce the same result. Madeline was pure and fun and beautiful on the inside. That was the magic behind it. If I showed my true colours, I knew people would shy away. They wouldn't like what they saw. She was better than me, and I knew it. She was deeper, more interesting. Just special. It was why Adam had chosen her and why I would continue to hide in corners and let her shine.

Pete's cousin Ben walked into the room, nodding my way. He was tall, almost as tall as Adam, and I was pretty sure he was the same age as him, twenty or twenty-one. He was good-looking and he knew it, which meant I was a stuttering mess whenever he was nearby. He raised his can of beer in a silent cheers, his eyes meeting mine. I looked away, counting silently to ten, and when I looked back, he was already talking to someone else.

I bit my lip, angry at myself for being so embarrassingly shy. Knocking back my beer, I hoped the alcohol would help me to at least act like something resembling a normal person. One who didn't have to overthink every single word and action or spend every second of parties like this desperate to hide, feeling like I was balancing on a tightrope waiting for everyone to watch me fall.

It was my lack of self-confidence that had ruined my chances of being with Adam, the reason I'd never got up the guts to ask him out before Maddie sunk her claws into him, and it was also why every single night for the past two months I'd woken in a cold sweat from the same nightmare.

I had dreamed of being a surgeon since I was a little girl, carefully cutting holes in the bellies of my teddy bears, sneaking needles and thread from my mother's sewing basket to practise stitching them back up. I'd never doubted that I could do it. But now, with the first year of my five-year degree in medicine under my belt, the reality of my plan had begun to set in, and with it, the doubts.

In my nightmare I was dressed in scrubs, surrounded by people in blue masks, their eyes penetrating as they watched me on the verge of making a catastrophic decision. I saw the pucker of their foreheads, aware that they disagreed, yet still so sure of myself. Ignoring them, I raised the scalpel, ready to make the incision. Each time, the blade cut into a new place on the prone patient: the stomach, the liver, the heart. But the result was always the same. The bloom of blood, far greater than expected, the gasp of the anaesthetist as the monitor began to beep frantically. The clatter of the scalpel as it hit the tiles. I would wake shaking and crying, certain that I was seeing my future, doubting that I had what it took to be the surgeon I'd always hoped to become.

I closed my eyes, forcing back the self-pitying thoughts, then stood up, determined to go and find another beer, to at least try to push myself a little way out of my comfort zone. Halfway to the door, Madeline's mobile phone began ringing, the tinny rendition of 'Tubular Bells' filling the room.

I paused, watching her slide it from Adam's shirt pocket, kissing the tip of his nose as she flipped it open. 'Hey, Dad,' she said, and I marvelled at how easily the words came. She didn't leave the room to take the call, as I would have done. She didn't even lower her voice. 'What?' she asked, a frown puckering her forehead. I stared, watching as her expression changed, almost in slow motion, her mouth going slack, the blood draining from her face. She held the phone out to Adam, silently.

He took it, shaking his head in confusion.

'Mr Lloyd? Everything okay?' he asked, his eyes on Madeline's blanched face. 'No... Oh shit,' he breathed, his smile falling instantly. He cut the call, flipping the phone shut, his free hand gripping Madeline tightly as his eyes found mine. The whole room was suddenly silent; someone had turned off the music and everyone seemed to be waiting for him to speak.

'Adam?' I heard myself ask. 'What? What is it?'

He shook his head again, looking shocked. 'It's Nola,' he said, his voice cracking as he said the name of Maddie's sixteen-year-old sister. 'She's dead.'

CHAPTER TWENTY-ONE

Madeline

You think you know who you are, how you would react if faced with a challenging situation. I always thought I would be brave if I lost someone I loved. Not that you ever consider things like that when you're nineteen, not really, but I'd had my fair share of morbid daydreams, my *what ifs*.

I pictured myself reacting with serene stoicism. I'd be calm, wise even. But at nineteen years old, these ideas are just too abstract to really consider. It's like listening to a ghost story around the campfire. It gives you chills, but then you move on.

The reality, the crushing desperation to claw back what you had, to offer up yourself in exchange for your loved one, is something altogether more terrifying. A raw, unrelenting longing that leaves you unable to move forward, or even to grieve. When I eventually grasped that Nola was never coming back to me, it felt like some evil thing had crawled into the pit of my belly and begun to devour me from within.

It had been six months. Six of the most awful months of my life, and I had never felt so utterly alone. I'd had a life I wouldn't have swapped for the world. The most loving, open parents, who accepted me just as I was, who never tried to take my freedom or control me the way I'd seen Laura's do. The perfect sister – and she *had* been perfect. We'd never had the hair-pulling, face-scratching screaming matches I'd heard were common amongst sisters. We'd been close. We'd talked, openly and honestly, in a way I missed more than ever now.

She'd known, even before Laura had, when I realised I was falling in love with Adam. She'd been the person I trusted enough to tell when I'd missed a period at seventeen. Rather than calling me stupid and blaming me for not being careful, she'd held my hand, telling me it would be okay, whatever happened, until I believed her. We'd spent four days huddled in her single bed, waiting, *hoping*, before it finally arrived and we breathed a shared sigh of relief. Adam hadn't ever known about that.

She'd taken my clothes and I hers, but I was glad to share with her. Our parents had raised us with Buddhist values, kindness, gratitude and mindfulness being at the forefront of everything they did, and each morning, it was our habit to make a mental list of all that we were grateful for in our lives. Nola was never left off mine.

It was this habit of addressing our feelings then letting them go that made her death all the more shocking. When our great-uncle Conrad had died in his sleep at the grand age of ninety-four, Mum and Dad had smiled and talked about his energy moving forward. They'd told us that death was nothing to fear, just another step on the path, a new beginning. Grief didn't even come up. We wore our most colourful clothes to his funeral, and I felt sorry for all the people dressed in black, heads bowed, tears falling into their laps. They didn't understand, clearly.

But when Nola died, it was different. I don't know if they stopped believing, or if they never really did believe to begin with. But at Nola's funeral, there were no bright colours. Mum and Dad talked of loss, of anger, and there was never any mention of the promised new beginning. Their grief ran so deep there was no way to reach them. And so, for the first time in my life, I was alone. I had lost Nola, and in the aftermath, I'd lost my parents too.

I didn't mean to stop eating. Or to get ill. I didn't ever sit down and decide that the only way out of this mess was to starve myself.

But that was exactly what happened. As the months passed, I felt my own grief twist into something far darker, a rabid monster of a thing that inhabited my body. And it seemed only right that to get rid of it, I would have to starve it out. It wasn't out of hatred for myself but for the darkness inside me. I wanted it gone. And I won't pretend it didn't have positive effects too. Four months after Nola's death, one rainy Sunday afternoon, my mother walked into the kitchen and stopped in her tracks, looking at me as if seeing me for the first time. Whatever she saw frightened her enough to snap her out of her grief and become my mum again.

I watched Adam's lips moving, his eyes on mine, pleading almost, as he continued his speech. It was the same every day. He would come to the hospital where I was being held prisoner and beg me to get better and come back to him. And I would try to say the right things and fail horribly. His voice seemed to be coming from far away, and I watched in detached interest, knowing this new effect was probably down to the antidepressants being forced down my throat by the nurses I'd grown to distrust. They never listened, and I'd quickly realised their promises meant nothing. They had a habit of telling me what I wanted to hear, then going back on their word moments later. I had told them I didn't consent to the drugs. I'd felt the change in me within days of taking the first one, the numbness that washed over my mind, dulling the colours, muffling the sound. I felt like I'd died too, like my poor, beautiful Nola.

I still couldn't believe what had happened. Sudden death syndrome, they'd called it, a term I associated with babies left to sleep in cots with no one to watch over them. Not healthy sixteen-year-old girls. Not Nola. But that was what had happened.

She'd been in the living room, watching the soaps with our parents, curled up on the armchair where any other night I would have squeezed in beside her, painting her nails or plaiting her hair. She'd fallen asleep, her head on the armrest, and when Dad went to wake her, she was cold and stiff. The coroner said she'd probably been dead around an hour and a half when they realised. It was crazy. The stuff of nightmares. She'd died right there, right in front of them, and they'd just kept watching *Casualty* without ever knowing.

'Maddie, are you even listening?' Adam asked, the agitation in his voice breaking into my thoughts.

'Yes, I…' I stumbled over my words, not sure what he expected from me.

He sighed, dropping his head into his hands. I knew I should feel something – sadness, guilt – but the pervading sense of numbness overrode anything else that might have lingered beneath the surface. Adam looked up, and I realised he was close to tears. 'I feel like I'm losing you, Maddie,' he said softly. 'I know you need to be in hospital, I get that, but it's been two months, and as far as I can tell, you're no better than you were when you came here. Are you trying? Do you even *want* to get better?'

I stared at him, trying to work out why he cared, why it even mattered now. I wasn't the girl he'd fallen in love with on the school field all those years ago; I wasn't the person who could make him laugh until tears streamed down his cheeks, or make his words fade away as he gave himself up to the feeling of our bodies pressing together. I was a shell. Nothing more.

'Maddie,' he continued, 'I'm not leaving you. I won't. Because you know what? Nothing has been the same since I met you, and I won't go back to being just Adam. You can't feel it now, and that's fine. But you will. You'll come back to me, and I will be waiting.' He leaned forward, grabbing my hands, squeezing them tightly, almost painfully.

'I… I do love you, Adam. At least, I think I do. But it's buried, you know, under this heap of darkness, and I don't know if I'll be able to find my way back to you,' I admitted. 'I don't know if I even have the energy to try. I'm sorry,' I said, as I watched a tear slip from the corner of his eye.

'Don't be. Just get better. *Try*, Madeline, because I fucking miss you. If you won't get better for me, do it for her. Do it for Nola, yeah?' He grabbed my chin, pulling my mouth to his, kissing me with rough passion.

Pulling back, he sighed. 'I have to go. I'll see you tomorrow.' He didn't wait for a reply as he turned, walking away.

CHAPTER TWENTY-TWO

Laura

'Hey, Paula! Paula, wait up!'

I paused on the pavement outside Adam's grandparents' house, looking over my shoulder in the direction of the loud male voice. It took me a second to recognise the tall, broad-shouldered guy jogging towards me, but then I caught his cheeky grin and felt myself flush. Ben Roley, Pete's cousin. I'd met him at a few parties now, seen him across the room a handful of times, and we'd had that moment the night Nola died, before Maddie got that awful phone call, but we'd never spoken properly, in the cold light of day.

I folded my arms across my chest, feeling suddenly frumpy and embarrassed. I wished I'd bothered to put some make-up on, or worn a pair of heels rather than my old scuffed trainers. But then, I reasoned, I would probably feel ridiculous tottering round Adam's estate all dressed up with nowhere to go.

'Hey.' Ben grinned, coming to a stop in front of me.

'Laura.'

'Huh?'

'It's, uh, Laura. Not Paula.'

'Oh, gotcha. The man in?' He nodded towards Adam's front door.

I shook my head. 'No. His grandad said he went to visit Maddie, then went out straight after dinner. Some party or something.' I shrugged, hoping he couldn't see how hurt I was.

It was kind of an unspoken arrangement that with Maddie out of the picture, Adam and I would spend our evenings together, carrying on the same pattern we'd followed before she went into hospital. It made sense to me that we'd try and keep things the same as they'd always been.

Only, the past few weeks, Adam had been pulling away from me. Not returning my calls as often as he usually did, making plans with other friends. He said he wanted to catch up with old schoolmates, and that maybe I should do the same, but it had quickly become apparent that I didn't have any friends other than him and Maddie.

I'd thought I had plenty, but as soon as they'd got the gossip on Maddie's hospitalisation and shaky mental-health situation, the calls had quickly fizzled out. I'd heard about parties on the grapevine, parties that I knew I'd have been invited to if Madeline were home. I should have realised they were only interested in her. She was missed and I wasn't. I'd been dropped by them all, and now Adam was slipping away from me too and I had never felt so alone.

'Ah.' Ben nodded. 'As it happens, that was why I came by. To invite him to a party. John Wills's. You know him?'

I shook my head, keeping my lips pressed firmly together. It hardly seemed fair that Adam had two party invites and I was left alone for the fifth night running.

'Nah, I doubt you would. He's a friend of a friend from uni.' He folded his arms, flexing his biceps. I wondered if he was doing it on purpose to impress me. I half turned to leave, not wanting to embarrass myself by saying anything stupid.

'Hey,' Ben said, before I could mumble a goodbye. 'What are *you* up to? You should come.'

'Me?'

'Yeah, why not? You got anything better to do?'

I blushed, looking down at my scuffed toes. I considered making something up, but I'd never been much good at lying convincingly, and I couldn't think of anything to say. 'No,' I said finally, looking up at him.

'Cool. So come.' He stepped back, nodding for me to follow.

'What, now? Dressed like this?'

He frowned as if he couldn't see the problem with my oversized hoodie and unflattering jeans.

'Yeah, why not? Anyway, it's right over the other side of town. I can give you a lift.'

I glanced back towards Adam's door, wishing he was in there. That he'd come to the pub with me and we could chat, just the two of us. But since that wasn't going to happen tonight, what did I have to lose?

'Okay.' I nodded, meeting Ben's questioning gaze. 'Let's go.'

The air was thick with cigarette smoke, the bass-heavy music vibrating through my nervous system as we pushed past the scantily dressed bodies into the living room. The women in the hall were older than me by a good few years, and they eyed me suspiciously as I passed, adjusting their minidresses, flicking back their bleached blonde hair. I didn't recognise anyone.

Ben reached across a cluttered table, then pushed a cheap-looking alcopop into my hand. I looked around for a bottle opener and he grabbed the bottle, his hand covering mine as he used his teeth to prise off the cap. He released me with a grin, and I took a sip, trying not to appear flustered, though he made me nervous.

He was so good-looking, different from Adam, but still definitely in the same league, which meant way out of mine. He leaned forward, his lips grazing my ear, and I shivered. 'I'm just going to find John. Why don't you say hi to the girls? They're cool.' He pulled back, flashing me a wink that made my mouth go dry before disappearing into the next room.

I looked over my shoulder to where a group of girls were laughing and dancing, handing round shots. None of them so much as glanced my way. I felt awkward, standing there holding my overly sweet drink, dressed like a slob. I should have said no to the invite, gone back home and spent the evening getting ahead on my reading for next term. I definitely shouldn't be here.

I craned my neck to see if Ben was coming back. He wasn't, and I could hardly go looking for him. He might like me. *Maybe.* But that would quickly change if I turned into some desperate hanger-on, following him around like a lost little puppy.

'Hey, you want a shot?'

I looked up to see one of the girls holding out a glass towards me.

'Uh… I guess so.' I took a tentative step forward. 'What is it?'

She shook her head, her eyes bloodshot, and I realised she'd had more than her fair share already. 'Nope. First you drink. Where's your sense of adventure, babe?' She moved closer, lifting the glass to my mouth, her fingers grazing my lower lip. 'Drink,' she purred.

I cupped her hand, tipping back the glass, swallowing before I could change my mind. The alcohol hit my throat, making me cough loudly. She laughed, dropping the shot glass into the mess on the table. It landed with a tinkling sound, rolling into a pint glass filled with a mysterious purple liquid, seemingly undamaged.

I grimaced. 'What the hell was that?'

'My secret recipe.' She winked. 'Half gin, half tequila and a teensy sprinkle of MDMA.'

'You're joking? You just gave me drugs?'

'Hardly. Barely a taste.'

I felt the bottom drop from my stomach as I realised she wasn't kidding. I'd never even smoked pot, let alone taken a pill. 'You should have asked!' I said, my voice harsh. 'I don't want to lose control. I don't like the thought of it.'

'Relax,' she slurred. 'I doubt you'll even notice it. It's nothing.'

I shook my head, wondering if I should go and stick my fingers down my throat in the bathroom. Bring the whole lot back up. It was exactly what my mum would tell me to do. The truth was, the thought of being high or out of control – or whatever it was they called it when you took Ecstasy – in front of a bunch of random people made my insides squirm. The embarrassment I would have to suffer in the aftermath made saying no all too easy, though I knew Maddie and Adam had experimented with this kind of thing before. Never when I was with them though. I would have ruined their fun pointing out all the things that could go wrong. I began listing them in my mind now, picturing being kicked off my medical degree having been discovered out of my mind on drugs. 'I'm going to the bathroom,' I announced.

The girl grabbed my wrist. 'Ben's into you.'

I spun around to face her. 'What?'

'He *likes* you. He broke up with Siân last month and I haven't seen him with anyone since. But now here he is. With you.'

'That doesn't mean he likes me.'

'He wouldn't have brought you here if he didn't.'

I pursed my lips, wondering if there was any truth to her words.

'I mean,' she continued, 'did he *have* to bring you?'

I shrugged. 'No. I guess he didn't *have* to. But I thought he was just being polite.' I folded my arms. 'You really think he likes me? I'm not his type.'

'You're pretty. And I bet you've got a nice body hidden in there.' She reached forward, slipping her hand under the bottom of my hoodie, gripping my waist, and I laughed, shocked. 'Yep. Smoking hot. Trust me.'

'Yeah, I always trust people who spike my drinks the moment I meet them,' I said, rolling my eyes.

She gave an easy laugh and reached across the table, grabbing a bottle of vodka, twisting the lid free. She took a deep swig, then handed it to me.

'Just neat voddy. No extras, I swear.'

I stared at the bottle in her perfectly manicured hand, indecision plaguing my thoughts. I could go and throw up in the bathroom, then call a taxi to take me home before I made a fool of myself. Or for once, I could let go of my self-imposed rules and have fun. Maybe Ben *did* like me. Maybe this could be the start of something special. Something that was just mine. I sighed, grabbing the bottle, and knocked back a bitter swig, coughing as it burned my throat.

'Good for you.' The girl grinned, swaying slightly. 'Now go find that man and stake your claim.'

I nodded, my head already beginning to swim, a liquid warmth spreading through my limbs. I backed away from her, grinning, then turned, weaving my way through the crowd. The tension I'd been filled with on arriving had ebbed away, replaced by a calm glow as I slipped past people, my hands grazing bodies, enjoying the connection with everyone I passed. People smiled at me, patting my back, noticing me, and I wondered if it might always have been this easy, if only I were willing to try.

I walked into the dining room, then the kitchen, looking for Ben amongst the groups congregating here and there. The music was louder towards the back of the house and I felt my hips sway in time to the rhythm as I moved through a wide hallway towards a wooden door. Pushing it open, I realised it was a snug, two long, cosy-looking sofas pushed up against the walls, a Tom Cruise movie playing on the heavy-backed TV sitting on the pine stand in one corner.

A couple were sprawled over one of the sofas, kissing noisily, the girl straddling the guy's lap. I blushed, shocked, as I realised she was topless, and was just about to step out discreetly when the guy pulled back and I saw his face in profile. *Ben.*

I heard a gasp and my hand flew to my mouth as I realised the sound had come from me. Ben and the girl stopped kissing, both turning to look at me simultaneously. The girl frowned, and Ben flashed me a wink before turning his attention back to her.

I stumbled backwards into the hall, pulling the door tightly closed behind me. What an idiot I had been to ever think someone like him would be interested in me. I should have left. Should never have come. A wave of dizziness washed over me and I gripped the edge of the radiator, leaning my forehead against the cool wall, waiting for it to pass. Instead, it intensified. I felt suddenly frightened and exhilarated all at once.

'You okay there?'

I raised my head. A man, dark-haired, light stubble coating his chin, stood at the end of the hallway watching me. 'You need to sit down?'

I shook my head, turning slowly to face him as he walked towards me. I expected him to stop a few feet away, but he kept moving forward until his body was pressed right up against mine, my back firm against the wall. I could feel the hard edge of the radiator digging into my hips, but it didn't bother me. My mind was awash with a jumbled mass of thoughts. His aftershave smelled good, his body felt good, he didn't look like Ben or Adam. His crotch was pressing against mine, his nose was slightly crooked and the colour of his shirt seemed to change the more I looked at it.

'This okay?' he murmured, his hazel eyes locking on mine. I heard a giggle from behind the snug door, and without thinking, I grabbed the back of the stranger's neck, pulling his mouth down on mine. He didn't fight, didn't pull away, didn't reject me, and in that moment, that was the only thing that seemed to matter. Someone wanted *me.*

He kissed me hard, then pulled back, grabbing my wrist, tugging me wordlessly towards the stairs. I let him. I didn't think as he led me up them, nor as he pulled me into a room with a double bed and a burgundy quilt. He kicked the door shut and pushed me down on the mattress. There wasn't the slightest flicker of doubt in my mind as he stripped me naked and yanked off his own jeans, climbing on top of me, his weight pressing my body into the softness of the bed. I felt like it couldn't be real. Like I was watching from the far corner of the room as it all happened to someone else. Someone completely different from me, because this was not the sort of thing Laura Burts would ever do.

The room spun, the ceiling a kaleidoscope of colours, and I felt that deep sense of fear bubble up once again, knowing it couldn't be real, that my mind was no longer my own. His face loomed above mine, his features morphing, blending, changing, confusing. I closed my eyes as he pushed my legs open, gasping as he shoved inside me without hesitation. He thrust fast, hard, painful, and I heard voices growing louder in my mind, calling my name, trying to get me to come to them. I shook my head, my eyes still firmly shut, too afraid of what I might see if I opened them.

He groaned, falling forward, his weight crushing me for a moment. Then he eased back. I felt a pinch sharp against my nipple, causing me to cry out, followed by a strange lightness.

I didn't know how long I lay there, waiting for the noise inside my mind to quiet, but when I finally opened my eyes, he was gone, and I was alone again.

CHAPTER TWENTY-THREE

Madeline

Now

I picked up the alarm clock from the bedside table, staring at the glowing screen. It was 1.47 a.m. and I had yet to sleep at all. The lamp cast a soft glow over the room, enough for me to see but not so much that it disturbed Tilly. I put the clock back and rolled over in bed, facing her. She was fast asleep on what had once been Adam's side of the bed, the only place she'd been able to settle since coming home from hospital.

Not that I'd done anything to discourage it. I wanted her close. The thought of her being out of my sight, even for a few hours, was enough to make my chest ache, my throat tight with fear. I needed to be able to see her.

I placed a hand on her forehead now, checking for a fever. Her skin was cool, but that did nothing to reassure me. I couldn't help but feel tense, the lingering doubt playing on my mind as I thought of all the possibilities the doctors might have missed. It wouldn't be like we were the first family to be the victim of misdiagnosis. I'd read the stories in those awful real-life magazines. The children who'd died after seeing countless professionals, all because they hadn't dug deeper, found the real issue. I couldn't let that happen to Tilly.

A sudden memory popped into my mind as I leaned back against the stack of pillows, my hand still resting on Tilly's arm. I'd been about seventeen, getting ready for a party I was going to with Adam. Nola had appeared in my doorway, her elfin face smiling, her wide almond eyes gleaming with excitement, half shielded by her thick black fringe. At fourteen, she was already stunning. She was like a cartoon character, all sharp edges and oversized features. We didn't share a single attribute physically, her looks coming from our dad's side of the family, mine very much mirroring our mum's, but our personalities were virtually interchangeable. She was funny and brave and shocking and wild, and I loved her for it.

I'd grinned, gesturing for her to come in. I was wearing a purple Wonderbra and matching lacy boy shorts, my hands on my hips as I tried to choose between a denim miniskirt and a flowing tie-dye dress.

'Go with the skirt,' she said without my needing to ask as she flung herself casually across the bed. Nola always knew what looked good on me, as only a sister could, and I'd been hoping she'd be around tonight. I loved these evenings together, talking about whatever was going on in our lives whilst picking out outfits for each other. She was more edgy in her style; I was more bohemian, but that only made choosing clothes for one another all the more fun. On the nights when she was out with her own friends, I always missed our chats.

'Thanks,' I said and grinned, wrinkling my nose as I stepped into it, pulling the zip up. 'You look nice.' I smiled, leaning over to touch a tiny silver star that dangled from a bracelet on her slender wrist. It was new, as was the silky black top she wore. 'What are you up to tonight?'

She bit her lip. 'Got a date.'

'No! Really?' It had been a few months since we'd broached the subject of dating, but last time we'd discussed it, Nola had seemed set on her intention to stay single for the foreseeable future, though she always loved hearing about the dates Adam and I went on. She was still so young, and I was glad she was happy to wait until she was ready rather than get swept up in the peer pressure from her friends. It was all too easy to fall into that trap, and I was so proud of her for sticking to what she wanted to do, taking her time, enjoying her hobbies and friendships before romance complicated her life. However, there had clearly been some developments since our last talk, and the fact that I hadn't been aware of them caught me off guard.

'Don't sound so surprised, Dee Dee.' She laughed, flinging a pillow at me.

'I didn't know there was someone you liked,' I said, trying not to sound hurt that she hadn't confided in me.

'I wasn't sure myself.' She shrugged. 'But, well…'

'What?' I sat down on the edge of the mattress next to her, putting on a pair of oversized gold hoop earrings as I waited for her to answer. She was unusually subdued, biting the skin around her nails as she fidgeted on the bed. If I hadn't known her better, I'd have thought she was nervous, but that was ridiculous. She knew there was nothing she couldn't share with me; we'd never kept secrets from each other.

When I'd accidentally smeared ink from my leaking fountain pen on Mum's favourite silk dress, I'd told Nola first. When she was being bullied by a group of girls back in middle school, it was me she'd confided in and asked for help. We were a team, a pair, and the idea that she would be afraid to tell me about her crush surprised me. Perhaps it was more than a crush though. I had only been a year older than she was now when I'd met Adam, and that had turned into something far more serious than I'd expected.

She took a breath, rolling onto her back on the bed beside me. 'Her name is Amy,' she said softly.

She was watching me closely looking for a reaction, and suddenly I understood the source of her nerves. I nodded for her to continue.

'We've sat next to each other in maths for a year now. At first I thought it was just in my head, but a few months ago I realised she was feeling something for me too. She started looking at me differently – there was a spark between us that just kept growing. I didn't want to mess up our friendship in case I'd got the wrong end of the stick, but when we walked home from school last week, she asked if I wanted to go out, and I couldn't have said yes any quicker. She's incredible, Dee Dee,' she finished, her cheeks flushing as she closed her eyes, as if she was picturing Amy now.

'Wow!' I giggled. 'You've got it bad.'

'Shut up!' She grinned, opening her eyes to meet mine. 'I'm not saying I'm gay, you know? I'm just…' She shrugged again.

'Exploring your options?' I offered.

'Yes. Yeah, exactly. That's okay, isn't it?'

'Nola, you're *fourteen*. You don't have to decide anything yet. Not ever, if you don't feel like it. We don't have to put a label on anything. You just do what feels right. And have fun, okay?' I said, poking her in the ribs. 'But this Amy,' I asked, suddenly worried, 'she knows how you feel now, right? She doesn't think this is just a night out with a friend or something?'

'No, she knows. We talked a lot after she broke the ice. It's been so good to finally let it out in the open. I've felt so confused with her up until this week, never really sure if it was just wishful thinking on my part or if she actually liked me that way. Turns out she was thinking the exact same thing about me this whole time. You'll like her,' she added, and I smiled, sure that she was right. 'She's really cool. She knows who she is and she's not afraid of it. She shaved her hair, you know? It's… What do you call that cut that boys get? Like Daryl down the road?'

'Short back and sides?'

'Yeah. But the top is longer; it flops over her eyes and…' She shuddered, her eyes drifting shut.

'You really like her.'

'We'll see.'

'Hey, I suppose I should thank you for making it easy for me. At least I don't have to give you the talk about getting pregnant yet,' I said, getting up from the mattress and heading across the room.

'Ha! You think Mum and Dad would let you take that from them? I've known that shit since I was seven. And besides, are we just going to gloss over your little pregnancy scare at Easter? I think I can do without *that* kind of advice,' she teased.

'Not funny yet,' I said, grimacing as I remembered how nervous we'd both been when I'd missed a period. It was strange to think I could be heading towards the end of a pregnancy with Adam's baby right now if things had worked out differently, but I was relieved it hadn't. We had plenty of time for babies in the future. Right now, we were having fun and enjoying our freedom. And Nola was right, after what happened at Easter, she probably knew everything when it came to safe sex. If there was one good thing to come out of that nerve-racking week, it was that it had drilled into her the importance of using contraception.

'Are you going to tell them about tonight?' I asked.

'I might. I haven't decided yet. Knowing Mum, she'll throw me a coming-out party, and I'm not even sure myself yet. Don't get me wrong, I'm grateful that our parents are so open. I don't think there's much we could do that would shock them or that they wouldn't support us with.'

'No,' I agreed. 'We are lucky. You've met Adam's grandparents, right? I don't think I realised just how easy we have it until I got to know them.'

She grimaced comically. 'Exactly. And I know that if and when the time comes to put a label on my sexuality, Mum and Dad will be completely on side. But she'll want me to talk about it, share everything with her, and she'll be so excited about the prospect of being a supportive mother that she'll smother me with it. Right now, I need space to think, to work out how I feel before

I have to try and explain it to them. I don't want to be rushed into making a choice, so don't say anything yet, okay? When I'm ready, I'll talk to them.'

'Course,' I agreed. 'But you can talk to me. I won't go on about it, but I'm here any time you need me.'

'I knew you would be like this; I don't know why I was even nervous about telling you.' She got up from the bed, looking relaxed and happy. 'Thanks, Dee Dee.'

'Nols,' I said, grabbing her wrist as she passed me. 'I love you.'

'I know.' She squeezed my hand and I watched her go. 'Love you too,' she sang as she left the room.

I blinked up at the ceiling now, realising my face was damp with tears. It was in the dead of night that I always found my mind drifting back to my sister. I couldn't stop myself replaying the memories, trying to imagine what she would have been like if she hadn't died. What *I* might have been like. I knew I wasn't the same person I'd been before I lost her: I was cocooned in fear, terrified of losing my daughter the way I'd lost Nola.

Maybe if she'd been to a doctor, she could have been saved. We would never know if there was something lurking inside her body, waiting to strike. The autopsy had drawn a blank, but that didn't mean there weren't answers that could have been found while she was still living. I couldn't let it happen to my family twice – I just couldn't.

I wiped my eyes on the bobbled pale-pink cotton of my pyjama sleeve, rolling back onto my side to face Tilly. She was so perfect. So beautiful.

She stirred and I leaned my head on my hand, watching her. 'Tilly?' I said softly. 'Do you want a drink? I have some water here for you.'

'Mummy?' she asked, blinking sleepily. 'Is it morning?'

'No, baby, it isn't. It's still night.' I helped her to sit up and pressed a glass to her lips.

She pulled back, shaking her head.

'Just a few sips, sweetie, that's it. You need to keep hydrated.' I smiled as she gulped down the water, relieved that she hadn't put up a fight. Without a cannula, this was the only way to keep her hydrated, and I wouldn't let her down.

She lay back down on her pillow, closing her eyes. After a few moments, she spoke. 'My legs hurt, Mummy. And I feel sick.'

I frowned. 'Shall I rub your legs for you?'

'Yes,' she whispered. 'On the knees and ankles. They're so sore.' She blinked, then opened her eyes again. 'I need to sit up.'

'Okay, let me help you.' I propped some pillows up behind her. 'Do you want more water? Some food, maybe?'

She shook her head. 'No, I'm…' She pressed her hands to her lips, but it was too late. Before I could do anything at all to help, her mouth opened and she vomited through her fingers onto the duck-down duvet, her tiny shoulders heaving.

I jumped out of bed, rushing around to her side. The moment she stopped throwing up, I flung back the ruined duvet, lifted her into my arms and ran to the bathroom, setting her down beside the sink. 'I'm going to get you a bowl. If you need to be sick again, do it in there,' I said, pointing to the sink.

I ran down the stairs, taking them two at a time, dashing into the kitchen to grab the washing-up bowl from the sink. I flung open the cupboard, reaching for the Dettol too. There was a crash on the ceiling above me, and I spun, dashing back upstairs, my heart thumping painfully in my chest.

'Tilly!' I yelled, rushing towards the open bathroom door.

I flung it wide and gasped. Tilly was flat on her back beside the bath, her eyes closed, her lips tinged with a terrifying hint of blue.

'Tilly!' I screamed, squatting down beside her. 'Baby, wake up, wake up now!' I gripped her shoulders, squeezing tight. 'No, no, no!' I yelled. I pressed my ear to her mouth, almost crying with relief as I heard a shallow breath fall from her lips.

'You hold on, baby,' I cried. 'You're not going anywhere.'

CHAPTER TWENTY-FOUR

The ambulance ride had been a blur this time around. There had been no time to think, to plan what I had to say. Tilly was evidence enough that we needed to be taken seriously. The paramedics had roused her en route, and now we were back on the children's ward, an oxygen mask covering her small face, yet another cannula jutting out of the crook of her elbow. It felt like Groundhog Day.

The whole room smelled strongly of vomit, and I knew I looked a mess, my hair unbrushed, my old pyjamas in serious need of upgrading. Tilly wouldn't stop crying, tugging at the mask, begging to leave as she thrashed in the bed. Every time she rolled from one side to the other, she winced. I could see the pain written on her face.

'She needs medication. Her legs are hurting!' I insisted to the nurses in the room.

'She can have Calpol – I'll get it now.'

'No, not oral. It's no good. She'll be sick again!'

The sister nodded, placing a hand on my shoulder, and I fought the urge to collapse into her arms and sob like a baby. I couldn't think about what any of this meant, not yet. It was too scary, and I knew that as soon as I opened those doors, the fear would engulf me. I couldn't afford to crumble; I had to stay strong. 'We can ask the doctor to write up IV paracetamol,' she said gently. 'But there's been a major emergency downstairs in A&E. It could take an hour before they get to Tilly. Shall we try the Calpol for now? I would hate to leave her in this much distress until then.'

I bit my lip, feeling backed into a corner, then gave a resigned nod. 'Fine. But I don't think it will work.'

She squeezed my shoulder, then left to go and get the medicine. The other nurses followed, leaving us alone. It had all happened so fast. I felt ridiculous trying to talk to them dressed in my pink pyjamas, but I hadn't had a chance to even grab a jumper before we were piled into the ambulance. The only thing I'd thought to bring was my phone, and that was almost out of battery. Tilly yanked at the oxygen mask again and I rushed towards her, holding my hand over it. 'No, sweetie, don't fight it. It's helping you.'

'It's hurting my throat. I don't want it!'

I shook my head. 'I wish I could swap places with you, Tilly. I would do it in a heartbeat.'

The door opened and the sister came back in, bearing a tray. 'Calpol,' she announced, holding up the syringe. 'Here, Tilly. Let's get that mask off you and give you some medicine.'

'Are you sure she can breathe without it?' I asked, blocking her path. 'I don't want her to pass out again. Her lips were blue, before the ambulance arrived – they were *blue*,' I repeated, needing her to understand the severity of the situation.

She nodded. 'I know, but she's stable now. This was a precaution really, but her stats are looking much better. She can take it off.'

'Shouldn't you ask a doctor?'

She raised an eyebrow. 'Let's give her the paracetamol and see how she does, okay?'

I nodded reluctantly and took the syringe from her hand. 'Okay. I'll give it to her – she won't take it from you. She's afraid of nurses since our last stay.'

'That's not a problem. I'll just stay so I can witness it, then I can sign it off.' Her tone was sunny but her words set me on edge. I didn't need a witness to attest to the fact that I'd given my daughter a bit of Calpol. I was just about to argue the point when Tilly cried out, her hands wrapping around her stomach as she curled into a ball. I sucked in my irritation, turning away from the sister.

'Let's take this off you, sweetie,' I said softly, slipping the mask away from her face. A red line ran around her mouth where the strap had been adjusted too tightly, and her lips were dry and cracked. 'Can she have some water first?' I asked, my eyes not leaving Tilly's.

'Yes, of course,' the sister said. 'I'll grab you a jug. One moment.' She left the room and I helped Tilly to sit up.

'Are you feeling sick, sweetie?'

She nodded.

'I have some medicine for you to try. Do you want it?'

'Okay,' she croaked. I held the syringe to her parted lips, pressing down on the end. Tilly swallowed thickly, then grimaced. I walked to the little table, placing the empty syringe back on the tray just as the sister returned.

'I just gave it to her,' I said, taking the jug and the plastic cup from her hand. I poured a little water into the bottom of the cup and handed it to Tilly. 'Here, sweetie, rinse your mouth out.'

The sister picked up the empty syringe. 'And she had all of it?'

'Yes.'

'Are you still feeling poorly, Tilly?' she asked, stepping up to the bed. Tilly nodded and pressed her lips together.

'Sick bowl,' I yelled. 'She's going to throw up!'

The sister grabbed a disposable bowl from the cupboard beside Tilly's bed and thrust it under her chin just in time. Tilly gagged, emptying the contents of her stomach into the bowl. I rubbed her back, furious that I'd given in so easily. I should never have agreed to give her the oral paracetamol in the first place. I knew it would never work.

'You see?' I demanded as she finally finished. 'She can't keep anything down. It's unfair to make her try. You need to bleep the doctor now – she needs to be assessed,' I insisted, wiping a paper towel over Tilly's damp mouth and tossing it across the bed.

The sister glanced at the balled-up tissue, raising an eyebrow, then gave a grim nod. 'I agree. I'll see if I can get hold of one of them. It's always this way with night admissions, I'm afraid. We're just stretched so thin and the poor doctors are pulled in every direction.'

'Well pull them this way, for goodness' sake.'

She nodded and left the room. I kissed Tilly on the forehead, helping her to lie back down, and watched her eyes sink closed. She was exhausted, poor baby. I should have been too; it was nearly four in the morning and I hadn't slept at all, but I was wired, buzzing with adrenaline after the events of the night. I watched Tilly drift into a fitful sleep and sank down into a chair beside her bed.

I knew I had to call Adam. I really didn't want to; I could only imagine how angry he would be when I told him we were back here again. But the longer I left it, the harder it would be. Perhaps it was easier to just get it over with.

I leaned across to the table, sliding the phone towards me, staring bleary-eyed at the screen. With a sigh, I keyed in the passcode and leaned back against my seat, pressing the phone to my ear. I watched Tilly's face, hoping the sound of my voice wouldn't wake her. I didn't want to risk stepping out into the hall in case she needed me.

The phone rang four times and I was beginning to think it would go to voicemail when finally Adam answered. 'Maddie, what is it? What time is it there?'

'It's four in the morning. Where are you?'

'I'm in Florida. It's just gone 11 p.m.'

'You're working?'

'Of course I'm working. Tell me you haven't gone into another panic over Tilly. I can't think why else you'd be calling at this time.'

I bit my lip hard, tasting blood. 'We're in hospital. She was unconscious, Adam, her lips were blue. If that's not a good reason to panic, I don't know what is.'

'You didn't call another ambulance?'

'Of course I did! What choice did I have?'

'Oh, Maddie…' I heard the tightness in his voice, as if he were trying to stop himself shouting. 'You can't keep doing this. You just can't. Is she okay?'

'She's going back to sleep now. But she needed oxygen. And she's being sick again.' I chewed my fingernail, feeling inexplicably nervous. 'Adam, I *need* you to be on my side here. I can't fight you on this. Please just accept that I'm seeing it first-hand. She's ill. Do you think I *want* her to be like this? That I get a kick out of riding in an ambulance?'

He was silent for a moment. 'I think you feel it's necessary, but I've seen her after every one of these episodes, and every single time she's been fine. She's never been critical, and if you keep rushing her to hospital for every little thing, they're going to start looking at *you*. They're going to think you're one of those helicopter mothers or something.'

I squeezed the phone in my palm, biting back the words that sprang to mind. How many times had Adam called me that very thing? Accused me of being pandering and overprotective when I'd simply been trying to get him to see what was happening right in front of his face. How hypocritical of him to act like he didn't think of me that way too, when we both knew he was the first person to make that accusation.

'How can they?' I pushed. 'How could *anyone* think that after what happened? She collapsed and wouldn't wake up! What is there to overreact about? What would *you* have done?'

'I don't know,' he admitted. 'But I don't know what you expect them to do. The tests are all negative. It's nerves, *anxiety*, not a medical emergency. I feel like you're escalating things since you've been alone. It's not good for you,' he added softly. 'Listen, I was going to call when I got back to discuss this anyway.' He paused, and I took a deep breath, considering hanging up. 'Maddie, I want us to sit down when I get back and have a conversation.'

'About what? Because unless it's how you're going to step up and help get the support your daughter needs, I'm not interested.'

'Not about her, no. About *you*. Your… fears. I think we need to look at the whole picture here. The tests are coming back negative and yet you keep finding yourself in this position. I know you get scared, Maddie, and I don't blame you for that—'

'You're unbelievable. Don't you dare, Adam. Don't make this be about me, because it's not. You know it isn't.' I cut the call before he could reply and slammed the phone down on the table. Tilly stirred and I got up, feeling her forehead for the thousandth time that night. How dare he turn this around, make *me* out to be the problem when I was the only one who even seemed to care about what was happening to our daughter. He was doing this to get to me. To punish me for leaving him. For refusing to fight for the marriage I no longer wanted to be in. I knew he didn't really believe I was capable of making this up. I would never do anything to hurt my daughter. Never.

I was suddenly exhausted, my head spinning, flashbacks of the ambulance ride bursting in bright colours across the canvas of my mind. I'd been terrified, though I hadn't shown it at the time. All I could think of was her. Getting her here, where she could be safe. But now, in the still quiet of the children's ward, with the background noise of beeps and hushed voices from outside the door, it hit me: I could have lost her. If she'd been sleeping in her own room, I might not even have realised she was in trouble until the morning. What would have happened then? It didn't bear thinking about.

I climbed up beside her on the bed, needing her close. I was just letting my eyes drift closed when I heard footsteps. The door opened, and I looked up as a man in a pair of blue scrubs came into the room. I knew instantly that he was a doctor. I struggled to sit up as he flicked on the overhead light, blindingly bright. Blinking hard, I focused on him.

'I'm Dr Keifer,' he said, approaching the bed. His hair was white, and he wore thick glasses. His mouth was hard and unsmiling, and I got the sense he was none too happy at being summoned from whatever it was he'd been doing.

I nodded. 'Thank you for coming to see us.'

'Can I have a look at her?' he asked, not waiting for me to move off the bed. He walked around to the opposite side, peering over the top of his glasses. Tilly, thankfully, remained sound asleep. He pressed a thumb on the back of her hand, tutting, then pulled the collar of her nightdress down, feeling along her collarbone. 'She's dehydrated. Has she been drinking?'

'I've been offering her drinks hourly since we were discharged, using the water bottle Dr Wallis suggested. She has taken little sips, but she's been sick several times tonight.'

'Hmm.' He lifted her nightdress, pressing her stomach gently, then lowered it back down. 'She's very small for her age.'

'Yes. I know.'

'What are these bruises?' he asked, fixing me with a penetrating stare. His pupils seemed magnified through the thick lenses of his glasses. I looked to where he was pointing, surprised to see dark purple bruises spreading over both Tilly's shoulders.

I shrugged. 'I think they must be from when she collapsed. She was unconscious in the bathroom, you see – that's why I called the ambulance. I tried to rouse her.'

'You must have pressed quite hard.'

'No, nothing like that. She bruises so easily; the slightest bump is all it takes. Look at her legs – she's covered, and those are just from playing.'

He pursed his lips, watching my face, and I felt myself grow flustered.

'I was just trying to wake her up. It was very frightening,' I added firmly.

He nodded, looking back down at her. 'Dr Wallis discharged you following a series of tests, correct?'

'That's right. Nothing was found, but clearly something has been missed.'

'How so?'

'What do you mean?'

'What makes you think that something was missed?'

'Because she collapsed, of course. And she's still being sick and nothing has changed. I told him when he discharged her that he was rushing into it, and tonight has proved just that.'

'I see,' he said, rubbing his lips together thoughtfully. 'And Dr Wallis saw these bruises?'

'Well, not the ones on her shoulders, no, because they weren't there. But I'm sure he saw the ones on her legs. I think I mentioned it – there was such a lot to tell him, I can't remember...' I admitted, my words spilling out faster than I would have liked. I took a breath and knotted my fingers together, digging my nails into the tops of my hands as I fought to regain my composure. Tilly stirred, rolling over, and I reached out, placing a hand on her back, rubbing in soothing circles. I didn't like the way the doctor was looking at me, nor the direction this conversation was going. He sounded accusing rather than understanding. 'Where is Dr Wallis?' I asked. 'I'd like to speak with him if I may.'

'He's not here.'

'Well, in the morning perhaps?'

'Dr Wallis is on annual leave for the next two weeks. You're stuck with me, I'm afraid. Now perhaps we'd better have a little chat in the hall, so as not to disturb Tilly,' he suggested.

I frowned. 'I'm not leaving her alone. She might need me.'

'I'm sure one of the nurses can stay with her.'

'Why? What more is there to say? You can see for yourself that she isn't right. So what happens next? What other tests can we can do?'

He shook his head. 'I'm not happy about this bruising,' he muttered, more to himself than to me.

'Are you thinking it's a sign of a particular condition?' I asked, trying to steer him back on track.

He raised his eyes to look at me. 'That remains to be seen.' He tapped his fingertips on the edge of the bed thoughtfully. 'I'll order some fluids to be put up – she is very dehydrated again,' he said in a tone that suggested this was somehow my fault. 'And I'll be back round later in the morning to discuss this further.'

'Can you write up IV paracetamol for her? The sister said she was going to ask you to do it.'

'Yes. I agree, pain relief would be a good idea.' He frowned again and then gave a brief nod and left.

I stared after him feeling suddenly sick to my stomach. I was shaking too, I realised. I didn't like him, this Dr Keifer. Who did he think he was, coming in here with his barely concealed accusations? Did he really think I would call an ambulance if I'd hurt her on purpose? Of course I wouldn't! And surely any child would have bruising after being found unconscious? Maybe I *was* a bit rough in my panic, but he couldn't possibly think I'd done it to her in anger?

The way he'd looked at me, like a judge waiting knowingly for a confession from the accused, made me frightened. Not for myself, but for Tilly. Because if he focused on the wrong thing now, then the real cause would go undiagnosed and she would be the one to suffer.

CHAPTER TWENTY-FIVE

Laura

Then

'So you're saying it wasn't wrong? I'm really…'

'Pregnant, yes.' Dr Raymond nodded, his face impassive. 'I can't tell you how far along, unfortunately – you'll need to book in for a scan to determine that.'

I squeezed my eyes shut, leaning back against the chair in the cosy GP surgery I'd been visiting since I was born. I wouldn't need a scan to tell me exactly how pregnant I was; I already knew. 'What happens now?' I asked, jutting my chin out as I faced Dr Raymond's carefully blank expression.

'Well, that will depend on how many—'

'Eight. It's Eight weeks.'

He steepled his fingers below his chin. 'Laura, you're young. You have so much ahead of you. Your dad told me you're planning to train as a surgeon.' He sounded impressed. 'You've always had a good mind; even as a child you were such a bright little thing.' He smiled gently, leaning forward in a fatherly fashion. He'd always been candid in our conversations, blurring the lines between family friend and professional, and I could tell he was about to bend the rules and speak his mind now. 'Look, I can't tell you what to do. That choice is yours to make. But you are at a crossroads in your life, and you need to think this through.' He tapped his pen on his desk, clearly wanting to say more than he was able to. 'Is the father around for you to talk to?'

I shook my head, my cheeks hot. 'You won't tell my parents, will you?' He and my dad had been friends since before I was born, and they frequently met up to play golf and talk about politics and family life.

'You know I couldn't even if I wanted to. But will *you*?'

'No. Not yet anyway.'

He pursed his lips thoughtfully. 'I'll refer you for that scan. Is there *anyone* you can talk to? This isn't something you should have to deal with alone.'

I thought of Maddie, her blank gaze as she stared out of the window, the stilted small talk we'd made as we discussed her future when I'd visited the psychiatric unit yesterday. I couldn't tell her this. She was barely coping with her own issues – I had no right to pile my problems on top of her.

I nodded slowly. 'I have a friend I can discuss it with,' I said softly, hoping I was right.

I left the surgery, resisting the urge to cup my flat belly as I slipped between two parked cars, and walked to the bus stop. The number 1A to take me home went by without me raising my arm. Instead, I flagged down the number 7 and settled myself at the back, heading to the estate where Adam lived.

'But... whose is it?' Adam asked again, pacing back and forth in front of the bench. A couple of pre-teen boys on bikes raced along the boardwalk, swerving recklessly around Adam, who barely seemed to notice them pass. The sky out over the sea looked ominous, the clear watery blue of the afternoon being replaced in increments as the wind blew the heavy grey clouds towards us. Shivering, I pulled the sleeves of my jumper down over my wrists, bunching the material in my fists nervously.

We'd come down to the seafront so we could talk without his grandparents popping in to offer cakes and gossip about their new neighbours every five minutes. Adam had come without a fuss, and I'd been grateful that for once he was able to spare some time for me.

Now, though, I wondered if I'd blurted out my news too quickly. He seemed to be struggling to take it in, and I couldn't blame him. It was hardly what anyone would expect from a wall-flower like me. I was still in shock myself. I stared past him, out to sea, watching the gulls swoop every now and then, opportunistic as they targeted the couples huddled together on the cold shingle with their bags of chips. The air smelled of salt and fried food, and there was guitar music drifting from somewhere nearby, half lost on the whistle of the wind.

'I don't know,' I murmured. 'I was… drunk. This is humiliating for me, Adam. Please, don't make me go into any more detail than that.'

I looked down at my lap, feeling ashamed at having to admit the truth. It hadn't escaped my thoughts that my baby, the child that was growing within my body at this very moment, would be forever fatherless. How could I tell my parents that I didn't even know his name, let alone what he did for a living, what kind of man he was? I could already picture the look of disgust on my dad's face. He would feel like I'd let him down, and perhaps I had. This was hardly what I'd planned for my future: being a single mum before I'd even reached my twenties. I sighed, glancing up at Adam, seeing the disbelief in his eyes. I'd surprised him – that much was clear. 'I don't know who he is,' I repeated softly. 'All I can tell you is that he's not going to be around. He's nobody.'

Adam stopped pacing to look at me. I avoided his stare, turning my head to gaze out at the choppy ocean.

'Laura, this isn't like you.' He sat down beside me, taking my hand, and I felt a warmth spread through my fingers, my breath catching in my throat. 'Did something happen... Did this guy... did he hurt you?'

I shook my head, finally meeting his eyes. 'Adam, please, I've told you, I don't want to go into this.' I knew my answer made what he was asking sound like a real possibility, but the truth was, I couldn't remember all that had happened that night. My memories were disjointed, blurred and unreliable. I couldn't even picture the man's face now. I'd woken up the morning afterwards in my own bed with no memory of even leaving the party, and when I'd remembered what I'd done, I'd felt half embarrassed, yet half proud that I'd broken out of my boring mould for once. I'd done something brazen and out of character, and perhaps it would make me more confident in the future. It was the kind of wild, crazy night Maddie would have had if she'd been single, and I could just picture her expression when I told her about it.

I'd wanted to surprise her, to see her face light up in disbelief the way it once had when she'd been well and we'd shared secrets. But then I'd realised she wouldn't react that way now. I doubted she would even raise an eyebrow if I told her my story. She'd been like a shell of a person for such a long time, I was sure that if I confided in her, I'd only be hurt and disappointed by her reaction. It wouldn't be like telling my best friend. So I'd kept it to myself, hoping that one day she would be well enough to laugh about it with me, and let myself believe it was the beginning of a new, stronger, braver Laura who wasn't afraid of the world. It had seemed so liberating before I knew about the baby, but now it just seemed careless and stupid.

'Okay.' Adam nodded, not letting go of my hand. 'Okay. But what will you do?' he asked.

I shrugged, tears pricking at the backs of my eyes.

'Do you want to keep it?'

Did I? Could I? It was a question I'd avoided asking myself up until now. 'I think I do. I know it's crazy, Adam, but yes, I want to have this baby. It feels like a good thing,' I added, realising just how much I meant it. 'But how can I? How can I do this all by myself?'

'Laur, you're not all by yourself. You have me, don't you?' He slung an arm round me, kissing the top of my head. 'If you want to do this, we'll figure out a way to make it work, okay?'

I closed my eyes, relief flooding through me as he held me close. I hadn't realised until he'd spoken those words just how afraid I was. How completely alone I had been, not just today, finding out about the baby, but in every little part of my life. Without Madeline there to steady me, I'd been lost, unable to find my balance, but this felt like the start of a new chapter. It felt real. Adam was a man of his word and I knew that if he made a promise to support me, to help me to have the baby, then he would stand by that. He wouldn't let me struggle alone.

'We will?' I asked, my eyes filling with tears at the prospect.

'Of course.' He grinned and patted my belly, and I let out a shaky sigh, leaning into him, as I wondered whether this was how things were supposed to end up all along.

CHAPTER TWENTY-SIX

Now

I packed the last of the ham-salad baguettes into a basket, adding the little pre-packed pancakes that Tilly loved so much and a bottle of juice for Madeline. Not for the first time, I considered the unhealthy dynamic in our friendship, the one that frequently found me in the role of mother rather than equal.

I was certain she wasn't bothering to eat, and it annoyed me, because it was by choice. Perhaps not a conscious one, but all the same, I knew how her mind worked. She would suffer right along with Tilly every inch of the way, punishing herself for not being able to take her pain away. She was the type who never ate at a wake because it might seem disrespectful or diminish her show of sadness somehow, even if she'd barely known the deceased.

It meant that, unwittingly or not, she became a patient too, and much as I would have liked to just let her get on with it, make her own choices, I knew I wouldn't. I cared too much, even if she was irritating beyond belief.

When she'd called this morning to tell me that Tilly was back in hospital, my first instinct had been to grab my keys and run to her. The fear that swept over me was like a shower of freezing water, my only thought to keep her safe. But then, as Madeline had described the frantic ambulance ride, the difficult doctor she'd had to deal with, I had heard her. *Tilly.* She was chatting away in the background and suddenly I was no longer frightened, I was angry.

Why hadn't Madeline started the call by reassuring me that she was fine now, rather than letting me think she was in some critical state, still masked up and needing oxygen? Didn't she realise how her tone came across, how her words induced the deepest kind of terror? I only hoped she'd been more careful when she called Adam.

I covered the basket of food, gave Minnie an affectionate rub with my bare foot, then went upstairs to put on some make-up. I never wore much, but it helped me to feel confident, especially when I knew Adam was going to be around. He'd seen me at my worst, but that wasn't how I wanted him to think of me. Not that I should want him to think of me at all really.

I slicked a soft pink shade across my lips, pressing them together, then ran a brush through my sleek chestnut hair, still enjoying the chic swing of it over my shoulders from the new cut.

I was just placing the brush back on the dresser when the doorbell rang. I frowned. At 2 p.m. on a Saturday, it could only be the postman. I tried to remember if I'd done any more late-night shopping this week. It usually happened after a few glasses of wine, when I decided to revamp my frumpy image, scrolling through clothes on chic websites that looked great on the model but would no doubt make me look ridiculous and awkward. In a haze of tipsy confidence, I would recklessly add items to my basket, ignoring the fact that I would never actually be brave enough to wear them in the cold light of day. I cringed, remembering the leather miniskirt that had arrived, wrapped in fuchsia tissue paper, last week. I hadn't even bothered to try it on before I packed it up and returned it. The bell rang again and I ran down the stairs, feeling silly.

I flung open the door and instantly took a step back, my arms crossing self-consciously around my waist. 'Adam!'

'Hey. Can I come in?'

I stared at him, his chin covered with dark stubble, his clothes rumpled and creased. 'You must have got a flight straight away,' I said, stepping back to let him pass. 'Did *you* fly?'

'No.' He shook his head. 'I'd only just gone to bed when Maddie called. I had to let them down for the return flight and book my own ticket back.' He frowned, his voice weary. 'She has no idea the trouble she's causing for me. I can't let her keep doing this,' he said, heading into the living room and slumping down on the sofa. I watched, suppressing the feeling of happiness that always came with seeing him at home in my flat.

'But you didn't go straight to the hospital?' I asked, realising I was stating the obvious. I sat down on the armchair opposite him, leaning forward.

'I wanted to see you.'

'Oh?'

He put his head in his hands, groaning, and I felt a sudden pang of dread interwoven with undeniable excitement. I breathed in deeply, pressing my knees together, waiting nervously for him to continue. At last he looked up, his eyes bloodshot, his face pinched with worry, and my heart sank as I realised that whatever the reason for his visit, it wasn't about me. 'Laura,' he said, his eyes on mine, 'I need you to help me.'

I shook my head, confused. 'How? With what?'

'With Tilly. I'm not an idiot. I won't pretend this is all some elaborate story Maddie's made up. Something *is* wrong with her, and I can't deny it. You know how crazy she's become about food, the daily battles to get some nutrition into her. It's a problem that needs solving.'

'Right.' I nodded slowly, feeling embarrassed that I'd let myself think it might be about something else, just this once. I loved Tilly more than my own life, but I didn't see how I could help resolve the situation between Adam and Maddie. That was something I couldn't fix.

'But I don't think she's physically ill. She's hardly ever sick when she's with me – she climbs and jumps and runs all over the place without going on about this mysterious leg pain,' he said, pursing his lips. 'The child Madeline describes isn't the same one I see.'

'I'm not sure I understand what your point is.'

'Laura, you know how I feel about Maddie. Nothing has changed for me. I love her and I would never do anything to hurt her.'

I nodded tightly, trying not to let my face morph, displaying the desolation I felt at his words.

'But,' he continued, 'I don't believe she's in her right mind lately. I feel like she's letting her own fears cloud the situation, and poor Tilly is the victim.'

'You know as well as I do that Maddie loves Tilly more than anything. You're not trying to say you think she's... what? *Causing* this somehow?' I shook my head. 'She wouldn't, Adam. She'd never do anything to hurt that girl.'

'I'm not saying she's *doing* anything to her. Just building up the levels of fear and anxiety so that Tilly becomes almost too frightened to eat. Anxiety can make you sick. It can have all sorts of physical traits. You're a doctor, Laura. You know this.'

I nodded slowly. 'Yes, but...' I paused, shaking my head. 'Do you think Maddie's been lying about how bad things are at home?'

'No, not lying, but building them up in her head. Escalating little things to be catastrophic. She was having sleepless nights before I left. Worrying over things that were out of her control. It was why I thought it was a blip when she told me she wanted a divorce. I thought she was just having one of her moments, pushing me away out of fear. I never thought she'd see it through.' He sighed.

I nodded slowly, remembering the shock I'd felt when she'd told me her marriage was over. It had come out of nowhere and, like Adam, I'd never believed she would really divorce him. I had known Maddie was more restless in those last few months, and a couple of times she'd made strange offhand comments about even the best things having to come to an end, or something equally mysterious, but I'd never thought much of it. As open as she was in so many aspects of her life, as it turned out, she could really keep a secret when she wanted to.

On reflection, I was sure that she didn't speak about her marriage to me because she was still making up her mind. She wasn't one for taking advice, asking opinions. She would follow her intuition and do whatever it was she decided on in the end. And that was the first Adam or I really knew about it. By then, it was too late to convince her to consider anything else. Her mind was made up and there was no way for Adam to change it, no matter how much he wanted to.

He leaned forward and I focused on his face, the dark circles beneath his eyes, the new lines around his mouth. 'You know how she was after Nola,' he said softly. 'She's never got over that. From the moment Tilly was born, she's been terrified of losing her.'

'It's been almost fifteen years since Nola died, Adam. She can't be holding on to that fear after all this time,' I said, shaking my head. 'And it's not like she's been in and out of hospital with Tilly before. Not to this extent.'

'Because *I* was there to reassure her that Tilly was fine. To bring her down from this heightened sense of fear and force her to see things reasonably. I'm not there with her now, and to be honest, I was half expecting things to go this way. I'm worried about her, Laur. I don't know what goes on in that house when she's all alone, but it makes me uneasy. I feel like she's not herself, and we're only seeing the tip of the iceberg.'

I nodded. 'I can understand that. Lately I've been having a lot of the same concerns. I don't like that she's on her own so much,' I admitted.

'It's not as though I didn't try to keep things the same,' Adam said, his tone defensive. 'It was me who suggested coming over to the house at weekends so we could all spend time together, even after the divorce, but Maddie accused me of holding on to the past. She doesn't even like to let me in the house – it's as if she feels like I'm checking up on her or something.'

I had heard all this from Maddie's side too. In her mind, if she didn't put boundaries in place, Adam would never let her go. I could see her point of view, especially since Adam had made it clear that this wasn't the path he would have chosen given a say in the matter, but the result was that Maddie had spent more time alone over the past year than she ever had before, and perhaps those long, empty days had given her mind too much space to wander. To worry. I twisted my mouth, chewing on my lip. 'You're asking me to take your side over hers.'

'Yes.'

'Adam, I—'

'For T, Laura. For Tilly. I'm not asking you to do much. Just come to the hospital and back me up when I talk to the doctors. Tell them you agree with me that Tilly needs a good routine, firm rules around eating and support with her anxiety.'

'And how will she get that if she goes home with Maddie?' His eyes flashed guiltily and I sat back, shocked. 'Oh. You want her with you? What, you're going to just push Maddie out, is that it?'

'No. You know I'd never do that. But for now, and I'm talking short term, I want to have Tilly with me, where I can make sure she's in a healthy environment. I think it's only fair.'

'Adam, I don't know. Can you imagine what it would do to Maddie? What about *her* mental health? You know she's not taking care of herself. I'm packing food to take in because I'm sure she's not eating. If we take her daughter from her, it could push her over the edge. I don't want to see her back in hospital, Adam. You remember what it was like? How we couldn't reach her? She just checked out completely,' I said, my voice cracking as I remembered those awful visits to sit opposite the shell of the girl who had once been the most animated person in my life. I couldn't bear to watch her fade away from us again. 'I don't want to do anything that's going to push her to breaking point, and I'm afraid that what you're suggesting will do just that.'

He sighed. 'I know. Do you think I'm not terrified for her too? But I have to think about Tilly first. She's a child – *my* child – and I won't leave her where I don't believe she's safe. Look, Laur, I can't force you to stand with me on this, but I know you love Tilly. You want the best for her, don't you? Will you at least consider what I'm asking?'

I stared at him, lost for words. Finally, I nodded. 'I'll think about it,' I agreed. 'But you are asking me to betray my best friend.'

'For Tilly,' he repeated softly, his eyes meeting mine. He stood up, and I did the same, then he stepped forward, wrapping me in a tight hug, and I let myself be swept up in it, the feel of his arms around me, the smell of his skin, my head leaning against his solid chest.

After a moment, he pulled back, giving a half-smile. 'I should go. I need to get over to the hospital and see T. Will you come with me?'

'I'll follow you. I need to think first.'

He nodded. 'Okay. That's all I can ask, I guess. But let me ask you, Laur. Do you think Tilly is ill? That she's harbouring some condition that every single doctor, yourself included, has managed to overlook?'

He didn't wait for an answer. He pressed a kiss to my cheek and opened the front door, leaving me to stare after him, feeling more caught in the middle than ever before.

CHAPTER TWENTY-SEVEN

I walked briskly through the double doors into the hospital, conscious of how long I'd kept Adam waiting. I'd left my flat just half an hour after him, driving on autopilot to get here, but when I'd pulled up into the car park, I'd been no closer to making a decision. I didn't know what to do for the best. I agreed with Adam that we had to keep Tilly safe, but I couldn't stop myself from thinking of Maddie, knowing how much it would hurt her if I took Adam's side.

I'd sat in the car for close to an hour, the basket of food resting beside me on the empty passenger seat as I went over my options, trying to work out a solution that would benefit everyone and eventually coming to the conclusion that I'd been dropped smack bang in the middle of an impossible situation. No matter what I did, someone was going to get hurt. But as much as I loved Maddie and Adam, Tilly had to come first. I would do whatever was necessary to keep her safe. It was the only option.

I rounded the corner and pressed the button for the lift, rushing inside as the doors opened. An elderly couple stepped up behind me, both wearing hearing aids and leaning heavily on wooden walking sticks. The old man put out a wrinkled hand, preventing the door from closing as his companion made her way slowly inside the lift. I watched, feeling a swell of emotion at the gesture. It was the kind of unspoken chivalry I dreamed of. Someone to look out for me, to care enough to think about these little things, and it made me feel more alone than ever.

The man nodded, as if offering a silent thanks for my patience, and pressed a hand to the woman's crooked spine, steadying her as the lift began to move up. I felt sick, half tempted to turn around and go home. I grasped the picnic basket on my arm, pulling it close to me, the smell of the bread filling the tight space, making my stomach lurch.

The lift came to a rattling stop and the doors opened, the elderly pair making a slow exit before they slid closed, leaving me alone. I didn't have more than a few seconds to think before they were sliding open again, revealing the bright lights of the corridor leading to the children's ward. I stepped out cautiously and saw Adam leaning against the wall beside a rack of colourful picture books. He stepped forward, wrapping me in a hug.

'Hi. So?' he asked, stepping back to fix me with a hopeful stare. 'Did you come to a decision?'

I sighed. 'I hate this. You *do* realise what a difficult position you've put me in?'

He had the humility to dip his head. 'I'm sorry.'

'I'll come and speak to the doctors with you, okay? But I'm not saying anything against Madeline. And I won't lie, Adam.'

'I would never ask you to, Laur. You know I wouldn't.'

'Fine. Good. So we're on the same page. I'll explain what I know about Tilly's condition, but I can't speak as her GP, only as your friend. She hasn't been my patient for a long time.'

'But you know her. You know her as well as I do, Laura; she thinks of you almost like a second mother.'

I swallowed thickly, forcing back the wave of emotion his words had created within me, wondering if he knew just how much a statement like that would mean to me. I nodded silently, taking his elbow and guiding him towards the doors to the ward, keen to get the conversation with the doctor out of the way. 'So have you spoken to anyone yet? Have you seen Tilly?'

He nodded. 'I was in with her just now. She was sleeping, I don't think she got much rest last night. I asked the sister to bleep the consultant so I'm just waiting for him now,' he said. 'I told Madeline you were on your way.'

I nodded. 'This feels wrong, Adam. Going behind her back. Should we not all just sit down and talk to the doctor together?'

He shook his head. 'After I've had a chance to say my piece. You know what she's like, Laura. She'll go crazy if I so much as disagree with her. I just need to get my head round what's happening, see what the doctor thinks and make my side of the story heard. We can go and see T and Maddie straight after, okay? We'll explain that we've had a conversation.'

I shrugged silently and he gripped my arm, turning me to face him. 'Look, this doesn't have to become some huge thing. I'm not asking you to turn your back on your friendship with Madeline; I know what she means to you. But this is important. Tilly's my daughter too. Maddie is acting like she's the only one who cares, when we both know that's not true.'

'Okay,' I breathed, meeting his eyes. 'Okay. Well, let's get it over with, shall we?'

He stepped towards the double doors, pressing the buzzer, and we waited for a nurse to buzz us in. Adam headed straight for the nurses' station, and I followed him, my gaze flicking from side to side. I felt as if Madeline might jump out at me from a doorway or step out from behind the laundry cart at any moment, ready to accuse me of betraying her trust.

My hand tightened around the basket until the knuckles turned white as I stepped cautiously up to the desk behind Adam. A white-haired doctor with thick glasses was talking quickly on the phone, and he glanced up as Adam spoke to the nurse, holding his index finger towards him. He had the kind of easy confidence that let you know he was someone important here, a no-nonsense expression that made me nervous. He signed off the call and turned to us.

'Mr Parkes, I'm glad you're here,' he said in a voice devoid of emotion. He held out a hand. 'I'm Dr Keifer, the on-call gastro consultant. I believe you've had dealings with my colleague, Dr Wallis?'

'That's right.' Adam shook his hand briskly and I saw the way he pushed his shoulders back, his stance commanding. 'Can we talk somewhere about my daughter? Somewhere private?' he amended.

Dr Keifer nodded, casting a brief glance at me. I looked down at my shoes, dropping my hands to my sides. Adam followed his gaze. 'This is Dr Laura Burts. She's a close friend of the family and will be joining us.'

The consultant gave a short nod and stepped around the desk. 'Follow me.'

Adam walked closely behind the doctor and after a brief moment's pause, I reluctantly followed the two of them into a small room with a padded table taking up most of the space. Dr Keifer indicated a couple of chairs beside the wall and Adam sat down, nodding for me to join him. I lowered myself into the seat, conscious of just how closely the chairs were positioned. Adam's thigh was pressed hard against my own, and I felt the drum of my heartbeat stutter in my chest. Dr Keifer perched against the bed, his grey trousers crinkling the strip of blue paper that ran along its centre.

'The nurse led me to believe that you were the one to assess Tilly when she was admitted last night?' Adam said, getting right down to business.

'That's right. I'm on a twenty-four-hour shift.'

'And how was she, in your professional opinion?'

Dr Keifer clicked his tongue against the back of his front teeth. 'Tilly's case is not cut and dried. When she came in, she was tired, of course, but the nurses reported her as being disorientated before she fell asleep.' He rubbed his hand across his chin, fixing Adam with a piercing stare. 'I ordered some bloods to be taken, more routine than anything else, after I left her last night. I have just discovered that your wife—'

'Ex-wife. We're divorced.'

'Ex-wife then,' he said, a look of irritation crossing his features at having been interrupted. 'She refused to let them take bloods from Tilly.'

'That's odd.' Adam frowned, looking at me. 'She's usually the first to demand more tests.'

I shrugged silently, just as surprised as he was.

'She told the nurses that we had taken more than enough blood from her daughter and she wouldn't put her through it again. Now, it wouldn't be the first time we've been refused consent from a parent. However, coupled with Tilly's disorientated state, and the fact that she reportedly collapsed at home, it does present some questions.'

'Questions?' I asked, leaning forward.

He nodded grimly, his gaze barely registering me before he turned his attention back to Adam.

'Mr Parkes, to your knowledge, has Ms, uh…'

'She still goes by Mrs Parkes. Didn't want a different name from Tilly, so she kept mine,' Adam said gruffly, his voice betraying only the barest tip of the iceberg when it came to his feelings on *that* particular issue.

'Has she ever given Tilly sedatives to help her sleep?'

'No, never,' Adam said, shaking his head. 'Not that I'm aware of.'

Dr Keifer looked at me and I shook my head too. 'No,' I said. 'Not that I've ever seen. I'm sure she wouldn't.'

'Right. I had some concerns, given how disorientated and sleepy your daughter was, that could be behind her reluctance to let us take bloods. It's not unusual for a parent to question the tests we recommend, but I must say, I find her lack of cooperation quite concerning. She is very resistant to the idea of even leaving the room to discuss Tilly out of her earshot.' He pursed his lips. 'Tell me about the situation at home. Have you seen a decline in your daughter?'

I watched the way he stared at Adam, waiting for his reply. He seemed to be searching for evidence, and I felt the slow trickle of ice through my veins, the pulse on my throat vibrating rapidly.

'Madeline and I have differing opinions on Tilly's health,' Adam said slowly. 'She tends to jump to the worst possible conclusion every time Tilly has a blip. Tilly's always been a fussy eater, and I have no problem admitting it's an area we need to work on. It's been difficult because her mother and I aren't consistent – Madeline tends to let her eat whatever she likes, which is a bone of contention between us,' he said wryly. 'But where I think she needs firm discipline, routines, boundaries, Madeline thinks she's suffering from some hidden malady.' Adam looked at me and I stared back, frozen.

He continued. 'She's constantly taking her to the GP for the smallest hiccups. And I know she would hate me to say this, but I feel it's important. Her reactions are extreme, completely over the top. I mean, she builds up every minor thing to be something huge.'

'You're saying she could be making it up? Fabricating illness? That's a serious accusation.'

'No, not like that – well, not intentionally. But she has her own issues with food. A history.'

I dug my fingernails into the soft bare skin of my wrist, willing him to stop. This felt like the worst kind of betrayal, taking Madeline's darkest ebb and using it as a weapon against her now, years later.

Adam was finding his flow, oblivious to my discomfort. 'She was committed with an eating disorder after her sister died. Losing her so suddenly made Madeline very fearful. She's not doing it on purpose, but…' He shrugged, shaking his head slowly. 'I just don't think she's herself right now.'

'And you?' Dr Keifer said, turning to look at me. 'Do you agree with Mr Parkes's assessment?'

I chewed my lip, glancing from Adam to the consultant, then sighed, my shoulders slumping in defeat. 'She would never hurt Tilly; she's a good mother. But,' I conceded, the heat of Adam's thigh burning through the thin denim of my jeans, 'she *is* anxious. And since she's been alone, since Adam moved out, things do seem to have escalated considerably. I see Tilly several times a week, sometimes daily. And the picture Madeline paints doesn't always match up to what I see.'

'Right.'

'But I don't think she's doing anything malicious. She's just so afraid. Because of Nola.'

'Her sister,' Adam clarified.

The doctor nodded. 'I must say, I'm inclined to agree with you both. I know you don't believe Mrs Parkes means any harm towards your daughter, but I've seen a handful of these cases during the course of my career, and you would be surprised how innocent they can appear at first glance. And there are bruises on your daughter that her mother hasn't been able to explain, which is a real concern to me. When you arrived just now, I was on the phone to a colleague discussing the best course of action. I wouldn't forgive myself if I didn't act in Tilly's best interests from the very start.' He folded his arms across his chest, his eyes flicking down to the large gold watch on his wrist. He clicked his tongue against his teeth again and I cringed inwardly. 'With that in mind,' he continued, 'I am going to have to inform both social services and the police about what I have seen.'

'That seems extreme,' Adam said, leaning forward. 'Can't we just ask Madeline to agree to step back and let me take over primary care? I don't want Tilly to get caught up in something messy.'

'Unfortunately, no. I can't leave something like this in your hands. I have a duty of care. I would imagine social services will come to the conclusion to place her with you, but that isn't for me to decide.'

'Adam,' I gasped, my eyes widening. He placed a hand over mine on my knee, squeezing tight. This would kill Madeline. Tilly was everything, absolutely everything to her, yet here we were plotting and scheming to have her ripped away. 'We can't do this,' I whispered. 'Adam, it's not fair. You know she's a good mother. She isn't a danger to Tilly!'

He turned to me. He looked tired and concerned, but there was still a flash of satisfaction in his eyes. 'I know that, Laur. I do, but I have to keep my daughter safe.'

'And what if they feel that's not with you? What if they make her go into care, Adam?'

'I'm sure it won't come to that,' he said. 'There would be no reason for them to take her from me. Laura, you're a doctor. What would you do if you were in Dr Keifer's position? You'd have to make that call.'

I knew he was right. I would be duty-bound to protect a child I believed to be in danger. But this wasn't the same. This was Maddie and I knew they had blown things way out of proportion.

'I know it's not easy,' Dr Keifer said, standing up. 'These things never are, but it's my job to ensure that Tilly is in the safest possible environment. With everything you've told me, I can't sit back and do nothing.'

He moved to the door and I stood, reaching for the picnic basket I'd placed on the floor, my legs shaking. He turned to me with a grim smile. 'Look, this may be the catalyst your friend needs to seek help. It sounds as though she's been struggling for a while. This could turn out to be positive for her.'

I shook my head, knowing Madeline would never see it that way and that she wouldn't back down without one hell of a fight.

'Let's go and talk to her, shall we?' Adam said, stepping out of the claustrophobic room into the hall. His hands shook and I realised he was just as worried as I was.

'Should I come?' I asked, feeling suddenly intrusive.

'Please do,' Adam said, squeezing my arm in what I guessed was meant as a reassuring gesture. 'You can talk to Tilly and distract her while Dr Keifer and I explain the situation to Maddie. She's already insistent she won't leave the room.'

'She won't just walk away from Tilly, Adam. This is going to be messy.'

He nodded. 'So let's get it over with as quickly as possible. Okay?'

I paused, glancing towards the corridor that led to Tilly's room.

'Are you ready?' Dr Keifer called, already ahead of us. Adam nodded, giving me one final, pleading glance. Then he turned, walking away from me, and I took a steadying breath, wishing I could leave, go back to bed, undo my promise to come here and support Adam. Nothing about this felt right, but I was in too deep now to turn back.

I watched Adam disappear around the corner and then, swallowing down my self-disgust, I followed after him, my heels clicking against the hard flooring as I rushed to catch him up.

CHAPTER TWENTY-EIGHT

Then

The sound of a pebble on the glass brought a smile to my face and I closed the textbook I was studying, moving from my desk to my bedroom window to find Adam waving up at me. We hadn't discussed the fact that for the past two months he'd chosen to sneak in up the drainpipe of my parents' house, rather than ring the doorbell. It was clear to me that the situation was delicate. We didn't want my mum and dad asking questions, spreading gossip to Madeline's parents that might get back to her.

Not that there was actually anything to gossip about. Adam was a gentleman and I knew he was waiting for the right opportunity to talk things through with Maddie before he made any promises to me. But I'd seen him looking at my lips when I talked and sometimes when we were lying on my bed, watching a film, his shoulder would bump against mine, or he would touch my hand, so briefly I wondered if I'd imagined it.

In those moments, I wanted to be brave. But I wasn't Maddie. I would never have the guts to do anything that might cross a line I couldn't return from. So I waited, patiently, sure that soon he would tell me that he wanted to be with me. He practically had already when he promised he'd be there for me and the baby. I could imagine him bringing me flowers in the maternity ward, holding my newborn child so carefully in his strong arms.

I pushed open the window as he scrambled up the side of the house. 'You're going to fall one of these days,' I chided as he climbed over the frame into my neat pastel-pink room.

'Nah, I'm part monkey,' he said with a grin, ruffling my hair. There was an energy about him, a buzz of excitement in his hands, his eyes bright. I took a breath, feeling suddenly nervous. Was this it? Had he spoken to Madeline? Suddenly I felt unable to hold eye contact with him.

'Did you see Maddie today?' I asked, lowering myself onto the edge of my bed.

'Yeah, just now. Did you?'

'Not today. I had a lecture.'

He sat down beside me, and I felt my breathing stutter as his hand covered mine in my lap.

'She's coming home, Laur.'

My head snapped up as I yanked my hand from his.

'In two days' time. They said she's doing well. Obviously her treatment will continue at home, but she doesn't need to be an inpatient any more. She's come so far.'

I stared at him, confused. 'But... so where does that leave us?'

'Hopefully back as the Three Musketeers.' He grinned, and I wondered if he was deliberately misunderstanding my question. He couldn't be that oblivious to the closeness we'd shared over the last month.

'Are you still coming to my scan with me next week?' I asked, my words coming out shy and uncertain. It had been so easy to talk to Adam lately – we'd become comfortable in a way we'd never managed before – but now, I suddenly felt insecure, as if Maddie coming home would eclipse any confidence I'd managed to build. She still didn't know about the baby. It had seemed wrong to tell her when she was wrapped up in her own problems. I'd thought I would have ages before we had to have that conversation. And if I was being honest with myself, I had liked it being a secret between just Adam and me, making plans for the future, discussing the changes that would need to come if I was going to make this work. It had felt special, but as he looked away now, focusing on a spot on the carpet, I knew instinctively that it wasn't going to continue like this. He would want me to tell her, and then the intimacy between us would come to an end.'

'Next week?' He frowned. 'I thought it was in a fortnight?'

'It's Tuesday – 4 p.m.'

'Tuesday, right.' He nodded, sounding distracted. 'I'm sure it will be fine. I'll see what I can do,' he said, though he'd promised to be there with me when we'd discussed it just last week. At the time, he'd sounded as excited as I was about seeing the baby on the monitor, but now, there was no hint of that buzz. It was gone, and I could tell that his thoughts were wrapped up with Maddie.

'Look, don't tell her right away, okay, Laur? I know you're going to want to share this with her. She's your best friend. But coming home is going to be a big deal for her. Let's give her a week or two to come to terms with her new routines before we give her anything heavy to worry about.'

'Worry?' I repeated.

'Yeah, you know she's going to be shocked when she finds out. She cares about you so much, she'll be worrying about how you're going to cope as a single mother.'

'Right,' I said, absorbing the message behind his words. He'd never described me as a single mother before today, and I hadn't felt like one until now because I'd had him. But it couldn't be clearer what he was trying to say. *You're in this alone. It's your baby, not mine.*

Adam continued speaking, oblivious to the pain his words were causing me, the coldness sweeping through my body. 'Things have changed a lot for you since she was last home, and you know what Maddie's like – she's such a mother hen, she'll want to support you any way she can. I'm just saying give her a little while to settle in before you tell her. She needs to focus on her recovery. That has to be her priority.'

And yours, I thought sadly. He looked me in the eye finally and blinked, as if he were surprised by my expression. 'But we'll be there for you,' he added quickly. 'You know that, right?'

I stared at him, stunned. I knew him well enough to understand exactly what he was saying. Our little pretend play was over and it was time for him to get back to his real life, back to Madeline. I'd been stupid to ever believe he might make any other choice. It was *always* going to be this way. Adam with Maddie, and me alone. I guessed that the reality of Maddie coming back was starting to hit him, the responsibility of the commitment he'd made, his promise to support me now weighing heavy on him. I was a burden, a complication, and I suddenly knew if I was determined to have my baby, I would be doing it alone. Their lives would rush on without me and I would have to accept being left behind.

'Anyway,' he said, getting up off the bed, 'I'll double check about that scan appointment. I'm sure it'll be okay; I just don't want to leave Maddie alone too long.' He moved towards the window, lifting his boot up onto the frame.

'You're going?'

'Yeah, I want to get some stuff ready for when she comes home. I'm going to buy her a massive bouquet of tulips – you know they're her favourite – but the doctor said to steer clear of getting chocolates or anything like that, so she doesn't feel pressurised to eat. We're going to have to tread carefully with that kind of thing; she's still fragile,' he warned, a crease appearing between his thick eyebrows. 'I can't believe it's finally happening, Laur – after all this time she's finally getting out.'

'Me neither,' I said softly. 'Tell her I'm looking forward to seeing her in her own surroundings.'

'I will. I'll see you later then,' he added casually, his eyes already fixed on his feet.

I watched him climb out of the window and disappear down the side of the house without so much as a hug goodbye. I wrapped my arms around my waist as the first tears slipped from the corners of my eyes. They didn't stop.

CHAPTER TWENTY-NINE

Madeline

Now

I stared blankly down at the tree-lined street below the window, watching the passers-by come and go, wondering what their stories were. Did the old man with the bunch of wilted roses have a date, or was he heading to the graveyard to mourn his late wife? Was the woman chasing after the toddler on his tricycle harried and rethinking her life choices, or loving the adventure? There was a suited and booted man at the bus stop, who looked to be around thirty. He'd been sitting there for almost an hour, waving the buses on when they pulled over. Was he waiting for a friend? Had he lost his job but was too ashamed to tell his wife? I was grateful for the distraction as I watched them go about their lives, each of them perhaps lost in their own problems. It was a relief, at least, that this room didn't face the park.

I'd fallen into a deep, dreamless sleep just as the sun was peeking over the horizon, my head nestled against Tilly's in her narrow bed, my arm resting protectively over her waist as if someone might come in and snatch her from beside me as I slept. I'd woken several hours later shaking and disorientated, sweat drenching my already disgusting pyjamas, Tilly still sleeping soundly beside me. I wished I'd thought to ask Laura to bring me some things: clothes, toiletries. I had no idea how I was going to manage without leaving Tilly, and *that* was not happening. My phone had died just after the staff switched over for the day shift, and though the sister had a stash of chargers she'd brought in from behind her desk, the only one that matched my phone had turned out to be broken.

Tilly had woken and managed some toast around ten, chatting happily with the play specialist before settling down for another nap. I watched her now from my seat by the window, grasping the lukewarm cup of tea a friendly healthcare assistant had brought me. I couldn't understand how she could swing from one extreme to the other over and over again. There was no pattern to her illness, no reason for her to be in a critical state one minute yet absolutely fine the next, and I knew the nurses were beginning to think I was just overreacting.

I'd caught sight of Carrie – the one who reminded me of the Trunchbull – as she passed the window to our room, glancing away before our eyes could meet. She'd gone into the room beside us, her voice booming through the paper-thin walls, and the nurse who'd come in to see us had been a fresh face, a fact I was immensely grateful for.

I felt as though nobody was prepared to listen to me. Not Adam. Not Laura. And now, even the doctor I'd seen overnight seemed determined to misunderstand me. I hadn't liked the way he'd looked at me, the doubt in his eyes as I'd explained what happened. And though I hadn't seen him since, I knew from the nurse on night shift that he was none too pleased at my refusal to let them take yet more bloods.

I was shocked that he'd even asked. Poor Tilly had given them enough blood this past week to do every test under the sun. I was still waiting to hear the results of the cystic fibrosis test; it was crazy that they would even think of taking more so soon. Every time we had to hold her still and force her to have a needle pierce her skin, I felt like I was letting her down. I could see the betrayal in her eyes as she begged me to help her. *Protect her.* And I wanted to. My instincts yelled at me to shove the nurse to one side and wrap my little girl in my arms, to swear to her that I would never make her have to endure this again. I knew it hurt, and her fear made it all the worse, but the tests I'd agreed to were necessary. They were the only way we were going to find out what was causing her symptoms, but if they were going to find something in her blood, surely it would have been discovered by now? It seemed like they were just going through the motions at this stage, ordering more and more blood tests just to appear like they were doing something, and I could not agree to that. It was as if they couldn't see the small, frightened little girl they were trying to turn into a pin cushion. As long as they ticked their boxes, they didn't care what it did to her confidence, how much trauma they imprinted on her developing mind.

I looked up as the door opened, a cursory knock sounding too late for me to say 'Come in', and Dr Keifer stepped into the room with Adam following behind him. I rose to my feet, seeing the way the doctor's eyes flicked towards Tilly. There was no way I was letting him disturb her sleep to do another examination. He couldn't tell what was going on any more than I could. We needed tests. Proper, conclusive tests that could give us some real answers. I'd run out of ideas myself, but wasn't that why we were here? So that the doctors, the people who'd had years of training, could figure out what was going on. I was damned if I was going to take another brush-off, no matter how condescending he wanted to be.

I steeled myself for an argument, sensing his dislike for me. I wished I was dressed properly or that I'd managed to brush my hair or teeth. I knew I must look a state, but I didn't have the energy to care right now.

I stepped up to the end of the bed, barring his path to Tilly. The sound of heels hurrying towards the door caught my attention, and Laura rushed into the room, breathless. She glanced from Adam to me, then walked past Adam and the doctor, moving to stand quietly at the head end of the bed, her face tilted down towards Tilly, who was snoring softly.

Adam was uncharacteristically quiet, avoiding my gaze, and I frowned, waiting for his usual insistence that this was all just some misunderstanding. I was certain he'd been waiting for the moment the doctor appeared on the ward so that he could rehash *that* old argument. He'd probably seen him coming and run after him so as not to miss his chance. Instead, though, Dr Keifer cleared his throat.

'Mrs Parkes. I have just had a long conversation with Mr Parkes and Dr Burts about your daughter.'

'You've *what?*' I said, shaking my head. Adam stared at me, his expression blank.

'We felt it was necessary to chat amongst ourselves about Tilly's well-being,' the doctor continued.

'Any conversation about my daughter's care should involve me, *her mother,*' I said firmly. 'I bet he's been telling you she's fine, hasn't he? That I'm being overdramatic!'

Dr Keifer remained unruffled. 'I might remind you that I *did* invite you to discuss the situation privately with me, an invitation that was swiftly declined. You didn't want to step out of the room.'

'Because I didn't want to leave Tilly, not because I wanted you to go and talk behind my back!'

'Madeline, calm down. I just wanted to get my point across,' Adam said coolly.

Dr Keifer cleared his throat. 'Given the situation, I have to inform you that I have some serious concerns regarding Tilly's well-being. I have just informed your ex-husband of my intention to contact social services and the police to share those concerns.'

'What are you talking about? Adam, what have you said to him?'

Adam kept his eyes lowered as the doctor continued speaking. 'Obviously this is a difficult situation, but to save your daughter from being witness to an upsetting scene, I would very much recommend you come with me and wait in a private room until they arrive.' He removed his glasses slowly, taking his time to polish the lenses using a little chamois leather he'd pulled from his trouser pocket. I noted, with dream-like detail, that he'd changed from his scrubs since last night. With an unhurried movement, he placed his glasses back on his nose. I stared, frozen to the spot, shocked at what he was telling me.

'No,' I whispered finally, my mind snapping into action. 'I refuse. You don't have the authority to make me leave. I won't let you do this.'

'I understand your resistance, Mrs Parkes. But I'm afraid I have a duty of care to keep your daughter safe, and I don't believe she is in her current… situation. There are unexplained bruises on her collarbone, quite extensive ones that I have only previously seen in serious accidents and in cases where an adult has shaken a child.'

'You don't—'

'She's been admitted to hospital with severe dehydration and symptoms that seem to vanish within a short time without any intensive treatment, only to return with the same problems again and again. My nurses were concerned about her on admission last night, and to top it off, you have refused to let us conduct the necessary tests, or to leave her side for a moment. All in all, I'm concerned enough to open an investigation. I have no choice but to do so.'

'Is this about the bloods? Because I wouldn't consent to them? I told the nurse why! I explained it to them last night!' I turned to Adam, rage pulsing through my body, my senses alight with fury. I could not believe he could do this, not when I was barely holding it together, when my every thought had been for our child. To keep her safe! And now, what? He was standing by this man who was threatening me with the police just for trying to keep our child safe?

'Are you going to let them take her into care? Be looked after by strangers?' I demanded.

'I don't believe that will happen. Not when she has me.' His voice was gentle, but the words tore at my heart. So that was it. He wanted to push me out so he could take my place. Did he really think he could fix what I could not?

'You're doing this out of spite,' I accused, glaring at him. 'Because I wouldn't change my mind, invite you back to my home, my bed! You have never forgiven me for the divorce, and now you're using our child, *our daughter,* to get revenge on me! How could you? How can you put her in the middle like this? I don't even know you any more, Adam – you're pathetic!'

Adam folded his arms, fixing me with a piercing stare. 'This isn't my choice, Maddie. I never mentioned the police or social services. I just wanted to understand what was happening, what the doctor thought about Tilly's health. But I *am* worried. We all are. We just want to help Tilly – can't you see that? And I'm concerned about you. You've not been yourself lately and none of this has helped. If you just cooperate, work with us rather than trying to do this all by yourself, we can figure this out between us. I'm sure this will blow over in a few days, and in the meantime, some space would really do you good.'

'Are you serious? You want me to leave, is that right? Leave her when she needs me most?'

'Mrs Parkes, this doesn't have to become a scene,' Dr Keifer cut in, his voice a monotone, almost bored, as he watched me. His expression was one of distaste, as if he'd been dragged into a conversation he didn't have time for and couldn't wait to escape. His mind was already made up – there was no way to bring him back to my side.

'Laura,' I cried, spinning suddenly to face her. 'You know this is ridiculous! You can't possibly think this is right? Please,' I begged, tears springing to my eyes now, blurring my vision. 'Tell them. Please, Laura. You have to help me.'

She stroked her fingers gently through Tilly's hair, winding a curl round her finger, before raising her eyes to meet mine, and I saw the guilt written all over her blotchy red face. 'I'm sorry, Maddie. Really I am. But there's nothing I can do now. The doctor is right – he has a duty of care. And perhaps…' She wiped away a tear from the corner of her eye, then straightened up, pushing her shoulders back. I felt my stomach drop, knowing what she was about to say before she even spoke. She took a breath. 'Perhaps for now, this is for the best. For both of you.'

CHAPTER THIRTY

Laura

'Well I won't go. I will *not* let you do this. She needs me here.'

'Sweetheart, I'm sure you'll still be allowed to visit – you can still spend time with her,' I said, looking to Dr Keifer for confirmation.

'Perhaps. It isn't my decision, but I would imagine social services will allow supervised visits,' he said. Madeline flashed him a furious glare, and I was amazed at her strength, her presence. She was wearing her old PJs, the comfiest ones she owned, but also the scruffiest; they were baggy at the bum and there was a hole beneath the armpit. Her hair stuck out wildly and her feet were bare, but none of it made the slightest impact to her energy. The respect she commanded with her self-belief. She was so used to getting her own way, and I knew by the glint in her eye, she was ready to fight hard to let that pattern continue.

'*Supervised*? Supervised with my own fucking daughter?'

Adam had the grace to look abashed, his expression faltering. He looked at me, and I glanced away, feeling like I had already done enough damage. I didn't know how to make Maddie agree to leave, and if the police arrived with her still in the room with Tilly, it was going to get very messy. I didn't want a social worker turning up, seeing her like this, having *this* be their first impression of her. She needed to focus, calm down so they could hear her out, but if she kept being this stubborn, this irate, I knew they would want her to stay away entirely.

There would be no contact, not even with Adam hovering nearby. They would deem her unsafe. How could she not realise that? I knew Madeline well enough to see exactly what she was feeling. She was panicked, scared, but it made her seem erratic. Her passion to keep Tilly safe came across almost like paranoia, and I knew that her wild desperation to fight for her daughter, coupled with her history of mental illness would be a massive red flag for any social worker. Tilly's safety would come first, and if that meant stopping contact with a mother who appeared, quite frankly, unhinged, they would do it in a heartbeat.

'What about the tests? Your plan for Tilly? Have you even found out whether she has cystic fibrosis yet?' she demanded.

Dr Keifer nodded slowly, unfazed by her distress. 'Actually, yes. The results came back a few hours ago. They were negative, as Dr Wallis anticipated.'

The air seemed to leave her lungs as she processed this new information. I felt awkward, like I should offer to leave. This was a family disagreement, and yet if there were three people I considered to be family, Adam, Tilly and Madeline were it. So I stayed, slinking close to the bed, hoping that Tilly wouldn't wake up, because she didn't deserve to have to witness this.

'Let's wrap this up, shall we? I obviously have some calls to make, and I *do* have other patients to see today,' Dr Keifer said. I could have slapped him for his casual dismissal of Madeline's feelings. He was treating her as though she was an irritating diversion to his planned day. I knew he was in a difficult situation – as a doctor, there were never enough hours in the day – but didn't he realise he was asking her to tear her heart in two, to walk away leaving one half here? It was a situation that required calm, understanding, *empathy*, and it was apparent that he lacked any of those qualities.

He moved towards Madeline and she widened her stance, blocking his path to the bed. 'I'm going to show you to a private room, if you'll follow me. As we discussed,' he said pointedly. He reached forward as if to take her arm.

'If you touch me, you will regret it. I'll sue you. For assault.'

Adam seemed to suddenly emerge from his shell-shocked state. 'Madeline, please, let's not make this more difficult than it has to be. None of us wants T to wake up and see us at each other's throats.'

'But it's perfectly okay for her to wake up and find out I've abandoned her, is that right?'

He shook his head. 'I'm sorry. I didn't want it to come to this. I swear we're not doing this to cause you pain. I… I just don't feel like you're making the best choices for her right now. You need space to clear your head, get some perspective. And in a few days, when the dust has settled, you can come and visit her at mine. You know you're welcome. It will be nice for you to finally see my place.' He shrugged. 'It will be just like when she comes to me for the weekend. You'll barely notice she's gone.'

Madeline took a step back, her eyes wide with disbelief. 'You're planning on taking her home? Discharging her, despite the fact you don't have any idea what's making her ill?'

Adam looked over her shoulder at me and I bit my lip. Madeline spun around, looking from him to my frozen face. 'Oh, I see. *I'm* the cause. Of course. How perfect for you, and how fucking wonderful of you to let yourself off the hook like that. Because while I've been up all night clearing up vomit and nursing my sick daughter, been here through the cannulas, seen her in pain every day, had her collapse not once but *twice*, you've been sitting back, denying the issue and coming to the conclusion that it must be *my* fault. What? You think I decided I wanted a new hobby and watching my daughter suffer was pretty unbeatable, is that right? Instead of taking up dance or martial arts, I thought I'd just call for an ambulance to get my kicks? I cannot believe you would think for a second that I'm doing this to her!'

Tilly stirred, rolling onto her side, and I felt my stomach clench, hoping she wouldn't wake up. She did not need to see this. Maddie's hands were shaking visibly, a combination of fear and rage, and Adam watched her, his lip trembling. His eyes were soft, filled with love and regret. It made me squirm uncomfortably, the energy that pulsed from him, the unspoken longing. It was at these times that I let my jealousy consume me. He had *never* looked at me that way. And while he was still fighting this obsession for what they had once shared, it was likely he never would.

He'd always said, ever since we were kids of fifteen and Madeline implanted herself into his life, that he was awestruck by her. When she was wild and passionate, blazing with fire, making decisions based on her wants and desires with no care for rules and expectations, she was like a goddess. That had been what he'd called her, all through their marriage. *My goddess.* I stared at him now and had to turn away, embarrassed at the intensity of his emotions. Madeline gripped the end of the bed, her body tensed. She looked as if she were thinking through every option available to her, trying to fight her way out of the corner we'd backed her into.

She looked up slowly, her voice low and measured as she ignored the doctor, speaking only to Adam. 'I am not leaving my child. I need to advocate for her, because it's clear you're not capable of helping her.'

'Maddie, I—'

'And I want another doctor,' she demanded, flashing Dr Keifer a hate-filled glare. 'I want to see Dr Wallis, or at the very least, someone with half a brain. He never accused me of child abuse because my daughter is ill!'

Dr Keifer folded his arms. 'A new doctor is not possible now. This is a safeguarding issue, and whoever you see, the same result will stand. Now are you going to come with me? Or shall I just wait for the police to escort you out?'

Her mouth dropped, her face draining of blood, the flaming red spots on her cheeks replaced instantly with a ghostly white pallor. She glanced back towards Tilly, and I made myself as small as possible, sinking into a chair beside the wall, watching her through guarded eyes.

'Yes. You're right,' she announced suddenly, her voice shrill. 'I *will* leave. I will take my child and go to another hospital. One where they bother to educate their doctors.' Without pausing, she marched to the bed, lifting Tilly, still sleeping soundly, into her arms. Tilly didn't so much as stir, and I knew Madeline's hold would be gentle, despite her fury. She turned to the door, walking towards it with purpose. I watched, fascinated, as Adam stepped in front of her, blocking her path.

'This isn't the answer, Maddie.' His voice was thick and he sounded like he was holding back a flood of emotion. He placed a hand on her arm, and she looked up at him, the fight seeping out of her. I realised, with a sick feeling in the pit of my stomach, that she was crying. The tears were flowing relentlessly down her pale cheeks now, dripping from her chin onto Tilly's shoulder. I'd seen her cry a thousand times before, but I couldn't remember ever having seen her so utterly broken.

She opened her mouth to speak, then swallowed, looking up to the polystyrene-tiled ceiling, her breath coming in short, sharp bursts. I felt my own throat tighten and realised I was crying too. I wanted to go to her, to hold her and tell her it was going to be okay. I hated that I had contributed to this, but then I looked at the sleeping child in her arms and my resolve hardened. We had no choice – that was the only consolation. We had been pushed into this by her behaviour, and no matter how difficult it was, we had to keep Tilly safe. We would never forgive ourselves otherwise.

Madeline looked at Adam, not bothering to wipe her eyes. 'I'm not doing this for me. Can't you see that? I'm doing it for *her*. Everything I do, it's for her. Why would I make it up?' she whispered. Tilly's head lay heavily against her shoulder, the muscles in Maddie's arms tense with the effort of holding the dead weight of her. I'd carried a sleeping Tilly enough times to know that small as she was, it didn't take long to feel the strain in your arms.

'I don't think you're making it up,' he said softly, his eyes shining. He blinked, then cleared his throat. 'I just think you're not yourself right now. You're not thinking clearly.'

She shook her head sadly. 'I won't go,' she whispered. 'I can't.'

'Maddie…' His voice trailed off, as if he'd run out of words to convince her.

We watched as she turned back to the bed. She laid Tilly down with slow, gentle movements, then, without a word, climbed up onto the bed beside her. She pulled the thin blue blanket over the both of them, rolling onto her side, her arm covering her daughter.

Dr Keifer sighed and opened the door, gesturing for Adam to follow him out of the room. I glanced from the bed to the door, then followed the pair of them out into the corridor. 'I'm sorry it's had to come to this,' the doctor was telling Adam, his voice low and irritated. 'I had hoped she would be willing to avoid making a scene. I have to make those calls now, both to social services and to the police. I can't put it off any longer. I'll have the nurses put her on high alert – someone will remain outside her door and ensure she can't leave with Tilly – but this *will* be resolved today.'

Adam gave a brief nod and the doctor turned, walking quickly back down the corridor.

'Adam,' I whispered. He shook his head, and I could see he was close to tears.

'I need… I have to…' he choked, his eyes glistening.

'Go and get some air. Take a minute,' I told him, gripping the top of his arm. 'I'll stay here with them.'

He bit his lip, then swallowed thickly. 'Okay.' He nodded, wiping roughly at his eyes.

I watched him walk in the same direction as the consultant, then leaned my head back against the wall, forcing myself to breathe deeply. I yanked a tissue from my handbag, blotting beneath my eyes, then screwed it up in a tight ball, forcing myself into composure.

It had started now. There was no going back. The only choice was to push on and hope Madeline could forgive me. Which right now seemed laughable. I didn't know if I would even be able to forgive myself for the part I'd played in what had happened today.

CHAPTER THIRTY-ONE

Madeline

I couldn't stop shaking, my mind spinning with fruitless solutions and schemes as I bunched my fingers around the thin cotton of Tilly's nightdress, my knuckles turning white. I couldn't believe what had happened. That Adam and Laura, the people who had been my closest allies for as long as I could remember, could betray me so absolutely.

They knew what this would do to me. That it would rip me apart, destroy me from the inside out, but did they realise what it would do to Tilly? I wondered. No. They couldn't possibly understand the psychological effect their callous actions would have on her, or they would never stoop this low.

I tasted bile in the back of my throat and swallowed it back, unwilling to give in to my despair. I couldn't let myself fall victim to my fears. I had to stay strong. Keep fighting for my daughter no matter what.

I raised my head from the lumpy, plastic-coated pillow, listening hard for sounds of voices, movement outside the door, but other than the patients in the neighbouring rooms and the wheels of the medication trolleys, there was nothing unusual. Not yet, but they *would* come back. They had made it abundantly clear that this wasn't over.

I squeezed my eyes shut, pressing my face back into the pillow to dry my damp cheeks. I felt like I'd slipped into a nightmare.

I couldn't understand their motives. I knew Adam was angry with me, that he resented the fact that he could no longer have me, and he hated the inconvenience of rushing back and forth to hospital. He wanted to brush over anything that didn't fit his idea of perfection, and he blamed me for destroying his glossy, picture-perfect life, first by divorcing him and then by refusing to ignore Tilly's declining health.

But he couldn't seriously believe that I got pleasure out of her suffering? Like those awful mothers who force-fed their children salt water and pills, then basked in the sympathy and attention they got as a result. I knew he couldn't believe I would do that to our child. She was my life. My everything.

And Laura… rushing in to take Adam's side over mine. I pictured her now, the way she'd avoided meeting my eyes, clearly ashamed and yet doing nothing to help me. She'd blushed every time he glanced her way, like a flustered teenage girl wrapped up in her first romance. Could she really be thinking of Adam that way now, after all these years?

I had thought her crush on Adam had fizzled out after he and I became a couple. She'd never mentioned it again, and certainly when I'd been discharged from the psychiatric unit, there was no sign of any lingering resentment or jealousy. She'd slotted into our lives, never a third wheel exactly, but always there. A friend to both of us. Yes, I'd seen her cast wistful glances in his direction every now and then. But then Adam was a powerful man. A handsome man. He had the kind of charisma that warranted being stared at occasionally. I never took it as more than a passing interest on her part.

And yet, in the past year, since Adam and I had gone our separate ways, I had noticed subtle changes in Laura whenever she was around him. She blushed more often. She wore lipstick when she knew she would see him, and more recently perfume. I knew she frequently stopped by his place for a coffee and a catch-up, something I'd not given much thought to. They'd always been friends. It hadn't crossed my mind that there could be more to their relationship than that.

But now? Now she'd arrived to stand with him, against me, and that spoke volumes.

Did she think she could just step into my shoes? Push me out so *she* could be the one to comfort my daughter, and slip into Adam's bed now that I'd vacated my spot? I would never have believed it possible. But then today had opened up a whole new world of what my long-standing friend was willing to do to me.

Tilly stirred, her arm coming up to her head, her fingers rubbing at her eyes as she blinked against the daylight. She opened them slowly and saw my face, inches from her own. 'Hello, Mummy.' She smiled, patting my cheek with her soft little hand. 'Did you have a nap with me?'

'Just a long cuddle,' I said softly, leaning forward to kiss her. 'How are you feeling?'

'I'm not sure. Did I miss the daytime?'

'Not all of it,' I said quietly. 'Do you need to go to the toilet?'

'No.'

'Shall I read to you?'

She nodded, sitting up. I raised the head of the bed using the remote control as I'd seen Laura do, then propped up a pile of the wafer-thin pillows behind us. Reaching over to the bedside table, I pulled a book from the pile the play specialist had left for us. 'This one?' I said, holding up a story about a little girl who finds a kitten hiding in her play house.

'Yes, I love that one. Can we get a kitten, Mummy? When we go home?'

'We'll see.' I smiled, feeling a pain in my heart that wouldn't subside. 'What would we call it?'

'Uh, Millie? Or for a boy, Sparkles.'

'Sparkles?'

'Yes. He would have to have a glittery collar. And we could get him a fancy basket. Or he could sleep on my bed,' she continued. Her excited chatter filled my ears but not loudly enough to blot out the unmistakable sound of Dr Keifer's authoritative voice growing louder as he approached our room.

I froze, a smile fixed on my face, my eyes on Tilly's as my heart began to race, my stomach spasming violently. I gripped the closed book in both hands to stem the shaking that had begun first in my hands, then my lips, moving through me until my whole body was trembling uncontrollably.

'Mummy, you look chilly,' Tilly said, her little forehead creasing. She pulled the blue blanket higher up my body until it was covering my arms, then patted my knee through the material. 'That should warm you up,' she announced, proud of her efforts.

The door handle lowered, and her head spun in the direction of the click. 'Daddy!' she cried as Adam stepped into the room, closely flanked by Dr Keifer, two uniformed policemen and a woman in a smart navy suit. And Laura. She stepped silently in behind the others, her head bowed.

I wanted to leap from the bed and demand that she tell me what I'd done to deserve this. My fear and tension rolled around inside me, morphing into something darker. Hatred. I had never thought it possible, but right now, I hated her with an intensity I had never experienced before, because above anyone else, she was my friend. My very best friend since we were seven years old. And in one fell swoop, she'd destroyed that. I would never be able to forgive her.

Tilly leaned back against me, her eyes widening as she took in the stern faces of the visitors. Adam made to move towards her, and I glared at him, my arm reaching behind her back, holding her tightly.

'Madeline, it's time for you to go now,' Adam said, his voice quiet yet firm. 'Tilly, Daddy can take care of you tonight. Mummy needs to go and have a rest and a shower.'

Tilly shook her head. 'Mummy's about to read me a story.'

'I can do that.'

'I want Mummy to. You always miss parts out. Mummy said *she* would,' Tilly insisted, looking up at me.

'Yes, I did. And I will.' I cracked open the book, trying to focus on the page in front of me. The words danced and blurred; my hands shook.

'Madeline, please,' Adam said, moving towards the bed. I smelled his aftershave as he got nearer. I knew I would remember that scent as part of this moment for the rest of my life. Never again would I be able to breathe in the expensive cologne without feeling the need to run. To fight. I knew I would never be able to forgive him either, not now. He'd gone too far in his need to get his point across.

'No, Adam. I already told you.' I meant the words to come out fiercely. To force him to take pause. Instead they emerged as barely a whisper. A feeble croak.

'Go away, Daddy. You're spoiling it.'

'I can't, T. Mummy needs to go. These people want to have a little chat with her.' He made a gesture with his hand, though I didn't look up to see who it was intended for.

'Mrs Parkes, I'm Melissa Stoneham,' a husky voice said. 'From social services. If we could talk somewhere more private, I can explain the situation to you. This isn't something your daughter should be present for.'

'I'm not going anywhere with you.'

'Daddy, make them leave. They're scaring Mummy!' Tilly said, her voice growing shrill as her fingernails dug into my arm.

Dr Keifer cleared his throat. 'Mr Parkes. We've tried it your way. I know you thought it possible to talk this out again and make her see sense, but clearly it isn't going to work, and dragging it out isn't going to do any of us any favours. Unfortunately, if Mrs Parkes is refusing to cooperate, we have no choice but to do this… forcibly.' He glanced towards the police officers.

'What is he saying, Daddy? What does he mean?'

Adam strode around the bed, his footsteps slapping against the floor as he came to my side. He leaned forward, his voice low and urgent in my ear. 'Madeline, for God's sake, will you just go with them? I know you don't want this to get ugly. Tilly is watching – please don't make them have to drag you out of here. Do not make her the victim because you didn't win.' He stood back, breathing hard.

I sat stunned for a moment, the room buzzing with tension, Tilly's fingertips bruising as they pressed against my arm. I took several steadying breaths, raising my eyes slowly to meet Adam's, then gave the smallest of nods. He sighed, stepping back.

Swallowing painfully against the lump in my throat, I turned my body towards my daughter, pasting on a smile. 'Daddy's right, sweetie,' I said, my voice coming out shaky and shrill. I took a deep breath and tried again, managing to keep my tone steadier. 'I am a bit smelly, aren't I? I should pop home and have a quick shower. Freshen up. But you won't be alone. Daddy will look after you, okay?'

'No, Mummy, I want *you*,' she said, her eyes frightened as she gripped the collar of my pyjamas. 'I want you to stay.'

'I want to, baby, but I can't right now. I have to go, just for a while, okay?' I prised her tiny fingers from my clothes, moving away, my hands holding her wrists so she couldn't grab for me as I climbed backwards off the bed. I leaned forward, pressing a kiss to her forehead, then both cheeks, reminding myself not to fall apart. I had to keep going, just a few moments more.

'I love you. And I'll be back before you know it,' I promised, breathing in the scent of her soft, milky skin.

'Mummy,' she said, shaking her head. 'Mummy, no!' she screamed as I took a step back and turned away from her.

I couldn't pause. Couldn't look back. With my heart breaking, I walked to the door, not acknowledging any of the people standing by, watching my world being torn apart. I opened the door, walking through it with the blood-curdling screams of my daughter ringing in my ears. And then I began to run.

CHAPTER THIRTY-TWO

Laura

I stood at the entrance to the hospital feeling cowardly and ashamed of the part I had played in the scene I'd watched unfold. I hadn't said a word. She was my best friend in the world, almost a part of me we were so close, and yet, when she'd needed me most, I had kept my mouth shut and let it happen.

Tilly had been utterly distraught, refusing any offer of comfort from Adam. As the frightful entourage had filtered out of the room to leave us to deal with the aftermath of sending away her mother, Adam had tried everything to console her, but she'd just kept screaming, begging him to go and find Madeline, pushing him away when he tried to touch her.

It had been me who had finally calmed her down. I'd seen the weary despair written all over Adam's face and grabbed his arm, telling him to sit down and let me try. There'd been no fight left in him by that point. I knew the events of the day had caused him so much more pain than he was letting on. This was never his first choice. Nor mine.

He'd slumped in a chair by the window, looking utterly desolate, as Tilly screamed and begged for her mummy. I'd been so afraid she would push me away too. I'd been part of it. But like the coward I was, I'd hidden in the background, watching but not speaking, and perhaps that had helped. Because when I stepped slowly up beside the bed and reached out a hand towards her, Tilly had looked up at me with tear-filled eyes and held out her arms in invitation.

She'd melted into me as I lifted her shaking body from the bed, holding her tight against me, swaying from side to side as her shuddering sobs finally began to fade away. She'd clung to me as if she couldn't bear to lose me too, and I'd felt a sick satisfaction I was instantly ashamed of at how deeply she loved and trusted me. That she considered me almost as good as a mother. It made a warm glow spread through my limbs, my heart swelling as her small hands gripped the back of my neck, her breath falling against my cheek.

I had no idea what the future held for Madeline. Whether she would be committed again now that Tilly, the one thing she'd been focused on, the thing that held her together, had been taken from her. Would she unravel completely?

But for a second, just the briefest moment, with Tilly's weight in my arms and Adam needing my support more than ever, I convinced myself she would be all right, and I let myself believe that this could be my future. Him. Her. Me. We could be happy, if Maddie stepped back. We could be a family.

A stream of people had filtered in and out of the room – social workers, police, nurses – and each time, Tilly had stiffened up, burying her face against my chest. As the hours passed, we were given snippets of information. Madeline had been taken to the local police station for questioning. The social services team had held an emergency meeting regarding Tilly's immediate needs, and we'd been informed that they had decided to place her in Adam's care, for now at least, while they conducted their investigation. He had never expressed any doubt that they would come to this decision, but I had seen the tension around his eyes as he waited, the heavy sigh he'd let out when we'd been told the news.

A social worker had tried to speak to Tilly, but it had come to an abrupt end when Tilly had flown into a panic and screamed for the woman to bring back her mummy. She'd cried herself to sleep in my arms, and I'd sobbed silently into her hair before being interrupted by a softly spoken woman from the police who had been sent to take photographs of Tilly's bruises, thankfully an event she'd remained asleep throughout. The bruises had shocked me more than I wanted to admit. I didn't understand how they could be so dark, so big, and yet I knew in my heart it could never have been Madeline's doing. She loved her daughter too much to ever raise a hand to her.

I stood at the double doors of the entrance now, staring across the courtyard at the front of the hospital. I'd left Tilly sleeping, made a coffee in the little ward kitchen for Adam and then come down here to clear my head. It felt like days had passed since I last saw the outside world. I hadn't expected to see Madeline, but there she was, on a wooden bench thirty feet away, her head bowed, her hands clasped in her lap. I realised with a jolt that she must have been released after being questioned. I had expected that. They had nothing concrete. It was all speculation at this point. But I hadn't expected her to come back here. Her body was rigid, frozen, as if she were one of those statues, the kind I hated, of mothers who had lost children.

She was still wearing her pyjamas and I remembered she'd come here in the ambulance. None of us had even thought about how she would get home. I doubted she had money for a taxi. She wasn't even wearing shoes. Had she walked from the police station barefoot? The thought made my eyes well up, my throat seizing with emotion.

I wanted to turn away, walk back upstairs, pretend I hadn't seen her, but I knew I wouldn't. I closed my eyes, steeling myself, then, knowing I was walking into a fight I couldn't win, I stepped outside and crossed the courtyard.

She didn't look up as I approached. She was shivering slightly, the summer evening typically English, the weather switching between bursts of sunshine, blasts of nippy wind and now the thick black clouds spreading across the previously blue sky, threatened a downpour I hoped I would miss.

'Maddie,' I said, taking a seat on the bench beside her. 'What are you doing here?'

She stared straight ahead, her gaze sliding up the building to the colourful windows of the children's ward. She didn't bother to turn to me as she spoke. 'Where do you expect me to go, Laura?'

'I'm sorry. I didn't realise you'd come with nothing.' I reached into my handbag, pulling out my purse, and slid a twenty-pound note from it. 'Do you have your key? I have the spare here.'

She gave a choked laugh. 'Trying to get rid of me, Laura? Is it messing up your pretty little picture?'

'Maddie, I…' I shook my head, gripping the silver key between my palms so hard I thought it might break through the skin. 'I never wanted this to happen. Adam asked me to come with him to speak to the doctor. I never expected them to go this far. I thought he just wanted a few days to see if Tilly improved in his care.'

'Because I'm hurting her. That's what you think, isn't it? That I *want* her to be here.'

I shook my head. 'I don't think that. There's nothing simple about this, Maddie. But you know, if you are struggling… if there's been stuff going on with your mental health that I've missed,' I said, swallowing back tears, 'then I'm sorry. And if you want me to come with you to a therapist, or make a referral for you, I will. I want to help you. You're my best friend.'

She turned her head slowly, her eyes wide. 'No, Laura. You're someone I used to know. That's all. You're not my friend, you're a snake, a parasite, and if you think I can't see right through you, you're kidding yourself.'

I sat back, stunned, my hands shaking as I held out the money and the key. She didn't take them. Her phone lay beside her on the bench, and I slid the note and key beneath it and stood up, my legs shaking. 'I'm caught in the middle here, Maddie. I'm sorry you feel like I let you down, and yes, I did go behind your back, but only because Adam begged me to because he was worried about Tilly. I just wanted to do the right thing… for her.'

'And if it gets you closer to Adam, then that's a nice little bonus,' Madeline said, her head snapping up to stare at me. Her accusation shocked me. I didn't know if she was grasping at straws, or if she had realised the depth of my feelings for Adam. How much I wanted his support and felt needed when he wanted mine.

In all the years since she'd come home from hospital, I'd never shared my secret with her, the things that had happened in my life while she was away recovering from her grief. There had been times when I'd come close to admitting the truth. The baby she never knew about, the bond that had formed between Adam and me. The pain I carried constantly in my heart, pulsing through my veins, dulling everything around me.

Some nights, after a few glasses of wine, when it was just the two of us, I'd been tempted to tell her, but something had always stopped me. There was a part of me that wanted her to know instinctively, without my having to spell it out. I wanted her to care enough to ask what she'd missed, what I'd been going through in her absence. I knew it was unfair of me; she'd suffered so much, and she'd been so ill. I was grateful she'd made it through that dark time, but along with my joy at having her back in my life again, healthy and well, there was a sense of resentment. I had been there for her, but she had never thought to ask about me. I wanted her to look deeper, care enough to scrape away the flimsy pretence and see the truth for herself, but she never did, and my secrets remained unspoken.

I took a step back, unable to meet her intense stare. Her eyes were filled with pain, and despite her fury, she looked small, broken.

'I really am sorry, Maddie.' I glanced towards the hospital. 'You should go. They might try to escort you off the grounds.'

She shook her head. 'Go where?' she whispered. 'Where else would I be?'

CHAPTER THIRTY-THREE

'So, as I said, my sister insisted I come in, but I hate to have troubled you,' Mrs Kennedy muttered apologetically. 'I think it's silly really and I know how busy you are.'

'Not at all,' I said, fixing on a reassuring smile as my fingers flew across the computer keyboard. I had no recollection of even meeting her before, though her records showed that I'd been her doctor for nearly a decade. When it came to patients, it wasn't uncommon to have two extremes. The ones who came for every tiny malady, convinced it was the start of some horrible and rare disease, and the ones like Mrs Kennedy who couldn't seem to grasp that she was entitled to receive healthcare and I was here to help. I felt like dishing out gold stars to the sensible patients, the ones I saw when they had a real problem, who understood that I was available to help but that I wasn't someone to call in on because they were bored.

I saw from her records that Mrs Kennedy was sixty-two, though she looked far older. Her silver hair was cut short and permed tightly, and her lavender twinset smelled strongly of fabric softener. She was neat and straight-backed, and I could just imagine that her house was spotless, like my grandmother's used to be before she died. I would have liked to do a house call, if I'd had the time. I imagined she served tea from a warmed pot and custard creams on a floral-printed dish.

I hid a smile at the memory of my grandmother. She'd been a tiny woman, with a sing-song voice and open, loving arms. The type of woman who gave everything and couldn't stand to take anything in return. I bet she would have had hysterics over the trend towards self-care and 'me time'. There'd been none of that in her day. I would have put money on Mrs Kennedy falling into this category too.

'Mrs Kennedy,' I said with a smile, patting her arm, 'I'm here to help. Your sister was right to tell you to come.'

'So it's serious, then?'

'Not at all, but you don't need to wait for something dire to book an appointment. I know it's not always easy, but believe me, I've seen everything. You'd have to try pretty hard to shock me.'

She gave a tight smile, and I could see she was far from convinced. 'So what is it?' she said, eyeing the door, clearly keen to leave.

'Piles, Mrs Kennedy. I know you thought it could be something more sinister, but those lumps are simply plain old haemorrhoids.'

'Goodness,' she whispered, her lips pressing into a tight line as she stared down at her lap.

'To be honest, you've done very well to avoid them for so long. It's a common and curable condition. They should go away quite soon with the right diet and treatment.'

'So I'm not going to die?'

'Not from this,' I said, holding back a smile. I printed off a prescription, giving her a pep talk about taking it to the pharmacy. I was sure she'd have to summon all her courage to hand it over to the pharmacist. I also gave her a leaflet on fibre-rich foods, then waved her off and leaned back in my chair. I felt drained. The emotions of the last few days had made sleep impossible, and my worry over Madeline and what she might do now that she didn't have Tilly to keep her busy was a constant drip of fear in the back of my mind. I hoped she was eating and that she wouldn't hurt herself, but there was no way she would let me in to make sure.

I made up my mind to call her mum later to explain the whole situation. If I couldn't keep an eye on her, her mother would have to.

I looked at my watch, seeing that it was already 1.30 p.m. I hadn't had a chance to eat lunch yet and I was starving, but I wanted to drive round to Adam's place during my break and make sure he was coping.

Tilly had been discharged late last night after Madeline had finally disappeared from the courtyard. I'd carried her out to the car, wondering if Maddie was watching us from the shadows. I wouldn't have put it past her to leap from the darkness and snatch her daughter from my arms. She had never been one for doing as she was told, but I couldn't forget the way she'd tried to pretend everything was okay for Tilly's sake, and how she had left with that heartbreaking smile pasted on her trembling lips to make it easier for her child to bear.

No, she wouldn't make another scene. She wouldn't give up, not ever, but she'd find a more palatable way to fight. One that didn't leave Tilly traumatised and caught in the middle. At least, I hoped so.

I'd wanted to go back to Adam's, to settle Tilly, I told him, but he'd refused my offer, telling me he just wanted to get home to bed. Now, though, I needed to see them to check that he was okay and that Tilly had forgiven him for what happened.

I picked up my bag, glancing again at my watch. I'd had a cancellation this afternoon, and though I should have filled it and would likely be reprimanded by the surgery manager for not giving the appointment to someone else, I had left it open, allowing myself a full hour for lunch, reasoning that I'd spent many a day shoving in a stale sandwich in the spare two minutes I got to myself. I'd given up countless lunch breaks for my patients, so I was not going to feel guilty for taking one today.

I walked past reception, waving to Mica, the receptionist, without pausing to chat. I didn't want to get caught up answering the mountain of queries she would no doubt have for me. They could wait until later. I all but ran to my car, jumping into the driver's seat and shoving the key in the ignition, cranking up the radio with a sense of freedom as I drove out of the surgery car park.

Adam lived in a two-bedroom third-floor flat a five-minute drive away from the surgery. I knew Madeline thought he was living somewhere cold and grotty – she'd assumed as much when she heard that he'd rented a flat rather than buying a house – but she couldn't have been more wrong. The flat was in a converted museum on the outskirts of Brighton, huge picture windows flooding the place with light and gorgeous green communal gardens surrounding the whole building.

The place was full of little details: reconditioned cornicing in the sitting room, shining parquet flooring, and open brickwork in the kitchen. It could have been lovely, but Adam gave the distinct impression he hadn't made it his home just yet. Most of his possessions were still lined up in boxes in the hall; the only finished room was Tilly's, where he'd pulled out all the stops, buying her a beautiful canopy to go over her bed and hanging pictures on the walls. She had a cupboard filled with toys and books, and I'd had to warn him more than once that he was spoiling her. I knew he was trying to compensate for his absence in her life.

I pulled up into the allocated parking for his visitors, flipping down the sun visor to check my make-up in the mirror before pulling a tube of lipstick from my bag. I spritzed some perfume on my neck and popped a mint in my mouth, crunching it to pieces as I clambered out of the car and made my way to the door.

I pressed the buzzer, waiting impatiently for him to let me in.

'Laura?' His voice crackled through the intercom. 'Why aren't you at work?'

'I'm taking a lunch break. I wanted to check on you both.'

There was a pause, and I felt myself growing irritated, a heat spreading up my neck, but then a low buzz sounded and I pushed open the door, heading for the lift. I hoped I wasn't being too pushy. He'd never had a problem with me turning up unannounced before – I popped in at least once a week to have a quick cup of tea, or to bring a home-made casserole if I knew he'd had a long flight. I never liked to think of him sitting here exhausted and lonely with only a microwave meal for company. And it *had* been him who'd dragged me into the whole messy business to begin with. But maybe I should have called, I thought, stepping out of the lift and heading to the large wooden door at the end of the sun-dappled corridor. He was probably still shell-shocked from what had happened yesterday.

He had left the door to his flat ajar, and I pushed it open, stepping inside. I loved this building; the high ceilings and the sense of light and space were nothing like my own flat.

'Hey,' Adam said, stepping out of the kitchen, a pack of coffee filters in his hand. 'Not like you to pop by in the middle of the day.'

I shrugged, noticing that he looked far better than he had yesterday. His eyes still had a faint pink tinge to them, but he was freshly shaved and dressed in a pressed pair of chinos and a crisp white shirt, open at the collar to reveal a slice of tanned skin.

'Did you have a good night?' I asked, following him into the kitchen. 'Catch up on some sleep?'

He twisted his mouth, finding a pair of scissors to open the coffee filters. 'Not great,' he admitted. 'Tilly wouldn't settle. She's confused – understandably so – and taking it out on me in the extreme. I think she probably woke most of the building last night when I brought her in – she was screaming like I was killing her.'

He frowned, pulling a pack of ground coffee from the larder and scooping out a generous helping. 'I did think about calling Maddie so she could at least say goodnight, but in the end, I decided against it. I want to give her the chance to cool off, you know?'

The delicious rich smell of coffee rose around us, and I smiled as Adam poured the steaming liquid into the pink-striped mug he reserved for me, stirring a cube of sugar into it. He passed me the mug, his eyes meeting mine.

'And how is she now?' I asked. 'Is she in her room?'

'Yep. Avoiding me.' He gave a deep sigh, and I felt sorry for him. 'I've had to request a sabbatical from work. They told me to get her a nanny and be back in by the end of the week. They want me to take the London to New York flight. Can you believe that?'

'You can't, Adam,' I exclaimed, burning my tongue on my coffee in my shock.

'I know that. I've put in an appeal. Told them I'll take it unpaid.' He paused to pour his own coffee. He added milk but no sugar and set it aside. I liked knowing how he took it. That he would wait until it was barely lukewarm to drink it down.

He sighed. 'I think it will work out, but they're going to give me hell for it when I do go back. I hate letting them down.'

'You'll be fine. And this is important. Tilly needs you right now.'

He gave a grim nod. 'There's a social worker coming this afternoon to see how she's doing. I feel like I've opened up a can of worms with this thing, Laura. Like they're going to be on my back making sure I'm being fucking super-dad until the end of time.'

'They won't. Besides, you're a great dad. They'll see that straight away.'

He nodded, his eyes thoughtful as he sipped his coffee. I put my mug down and pointed towards the door. 'Can I go and say hi?'

'Yeah, I'm sure she'll be glad to see you,' he said, a note of bitterness clouding his tone.

'Adam... she *will* forgive you for this,' I said softly, stepping closer to touch his shoulder. 'You did it for her. But she's six, and she's had a hell of a week. She just needs some time.'

'I hope so.'

I left him to stew in the kitchen while I went down the hall to Tilly's room, pushing open the door to see her lying on her side, her eyes glazed as she watched a garishly bright cartoon. 'Hey, little T,' I said, sitting on her mattress. 'How are you, honey?'

She angled her head, trying to see around me to the TV screen, and I frowned. 'Tilly,' I said, my tone sharper, jolting her out of her screen coma.

'Hi, Auntie Laura,' she mumbled, her gaze flicking briefly to my face.

'Hey. I bet it feels good to be out of the hospital?' I smiled, stroking her hair back. I could tell instantly that Adam hadn't bothered to brush it. It was a mess of knots and tangles, so I reached for the pink brush on her dresser and drew her into my lap, working gently at the mass of curls as she continued to watch the television. I didn't mind, and I couldn't blame her for being subdued, not after the week she'd had.

I pulled her hair into bunches, plaiting them tightly so as to prevent further tangles. It should last until my next visit, at least. Tilly sighed heavily and I watched her close her eyes as if she were silently counting to ten, before opening them to stare blankly at the television again. I half wanted to get her talking, to make sure she wasn't in pain, but I didn't want to upset her. Instead, I kissed her cheek and left her to rest, heading back through the flat to find Adam. I had to be back at work in twenty minutes, and as much as I would have liked to stay, I couldn't let my patients down.

There were voices coming from the living room, and I popped my head round the door, surprised to find a woman sitting in Adam's armchair, a cup of coffee clutched in her hands. 'Laura.' Adam smiled, looking up. 'Come in. This is the social worker I was telling you about. Beatrice Caine, this is my good friend Laura. She's a GP.'

I walked forward, shaking the woman's outstretched hand, feeling awkward. I knew I should leave, but curiosity propelled me to stay. I crossed the room and sat down on the sofa, making sure to leave a sizeable gap between Adam and myself.

'So as I was saying,' Beatrice said, looking back to Adam, 'we've had a lot of conversation about the best course of action for Tilly, and we feel it best that she remain in your care rather than go into a foster home. I have to ask that while we continue to look into this, you don't allow visitation with her mother.'

'Right.' Adam nodded.

'The team at the hospital feel that it's important that Tilly gets into a good routine with her eating right from the get-go, to try to break any bad habits that have been formed.'

He nodded emphatically. 'I couldn't agree more. I'm sorry to say that her mother has really let things slip in that regard, letting her pick and choose what she wants to eat. I expect I'll have a difficult fight on my hands – Tilly can be stubborn – but I have no problem drawing a hard line. She'll be offered three healthy meals and two snacks per day, and if she refuses to eat, there will be nothing in between. We've already had several battles since she got home over this new routine, but the tests the hospital have done have all come back negative. The consultant said that she isn't ill, and I agree with him. We just have to be firm about it. She'll soon figure it out.'

He leaned forward, his tone confidential. 'She's suffering with a combination of bad habits and anxiety brought on by her mother's own issues.' He frowned. 'She needs boundaries, and I'm more than happy to be the bad guy if it breaks these unhealthy habits she's learned under Madeline's care.' His eyes were alight at the prospect.

Adam loved nothing more than fixing things. He was determined. Set on his goals. I watched the way the social worker smiled at him, nodding along in agreement, and hoped for Tilly's sake that his plan would work.

CHAPTER THIRTY-FOUR

Madeline

I was ready. For battle. For war. It didn't matter. I'd finally left the hospital grounds at almost 10 p.m. last night, my bones aching, a dreadful sense of numb defeat settling over me. I had half expected Adam to convince the doctors to discharge Tilly immediately, and though I knew I wouldn't try and take her from him, I wanted to see her. To kiss her goodnight and make sure she knew just how much I loved her. But she hadn't come out, and I'd resisted the desperate urge to go back inside. I knew it would only end in tears for all of us.

With my head pounding from hunger and dehydration, my body feeling as if I'd been hit by a truck, I had taken the money and the key Laura had left for me and climbed into a taxi. I'd forgotten about my bare feet until the driver pointed them out. It was just another thing on the long list of agonies, the pain colliding and growing until it blotted everything else out.

The house had been quiet as I let myself in, filled with dark shadows and strange noises, Tilly's absence a constant reminder of what had happened. The police had been calm in their questioning, yet relentless. The things they had asked, never accusing, but leading, probing, made me sick to my stomach. I couldn't be angry with them, not for doing their job, but I wanted them to see me and know that I could never harm Tilly, I loved her so much – I couldn't bear for them to doubt it. When they'd said they were letting me go for the time being, for a moment I thought they meant this horrible nightmare was over. That they believed me. That I could go back to my daughter and hold her in my arms again. But no. It was far from over. The nightmare was only just beginning.

I had walked around the empty house, turning on all the lights, locking the doors, and by some miracle, I'd fallen asleep on the sofa, the TV playing repeats of *Countryfile* in the background. I'd woken just after five in the morning, a squirming need in my gut, my hands fidgety with the energy I was suppressing, the instinct to go to her. It felt impossible to ignore.

I hadn't given into it though, nor the desperate melancholy that was calling me, wanting to suck me down into a dark place I would not escape from. Wallowing wouldn't help Tilly, and falling into a well of self-pity would only ensure Adam's victory. There would be time to process my emotions later, but for now, I needed to stay focused.

I'd forced myself to get up off the sofa, showering, untangling the matted knot of my hair, brushing my teeth and dressing in the smartest clothes I owned: a dark grey pleated skirt that fell to my knees and a white cap-sleeved shirt I had no recollection of buying. Perhaps Laura had left it here and it had ended up in my laundry somehow. It wasn't the kind of thing I would ever wear, but today I was grateful for it. I could play the part if I had to. Give them the type of mother they would respect and trust.

I'd dressed slowly, thoughtfully, as if I were preparing for an interview. I'd chosen my most boring jewellery, and a pair of black ballet pumps, and then I'd got to work. By 9 a.m., I'd sent long emails to fourteen lawyers and had the phone numbers of more than a dozen more who I'd have to wait to call. My inbox was full of queries from parents whose sewing projects were due any day now; I counted three from Susan Lake, who was waiting on that bloody octopus costume that still lay unfinished in the cardboard box I stored my projects in. My website reviews would be catastrophic after ghosting my customers for so long, the reputation I'd built over the past few years ruined in a matter of weeks. I wrote out a short paragraph apologising and explaining that I'd had a sudden family emergency, and copied and pasted it in response to each email, hoping they would be understanding.

Graham from the leaflet company had left a succession of increasingly irate voicemails on the house phone, the last telling me that since he hadn't heard from me, he'd found a replacement. I wasn't too worried about that. As cross as he sounded, Graham was a decent guy. I knew that if I called him and explained once things had settled down, he would give me my job back. There was never a shortage of work when it came to delivering leaflets door to door, and most people tended to move on from the job quickly.

I hadn't the energy to worry about work now. I'd spent an hour googling Tilly's symptoms, being led down wormholes, reading terrifying articles about children with leukaemia, then others about attention-seeking disorders. I knew it wasn't the latter, and I hoped more than anything that it wasn't cancer. I'd seen those children on the ward, the lost, ghost-like sheen to their round eyes, the bald little heads. It was impossible to imagine Tilly as one of them.

When Tilly was a toddler, I'd spent months surfing the internet, hoping to find a reason for her struggles. I'd presented every lead I'd found to Laura, only to have her dismiss them. Everything that seemed to be a possibility was quickly brushed aside, Laura pointing out all the discrepancies between Tilly's symptoms and those of whatever condition I'd struck upon, and I'd grudgingly had to admit that I'd got it wrong. Each time that happened, it made me doubt myself further, until eventually I'd stopped searching, placing my trust in Laura and the other doctors. But now I was on my own, and it was clear to me that I was the only one prepared to keep searching for a diagnosis that made sense.

I'd kept my focus on Tilly and staunchly resisted the urge to google results for parents who deliberately hurt their children or faked their illness to garner attention. I hadn't wanted to say it out loud, but I knew that was what everyone in that hospital room had been thinking, accusing me of. I'd seen a case in the news the previous summer, a mother who'd been putting salt in her infant son's formula to make him sick. Munchausen syndrome by proxy they used to call it, though an expert had said it was now more commonly known as FII: fabricated or induced illness. It made me feel ill, disgusted that the people who knew me best would ever believe me capable of such things.

The morning had passed in a blur of research and phone calls, and I still felt as though I had achieved nothing. A social worker had sent a text message telling – not asking – me that she would come round this afternoon to explain the situation more clearly. I had no idea what that meant, but I was ready for her. She was my link to Tilly. I had to make her understand that my daughter was unwell, and that without my advocating for her, she would suffer immensely.

I pressed the cordless phone to my ear now and glanced up at the clock on the kitchen wall, trying to keep the irritation out of my tone as I spoke to the difficult receptionist. 'I'm sorry,' she said, not sounding apologetic at all, 'but Mr Alliot is in court this afternoon. I'm happy to pass on your message, but I must warn you, he doesn't take this sort of case.'

'Well, can you recommend a lawyer who does?' I asked, rubbing my thumb and finger over the crease between my eyes, where a tension headache was building steadily.

'No, sorry,' she said, sounding bored.

'Great. Well, pass on my message. Thanks for your time,' I said through gritted teeth. I put the phone down and sighed, grabbing a pencil and scoring a line through *Alliot and Sons* on my notepad. Nobody seemed to want to take on a case against social services. Not that I had money to pay for a lawyer, but I was willing to sell everything I owned if it meant getting Tilly back where I could take care of her.

The doorbell rang shrilly, startling me out of my thoughts, and I stood, smoothing down my shirt, pinching my cheeks for colour as I went to answer it. I took a deep, steadying breath and pulled it open. 'Hello,' I said, offering what I hoped was a decent impression of a smile to the woman on the doorstep.

'Beatrice Caine,' she said, holding out a hand. 'I'm the social worker handling Tilly's case. May I come in?'

'Yes, of course.' I nodded, stepping back to let her inside. 'I'm Madeline, Madeline Parkes.'

'Yes, I know. Is there somewhere we can sit down?'

I nodded, leading her through to the living room. 'Can I get you something to drink? Tea? Coffee? Juice?' I offered, hesitating in the doorway.

She shook her head. 'No thank you.'

'Have you seen my daughter?' I blurted, grasping my hands together beneath my chin. She lowered herself onto the sofa, placing her briefcase on the floor, before raising her eyes to meet mine.

'Yes, I have.'

'Is she still being treated? They haven't discharged her, have they?'

'I'm afraid at this stage I can't pass on information of that kind, but I can tell you that she is doing well and her father is taking care of her wonderfully.'

I frowned, not missing the pink flush that rose to her cheeks as she spoke of Adam. So it was like that, was it? She'd fallen for his charm and already made up her mind that he was the hero in this scenario. Poor, harassed Adam having to take time off from his important career to deal with his inconvenient ex-wife and sick child.

It was funny, I thought. Nobody ever seemed to think *I* was a hero for the things I did: taking care of my daughter, working three jobs, keeping the house clean and cooking meals that never seemed to get eaten. It was expected. Presumed. But when the father stepped up, it was heroic. Selfless. I breathed in deep, pushing down my anger, determined to endear myself to her despite her obvious preconceptions about me.

'I think there's been a huge misunderstanding,' I said, sitting down opposite her, leaning forward with a smile. 'My daughter has never, not for one moment, been in any danger in my care. The idea is quite frankly ridiculous.'

'I understand your feeling that way, Madeline,' Beatrice said, unsmiling. 'My job is to explain the situation to you more clearly. I was told that things were a little fraught in the hospital yesterday, and my colleague didn't get a chance to discuss the case with you.'

'I was very upset. As you can imagine.'

'Of course. Now, we were contacted by a Dr Keifer regarding concerns about your daughter's welfare. Not only did she have unexplained bruising, but she'd had recurring admissions that had produced no result or diagnosis.'

'I've already told him that the bruises were from when she collapsed. I was trying to wake her. Tilly bruises so much more easily than other children. Look,' I said, hearing the tremor in my voice, 'I get it, you don't know me or our history and you've seen a set of circumstances and jumped to the most likely conclusion. But I'm telling you, I haven't hurt her. She's ill. Something is wrong with her. It's been growing steadily worse and I can't care for her if you won't let me bring her home. She needs to be here.'

Beatrice dipped her head, sighing as if my words were tiresome to her. As if I wasn't begging her to really think about the other possibilities. Without responding to anything I had said, she steepled her fingers. 'Mr Parkes also expressed concern about your mental state, which we felt was valid, considering your history.'

'That's really not fair. I was a teenager at the time and my sister had just died. Surely you can't hold that against me?'

'It's my recommendation that you be proactive here. At this stage, nobody is accusing you of anything, Mrs Parkes. You have to understand, we have a duty of care towards Tilly. If there's even the slightest possibility she could be in danger, we have to act.'

'But you won't bring her back to me?'

'We have to conduct our investigation. Now, if you *want* to be proactive and help your daughter, I would highly recommend a trip to your GP. As I understand, you have been struggling with ongoing anxiety. Your ex-husband mentioned that you previously received long-term psychiatric treatment for an eating disorder.'

'I don't know what he's told you, but that is hardly relevant now. It was *years* ago, and I can assure you I'm fine now.'

She nodded, though her expression was disbelieving. 'I'm only going on what those closest to you have shared with me. I'm sure you understand why this might be a cause for concern. I urge you to use this time to focus on your self-care. Seek the treatment that will help you most.'

I could have laughed. She wanted me to go and discuss my anxiety, when my ex-husband, my best friend and every professional who should have helped me had banded together to remove my child from my care. Did she not realise that without Tilly, I would never stop feeling scared, terrified about what was happening to her? That I was trapped with the knowledge that she was suffering and I could do nothing to help? As if I could just go and see my doctor and have everything magically fixed with the printing of a prescription, a few comforting words. It was insulting.

'You don't understand. You can't do this,' I whispered. 'Surely you can see how much I care for her? You must have come across cases like this before.'

'I've seen hundreds of cases where a parent has denied abuse, Mrs Parkes,' she said, rising to her feet.

'So you know that—'

'And in every one of them, the parent was discovered to be lying. Make of that what you will.' She picked up her briefcase and I sat frozen on the chair, unable to look away from the hard condemnation in her eyes. 'I'll show myself out,' she said. 'Consider what I said about that visit to the GP.'

I listened for the open and shut of the front door, the footsteps on the gravel driveway. And then I burst into noisy sobs, clutching a cushion in my arms, pressing my face into it.

CHAPTER THIRTY-FIVE

Laura

I stirred the jug of gravy, trying not to draw attention to myself as Tilly raged at Adam from the living room. I'd texted him at lunchtime to ask if he needed a hand with her, and when he hadn't replied, I'd decided to drive to his place straight after work. He'd buzzed me up without a word, and I'd walked in to find Tilly in hysterics, Adam more frazzled than I'd seen him in a long time.

It seemed that since my visit yesterday, he and Tilly had gone to war over her stringent eating habits, and neither of them had come close to backing down yet. Tilly was tired, hungry and emotional in the extreme. 'I don't care!' she yelled now. 'I want my mummy! It's not your day to have me anyway, and Mummy wanted to show me how to make vases on her pottery wheel. You've ruined it!'

'Tilly,' Adam said, his voice a warning. He was so black and white in these situations. I could tell he was losing his patience, thinking she was being rude and purposely defiant, but I knew that tone, the desperation behind her words. She was confused and scared and in need of comfort, and it was coming out as disobedience. I gripped the handle of the jug, forcing myself to stay put. It wouldn't do for me to try and step in now. Adam wouldn't appreciate my meddling.

I put the gravy jug on the table, frowning at the joint of pork, the greasy roast potatoes, the buttered spinach. Adam was determined to cajole her into eating a meal of his choosing, and he wasn't holding back. I could have told him he was wasting his time with a meal like this. She hated meat and said that she couldn't swallow potatoes, claiming they stuck in her throat and made her choke. If it were up to me, I'd have met her midway, compromised somehow. Even baby steps at this stage would be something. I heard him tell her to go and wash her hands and braced myself for the next blow-up.

Adam walked through the kitchen door, picked up a wine glass and filled it with a generous splash of Merlot. He took a deep sip, then put the glass down. 'How can it be this hard?' he said, taking a long breath, his eyes trained on the counter.

'She's struggling, Adam. She's confused, and she's missing Maddie. Have you heard from her?'

He shook his head. 'Not yet. T wanted to call her last night, but I didn't think it was a good idea… not yet.'

I pursed my lips, looking down.

'You think I'm wrong?'

'I don't know, but I think if this is the route you want to go down – holding out until Tilly gives in and eats what you want her to – well, it's going to get a lot worse before it gets better. It's not going to be a quick fix.'

Tilly appeared in the doorway, her expression guarded. 'What is it?' she asked me, ignoring Adam.

'Roast pork, potatoes and spinach. Gravy too.' I smiled, moving towards the table, pulling out a seat for her. She didn't move from the doorway.

'I want rice.'

'Just come and sit down, T. It's already cooked,' Adam said, slumping into a seat and picking up his fork. She looked down at her feet in a silent stand-off.

'What if we compromise?' I heard myself say. 'If you eat some meat and veg, I can cook you a bit of rice instead of the potatoes? How does that sound?' I glanced at Adam. He shrugged nonchalantly, though his shoulders had stiffened.

Tilly shook her head. 'I can't, Auntie Laura. I can't eat the pork. I tried before and it made my tummy hurt so much.'

'Just try, Tilly. That's all I'm asking,' Adam said, dropping his fork on his plate with a clatter. 'I *know* you're hungry. This really is getting beyond a joke. Just come and sit down now.'

I held my breath, watching the two of them silently. Tilly looked up slowly, her eyes meeting mine. She looked so sad, so very tired. 'I can't,' she whispered.

'Then you can go without,' Adam sighed. 'Go and get ready for bed.'

Tilly turned and left without another word. 'I'll go and help her,' I muttered, not meeting his eyes. I felt uncomfortable, *dirty*, as if I'd witnessed an abuse, though I completely understood why he felt he had to be so hard on her.

'Laur, you don't have to do that. Sit down and eat your dinner. You've been working all day.'

'It's fine. I want to,' I said, flashing him a quick smile. 'You have a break. I'm sure you need one.'

I left him before he could offer up another protest and went to find Tilly. She was sitting on the edge of her bed, a plush spaniel cradled in her arms, its head pressed beneath her chin. She didn't look up as I came in.

'Oh sweetie,' I murmured, sitting down beside her and pulling her into my arms. 'I know things are tough right now, but they will get better, and your dad's only trying to help. I understand that it doesn't seem that way sometimes, but he just wants what's best for you, sweetheart.'

She barely said a word as I helped her into her nightdress and brushed her hair. I half wanted to sneak her in something I knew she'd be able to eat, but then I thought of what Adam would say, how much more confusing it would be for Tilly, and I squashed down the urge. I tucked her in and read her a story, her little hand slipping into mine, her head nudging against my elbow as she drifted off. It never took long for her to give in to sleep; she was always so tired. A day of battling against everything would do that to you.

I slipped out of her bedroom and went to find Adam. He was sitting on the sofa in the living room, the TV on low, though it didn't look like he was really watching it. I knew I should leave, give him a quiet evening alone to think everything through, but the thought of walking into my silent flat, feeding Minnie before slipping into an empty bed, was far from appealing. I'd enjoyed tonight. Joining in with the cooking, putting Tilly to bed, knowing Adam was nearby and I wasn't alone for once. It felt right. Natural, somehow, and I would give anything for it to become a regular occurrence.

'You want another?' I asked, poking my head through the door, nodding to the empty wine glass on the table.

'Why not?' he said. I nipped into the kitchen, grabbing the bottle and an extra glass for me, noticing that he hadn't bothered to clear the table or wash up. I could do it later. It would be nice.

'Thank you,' he sighed, leaning back against the sofa as I handed him the wine. I sat down beside him, noticing how he didn't edge away. We were so comfortable with one another; years of friendship had forged a closeness between us that was special. Rare.

He gave a wry smile. 'Not just for putting her to bed… for everything.' He rubbed the heel of his hand against his eye sockets, then took another sip of wine before putting his glass down on the side table and turning to me, his arm slung across the back of the sofa. If he moved his fingers an inch, they would be on the nape of my neck.

'You and Maddie, you're like sisters. I know how hard it was for you to take my side over hers, and I'm grateful. I know it doesn't seem like it now, but I really feel it's what's best for T.'

'It wasn't easy,' I agreed, 'but these things rarely are. The situation is… complicated.'

'You can say that again.' He laughed. 'I still feel like I'm betraying Maddie any time I disagree with her. But she's not always right.'

'No,' I murmured.

'We're just lucky we have you, Laur. I feel like you're the glue that's holding us all together. You're like a second mum to T, you know? You being here, it's good for her. Everything would be so much more difficult if you weren't in our lives.' His fingers reached out, brushing the base of my skull briefly. He smiled, and I felt a strange sense of lightness, as if everything I'd waited for, everything I wanted, was finally happening.

I would never have let myself go there, even in my imagination, when he was Maddie's. But she'd made it so clear that he wasn't hers any more. She didn't want him. The life they had shared was over. And maybe now *I* could have a shot at happiness.

I thought back to those times when they were still married, when Adam had arrived back from a flight, Maddie and I chatting over coffee in her kitchen. The way he would walk up behind her, his hands sliding her hair to one side, his lips pressing down on the soft skin at her throat. I'd been jealous. Sick with longing. The way he'd looked at her, the intensity of love in his expression… it had been unbearable to watch. I'd never had that. Someone who couldn't wait to get home, just so they could sweep me up in their arms, who looked at me like there was no other woman in the world. What would it be like to stand in my own kitchen, laughing as my hair was swept aside, lips pressed to my skin as the child we loved slept soundly down the hall?

'So, I've been granted leave from work,' Adam was saying. 'My boss called today and we had a long chat. He gave in, so at least I won't have to deal with the stress of an appeal. I have a month to get this situation sorted. It's far from ideal, but really, what choice did I have?'

'It's a tough time,' I murmured.

'It really is. And I love my job. I've worked so hard to get to the position I'm in now. I hate letting the team down.'

'You'll be back before you know it. And I'm sure they understand that family has to come first.'

He nodded, his hand moving to my shoulder, squeezing it lightly. 'I'm so glad you're here,' he said. 'You've made today easier.'

I stared at him, wondering what he was trying to say, if his words carried as much meaning for him as they did for me. His hand remained resting on my shoulder, his fingers brushing lightly against the silky material of my shirt. I could feel my heart beating in my chest, the thump of it echoing in my ears. My fingers trembled against the stem of my glass.

I moved without intending to, my body angling closer, my hand reaching for the back of his neck as I lurched forward, my lips meeting his. My eyes closed, and for half a second, I felt as if I were the bravest woman on the planet, making the first move, breaking the barriers of our friendship, opening the door to something new. Something better.

And then it all came crashing down around me. Something felt wrong. I had spent so long reimagining that day on the school field when Maddie, fifteen and fresh-faced, had thrown down a challenge she knew I would never accept. What if I'd had the courage to approach Adam first? If it had been *me* he'd taken on a date, *me* he'd opened up to and subsequently fallen in love with? How would my life have turned out if I'd had the courage to go for what I wanted?

Every single thing that had happened to me since Adam chose Madeline, I'd twisted and blamed on my failure to act at that pivotal moment of my life. I had never been brave enough to share the strength of my feelings with Madeline, to admit that it had never been *just* a crush. It was so much more than that for me. I'd fallen in love with him without him ever knowing I existed, long before I'd even hinted to Madeline that I liked him.

I'd spent the best part of two decades certain that I had missed out on the love of my life, and that nothing would make sense as long as he was with my best friend, but now, with my lips pressed against his, I didn't feel the frisson, the sense of rightness I'd always imagined. It was like kissing my friend, my brother even – there was no spark. My whole life had been on pause, believing that I would forever long for something I couldn't have, and now that I'd finally crossed that line and reached out for it, the fantasy was falling to pieces in front of me.

I opened my eyes, pulling back to see Adam's expression darkening, his gaze hard. My wine spilled down the front of my shirt as I moved away, humiliated at what I'd done, the colossal mistake I'd made.

'What are you doing?' he demanded, his voice low and angry.

'Adam, I…' I blotted my shirt uselessly with a tissue from the box on the coffee table.

'You what? Thought you'd complicate the situation a little bit more?'

'I don't know what I was doing. Oh God, Adam, I'm sorry, I don't know what I was thinking!'

'Did you think I wanted this? Wanted *you*? Oh, now this is just great. I thought you were a friend, Laura. I thought you got it. I don't want *you*. I love Maddie. I always have. How she feels is irrelevant. How we manage our daughter's needs makes no difference to how I feel about her.'

'I'm sorry,' I whispered again, my cheeks on fire as I stared down at my lap. 'I got it wrong,' I admitted. Adam looked incandescent with rage – it was clear that he was in shock. He'd never expected this from me, never thought of me that way. It was so obvious now. Whilst I'd been pining for him, dreaming of the future we might have, he'd been oblivious. Blurring the boundaries of our friendship hadn't even crossed his mind. It was beyond embarrassing to realise just how wrong I'd got it.

He shook his head. 'Can you imagine what Maddie would say if she could see you now? You took her daughter from her and now you're trying to worm your way into her ex's bed. You're a fucking snake in the grass, Laura. I can't believe you would think that you and I…' He paused, shaking his head sadly, breathing hard, then groaned and rubbed his hands over his face. At last he raised his head, fixing me with a blank stare. 'I think you should go.'

'Adam, don't do this. Let's talk, please,' I said, balling up the wine-soaked tissue in my hands.

'There's nothing to say. How can I respect you after this? How can I trust you? I thought you were my friend. *Maddie's* friend. I don't even know where we go from here.'

I stood up, shaking, my throat thick with emotion. 'I'm sorry. I made a mistake,' I whispered. I turned for the door, determined not to cry until I'd got outside.

'Yeah,' he replied. 'You did.'

CHAPTER THIRTY-SIX

Madeline

Fifty-nine hours. That was how long it had been since I'd last laid eyes on my daughter. My skin crawled with the need to hold her, my heart racing every time I heard a car pass by the house, my imagination running wild. It was stupid. I knew he wouldn't just bring her back to me, but I couldn't stop myself from hoping. *Wishing*.

That first night without her, I had slept, guilty as it made me feel. I'd had nothing left in me after the trauma of the hospital. But last night, there had been no blissful oblivion. My mind had refused to quiet, tears streaming relentlessly down my cheeks as I pictured Tilly alone in her room in Adam's flat.

He wouldn't allow her to sleep in his bed, no matter how desperately she needed comforting. What if she wet the bed again? What if she collapsed in the night and he didn't hear? She might lie there all night, the life seeping out of her, and he wouldn't know until it was too late.

I'd tortured myself with possibilities, my temples throbbing, my eyes stinging with exhaustion but unable to close, until eventually, at three in the morning, with the full moon still high, I'd got up, grabbing a roll of bin bags from the drawer in the kitchen. I'd needed to stay busy to stop myself from doing something stupid. I was too exhausted and impatient to dare to touch my sewing machine, though I knew with each day that passed that I was getting further behind with my orders. But if I tried to do anything requiring precision now, I knew I'd end up in frustrated tears, with nothing but a pile of torn satin to show for my efforts.

With grim determination, I'd stalked back upstairs to my wardrobe, where I had pulled every single item of clothing from the rails and cubbyholes, stacking the lot in a mountain of brightly coloured fabrics on the bed. I'd spent the next two and a half hours trying everything on, making piles to donate, piles to keep and piles to sell. There wasn't much of value, but there were a few unique vintage pieces I could no longer fit into that might be worth something. Finally, with the task complete, I'd walked downstairs to the sofa, where I'd watched sitcoms through half-closed eyes until the sun rose.

Now, shaking with exhaustion and sick with worry, I sat beside the telephone, knowing I couldn't wait another minute. I'd run out of things to keep my mind occupied and was too tired to fight my instincts. I was determined to keep calm, though my heart thumped erratically against my ribs as I listened to the repetitive ringing.

'Hello?' Adam's voice answered.

'It's me,' I said quietly.

'Oh.'

'Please can I speak to her? I don't want to fall out; I just want to hear her voice,' I said, the pleading tremor in my own voice impossible to disguise. He was silent for a moment and I gripped the phone so hard I feared it might crack.

'I don't know, Maddie. I'm not sure it's the right time.'

'Adam, please,' I begged. 'I can't bear this... I—' I broke off, hearing the beautiful sound of my daughter's voice in the background.

'Is that my mummy?' I heard her ask. 'Let me speak to her, Daddy!'

Adam sighed, defeated. 'Fine. Five minutes though – that's all. And we need to discuss a proper timetable for future calls,' he added, with a clear note of warning. There was a crackle as I waited for him to pass the phone over, then Tilly's voice came on the line.

'Mummy?'

My face broke into a smile, my eyes blurring as I leaned my head back against the sofa in relief.

'Hi, sweetheart,' I managed, blinking back tears. 'Are you okay?'

She paused, and I wondered if she was waiting for Adam to move out of earshot so she could answer honestly. 'It happened again,' she whispered finally.

'What did, sweetie?' I asked, sitting up instantly, my spine rigid.

'I… I wet the bed.'

'Oh, darling. Did you tell Daddy?'

There was a long pause. 'I was too scared to. I just put a towel over the wet patch. That's okay, isn't it, Mummy? I didn't want to get in trouble.'

I squeezed my eyes shut, wishing I could reach through the phone to hug her. 'You didn't do it on purpose, sweetie. I'm sure Daddy would understand that,' I said, though I knew it was a lie. 'Did you eat breakfast?'

Her voice was barely a whisper when she answered. 'I haven't eaten anything since I got here. Daddy has made some new rules and I can't have any of the food I like. Only what he says. And I can't eat those ones, Mummy. They make my tummy hurt too much.'

'But you must have had something?'

'No.'

I sat back, stunned. So that was his plan: to starve our already underweight six-year-old until she broke. I felt a hot rage wash over me, my fingers trembling, my mouth going dry as I clung to the phone, to my only link to Tilly.

'I want to come home. To *you,* Mummy. Will you come and get me?'

'I—'

'Tilly!' Adam's voice called. 'Time to say goodbye. We'll call Mummy again soon.'

'No, I haven't finished!' I heard her yell. 'I want my mummy! I don't want you!' she screamed.

There was a muffled noise, and then Adam's deep voice was back on the line, Tilly crying desperately in the background. 'It sounds worse than it is,' he said, before I could even speak. 'Everything is under control. I'll speak to you later, okay?'

'Don't you dare hang up! Put Tilly back on the phone. I didn't even get to say goodbye!'

'As I said, it's not a good time.'

'Adam, you listen to me, you cannot starve her. I can't believe that social services would agree with you. I won't let you do this to her!'

'Madeline, trust me. I'm not going to cause her any harm. You need to let me try – you've had plenty of time to do things your way and it hasn't worked. Use this time to focus on yourself.'

'Adam—' The line went dead and I screamed into the handset, slamming it down. It rang almost instantly, and I yanked it up, slipping off the sofa onto my knees. 'Tilly?' I cried.

'No, Dee Dee,' replied a voice I wanted to cling to. 'It's your mother. I'm glad you're there. I'm coming over.'

'How did you find out?' I asked, my face pressed into my mother's shoulder as she hugged me tightly in the middle of my messy kitchen. Her skin smelled like coconut oil and her long dark hair wrapped around me like a comforting blanket. She pulled back to look me in the eyes, her hands rubbing soothing circles on the tops of my arms.

'Laura called,' she said, watching my face.

'Did she tell you her part in what happened? How she went behind my back and stole… stole…' I broke off, my throat tightening against a fresh wave of tears.

'She didn't sugar-coat it, Dee Dee. She's worried about Tilly. And you. She didn't know what to do.'

'So she decided to betray me. She's my oldest friend, Mum. She should have come to me first, but she took his side instead, because she wants him for herself.'

Mum gave a burst of sunny laughter, squeezing my arm. 'Oh sweetheart, Laura has always had a thing for Adam. You must have been blinded by your own love for him to have ever missed it.'

'So you think she planned this? That she's been waiting for the right time to make her move?'

She shrugged, turning to fill the kettle over the pile of dirty plates in the sink. 'I don't think so, no. But it doesn't matter anyway. She could turn up on Adam's doorstep naked and smothered in honey and he would still turn her down. He's got no romantic interest in Laura, Dee Dee. He's never looked at anyone the way he looks at you.'

I folded my arms, frowning. 'Well, I don't care either way. She can have my husband… ex-husband. I don't want him. But if she thinks for even one moment that she can steal my daughter…' I rubbed my fingers over my temples, feeling close to falling apart. 'They think I'm hurting her, Mum. Can you believe they would suspect me of making her ill? They know me better than anyone. They should be defending me, not making accusations. They keep saying I'm ill, going on about what happened when Nola died and making out that I'm not in control now. But I'm fine, Mum, I swear to you – they've got it wrong.'

'I'm glad to hear you say it. Laura did mention she had some concerns when we spoke on the phone,' she admitted. 'I would hate to think that you were going through something like that again, struggling to cope with it all by yourself. After everything that happened, you know you can always come to me? I would do anything I could to help, Dee Dee. So would your father.'

'I know.' I nodded, my eyes meeting hers. 'You would be the first person I would tell if I thought I was getting ill again,' I promised, pushing down my irritation at Laura for having caused her to worry. 'But I'm fine. It's Tilly I'm concerned about. She's the one everyone needs to be focusing on, not me.' I looked up suddenly. 'Do you think I'm capable of it? Of causing her harm, I mean? Do you believe what Adam and Laura have been saying?' I asked, hearing the tremor in my voice.

She put down the kettle and turned to me, a soft smile on her full lips. The sunlight glinted on her gold hoop earrings as she tucked an unruly strand of hair behind her ear. 'Darling, I know how much you love that girl. You would never do anything to hurt her. And I don't think you're ill either. I know you well enough to see that you're in a state because you're worried about Tilly, and that should be perfectly clear to Laura and Adam too,' she said firmly.

I breathed out a sigh of relief, grateful to hear that she was on my side.

'But,' she continued, holding my gaze, 'you are a fearful mother. I'm not saying you're mistaken that Tilly might be unwell in some way – you know her best and it stands to reason that you would see things that the rest of us miss. Even Adam. He gets a few short days with her before she's back with you, and that's not enough to pick up on the little things. But that's the point, Dee Dee. He needs to see it if he's going to be on your side. You've been asking him to fight a battle he doesn't believe in.' She shrugged, her bangles jingling as she crossed one bare foot over the other. 'He's a good dad. He always has been. He's not the bad guy in this situation.'

'So who is? *Me?*'

'Of course not, darling. You're doing what you think is right, and so is Adam. His goal is the same as yours. To protect Tilly. Listen, darling, if she really *is* ill, Adam will see that, won't he? He won't let anything bad happen to her. He will take action when it's needed. He's already proved he's willing to do what's necessary to keep her safe. Can you imagine how hard it must have been for him to take her from you, knowing how much it would hurt you? You *know* how he feels about you.'

I nodded. 'He loves me, yes. But he's also angry that I won't take him back, and anger can make people spiteful.'

Mum's eyes narrowed. 'Surely you know he's not doing this out of bitterness. Can you really say deep down that you believe he'd thrust poor little Tilly into the middle just to get one over on you? Come on, Dee Dee, you and I both know he's not like that.'

I looked down, shamefaced, as I acknowledged her words. It was true that spite and callousness had never been part of Adam's character when we'd been married. He'd been selfless, caring, generous and attentive. But people could change, and not always for the better.

Mum seemed to read my indecision. 'Trust him to be a parent. To find out for himself. Trust him to do what you've always done.'

I gave her a watery smile. 'How did you get to be so wise?'

'By living. Making my own mistakes and learning from them. And when it comes to parenting, there are always mistakes to make, opportunities to grow. I should thank you for my wisdom.'

She poured two cups of herbal tea, carrying them to the kitchen table. 'Come and sit down and rest for a minute. You aren't helping anyone with this relentless fidgeting.'

I sighed but did as I was told. It was comforting to have someone tell me what to do. I was lost otherwise.

'Now, I'm curious,' Mum said, pushing my cup towards me and gesturing for me to drink. I picked it up, taking a tentative sip. 'What *did* happen with you and Adam? You never have given me a straight answer. Why did you divorce? You always seemed so perfect together, though I know looks can be deceiving.'

'For the most unforgivable reason,' I admitted, bowing my head.

'What? You met someone else?'

'No. Worse than that.' I pursed my lips, looking up to see her warm, kind eyes watching me. There was no judgement in them. Only love. 'I changed my mind.' I shrugged. 'There was no big falling-out. No affair. I simply stopped loving him. Is there anything more unforgivable in a marriage?' I asked, offering a wry smile. 'I promised to love him till the day I died, and I broke my word. I couldn't help it. But he can't forgive me for that. I don't blame him for being angry, bitter. I broke his heart. But at some point, many years ago, he began to change, and so did I. We were too different to keep co-existing and I couldn't pretend any more.' I sighed. 'If there'd been someone else, it might have made more sense, been something to focus on. But without that, it hurt him all the more. I'm sorry, but that's the truth. He couldn't accept that I'd rather be alone than with him, not because I hate him, or because he's a bad person. He was never perfect, but then neither was I. But for me, it was the end of our story. I lived with that knowledge for a very long time before I had the guts to tell him.'

'I wish you'd told me you were feeling all of this, darling. I could have supported you.'

'I know you would have done. I just felt so guilty about it. You're supposed to keep trying, aren't you? But how long can you keep doing it when you know that the thing you had, that spark, has died?'

'It happens.' She nodded, sipping her tea.

'Not to you and Dad.'

'We've had our moments, our tough times. We nearly parted ways after Nola died.'

'I didn't realise,' I said, shocked at the idea that my parents could ever have considered ending their marriage.

'Of course not, sweetheart. You had quite enough of your own stuff to deal with back then. It was a hard ride for all of us, wasn't it?'

'I was selfish. I couldn't bear that I'd lost her, and then you and Dad, you were so sad, I felt like I'd lost you both too. I thought...' I didn't say what we were both thinking, that I had stopped eating to pull their attention back, nor the fact that it had worked so well.

'It was a long time ago, darling. And actually, it was focusing on helping you to get well again that saved Dad and me from our grief. It made us snap back and focus on the moment we were in, rather than longing for the past. We were lost for a little while,' she admitted.

'You know, before she died, Nola watched you like you were made of magic. You were so free, so very brave, Dee Dee. She admired that in you, and I know you inspired her to do the things she feared. Your energy was addictive to be around.' She put her cup down, reaching for my hand. 'We all struggled when we lost her. She took something from each of us with her, but she took your spirit and I think it's time you took it back. Let go of this fear that rules you. You wear it like a cloak, and it's hiding the real you. The brave, wild, wonderful girl you once were. You need to find her again, darling, and teach your beautiful daughter what it means to really live. You don't want her to grow up being afraid of her shadow.' She stood up, brushing her fingers through my hair. 'Find her.' She turned towards the sink, cup in hand.

'What if I can't?' I whispered. 'What if she's been lost for too long?'

She paused, looking back at me with a smile. 'Then you dig deeper.'

CHAPTER THIRTY-SEVEN

It only took me a second to realise what had woken me in the half-light of the dawn. My body moved on autopilot, jumping from the bed and running down the stairs, my heart pounding in my chest at the sudden burst of adrenaline. The ringing of the house phone was too abrasive for such a peaceful morning and I grabbed it, instinct already telling me who would be on the other end.

'Maddie? It's me,' Adam said softly, his voice nothing like the last time I'd heard it. It was shaky and uncertain.

'What is it? What's happened?' I said, standing in the doorway to the living room, my free hand gripping the frame for support.

'I'm so sorry, Maddie,' he whispered. My heart dropped, my knees giving way.

'What do you mean? Is she ill? Did she collapse again?'

He let out a shaky sigh. 'I thought I was getting somewhere, you know? She was stubborn, but so was I. I know she told you she hadn't eaten since we came back from hospital. She went three full days without a bite, just having little sips of water.'

I gritted my teeth, holding back my fury so that he would keep talking.

'She was hungry, and I knew that if I just stayed strong, she would give in.'

'And did she?'

There was a pause. 'Yes,' he answered. 'Last night.'

I closed my eyes, already sure of what he would say.

'She ate a small bowl of spaghetti bolognaise. I was so pleased – it was proof that she could do it. You're always saying she can't eat meat or gluten, but I gave her both and she seemed more energetic for a little while. But,' he said, 'it wasn't more than thirty minutes later that she threw up. Literally all over the rug in the living room. I was angry, Maddie. You have to understand, I thought she was doing it on purpose. You know it's possible – some children do, for attention or to get their own way. And she didn't even ask for a bowl. What else was I supposed to think?'

'Adam—'

'She didn't stop though. Every thirty minutes, she would throw up. After a few hours, it wasn't food any more, just bile, but it just kept coming. She couldn't even keep water down.'

I nodded silently. I knew those nights. I'd held her hair and rubbed her back. Washed her sweat-soaked body only to have her throw up all over herself once again.

'I got scared, Maddie. She started shaking and wouldn't stop. She looked so weak, so exhausted. And I realised what a fucking idiot I've been. I'm so sorry I didn't believe you. Seeing her like that was terrifying. That was no act; she's *ill*. Something is wrong.'

Tears were streaming down my face as he spoke, relief that finally, after years of fighting opposite corners, we were in this together. 'I'm coming over,' I said, wiping my nose with the back of my hand.

'We're not at the flat, Maddie. We're on the children's ward. I didn't know what else to do.'

'Then I'm coming there.'

There was a silence, then Adam sighed. 'The social worker told me that I wasn't allowed to let you visit. I promised I wouldn't.'

I closed my eyes, keeping my voice measured and calm. 'I think that's irrelevant now, don't you? You can't expect me to stay away when she's ill. She needs me, and it's not as if you can put any of this down to *my* actions. I'm not there, and still this has happened to her.'

'No, you're right. I just need to make sure they understand the situation. The last thing we want is to have it seem like we're going behind their backs. I need to call them, and I'll speak to the doctors too. Make sure they understand that you don't need to stay away any more. I can't believe I thought for a second that this could be all in your mind. I owe you an apology.'

'It doesn't matter now. All that matters is that we try and figure out what's wrong with our baby girl.'

'And we will,' he said. 'I promise you, we will. Together.'

I glanced at the clock on the dashboard as I pulled into the hospital car park. It was not yet 7 a.m., which meant the night shift would still be on. I felt drained, the thought of yet another battle with the doctors too much to bear. I had to hope that the ones who knew of our situation weren't working today, or failing that, that Adam had managed to convince them of my innocence. And why shouldn't he be the one to fix the situation when he'd been the reason it had come about in the first place?

I blinked back my anger, reminding myself that I had to move forward. It would do Tilly no good if I refused to let go of my resentment, and right now, she was all that mattered. I pulled into a space in the deserted car park and grabbed my bag, running to the entrance, following the now familiar route to the children's ward.

I was glad that today, at least, I was dressed in something other than old bobbly pyjamas. My dress, a sea of flowing green and blue cotton, fell to my knees, and I'd brushed my hair back into a high ponytail. I'd added earrings made of discs of blue sea glass and the silver charm bracelet my parents had given me for my twenty-first birthday. I might not feel the part, but at least I looked more like my normal self.

I followed an unfamiliar nurse into the children's ward, bypassing the desk and heading straight to the room Adam had told me they'd been given. Nobody stopped me as I walked briskly towards it, my head held high. The curtain was drawn across the window facing the hall, but Tilly's name was written on the whiteboard beside the door. I pushed it open, relief flooding through me as I saw her curled up sleeping on the bed.

Adam rose from his seat, his eyes red, his cheeks hollow and coated with dark stubble. Wordlessly he stepped forward, his arms outstretched. I paused, surprised at his vulnerability, half tempted to refuse his invitation. I was still so hurt, so angry at how he'd tossed me aside. But we would never get anywhere if I didn't at least *try* to forgive him. With a sigh, I stepped into the circle of his arms, feeling him slump against me.

'I am so sorry. I really am, Maddie,' he breathed into my neck. 'I should have known that you wouldn't…' He sniffed, and I wondered if he was crying. 'I hope you can forgive me,' he said, clearing his throat and pulling back.

I closed my eyes, then opened them, turning to face Tilly. 'For her. I can do it for her.'

He nodded.

'So, what have the doctors said?'

'Not much. She's got another cannula. It was awful.'

'I bet.'

'And they've put her on fluids. They got some blood when they did the cannula, which has been sent off, but they got a gas too. It said her sodium was high, but that's probably down to the dehydration.'

'Has anyone said what happens next?'

'No. I've just seen a junior doctor so far, who wasn't familiar with Tilly. I didn't bother to mention the social services thing to him.'

'Probably easier not to, but it will come up.'

'I called Beatrice Caine. Did you meet her?'

'The social worker? Yeah, we met,' I said, my stomach tightening at the mention of her name. 'What did she say?'

'She's calling another meeting. Isn't that what social workers do?' he said, his mouth twisting sardonically. 'I told her I was sure we'd made a mistake and explained the situation. She wasn't happy that I'd gone against their wishes and told you it was okay to visit, but she sounded swamped, which is a blessing for us. She said she'd be in touch.'

'I see.' I nodded, feeling sick with apprehension. Who knew what they would decide in the meeting? Whether they'd take Adam's word or decide he too was unfit to parent our child. I hated that my life and that of my daughter was in the hands of a bunch of strangers, but it was too late to undo that now. They were involved and we would just have to make the best of it.

I walked to the bed, watching Tilly's chest rise and fall. I wanted to reach out and touch her, but I resisted, not willing to disturb her precious sleep. I sat down on the chair beside her, waiting for whatever came next. Adam settled himself back in his seat, the room silent save for Tilly's steady breathing.

After an hour or so, with Adam dozing, his head lolling forward, I heard the familiar hubbub that signalled the arrival of the day shift. Soon we would be meeting a new nurse and we'd find out which doctor was on duty. I hoped that it was anyone but Dr Keifer. I didn't think I could stand to see his smug expression, those cold, mean little eyes again.

My stomach tensed as the activity increased outside our door: the cleaners laughing loudly, the nurses going in and out of rooms with medications, the breakfast trolley moving along with one squeaking wheel. My eyes roved from Tilly to the door and back again, over and over, my body coiled tightly, preparing for the unknown.

Finally the door handle to our room lowered, and my heart sank as Dr Keifer stepped into the room. He stared at me, clearly surprised. 'Adam, wake up,' I said. He groaned and blinked, wiping the back of his hand over his mouth and straightening up.

'Good morning,' Dr Keifer said, unsmiling. 'Mr Parkes, would you care to explain what is going on here?' He gestured towards me.

Adam stood up, frowning, and I saw the flash of irritation in his expression at the offhand way the doctor had referred to me. 'I'm afraid we've made a mistake. Madeline is not responsible for any of this. Tilly has been in my sole care since we were discharged, and yet here we are. I'm sorry to say, I jumped to the wrong conclusion. We all did.' His eyes met mine, and I smiled, grateful to have his support at last.

Dr Keifer shook his head. 'This case was referred to social services, and on their instruction, you may not be here until I hear otherwise,' he said, fixing me with a hard stare.

Adam shook his head. '*I'm* telling you though. We were wrong.'

'But I can't take your word for it, Mr Parkes. I need to hear it from social services. They need to sign off the case before I can discuss Tilly's care with her.' He was referring to me as if I wasn't even there.

'I called them first thing this morning. They are aware that Madeline is here and are having a meeting to discuss it. I haven't gone behind their backs. We're working on getting this whole mess sorted,' Adam promised.

I nodded in agreement. I was exhausted and confused as to why Adam's word wasn't enough. The doctor had disliked me from the moment we'd met, and it was clear that he wasn't prepared to let his mistaken judgement go. 'Look,' I said, standing up. 'I'm sure you can call social services to verify what Adam has told you, and we will continue to work with them to resolve this… confusion. But in the meantime, *you* need to work out what's wrong with our daughter and figure out what you've missed, because you *have* missed something.' I nodded to Adam. 'I'm not going to leave, but I'll wait outside for now if the doctor is going to be stubborn about it.' I threw a last glance back at Tilly, then walked to the door, stepping into the hall.

Long, bright strip lights ran along the ceiling, making up for the lack of natural light in the corridor. I leaned against the wall, my gaze fixed on the door. A little girl hooked up to a drip stand was toddling towards me, dressed in only a T-shirt and a nappy. She was pushing a little pink pram at breakneck speed, her frazzled mother chasing along after her with the drip-stand.

'Slow down, Pearla!' she chided, gripping the back of the little girl's T-shirt. 'You need to go slowly so Mummy can keep up.'

The little girl gave a serious nod, turning back to the pram and setting off at a much more reasonable pace. The mother glanced at me as she passed, and I offered a smile of solidarity. I was grateful that I hadn't been here in those whirlwind toddler years. At least Tilly was old enough to understand a bit more.

The door to her room opened, and Dr Keifer stepped out. He saw me, then pointedly looked away, walking past me as if I were no more than an apparition. I shrugged. If he was determined not to like me, then I wouldn't waste my time trying to change his mind. I had far more important things to focus on. Adam appeared at the door and held it open for me as I went back to my seat beside Tilly.

'Well?' I asked.

'You're not going to like it,' he said, pursing his lips. 'I can tell you, *I* don't.'

'What do you mean?'

'He thinks it's psychosomatic. He was convinced it was you talking her into it or making her anxious. I think he still feels you're the root cause, despite the fact that you've not seen her for days. But he's stuck on this notion that Tilly is somehow making herself sick through her own mental issues.'

'You don't believe that, do you?' I asked, my eyes widening. We'd only just got past *me* being the victim of the witch-hunt. I was not going to have him point the finger at Tilly.

'No. I don't. I get what he's saying: these things do happen and they can be serious. The mind can have powerful effects over the body. I *do* understand that.'

'But that isn't what's going on here. Not for Tilly.'

'No, I don't think so, not having seen the way she was last night.' He shook his head, his gaze going to her wrapped up in the blue hospital blanket on the bed. 'He mentioned self-harm, Maddie. He thinks she could be doing it on purpose.'

My mind flashed back to my own illness: the therapy room at the mental hospital I'd been forced to endure, the hunger pains, the sheer determination to gain some control over a life that seemed to be spiralling faster than I could handle. 'No,' I said resolutely. 'Not Tilly. She has no reason to do that. And she's too young.'

'That's what I told him. I'm not sure he was listening though – it's as if he's already diagnosed her. He said he's seen cases of self-harm in children as young as five.'

I shook my head, hating Dr Keifer for being so blind to the reality of our situation. His judgement was clouded by his preconceived ideas. 'So what happens next?'

Adam sighed, rubbing his palm over the stubble on his chin. He looked broken. 'I convinced him to test her for food allergies. It's been years since we last looked at that, and there's a chance the tests she had as a toddler missed something. He wasn't keen, but it's a start. As for the immediate solution…'

'What?' I pressed, seeing the hesitation in his eyes.

'She can't eat. And she can't stay on just intravenous fluids indefinitely. They want to put a tube in through her nose – he called it a nasogastric tube, I think. It goes into her stomach.'

'And we force-feed her through it?' I said, realising what the doctor intended. 'What? Milk?'

'Some kind of formula. He said we have to get past her reluctance to eat. And he wants her to speak to a child psychiatrist.'

'You told him no though?'

'I tried. And I told him we wanted a second opinion, but he said he can't let her starve.'

'Of course not, but force-feeding her isn't the answer. They need to get to the bottom of what's causing her symptoms. The sickness, the pains, the bed-wetting. She can't be the first child in history to have these issues.'

He shook his head sadly. 'I know. And I don't want to put her through it any more than you do. But she *does* need nutrition. He said the formula he wants her to have is a good one for children with digestive issues. Maybe it will help, build up her strength at least, while we keep pushing for tests.'

He stepped forward, his palm cupping my cheek. 'I am not giving in, Maddie. I'm just trying to find a compromise so we can get her the help she needs. It's only temporary.'

I nodded, not seeing a way around it. 'I want to be there for her when they put the tube in,' I said, my voice firm. 'I *need* to be.'

'Okay.' He nodded. 'I'm going to call the social worker again. We'll get this fixed.' He headed for the door, his shoulders rigid with tension.

'I hope you're right, Adam,' I said softly. 'I really do.'

CHAPTER THIRTY-EIGHT

Adam came back into the room with a burst of energy. 'It's sorted. They've had a meeting and spoken to the police again. The police have said that after analysing the photographs of Tilly's bruising and speaking with you, they don't have reason to believe that she's at risk in your care, and at this stage they don't have any reason to think you've intentionally hurt her.'

'Of course I haven't!'

He winced. 'They've agreed that you can stay. They want to visit to have a chat before they sign off the case, and' – he paused, looking awkward – 'they said until that happens, you have to be supervised, either by me or one of the nurses when you're with her.'

'That's fine. As long as I can stay.'

'I still have to do the nights.'

I nodded, reminding myself that it could be so much worse. 'Fine.'

He walked to the window, his eyes not meeting mine. 'I called Laura too. I thought, you know, we should at least tell her what was going on.'

'Why? So she can meddle some more?'

'Maddie, I *asked* her to.'

'How and why it came about doesn't matter,' I said, realising how angry I still was with her. Somehow her betrayal hurt more than Adam's. I didn't know if I could ever look at her the same way again. 'She isn't coming here, is she?'

'No. I told her it wasn't a good idea.'

'Good.' I folded my arms, leaning back in the chair. Adam sighed, his back towards me as he continued to stare blankly out of the window. I wondered if he realised how Laura felt about him. My mother had guessed years ago, she'd told me. How had I missed it? I thought about asking him if anything had ever happened – if he'd been tempted; if he still might be – but I shook the urge away. It was none of my business. Not any more.

I sighed, reaching forward to slide my hand beneath Tilly's, needing to feel the heat of her skin, to remind myself that she was still strong, still fighting.

She stirred, squeezing back, still half asleep. 'Mummy?' she whispered.

'Yes, baby. I'm here.'

She opened her eyes, turning her head towards me, her face breaking into a smile as she reached her arms out to me. I lifted her up, holding her as tightly as I could without hurting her, feeling the way she gripped my dress, one hand tight around the back of my neck. 'I dreamed you would come,' she said, kissing my cheek.

'Well, it must have been a magic dream, because here I am.' I looked towards Adam, seeing a smile transform his weary face as he watched us.

The door opened without warning and Tilly tensed, burying her face against my throat. A grey-haired nurse with a sticker of a kitten on her dress came in, holding a blue tray. 'Are we ready?'

'For what?' I asked.

'The doctor has asked me to place an NG tube for Tilly,' she said softly, her eyes kind as they met mine.

'I don't want another needle, Mummy,' Tilly whispered.

'It's not a needle, T. It's a tube that goes in your nose. It feels a bit funny, but it's not painful. Like a tickle,' Adam said, keeping his tone light.

'Can't we go home, Mummy? I don't like this.'

'I know, sweetie. Neither do me and Daddy. But we have to get you better first, don't we? And,' I said, meeting Adam's eyes, 'the doctor thinks this might help.'

'I hope you're right, because I'm getting fed up of all this,' she said crossly.

The nurse laughed kindly. 'I don't blame you, angel. Now, let's get this over with nice and quickly, shall we?'

It was anything but quick. Tilly fought and sobbed as Adam and I held her still, the nurse's hands shaking as she tried to insert the tube. Eventually she got it in, taping it to Tilly's cheek, and hurried out looking shaken and guilty. Afterwards I held Tilly cradled against my body on the bed, feeling sick and disgusted with myself for what we'd put her through.

'It will be worth it,' Adam said. 'If she tolerates the feed, she'll start to regain some strength.' He squeezed my shoulder and I looked up at him, lost for words, my eyes blurring with tears as I realised we were finally on the same page again.

The nurse returned a few minutes later. 'I have Tilly's feed here.' Tilly didn't speak, didn't even raise her face to watch as the nurse took the end of her new tube, attaching it to the giving set that ran through the feeding pump.

'All done. It will run continuously at a low rate. Hopefully within a few hours Tilly will be feeling much more like her old self. Let me know if she's in any discomfort and we can see about adjusting the rate.'

Adam nodded and she left quietly.

We watched the purple pump, listening to the whirr and tick as it fed the formula through the line. Tilly sighed and I switched on the TV beside the bed to distract her. She leaned back on the pillow, her eyes glazing over almost instantly as she stared up at it.

Neither Adam nor I spoke. We seemed to have run out of things to say. There was no energy for small talk, no desire to pretend it would all be okay. We were both as lost as each other.

The cartoon finished and another began. Tilly stretched, her fingers fidgeting against the sheet.

'Do you feel okay, sweetheart?' I asked softly. She didn't answer. Adam moved back to his place by the window and I realised I would have to get him some lunch, since he wasn't allowed to leave me unsupervised. I was just about to offer when Tilly rolled onto her side and vomited through the bars of the bed, white, frothy liquid splashing in a wide circle on the floor.

'Shit!' I heard Adam yell as I jumped off my side of the bed, grabbing a handful of paper towels from the dispenser on the wall. I blotted her mouth dry, but she retched again, choking on the frothy liquid. Adam grabbed the call button, pressing down hard. 'We need to turn this thing off!' he yelled as Tilly rolled onto her back, trembling and moaning in pain. I pulled her into my arms, the sweat from her brow damp against my cheek.

The door opened and a nurse rushed in. 'Oh dear,' she muttered, looking down at the mess.

'She's not tolerating the formula,' Adam said briskly. 'We need to turn it off now.'

'I'll go and ask the doctor.'

'Not before you turn this thing off. She's being sick, for Christ's sake!'

The nurse bit her lip, then gave a reluctant nod. 'I'll pause it,' she agreed. 'Just while I go and ask. I'm not sure what the plan is if she doesn't tolerate this feed. They may want to try another.'

'Not today they won't,' Adam said firmly. 'Not after this.' I watched him, relieved that at last he was thinking like me.

The nurse paused the pump and rushed off to find the doctor. Adam was shaking, his face contorted with anguish. 'Madeline, I'm sorry,' he said, turning to face me, running his fingers through his messy hair. 'I keep pushing, talking you into things, but I'm pushing in the wrong direction. You said this wouldn't work. I should have listened.'

'You didn't know this would happen,' I said, although I had been sure it would. 'And it wasn't like Dr Keifer presented you with a whole lot of options.'

Tilly rocked on her side, her arms wrapped around her stomach as she groaned.

'Is it hurting, baby?' I asked.

'It feels like my stomach is being squeezed and twisted by a giant,' she moaned.

A sharp rap sounded at the door and Adam and I both looked towards it as Dr Keifer entered. He glanced from Adam to me, his face thunderous. 'My nurse tells me you've insisted on turning off Tilly's feeding pump?'

'She's been sick,' Adam replied, saving me from having to engage with the odious little man. 'It's not working for her.'

Dr Keifer frowned, shaking his head. 'Let me look at her.' He strode over towards where Tilly lay against my side, and I felt an overwhelming instinct to cover her body with my own, to keep her safe from him. I didn't trust him. The relationship was broken beyond repair and it was clear that we needed to request a new doctor. I wished Dr Wallis were back from his holiday. He had been the polar opposite to Dr Keifer: kind, understanding, helpful.

'Can you roll onto your back, Tilly?' he asked, his voice harsh. She ignored him and I saw the irritation in his expression. He didn't realise she wasn't being naughty or stubborn. She was terrified of the man. He'd been there when I'd been forced from her room; he'd ordered the tube that now dangled from her left nostril and then the feed that had caused her this pain. As far as she was concerned, he was the reason bad things kept happening.

He tutted, folding his arms. 'Tilly, I need you to cooperate.'

'That's enough!' Adam said, stepping between Dr Keifer and the bed. 'If she says it hurts, then it hurts.'

'As we discussed before, Mr Parkes,' the doctor said, lowering his voice as if he could cut me out of the conversation, 'I'm almost certain these pains are psychosomatic. If you'd allow me to do my job, I can help her.'

'I disagree. But whether my daughter's symptoms stem from a physical or mental root is beside the point. I expect you to treat her with professional care and empathy and I will not stand for anything less.'

Dr Keifer's eyes widened, and I hid a smile as he spun, storming out of the room, closing the door firmly behind him.

'Thank you,' I said. 'For standing up for her.'

'Making up for lost time,' Adam said, his mouth hard. 'We need to request a new doctor. This one isn't right for Tilly.'

'That was just what I was thinking.' I rubbed Tilly's back, wishing I could make everything better for her.

'We'll find an answer,' I said, unsure whether I was trying to convince her, Adam or myself. 'We'll just keep searching until we do.'

An hour or so passed with Tilly crying and complaining, retching into a cardboard sick bowl, bringing up nothing but frothy white gunk that stuck in her throat and made her cough. Gradually the discomfort eased, which I was grateful for, and yet I knew she needed food, *nutrition*. Adam was right: she couldn't go indefinitely on IV fluids alone.

She was sitting up and looking a little better when the door opened and a woman poked her head around it. 'Knock knock,' she said, stepping inside. She had a soft, quiet voice and wore a lilac skirt-suit made of some fusty, thick material that looked hot and itchy. Despite the August heat, she wore thick, tan-coloured tights and black patent court shoes that shone brightly.

'Hello,' she said smiling. 'My name is Dr Sway, but you can call me Millicent. I am a child psychiatrist. I have been requested to come and see your daughter.' She spoke precisely, her words clipped and unnatural-sounding.

I nodded. 'Thank you. We've already told the doctor that we don't believe Tilly's symptoms stem from her mind,' I said. 'There is a direct correlation with food. We're quite sure her issue is a physical one.'

'I see. I have just been reading through Tilly's notes, and there *are* some aspects that have raised red flags for me. I would like to speak to her.'

'Right,' I said, feeling instantly uneasy.

Tilly was sitting up, watching the conversation between us.

'Tilly, Millicent here wants to ask you some questions.'

'Actually,' Millicent said, smiling again, 'would you mind waiting out in the hall? I find children tend to clam up when Mum and Dad are hanging around.'

'No,' Adam and I both said simultaneously. 'Not a chance,' he added.

'It really would be better.'

Adam's eyes met mine and I gave a tiny shake of my head. I was so aware of my words now, almost afraid to object out loud for fear it could be used against me. It was such a relief to finally have Adam speak up and take my side. 'We're not leaving her,' he said, fixing Millicent with a confident stare.

'I see.' She gave an exaggerated sigh and stepped up to the bed on Tilly's side. 'Would you mind giving us some space, at least?' she asked pointedly, looking at me.

I kissed Tilly's cheek and climbed down from the bed, going to stand beside Adam.

'Well,' Millicent said. 'I have a few things I would like to ask you, Tilly. Is that okay?'

Tilly glanced at her, then looked back at her lap, pulling her knees up to her chest.

'Now, let's see,' Millicent went on, as if Tilly had replied. 'Tell me how you feel about food right now, Tilly.'

'It makes me sick.'

'Okay.' She rattled off a list of questions, jotting down notes in a tiny notebook, Adam glancing nervously towards me. Tilly was cooperating, albeit in brief, uncomfortable sentences. She looked shy and fed up, but she didn't look like a troubled child.

'And finally,' Millicent said, stepping closer to Tilly so as to block her from our view, 'how do you feel about yourself, Tilly?'

'I don't know,' I heard her reply, her tone confused. What a question to ask a six-year-old! I frowned, hoping the woman would hurry up and leave so that I could comfort Tilly. She'd been through so much in such a short space of time, forced to speak to so many people who probed her with questions and poked her with needles.

I wished they would dig deeper and figure out what was wrong so that we could begin some sort of treatment. Even if it was something awful, it would be better than this limbo. I just needed to know now. Whatever it was, we would deal with it. We would find the best possible solution to help her, but without answers, without a diagnosis, we were powerless. All I wanted was to take her home, where she belonged. Hospital was no place for a child.

'What I mean by that, dear,' Millicent continued in her clipped tone, 'is if you had to describe your body, what would you tell me?'

'It's broken,' Tilly said simply.

'I see. Well, thank you, Tilly. This has been very helpful. I'll go and have a little conversation with Mum and Dad now.' She turned, tight-lipped, and walked towards us, her heels clacking ominously. 'May we step out into the corridor for a moment? I would prefer not to discuss this with little ears around.'

Adam and I followed her out, closing the door quietly, and she turned to face us.

'I suspected from her recent medical history and my conversation with her consultant—'

'You mean Dr Keifer?' I interrupted, my heart sinking.

'Yes, that is correct. Anyway, as I was saying, I had a feeling that the situation might be complicated with Tilly. And I was right. It is my view that she would benefit from a residential placement in Clarence Halls.'

'What's that?' Adam asked, folding his arms tightly across his chest. He towered above the psychiatrist, but she didn't seem fazed in the slightest.

'It is a treatment facility providing psychiatric care to children and young adults. They are equipped to deal with both eating disorders and self-harm. I can't be certain which is the root cause of Tilly's symptoms, but I am quite sure it is one of them.'

My hand shot out, gripping Adam's arm for support. I felt like I was falling. Like we'd arrived in a world where nothing made sense and we were the only ones who could see it.

'You're wrong,' Adam said, his hand covering mine. It was clammy, though his face was hard and determined. 'She's not going there.'

'You need to consider your daughter's best interests here, Mr Parkes. I called ahead prior to my conversation with your daughter – I suspected it might be wise – and as luck would have it, they have a bed for her. It can often take weeks, *months* even, to secure a place, but they had an unexpected cancellation.'

'You cannot take her there, not without our consent!' Adam said firmly.

'I spoke with Beatrice Caine, your child's social worker, earlier today and I have had a meeting with Dr Keifer too in order to get a clear picture of what's been happening. I would really prefer this not to become a battle. You must understand that we are all on Tilly's side. We want to help her.'

'But you have this wrong,' I said, finding my voice at last. 'She doesn't need a psychiatric placement, she needs a gastroenterologist.'

'I'm sorry, but I don't agree. Now, the ideal solution as I see it is to admit Tilly. Mr Parkes, you will be permitted to accompany her if you consent to the treatment.'

'And if I don't?' he demanded, breathing heavily. 'No,' he said, shaking his head. 'We won't consent to this. You can't go against our wishes surely? We are her parents!'

'In most situations, you would be right, but Tilly's case is unusual, and I'm afraid that without proper care she is going to be at serious risk. That changes things considerably. She has been admitted for severe dehydration on more than one occasion, and paramedics have had to be called to the home after she collapsed. This is not a situation we can treat lightly. Dr Keifer, social services and I all feel that we need to do whatever is in Tilly's best interests. And *this*, I believe, is it. I'll be sharing my recommendations with Dr Keifer and Beatrice Caine, and if they agree, Tilly will be transferred to Clarence Halls this afternoon.'

'You've got to be joking!' Adam snarled. 'You think you're going to put her through the trauma of being locked up in some unit? Not a chance!'

I stared up at him, unable to speak, my body juddering with adrenaline. I could not understand how they could have got this so very wrong. How I could be separated from my child again. 'We'll fight. We'll get a lawyer,' Adam said, his fingers pressing bruises into the back of my hand.

'You wouldn't be the first,' Millicent said, dipping her head in an infuriating little nod. 'But for now, if you won't work with us, I suggest you go and say your goodbyes.'

CHAPTER THIRTY-NINE

Laura

I watched another patient leave my room, closing the door behind him, and hoped I'd given him the right advice. I felt tense, ready to bolt should the need arise. I couldn't seem to absorb the things my patients were trying to explain, my mind drifting to Tilly every few seconds. Adam had called before lunch to tell me that he and Maddie were back in hospital with her, and that it was serious.

The fact that it was him saying this rather than Maddie made it all the more terrifying, because Adam wasn't the type to exaggerate. He'd sounded so worried on the phone, but I hadn't missed the brisk, businesslike tone to his voice, the coolness as he said he couldn't chat. He hadn't mentioned the kiss, not even to laugh it off, and that scared me. I couldn't stand to lose him.

He'd told me not to come. Expected me to stay away while the little girl I loved as if she were my own lay seriously ill in a hospital room. I felt used and excluded, and beneath my hurt, an intense anger simmered at the realisation that they could just cut me off as easily as ripping off a plaster. I glared at the clock in the corner of my computer screen, knowing I should buzz for my next patient, yet not making any move to do so.

I leaned back in my chair, closing my eyes, remembering the call that had come the night Madeline went into labour. They'd been living in a little two-bedroom flat a few roads back from the seafront at the time, and though I'd expected Madeline to want her mum with her for the birth, she'd asked me instead.

I'd agreed instantly, filled with terror and excitement at the prospect of watching a new life enter the world. It was impossible not to think of my own pregnancy, the child I never got to hold or kiss or feed, but I pushed down my trepidation and told her I wouldn't miss it for anything.

I'd arrived to find the flat had been decorated with fairy lights, a dozen beeswax candles casting a buttery glow over the small living room, the French windows open to the little courtyard at the back, letting in a blast of air that bordered on chilly. I'd pulled my scarf tighter around my neck, moving straight to the makeshift nest Adam had created for Maddie on the carpet, the thick duvet spread beneath her knees as she rocked back and forth on a huge inflatable birth ball.

Her face was red, her brow glistening with sweat as Adam pressed a glass of iced water to her lips. Her hair was tied haphazardly on top of her head, curls springing free at random angles. Aside from a turquoise and fuchsia silk scarf she'd tied to fashion a headband, she was stark naked.

I should have expected as much, but even so, I felt my cheeks redden as I lowered myself down on the quilt beside her, unable to meet Adam's eyes. Her hand reached out towards me in a silent plea, and I took it, feeling the crush of her contraction as she shared her pain with me. When it finally died away, her head dropped down to the big purple ball, her eyes closed as she caught her breath.

She opened them again slowly, smiling as she looked up at me. She was beautiful, her body ripe and soft, yet somehow strong enough to do this. I felt a sudden pang of jealousy, bitter and burning in my gut, and dropped her hand, leaning back. Maddie didn't notice. Another contraction seized her, and Adam moved to stand behind her, his eyes on the door. 'The midwife should be here by now,' he muttered.

Madeline gave a low moan, breathing through the pain as the doorbell rang. I jumped up, glad to have something to do, a reason to move away. I buzzed the visitor in without bothering to speak into the intercom, then went back to the living room. 'Midwife's here,' I said.

'Come here. I want you right with me when it happens,' Madeline said, her eyes shining up at me.

She sat back on her heels, her breasts bouncing heavily in preparation for the job they had ahead. Not for the first time, I felt stunned by her deep, unshakeable sense of self-confidence. She didn't apologise for her nudity, didn't even mention it.

Even when she'd stopped eating and been committed, it had never been about self-hatred for Maddie. It was about control. Taking charge of her life and, in some ways, the lives of her parents. But I would have bet everything I had on the fact that she'd never once looked at herself in the mirror and wanted to change everything she saw. It must be nice to feel so secure.

Reluctantly I moved back to my spot beside her, glancing over my shoulder as I heard someone enter. 'Julia!' I exclaimed. In place of the expected midwife, Madeline's mother sashayed in, kicking off her boots to reveal her dainty feet, tiny flowers tattooed across both of them.

'Hello, darling.' She smiled, leaning down to kiss my cheek. 'Hello, Adam,' she said, holding out her arms for him to step into. She gave him a hug that went on for long enough for me to feel uncomfortable, though Maddie didn't seem to mind. Finally she pulled back and looked down at Madeline. 'How's my baby?' she asked.

'Close, I think,' Maddie replied, smiling serenely.

'Good.'

'The midwife is really taking the piss though,' Adam said, pulling his phone from his pocket and frowning.

'She's not late. I told her not to come,' Maddie said, her hips beginning to rock slowly back and forth.

'That's what *I'm* here for, darling,' Julia said, patting him on the chest.

'*You're* going to deliver the baby?'

'Absolutely not. Dee Dee is. I'm just here to support her.'

Adam looked down at me and I shook my head, bewildered. I'd seen a fair number of deliveries during the course of my medical degree, but it seemed a long time ago now. I hoped they weren't expecting me to get stuck in. I was irritated that she hadn't thought to mention that there wouldn't be a midwife present. I would've had second thoughts about being here if I'd known.

Adam opened his mouth to speak but clamped it shut as Madeline tensed, gasping and moaning as the contraction overtook her. Julia squatted down behind her, peering between her legs. 'I see it,' she announced. 'I see the head! Keep going, Dee Dee – you're so close.'

'I know,' she gasped, her hand darting out, grabbing mine again. This time, I didn't pull away. I watched, half terrified, half fascinated, as Julia's eyes widened, a smile breaking across her face as Madeline gave a scream that sent shivers down my spine. Adam lowered to his haunches, cupping Maddie's cheek, and she grabbed his collar, pulling him close, kissing his lips with a level of passion that felt wholly inappropriate to the situation.

I felt like a voyeur, and yet I couldn't seem to tear my eyes away, my hand still clamped in her warm palm as Adam's eyes clouded and drifted closed. She pulled back slowly and smiled, and I felt my heart break as he gazed at her, his expression filled with something far stronger than love.

Her brow creased, her shoulders tensing as she let out a breathless gasp. With one final push, the baby slid from her body into Julia's outstretched arms. My heart seemed to stop in my chest as I looked at her. *A girl.* A tiny baby girl with a mass of hair and big, dark eyes, so very alert, so full of life. She was perfect.

'Here, Mummy,' Julia said softly as Madeline sat back breathlessly against the base of the sofa. 'Say hello to your daughter.' She placed the baby against Madeline's breast.

'That was pretty amazing,' Adam murmured. '*You* were amazing.' He kissed Maddie again, then looked at me. 'You're crying, Laur,' he teased.

I touched my cheek and realised he was right.

'She's happy to be an auntie.' Julia smiled. 'Aren't you, darling?'

'Yes.' I nodded. 'I am.'

That night had been the beginning of a fresh new page for me. Tilly had dulled the ache I'd carried for so long, filled the emptiness left by the baby I should have called my own. She'd healed me without ever realising I was broken. But now, I thought, tapping my desk with my fingertips, now I was alone once again. Cut off from the people I'd thought of as family, with nowhere left to go.

CHAPTER FORTY

Madeline

'I can't believe they took her,' Adam said, slumping into the far corner of the sofa. I stood in the living-room doorway, still shell-shocked. It should have felt awkward having him back in the house after so long putting up barriers, but after today, it didn't seem to matter any more. The problems that had once been monumental in my life now seemed like silly insignificant complaints.

'I can,' I said softly. 'This isn't the first time for me, remember?'

He looked up, shaking his head. 'I can't believe they think she could be doing any of this on purpose.' He ran his fingers roughly through his hair. 'Maddie,' he whispered, his eyes haunted, 'she must be terrified.'

'Don't. I can't stand thinking about it,' I said, holding up a hand. That final scene as they'd taken her, the police escort they'd brought in to keep things running smoothly, Tilly's panicked expression as she realised that this time, neither Adam nor I was going with her. She was *six*, for goodness' sake – she needed us. We'd been treated like criminals, like it was *our* fault she was ill. I knew Dr Keifer hadn't let go of his belief that I was the root of all her issues.

When it had become clear that they were going to take her regardless of our wishes, we'd tried to backtrack, to get them to let Adam go too, if only to make sure that he could advocate for her and comfort her through whatever was coming next, but the police had blocked his path, telling us there would be a multi-disciplinary meeting tomorrow morning where we could air our grievances. They didn't trust him not to remove her from the psychiatric unit the moment they left. We'd fought too hard to turn back.

It had been the two of us battling against a sea of blank faces, their decisions already made despite our protests, and in the end, we'd had to watch them take her away, utterly helpless and racked with guilt.

I looked at the clock, seeing that it was nearly 1 a.m. I hoped Tilly was sleeping. That she wasn't screaming for us. Adam leaned back against the sofa, and I realised tears were streaming silently down his cheeks. He'd never been a man to cry, but then he'd never had to fight so hard and walk away the loser before either.

'Don't,' I repeated.

His head snapped up to look at me. 'Don't what?'

'Cry. Give up. Let them win.'

'Maddie, give me a break.'

'No,' I said, folding my arms tightly across my chest. 'We don't get to fall apart right now. It doesn't help her, not one bit. She can't fight for herself, Adam. We're her support! We're all she's got in this world and we are *not* going to let her down.' I gripped the frame of the door, breathing hard. 'So,' I continued, straightening my shoulders determinedly, 'here's what's going to happen. I'm going to go into the kitchen and make a pot of coffee while you dry your tears, and then I'm going to come back and we are going to find out what's wrong with our daughter. There are other people out there who have been through this exact same thing – there have to be. We both know she's ill. If we find out what it could be, we can help her.'

'On the internet?'

'Yes, on the internet.'

'Maddie, I don't know...'

I shook my head, unwilling to negotiate this time, then turned, walking to the kitchen with my shoulders back, my head held high. I didn't care if he thought me harsh. Yes, I would have loved nothing more than to crawl into bed to sob myself to sleep, but I couldn't do that to Tilly. I would not give up.

I made a strong pot of coffee, grabbed a packet of biscuits and two mugs and put it all on a tray, carrying it through to the living room. I pushed open the door to find Adam, dry-eyed, sitting up with my laptop open on the coffee table in front of him. He fixed me with a determined stare.

'You're right,' he said, his voice fierce with emotion. 'We're going to fight for her. And we won't give up until she's right back where she belongs.'

'With a diagnosis to help her get better,' I added.

'With a diagnosis,' he agreed.

The sun had cracked its head over the horizon more than an hour ago, the buttery light streaming in through the open curtains in the living room. Adam leaned back on one end of the sofa, the computer on his lap, his brow creased as his pupils followed the text on the webpage. I tapped away on my phone screen at the opposite end, saving articles, discarding others. We hadn't stopped – not to rest, nor to cook. We'd silently worked our way through the pot of coffee and the packet of biscuits, pausing to share snippets of information every now and then, leading one another down rabbit holes on the internet.

My thoughts kept drifting to Tilly, my chest tightening as I pictured her waking alone in some cold, harsh environment. I couldn't begin to imagine the damage this would do to her psychological well-being in the long run. Ironic, really, that the people who were supposed to be fixing her broken mind had probably done more harm than everything else combined. Adam had made a fresh pot of coffee after we'd worked our way through the first one, and I poured a cup now, taking a sip, my hands shaking from excess caffeine and exhaustion.

'Maddie,' Adam said, sitting up straighter, a sudden urgency to his body language. 'Listen to this.' He cleared his throat and I leaned towards him, waiting. He pulled the laptop closer, his eyes wide as he read.

'Symptoms of this condition include but are not limited to: joint pain, digestive disorders, pelvic and bladder dysfunction, anxiety disorders and fragile skin that bruises easily.' I nodded, biting down on my lip. 'It can also be associated with postural tachycardia syndrome, otherwise known as PoTS, in which parts of the nervous system malfunction. This can affect breathing, heart rate and blood pressure and cause fainting and collapse.'

This was it. It had to be. It summed up Tilly to a tee. The bed-wetting. The eating problems. The random fainting – even the bruising Dr Keifer had all but accused me of. 'Adam,' I breathed, reaching forward to grab his hand, squeezing it tightly. 'What's the condition? What is it?'

'I think this is it, Maddie,' he said, his eyes shining as he looked up at me. 'It's called hypermobile Ehlers-Danlos syndrome.'

I shook my head. 'I've never heard of it.'

'Me neither, but it's as if they're describing Tilly. It says it's rare. That it's only just beginning to be recognised in medical circles.' He stood up suddenly, his energy palpable.

'What are you—'

'Get your shoes on,' he commanded. 'We're going to the hospital, right now. We're going to get our baby back.'

The shock of Adam's sudden internet diagnosis had worn off before we reached the hospital, replaced by a determination that pulsed through my body in a constant tattoo of adrenaline. I was no longer afraid of offending the medical staff, of saying the wrong thing. They'd taken my daughter already. There was nothing left to lose.

Now I was armed with information that could change everything, and I would not leave until they'd heard us out. I wanted tests. Specialists, and this time, they would be the right ones. The people who could actually help us. I marched ahead of Adam, having grabbed the door before it could close when another parent left the ward, and we made directly for the nurses' desk, coming face to face with Carrie, aka the Trunchbull.

She looked up at me, a frown puckering her forehead, her tight bun as severe as ever. 'Tilly's not on the ward, is she?' she asked, looking up at the whiteboard fixed to the wall behind us.

'No. She's in a psych unit,' I said sharply. 'I want to speak to Dr Keifer.'

She looked taken aback at my commanding tone. 'You can't just come onto the ward if your child isn't a patient.'

'She *should* be a patient. Unfortunately, due to the poor judgement of Dr Keifer and his team, she's in the wrong place. I need to speak to him. Now.'

She pursed her lips. 'He isn't on the ward; he's in a meeting.'

'Then we'll speak to whichever consultant *is* available. I don't care who.'

'This is really not how things are done. You can call and make an appointment with his secretary.'

'No, I cannot. Now listen, Carrie. My daughter, my *six*-year-old child, has been taken from us, and we have reason to believe they have made a big mistake. I'm not leaving until someone hears us out.'

'What's going on here?'

I spun round, coming face to face with Dr Keifer. The sight of him made my blood run cold, but I didn't flinch. I stepped forward, meeting his beady-eyed glare with a confidence I hadn't felt in a long time. 'We need to speak to you about our daughter.'

Adam nodded, moving to stand beside me. 'We think you've made a mistake.'

Dr Keifer snorted dismissively. 'Of course you do.' He half turned, as if he'd heard enough.

'Ehlers-Danlos syndrome,' Adam said loudly.

Dr Keifer paused, his brow knitting. 'What?'

'You've heard of it?' I asked.

He turned slowly back to face us, his lips pressed into a thin line.

'Excuse me, Doctor,' Carrie interrupted, casting a glance in my direction. She held the receiver for the ward telephone in her hand. 'I, uh, have the psych ward on the line.'

'About Tilly?' I asked, gripping the edge of the desk. 'Is she all right?'

Carrie ignored me, speaking directly to Dr Keifer. 'He wants to talk to you.' She handed him the phone, and I held my breath, watching his expression change as he listened.

At last he placed the receiver down with a resounding click, and his eyes lifted to meet mine. 'Interesting timing,' he muttered. 'He tells me Tilly has been unable to keep anything down. He believes her symptoms are physical, not mental. They want to send her back here immediately.'

'She's coming now?' I asked.

'Yes.' He clicked his tongue against his teeth. 'Ehlers-Danlos syndrome... it's rare. I've not seen it before.'

'But it could be?'

'Yes,' he conceded. 'You may be right.'

CHAPTER FORTY-ONE

Adam's hand was in mine and I was glad. I needed his strength and I knew he needed mine just as much. We stood in the empty bay on the busiest part of the ward, having finally been summoned from the parents' room by the ward sister. 'The paramedics have just called up to let us know they're transferring Tilly from the ambulance now,' she said. It wasn't the same sister we'd met before, but the way she spoke to us, almost apologetic in her manner, made me certain she knew our story.

I nodded silently, fighting the urge to run down and meet her halfway. I didn't want to miss her and have her arrive to find me absent. The sister placed a stack of sick bowls on the table at the end of the bed, checked the oxygen on the wall, then excused herself quietly. I was aware of being watched, the other parents on the bay casting curious glances in our direction. Adam squeezed my hand and we continued to watch the door.

I heard the familiar activity in the corridor, the loud clatter of the stretcher bouncing against the door, the quick footsteps of the nurses going to greet the new arrival. I moved without thinking, my hand slipping out of Adam's grasp, my body propelled towards the noise. As I stepped out, I saw the long white stretcher, the tiny, terrified girl lying in the centre of it, her gaze darting around, panicked as the adults talked above her head. I felt Adam step out behind me, a shuddering breath escaping his lips as I lurched forward. 'Tilly,' I murmured, the word sticking in my throat. It was enough. Her eyes locked on mine, filling instantly with tears.

'Mummy!' she yelled, shocking the paramedics and nurses into silence. They looked from her to me, then stepped aside, continuing their handover. I rushed towards her, my arms outstretched as I pulled her into them, burying my face in her hair, my tears falling fast. Her whole body shook as she clung to me, grabbing fistfuls of my hair, her lips pressed against my collarbone.

'It's okay, sweetie. I'm here. Daddy too. You're safe, darling. I won't *ever* let this happen again,' I promised, certain that I would do absolutely anything to keep my word. I felt Adam beside me, his arms wrapping around us, his hands shaking as we blocked the corridor with our emotional reunion.

I didn't care.

Tilly was curled against my body, her hand gripped in mine, even in sleep refusing to let me go. I wouldn't have tried to leave anyway. After the nurse had settled her on the ward, hooking up a bag of glucose and saline to her cannula, she'd left the three of us alone and Tilly had fallen apart, telling us, through a haze of tears, every horrible detail of her experience at the psych ward. I'd realised right away that she no longer had the NG tube dangling from her nostril, and she'd confessed that she had pulled it out so they couldn't keep making her sick with the 'horrible milk'.

It was going to be a long road to recovery after what she'd been through. She would probably need therapy to process the trauma of these past few weeks, but she was here with us now, and I hoped that from this point onwards, things would begin to look up. They had to.

'Hello,' called a voice from behind the curtain surrounding our little cubicle.

'Hi, come in,' Adam said, sitting up straighter in his seat. A woman of around thirty in a pretty blue dress, with a long, thick ponytail and big brown eyes, stepped through the gap in the curtain. She held a folder against her chest. I felt my body tense as I shot a glance towards Adam.

'I'm sorry to interrupt,' she said. 'I promise I'll keep my voice down so as not to wake her.' She smiled, nodding towards Tilly. 'She's had quite the time of it, hasn't she?'

I nodded, pressing my lips together, unsure where this was going.

'I'm Dr Varma. I'm a genetics specialist and I've been asked to come and speak to you about a possible diagnosis for your daughter.'

I felt my face break into a smile, relief flooding through my body. I'd waited so long, too long, for this. Finally someone was prepared to hear what I'd been shouting from the rooftops. 'Thank goodness,' I breathed.

'Did Dr Keifer speak to you? About the possibility of a condition called Ehlers-Danlos syndrome?' Adam said, rising from his seat.

'He did. And I've been reading through Tilly's medical records. I see that she's always had issues regarding eating, but these have escalated over the past year or so.'

'Yes, that's right,' I said, leaning forward, moving carefully so as not to wake Tilly.

She fixed me with an empathetic smile. 'Tell me, from your perspective, what are her primary symptoms?'

Dr Varma nodded as she listened, her fingernails tapping lightly on the back of the folder in her arms. 'That is very helpful, thank you. So, I have also read through the results of all the tests Tilly has had so far, and obviously none of them have flagged up positive. I'm sure you would like me to tell you we can do a blood test and get a concrete diagnosis of Ehlers-Danlos syndrome.'

'Yes, can you do that?' I asked.

'A blood test *can* help to confirm certain kinds of EDS. I'm not sure if you're aware, but there are actually thirteen different types of this condition, some of which are extremely rare. As it happens, the type I believe Tilly could have is actually the most common. It's called hypermobile Ehlers-Danlos syndrome, and sadly, there is no test to confirm it at this point in time.'

'So what do we do? How do we know for sure?' Adam frowned.

'You speak to a genetics specialist. *Me*,' she said with a smile. 'And based on all the information I have, I'm confident that we *are* dealing with a classic case of hypermobile EDS. However, the best way to give ourselves proof of this is to treat her.'

'What does that involve? Is there a cure?' I asked.

She sighed, shaking her head slowly. 'No. I won't sugar-coat it, Mrs Parkes. There is no cure.'

I glanced at Adam, seeing his shoulders slump, his face go slack, and I knew I was a mirror of his defeat.

'But that's not to say there isn't a lot we can do. Tilly's biggest struggle is around food. She's lost a lot of weight in the past year and she isn't getting the nutrition she needs for her body to develop and grow. The first thing we're going to do is to stop forcing her to eat when it's clear she can't manage it. Often I would recommend a hypoallergenic formula, but I can see Dr Keifer has already tried that and it did not go well.'

'I don't understand? We stop feeding her completely?' I frowned.

Dr Varma smiled. 'Through the digestive system, yes. We're going to put Tilly on an intravenous feed called total parenteral nutrition, or TPN. It will deliver all the calories, nutrients, hydration, everything she needs, direct to the bloodstream, bypassing her digestive system entirely. If I'm right in my diagnosis, we will see quite a quick improvement in Tilly's quality of life. She'll have more energy, her digestive system can rest and hopefully begin to recover, and she can start to regain some weight.'

'It sounds like science fiction,' Adam said, scratching his chin.

'I know. But this type of feeding has actually been around since the sixties, though it's come a long way since then. Tilly will need a very minor operation to place a central line into one of her main arteries, and once you've been trained and we know it's working for her, you can continue this at home.'

She paused, looking from Adam to me. 'It's a lot to take in, I know. It's overwhelming to begin with. You'll be learning a lot of new things and I'm sure you'll have plenty of questions. But I have treated many children with Ehlers-Danlos syndrome, and although it seems daunting, you'd be amazed how quickly you'll adapt, plus the improvements it can make to Tilly's quality of life will make it all worthwhile. And,' she added, her smile slipping, 'as much as I would like to say this is just one of your options, the reality is that TPN is what we opt for when we've tried everything else. I believe that is the case here.'

'Will she be on it forever?' I asked softly.

'Who can say? She might begin to digest food better in six months, or a year. Or it could be that yes, this is a permanent solution. It's one of those conditions where there isn't a lot of information and there haven't been many studies. It's still quite unheard of, which is why you have had such a tough time getting a diagnosis.'

'Was it our fault?' Adam said suddenly. 'Our genes?'

'It's not something you should think of as your fault. No parent would purposely pass on a faulty gene to their child. It's just life. Nature. Sometimes things don't follow the expected path. But that isn't something you can carry guilt over,' she added, her eyes soft as they met his.

He dipped his head, and I knew he hadn't taken her words on board. 'Can you test me? I need to know…'

'I can. If it will give you peace of mind. But as I said, if it's hypermobile EDS, there's no test to determine that. I can give you a blood test to see if you're a carrier of one of the other subtypes, but that won't make any difference to Tilly. You can't undo the past, Mr Parkes. All you need to worry about is what you do next.' She stepped towards the curtain, then paused. 'I'll ask the nurse to move you into a room, rather than the bay, so you can get some peace and quiet. I'm sure Tilly needs it after the last few days. I'll also write a referral for her to see the rheumatologist, who can help her with the pain she's been having in her joints.' Her eyes met mine and I nodded. 'I'll leave you to it for now, I've given you a lot to think about.'

'Thank you,' I said, feeling strangely light. It was a lot to take in, but it was what I'd wanted. A diagnosis. A plan to help her. I had known for a very long time, perhaps since she was a tiny baby, that something wasn't quite right. My instincts, the ones I'd always been told were paranoia and helicopter parenting, had turned out to be spot on. I wished that she'd been diagnosed with something curable. Something that could be fixed. But it almost didn't matter, because we had what she needed. We had support, someone who believed us and was willing to help us get through this and make life better for Tilly. That was all I had ever wanted.

CHAPTER FORTY-TWO

Laura

I stood in the corridor to the children's ward feeling like an intruder as I watched Adam and Maddie huddle around Tilly's bed through the window to their room. Maddie was talking to Adam, her words too quiet for me to hear through the glass, but there was a change in her body language. His too, I realised. There was no sense of tension in either of them now – it was as if the fight had left them.

The realisation terrified me. Was it because the worst had happened? Had Tilly been handed a death sentence in the form of a diagnosis? It wasn't fair that they'd neglected to keep me in the loop. That suddenly the makeshift family I'd always relied on had been taken from me, and now I was left imagining the worst.

I could understand their anger towards me. Maddie's especially, after what I'd done to her. But still, they knew how I felt about Tilly. They couldn't just cast me aside as if I didn't matter. I took a steadying breath. I should leave. It was clear I wasn't welcome, and Adam had told me I shouldn't come. But I couldn't do it. Instead, I sidestepped towards the door, pushing it open. Both of them looked up instantly as I entered, and I cringed inwardly as I saw the disappointment in their eyes.

They didn't want me here.

'How is she?' I asked, moving closer to the bed where Tilly lay, her hair fanned out on her pillow, mouth ajar as she slept.

'Why are you here?' Madeline asked, her voice cold as she stepped between me and the bed. I glanced towards Adam, who didn't move. Of course, he wouldn't speak up for me now. I was clearly going to be the bad guy in this.

'I need to know that she's going to be okay. I love her, Maddie. You know I do.'

'Yeah, I know. You love her so much that you wanted to take her from me and keep her for yourself,' she hissed through clenched teeth.

'Laura, you should leave. This is family stuff,' Adam said pointedly, moving to stand beside Madeline. His words cut through me like a knife and I took a step back, gripping my stomach, my eyes wide.

'I *am* family. I have never stopped being there for you. You're being unfair, both of you.'

'I'm sorry you feel that way,' Madeline said, her arms folded. Her lip trembled and I could see how close she was to tears. 'But right now, I have more important things to think about than your feelings, Laura.'

I shook my head. 'It's never about me though, is it, Maddie? It's always you: your problems, your feelings. Do you care that I miss her? That she wants me here?'

'She hasn't asked for you.'

I looked to Adam, wondering if he would jump in with a peace offering. For years, I'd been the mediator, the one who bent and compromised to keep everyone happy. I would never have gone behind Maddie's back if it hadn't been for Adam begging me to take his side, persuading me it was in Tilly's best interests. 'You're going to let me take the blame here?' I said, fixing him with a penetrating stare. 'I make one mistake, give into my feelings *one* time, and that's it? Game over? I'm pushed out forever?'

'What's she talking about, Adam?'

'I don't know,' he snapped, glancing down at Tilly, a flush spreading across his cheeks. He looked up, his expression hard. 'Laura, we need to focus on T right now. I'm sorry you feel left out, but, God… you need to give us some space, okay? Don't you realise what we've been going through? You can't keep clinging to our family just because you feel guilty for getting rid of your own!'

I gasped, stunned at his words, my hands going to my mouth as if to stifle a scream. Adam's eyes widened. 'Shit, Laur, I… I'm sorry. I didn't mean…' he stammered. 'It's been a really trying week. I'm exhausted. I didn't mean to say that, Laur, I'm sorry.'

But it was too late. Maddie turned to me, her face pale. 'What does he mean, you got rid of your own? Did you… Was… was there a baby, Laura?'

'How could you?' I whispered, my eyes on Adam's.

'Laura?' Maddie said, taking a step forward. 'Is it true? You had an abortion?'

I turned to her, fury spilling over like wildfire, my limbs tingling with the effort of holding my emotions in check. I wanted to scream. To fall to my knees and sob, but not here. Not in front of these people I no longer recognised. 'I did *not* get rid of my baby,' I hissed. 'I *wanted* her. More than anything. I would have given up everything to keep her, but I lost her and you two were so wrapped up in *your* life, *your* problems, *your* grief that you never even saw my pain! Because, like I said, it's never been about me, has it? Not ever.'

'Laura, I never knew…'

'You never thought to ask.'

Adam stared at me, stunned, silently recalculating everything he'd mistakenly assumed he knew about me. It didn't matter now. It was time to stop pretending, fantasising, wishing for something I could never have.

I cast a last, mournful glance at Tilly, the rainbow baby who had never really been mine, and with a silent prayer for her recovery, I turned and walked away from the people I had once loved more than my own life.

CHAPTER FORTY-THREE

Then

'So, Maddie wants to go to the beach tomorrow. I said we'd get a few people together, make it a kind of reunion, you know? Celebrate her freedom,' Adam said as I held the phone to my ear.

'Right. Yeah, okay.' I twisted the cord around my finger, picturing his face. Maddie had been home three weeks, and this was the first time he'd even bothered to call me. Her mum had told me she was sleeping when I'd gone over to welcome her back, making it clear that she wanted Madeline to adjust slowly back into real life. She said something about not causing her any stress, not that I ever would.

'So, you'll bring food, yeah? Burgers and stuff? We'll barbecue.'

'I suppose.'

'Cool. I've got to go – Maddie's waiting to watch a film.'

'Should I come over?' I asked. 'I haven't seen her yet.'

He hesitated, clearing his throat. I wondered if he'd thought about me since she was discharged. If he realised that with him back in full swing in his role of Madeline's boyfriend, I was now utterly alone? Did he even care about me or the life I was carrying inside me, or had I just been a way to fill his time? Someone to listen to his worries and then be tossed aside when I'd served my purpose.

'Maybe not tonight. We're kinda looking forward to some alone time, you know? But I'll see you tomorrow. It will be just like old times, okay?'

'Yeah. Cool,' I said, trying not to let him hear how hurt I was. I hung up, staring blankly down at the phone.

'Was that Madeline?' Mum called from the kitchen.

'Yeah,' I lied. 'I'm seeing her tomorrow.'

'Oh, I'm glad she's doing better. She's such a sweetheart.'

'Yeah,' I sighed. I turned from the phone and headed up to my room, switching on the TV and flicking through the channels. I settled on a soap, glad to lose myself in someone else's problems for a while, then slumped down on my single bed, sliding the notepad out from where I'd hidden it between the bed frame and the wall. I crossed off another day on the makeshift calendar I'd drawn out, adding up the time that had passed so far.

Nineteen weeks and six days. Tomorrow I would hit the halfway point in my pregnancy. It felt like a warm glow inside me, a happy little secret I didn't want to share. Only Adam knew, and the last time I'd seen him, he'd practically told me to make the whole mess go away. But it wasn't a mess. Not to me. I had felt the way the life pulsed deep inside me. The soft flutters and, more recently, the kicks and nudges that shouted from within.

I gripped my stomach, smiling. I'd planned it all out. I would pause uni for a year or so, until the baby was old enough to be left with my mum while I went to lectures. I'd work hard, stay focused and get my degree. Of course, I could no longer be a surgeon. Not with no support from the baby's dad, and since I didn't even know the guy's name, there wasn't much chance of tracking him down.

But I could still do medicine. I would be a GP – the hours would be far more suited to a single mum – and maybe, with Madeline and Adam's help, it would all work out. I leaned back against the pillow. I would tell Maddie tomorrow. I'd supported her through the roughest year of her life and I knew she would do the same for me now.

I was daydreaming about walking through the woods, hand in hand with a chubby-cheeked toddler, when a sudden cramp shot through my abdomen and I gasped, reaching for my belly. It passed quickly and I rolled onto my side, breathing hard. A moment later, I was hit with a second cramp, this time strong enough to make me cry out. I pulled myself up to stand and blanched as I felt the gush of warm fluid from between my legs, my jeans turning crimson.

I was too shocked to move, to call out for help. I knew I should ring for an ambulance, but it seemed too sudden. Too surreal.

Another wave of pain rippled through me, dragging me back to the present moment, and I stumbled for the bedroom door, darting onto the landing.

I could hear Mum talking on the phone, which meant it was 9.30 p.m. Dad always called from his night shift to make sure she was okay. Her laugh echoed up the stairs as I reached the bathroom, pushing the door closed and sliding down it onto the cream lino.

I pulled off my sodden jeans, tossing them into the corner of the room. Another pain shot through me and I gripped the edge of the bath, moving onto my knees. Was this labour? Was it supposed to feel like I was tearing in half? Like my insides were ripping? I had a sudden urge to bear down and tried to fight against it. 'No,' I whispered. 'Not like this, not yet!'

I felt a pressure swell and bulge and reached between my legs, pulling my hand away in shock as I felt something alien emerge. Slowly I moved my hand back, cupping the tiny round form that I knew must be my baby's head. 'No, baby, no,' I sobbed. 'Not yet, not yet…'

I groaned, the pressure mounting, and then in one quick motion, the tiny body slid from mine, landing in my outstretched palms. For a moment, I didn't look down. I waited, eyes squeezed shut, longing for a sound. A gurgle, a cry. Anything to let me know that there was still hope. But there was only silence.

With a choked sob, I looked down, seeing what I already knew was there. It was a girl. I'd hoped it would be. A little girl to share stories with and shower in the never-ending love I held in my heart for her. Her eyelids were fused shut, her minuscule fingers bunched into translucent fists she held pressed against her unmoving chest. She was so tiny she fitted in the palm of my hand with room to spare.

'I wanted you,' I whispered. 'Come back to me, baby girl. I wanted you so much.' I brought her to my face, kissing her delicate skin. And then I fell apart.

CHAPTER FORTY-FOUR

Now

'Laura, wait!' Madeline called, her footsteps growing louder as she ran after me. I didn't stop, didn't even glance over my shoulder as I made for the main doors of the hospital. I rushed out into the bright August sunshine, intent on getting back to my car and as far away from this place as humanly possible.

'Laura!' Madeline yelled again.

I dashed forward into the courtyard, coming to an abrupt stop as a nurse pushing an old man in a wheelchair cut directly across my path. I tried to sidestep, but a hand grabbed my arm, pulling me back.

'What?' I yelled, spinning to face her. 'What more is there to say, Maddie? You're upset because you didn't get all the juicy details, is that it?'

'How could you not tell me?' she breathed. 'Adam said it was… after Nola.'

'Yeah, exactly. You weren't really in the right frame of mind to deal with my issues back then, were you? And when you came home, you and Adam went out of your way to pretend nothing had changed.'

'But it had… right? You fell in love with him while I was away, didn't you?'

I shook my head, turning away. 'I'm not going to discuss my feelings with you, Maddie. You've made it perfectly clear that I'm not part of your little family unit any more.'

She shook her head. 'I'm sorry, okay? I was fucking angry at you. Can you blame me? You helped them to take my daughter when I was the only one who believed she was ill. You thought *I* could be the reason we were here! I mean, what did you expect?'

'But *Adam* got your forgiveness, didn't he? He's up there, comforting her, staying informed. But me? I'm shut out in the cold!'

'He's her father, Laur.'

'And I'm—' I broke off, shaking my head. 'I'm nothing. To you or to her. You've made your point.'

'Don't say that. You're not nothing. You're my best friend. You're her auntie, practically a second mother to her.'

'Not any more.' I turned, walking towards the car park, desperate to get away from her.

'Ehlers-Danlos syndrome,' she called.

I paused, frowning.

'That's what she has. Hypermobile Ehlers-Danlos syndrome… Have you heard of it?'

I turned to face her and saw the agony in her expression, her hands curled into fists at her sides.

'Are you sure?'

'Not one hundred per cent. The genetics specialist thinks so though. She said she's got to have an operation, some central line thing. They want to feed her intravenously.'

I shook my head. 'Can they do that?'

'You're the doctor, not me.'

I felt out of my depth. I'd never even heard of the condition, let alone diagnosed anyone with it.

'Is she… will she recover from it?'

'There's no cure. They said we'll manage it. Make her life more comfortable. I don't know what that means… I was too afraid to ask.' Her voice cracked and her eyes filled with tears. I absorbed her words, my blood turning to ice in my veins as I realised Tilly really was ill. This wasn't just a fussy phase. This was serious, and I hadn't picked up on it. I moved without thinking, stepping towards her, pulling her into my arms, vaguely aware that I was crying too.

'I'm sorry I doubted you,' I said, drawing back, wiping my eyes on the back of my hand. 'I should have supported you.'

'I'm sorry I wasn't there for you when you lost your baby.'

I sniffed, grateful that she'd said *baby*, rather than simply referring to it as a miscarriage. It acknowledged how great the loss had been for me.

She took my arm, leading me to a bench, pulling me down beside her. 'Do you love him, Laura? Because if you do, tell me. I won't be angry.'

I shook my head. 'No,' I said, feeling clearer than ever before. 'I don't.'

I looked up at her, meeting her eyes. 'I thought I did. For years, really, ever since I got pregnant and Adam said he would take care of me.'

I felt her flinch beside me but didn't stop. I had to explain, to make sense of it all. 'At the time, it meant everything to me,' I admitted. 'I was so utterly alone.' I paused, swallowing back the tears, determined to get the words out. 'When I lost my baby, I felt like *he'd* slipped through my fingers too. It was a very lonely time for me. And then, when Tilly was born, I was so happy for you, but at the same time, seeing the three of you together was a constant reminder of what I'd lost.' I shrugged. 'I couldn't watch you with her without thinking of my own daughter. It broke my heart.'

Madeline shook her head. 'You never told anyone the truth? About your baby girl? You let Adam believe you'd got rid of her?'

'We never had a conversation about it. He was supposed to come with me for a scan, but he didn't make it, and when he asked how things were going a few weeks later, I just said there wasn't a baby any more. I couldn't bear to get into it with him – it was

too raw. I thought he might bring it up again after he'd had time
to think. Ask what really happened, but he never did. I guess
he assumed I'd changed my mind about keeping her, and it was
easier to let him think that than to explain. It was just too sad;
I didn't know how to tell him, and he was so wrapped up with
you that I didn't feel able to confide in him.'

'Mum knew. She had to help... after. She was actually bril-
liant – she kept my secret because I asked her to. She didn't even
tell my dad. We never spoke about it after that day. I think she
wanted to protect me from reliving the pain, but it didn't work.'

I pursed my lips, clasping my fingers tightly in my lap.
'Maddie, I never tried anything with Adam when you were
together. I want you to know that. I wouldn't have done that to
you. It would have been wrong. You were married, and besides' – I
offered a dry smile – 'he would have turned me down flat and
I would have lost both of you. But yes, when you divorced, I'll
admit, I wondered if there might one day be a chance for us.'

'Maybe there still is...'

'No.' I shook my head. 'Don't you see? It was never about him,
not really. I thought it was. I thought if I had him, everything
would be okay; my life would somehow make sense, but it was a
fantasy. For a short time, when you were ill, I felt like something
was happening, and I've been trying to get it back ever since. But
not for him. For *her*. It's always been about her. I can admit that
to myself now. Adam was just a distraction from what was really
causing my pain. I guess I just wasn't ready to face it. I'm still not
sure I'm strong enough to let her go.'

'You know she was a girl?' she whispered, reaching for my
hand, gripping it tightly.

'Yes. And when I lost her, part of me died too. I know it
doesn't make sense...'

'No, it does,' she said, squeezing my fingers. 'It really does.'

I smiled weakly. 'I thought I wanted him. That he would fix me somehow. I never told you this, Maddie, but that summer when we were fifteen and you dared me to ask him out, it wasn't because I didn't care that I couldn't summon the courage to go over to him. It was because I cared too much. I'd convinced myself I loved him, that he was everything I wanted, and I was terrified he would reject me. I barely knew him – looking back now I can see it for what it really was: a teenage crush that I allowed to morph into something bigger. I was projecting so much onto him, making him into something perfect.

'It should have stayed a crush, and maybe it would have done if things had gone a different way, but when I got pregnant, he was by my side from the moment I told him, there for me in a way nobody had ever been before. I remember how he defended me whenever Dad was being an arse, going on about how great my brother was and putting me down in the process. Adam wouldn't stand for it, and that only made my fantasy grow more out of control. I convinced myself that I'd missed my chance with him, that he was supposed to be mine.

'He pushed me to get out of my comfort zone, gave me confidence I'd never felt before. He was so kind. When I was throwing up from the morning sickness, he would bring me his grandmother's home-made chicken soup, because he knew it was the only thing I could manage to keep down. He made me feel special without ever trying, because that's just the way he is. He's a good person, and maybe I hadn't experienced enough of that.' I sighed. 'But I loved you too, Maddie. And I valued our friendship beyond everything else, so I never did anything to risk losing you. All these years I've let myself wallow in misery, telling myself that if I had made that move first on the school field, been brave enough to tell you how I really felt, my life would be completely different now. If I had Adam, I'd be braver. I'd have pushed on with my dream of becoming a surgeon. My parents would be proud of me. Maybe I would even be a mother.'

I glanced up from my lap and shrugged, looking Madeline in the eye, needing to tell her everything before I lost my nerve. 'I let the fantasy take over, and it took me a very long time to realise that it wasn't him I wanted. It was the idea of him. Watching the three of you upstairs just then, the way he looked at you… *that's* what I've been longing for. The connection. The closeness. The family. Adam was always yours. I could never make him want me the way he does you. Even now, with the divorce, the stuff with Tilly, he loves you. It's unconditional and it will never belong to me. I don't need him to love me. I need to love *myself*, be my own source of courage, rather than making excuses for living a half-baked life. I can see that now.'

Madeline sat back, absorbing all that I'd told her, her face pale. I felt strangely free. 'I'm so sorry, Laura,' she said at last, her eyes glistening. She wiped away a tear as it rolled down her nose and sniffed. 'I should have known, *asked*. What kind of a friend misses all that? I had no idea,' she admitted, shaking her head sadly. 'I wish I'd been there for you when you needed me. God, you must have hated me for being so self-absorbed.'

I gave a wry laugh. 'No. I've never hated you, Maddie, not for a moment. I've spent a long time being jealous of you, trying to slot into your family, mirror your life. Daydreaming about your husband even, for goodness' sake. It's all been out of cowardice really. I haven't been brave enough to go out alone and get the things I want, because I've been too afraid of failing. But I have never hated you.' I squeezed her hand, smiling. 'I admire you. You've always been so much stronger than me, so unapologetically *you*. You aren't afraid to show the world exactly who you are, and it's time I took a leaf out of your book. I can't keep hovering in the sidelines of your life – it isn't healthy. I need to go out and get a life of my own. Discover who I am.'

'Laura, you don't have to do that. You can come up to the ward with me now,' she said. 'We can work this out. Adam didn't mean to be so harsh – it's just been one hell of a night. He's tired, and he was so upset that he'd hurt your feelings.'

I shook my head, rising to stand. 'I understand that, but I can't come back up with you now. This is about you and Adam and Tilly. The three of you are going to need each other to get through what comes next. And I need to step aside.' I smiled. 'You should get back to your daughter. You want to be there when she wakes.'

Madeline glanced towards the hospital and I saw her desire to get back inside.

'It's okay,' I said, nodding. '*I'll* be okay.'

She stood to face me, wrapping me in a tight hug. 'What will you do?' she murmured, holding me tight.

'Live,' I whispered into her hair. 'Without obsessing over what I've lost.' I stepped back. 'Now get yourself inside to that beautiful girl, okay? And tell her Auntie Laura loves her. I'll come and visit soon, when things have settled. And I'm always going to be at the end of the phone if you need me.'

She nodded, turning reluctantly back to the hospital. I stood shielding my eyes from the sun as I watched her approach the doors, turning at the last minute to wave. I copied the gesture, smiling as she disappeared through the double doors, sure that from now on, everything was going to be different.

CHAPTER FORTY-FIVE

Madeline

'Come on, Mummy! I don't want to miss it!'

I smiled, grabbing the last holdall from the floor and casting a final look around the hospital room to make sure I had everything. Adam had taken most of our bags down to the car and this was all that was left. It was amazing how much stuff we'd managed to accumulate in just six weeks. The room looked stark now, without Tilly's dolls lined up on the bed, her boxes of colouring pencils, craft stuff and Magna-Tiles, which we'd brought in from home to keep her entertained. It felt strange to be leaving.

The end of a black cable was poking out from the chair by the window – Adam's phone charger. I walked across to grab it and paused as I looked down on the world outside the hospital, seeing a mother and her young daughter heading into the park.

I smiled, forcing myself to remember the resentment I'd felt that first day here, when I would have cut off my own arm to be able to trade places with any one of those parents out there. I had hated them for their freedom, but I knew now that the hatred I'd felt had only been masking the real emotion: fear. Terror, in fact, that I might lose my child while they got to keep theirs, oblivious to my pain, the agony of every parent who'd had to say goodbye. But I didn't feel afraid now.

'Mummy!' Tilly called, appearing in the doorway again. 'He's coming now!'

'Go ahead. I'm right behind you.' I smiled, turning away from the window and following her into the corridor.

In the six weeks since that conversation with the genetics specialist, Tilly had transformed into a new child. Her eyes sparkled with a light I hadn't realised had been dimmed. The intravenous feeding had turned out to be exactly what she needed. Within days of starting it, she'd had more energy than I had ever known her to have. She'd put on weight quickly and now had soft rounded cheeks that made her once-gaunt face full and beautiful. I'd never realised quite how thin she really was, but seeing her healthy and vibrant now made me sad for how much she'd had to struggle without any support.

I pulled the strap of the holdall over my shoulder, watching her skip down the hall, unable to stop myself from grinning as she dashed into the playroom and slotted herself into the crowd of children, both patients and siblings. Some were new faces, but many were now firm friends, among them John, a little boy with leukaemia, whose dad nodded to me as I entered. Tilly had squashed herself down beside John with a grin on her beautiful face, and the two of them were leaning forward, their small fingers threading through the soft golden fur of Bertie, the therapy dog, who visited the ward twice a week.

It had been six weeks of intense change for Adam and me. We had been trained in everything we needed to know, from how to prepare a drip in an aseptic environment, avoiding pushing bacteria into the central line that now protruded from the left side of Tilly's chest, to how to change her dressing and recognise sepsis, the biggest risk associated with the central line. It was placed in a vein than ran directly to her heart. If we made a mistake, we could quite literally kill her.

It was overwhelming and frequently emotional. Adam, used to flying hundreds of people over an open ocean, had fallen apart the first time he'd had to clean and flush her line, terrified of getting it wrong. I'd sobbed in his arms when I realised she couldn't have a cake for her birthday in the autumn. We'd crumbled to pieces time after time. But then we had wiped away the tears and got on with it, because it was clear that this was what she needed to thrive and live the best life possible.

She'd had countless visits off the ward to the rheumatology department and had a list of daily exercises to help with her joint pain. So far, she was managing well without pain relief, but the team had told us that they would continue to assess this as she grew and adapt her plan as necessary.

Despite everything, I felt safe. I knew I wasn't fighting this alone any more.

I stepped out of the playroom into the corridor to see if Adam was on his way back from the car yet and bumped straight into Dr Wallis, sporting a yellow and black polka-dot shirt that brought a grin to my face. 'Madeline,' he said with a smile. 'I hear you're off?'

'We are. We got a delivery from her home-care company yesterday and we're all set up. It's going to be strange to leave this place.'

'It's a big change, but you can see how worthwhile it's been,' he said, nodding towards Tilly, who was telling the other children facts she'd learned about golden retrievers. They were hanging on her every word, her vibrancy magnetic. 'I'm just sorry we didn't get to the bottom of it sooner.'

I nodded. 'And I'm sorry you were in Bali and we got stuck with Dr Keifer,' I said, pulling a face.

'He's an acquired taste,' Dr Wallis agreed in a low voice. 'But you know, the condition hadn't occurred to me either. Up until now, I've only heard of one other case, and that was in a grown man. I spoke to a colleague in London, and she said that it is becoming more recognised.' He patted my shoulder, offering a warm smile. 'I'm sorry I didn't know enough to prevent you from all you went through.'

'We got there in the end. That's all that matters,' I said, though I knew it would take a long time to process the full impact of everything we'd been through. I still had nightmares about doctors in white coats and social workers in fusty tweed skirts bursting in to snatch Tilly from me.

Dr Wallis nodded and continued on his way, and I turned to see Adam coming towards me.

'You ready?' He smiled, coming to stand in the doorway beside me.

'You know the rules,' I told him. 'We don't leave until Bertie goes.'

'You spoil her,' he said, grinning, but I knew he didn't mean it.

I smiled. Everything had changed between us now. We'd been forced to spend endless hours in each other's company over the last six weeks, and although it had been uncomfortable, it had forced us to talk in a way we'd not managed since the divorce. I'd opened up about the fact that I loved him as a person but I just didn't feel *in love* with him any more, while he'd talked about his hurt that I could change my mind when I'd promised to love him forever. His bitterness was fed by feelings of rejection, and my coldness was rooted in a desire not to lead him on.

We'd cried, hugged and explained our feelings to one another. And in the end, we'd formed the basis of a friendship, a partnership where we were joined by the love we shared for Tilly and the respect we had for each other. We would never be a couple again, but we could be the best of friends and Adam had accepted that.

Tilly stood up, casually throwing her arm around John's shoulder as they stepped back to let Bertie pass. She whispered something to him and they both giggled. Then she skipped out to meet us.

'You ready, little T?' Adam smiled, holding out his hand.

'Yes,' she said, nodding. 'Let's go home.'

EPILOGUE

One year later

'So, come on,' I teased, as Adam's horse trotted ahead of mine, the sound of hooves ricocheting off the pebbles, the smell of salt water in my nostrils. 'Are you going to tell me all about your hot date or not?'

'Not!' he said, pulling a face.

'Because she was awful?'

'Because she wasn't… and it's weird.'

'Weird how?'

'Talking with my ex-wife about the woman I'm dating. It's strange.'

I laughed. 'Really? Even now? The only weird thing is that you haven't been snapped up sooner.'

'Thanks, I think. Big words from the wife who rejected me.'

I didn't flinch. There was no spite in his words now, no bitterness in our relationship. Over the past year, Adam and I had grown closer than ever. Our friendship had bloomed, and Tilly loved the days we spent together as a family, even if Adam said we were too modern for our own good.

In the end, I had convinced him not to go for the test to see which of us was the carrier of the gene that had caused Tilly's illness. It would only have brought more guilt and sadness to one of us, and there was no point in wasting time with that.

Tilly was ours. Our wonderful, fascinating, brave little girl who just so happened to have Ehlers-Danlos syndrome. It wasn't something to be sad or sorry about. The truth was, her diagnosis had brought us more happiness and relief than we'd known in years. The not knowing had been the hardest part, at least for me.

Adam's horse startled as a cool wave washed over its ankle, lurching away towards drier land. Adam gasped, his face turning white, letting out a breath as he realised the bay wasn't about to bolt.

'Why are we doing this again?' he breathed.

'Because she loves it and *you* need to broaden your horizons.' I grinned, adjusting my reins a little tighter and pressing my heels into the flanks of my silver gelding to catch him up. His horse whinnied as I came up alongside and he flinched. 'Relax. Your seven-year-old daughter is doing it. You can too, Captain Parkes!'

We both looked along the beach to where Tilly was cantering her muscular bronze pony in the froth of the waves, her long curls streaming out behind her from beneath her purple velour riding helmet.

We'd signed her up for lessons at the local stables two months after leaving hospital, after reading about how horses could be wonderful therapy animals. Outwardly Tilly had displayed very little evidence of the emotional scars she carried, but I knew they were there, lying dormant, ready to emerge one day. She hadn't wanted to talk to a stranger, and she'd brushed off our attempts to bring up the topic, so horses had seemed like the only option left.

And it had been incredible. Tilly had, as it turned out, a natural affinity with the animals. She'd bonded instantly with every single horse in the stables and was surprisingly agile for a girl who'd barely managed to walk a few months earlier. She'd picked up the skills quickly and now rode rings around Adam and me, although we did our best to keep up. Watching her gave me a deep sense of joy.

Of course, there was probably some rule about setting a seven-year-old loose on Brighton beach without an adult controlling the reins, but as Tilly was always reminding us these days, rules were made to be broken, adventures were waiting to be had. She was a different girl now, and I saw so much of my younger self in her wildness. She brought me back to the person I was meant to be.

Adam slowed beside me, flashing me a strange look.

'What?' I asked.

'I saw Laura yesterday. She's been offered a surgical residency at the hospital she had her heart set on. She starts in two months.' He grinned. 'She's really doing it, Maddie – she's going to be a surgeon.'

'Oh wow,' I breathed, breaking into a smile. 'Oh, Adam, I'm so proud of her!' Laura had transformed almost beyond recognition in the past year, the most notable difference being the change in her confidence. We saw less of her now, she was so busy with everything going on in her life, but the time we did spend together felt more authentic than it ever had before. There were no secrets between us now.

She'd moved out of her rented flat and bought a place of her own, a beautiful little cottage in a semi-rural village just outside Brighton. She'd never been a fan of the crowded streets and cafés of the city, complaining they made her feel claustrophobic, but now she had the best of both worlds, popping into Brighton whenever she liked, but escaping back to the tranquillity of her new home at the end of a busy day.

She'd taken up salsa dancing, something that had shocked both Adam and me, though we never said a word, and three months into her course she'd met Phil. Bald, confident and utterly hilarious, he was a man I would never have put her with, but somehow it just worked. Her face lit up when he walked into a room; he treated her like a queen. The two of them were in their own little bubble, and I realised there was so much I'd never known about my friend that I could now see in this new-found happiness she'd embraced. She was vivacious and funny, and I felt like our friendship was stronger than it had ever been.

And now she had the final puzzle piece. She was going to give up the job that had always been her second choice and go for what she really wanted. I couldn't have been happier for her.

'She'll be a wonderful surgeon,' I said. 'I want to celebrate this with her. Let's take her out to dinner this weekend. Somewhere nice.'

'Great idea. And Phil, of course,' Adam said. We shared a smile, our eyes meeting.

'Mummy, Daddy!' Tilly called, tearing us from the moment. I looked ahead to see her cantering towards us, a wide smile on her face, her eyes sparkling with light and life. 'Do you need me to show you how to canter again, Daddy?' she asked, looking at him earnestly.

'I think he does, sweetheart.' I grinned. 'I think we both need you to show us the way.'

She gave a tinkling laugh and reached over, patting Adam's horse between the ears. 'Come on, Archie,' she murmured. 'Let's have an adventure.' She grabbed Adam's ankle, showing him where to press down on the horse's flanks. 'Got it?'

'I think so,' he said uncertainly.

'Then let's go!' She spun her pony around, leaning forward as she set off across the shingle.

Adam glanced at me. 'Are we really doing this?'

'We are!' I laughed. We shared a decisive nod, then, with a deep breath, loosened the reins and kicked down, the horses lurching forward as we cantered after our daughter, letting her lead the way.

A LETTER FROM SAM

I want to say a huge thank you for choosing to read *One Last Second*. If you enjoyed it, and want to keep up to date with all my latest releases, you can sign up at the following link. Your email address will never be shared and you can unsubscribe at any time.

www.bookouture.com/sam-vickery

This story has been especially personal for me because I know exactly how it feels to have a child who has a chronic medical condition. With my daughter, there was never any doubt that we needed urgent medical care. From the moment we arrived at the hospital when she was just two days old, we were surrounded by the best support we could have possibly imagined. Paediatricians, surgeons, gastroenterologists, radiologists and nurses were all with us from the start, never doubting our words or telling us we were overreacting. What I came to realise is that if a child has a condition that presents itself in the extreme, you don't have to fight for support. In fact, we often wished we could be given more space in those early days!

During our many stays in hospital, being rushed to the front of the queue, bypassing A&E, being heard and taken seriously, I have often thought about how difficult it must be for those parents who have a child on the cusp. Surviving, but not thriving, perhaps with a condition that increases in severity slowly, so that only those closest to them can really see the changes. How hard must it be to know that something is very wrong, and yet have nobody there to figure it out with you? What if your child's symptoms were even blamed on your parenting style?

And *that* is where the inspiration for this story came from. I've wanted to write a hospital-based story for some time but held back as I knew that this was going to be a reminder of a lot of my own experiences as a mother. Madeline's determination to stay by Tilly's side, to protect her and comfort her, is something I relate to intensely. Between my husband and myself, we have never left my daughter alone without a parent to advocate for her, even during the stay in neonatal where we were given no bed and not allowed to sleep. We adapted our entire lives in order to ensure she was never on her own, and I could not have provided that care without my husband there to take turns with me. How hard must it be not only to lack the support of a second parent, but also to have to fight against their unwillingness to take your child's illness seriously?

The condition Tilly is diagnosed with, Ehlers-Danlos syndrome, is one that has been gaining attention over the last few years. It is the epitome of an invisible illness, one that is not easily diagnosed and that can have a multitude of symptoms and characteristics. The struggle for those who have this condition, both children and adults, is still very real, and they might have to face many battles in order to get the support they need to thrive.

I hope you've enjoyed reading *One Last Second*. If you did, I would be very grateful if you could leave a review. I'd love to hear what you think, and it makes such a difference in helping new readers to discover one of my books for the first time.

I always enjoy hearing from my readers – you can get in touch at www.samvickery.com or find me on my Facebook page.

Until the next time,
Sam

SamVickeryWrites

www.samvickery.com

ACKNOWLEDGEMENTS

It's not often I thank someone for making me work harder, but I am so grateful for the support and guidance of my wonderful editor, Jennifer Hunt, who has helped me to transform the initial spark of this story into something far bigger than I'd imagined and pushed me to keep going that extra step further.

To all of the team at Bookouture, I want to say a massive thank you for welcoming me so warmly and making me feel so looked after. Handing over a book is a nerve-racking experience but I've never been in any doubt that it is in safe hands with you. To the online community of Bookouture authors, who have made me laugh and welcomed me from the very start, I could not be more grateful to be a part of such a friendly, supportive and generous group of writers.

To the general practitioner who willingly answered my questions and helped me to correct the inaccuracies in my plot, thank you!

An unusual one next: to the wonderful doctors and nurses who take care of my daughter, some of whom feel like members of the family, I could not be more grateful for the relationship we have built over the years, the respect and trust we share for one another and the fact that you accept my parenting style without questioning my sanity – for the most part! Our time in hospital has given me more inspiration for stories than I could ever have wished for, but you'll be relieved to hear that none of the characters in this story are based on any of you.

To my mum, who reads all of my drafts, even though they make her cry and I know she would prefer a rom-com, thank you, I appreciate your support so much.

To my husband, Jed, and my children, Viggo and Aurora, thank you for always believing in me, for giving me time and space to work, and for listening to me talk at dinner each night about all the highs and lows that come with writing a book. You make all of this worthwhile and I love you beyond all measure.

And lastly and most importantly, thank you to my readers, both new and old, who have taken the time to pick up this story. I am so very grateful to you for your support and I hope you've enjoyed reading this book as much as I loved writing it.